HER WICKED PROPOSAL

The League of Rogues - Book 3

LAUREN SMITH

This book was previously published in 2016 by Samhain Publishing. This is a republication of the original version.

ISBN: 978-0-9974237-8-5 (e-book edition)

ISBN: 978-0-9974237-9-2 (print edition)

For Meg, my beloved childhood dog who went blind in the prime of her life. You taught me true strength comes from surviving through adversity and how to count your steps when climbing stairs. You are deeply missed.

L eague Rule Number 5:
     A man's best lover is a spirited lady, but one should treat spirited ladies the way one would a wild horse, with a firm hold and gentle voice.

EXCERPT FROM *THE QUIZZING GLASS GAZETTE*, APRIL 21, 1821, The Lady Society Column:

LADY SOCIETY IS IN MOURNING. THE DANGEROUS RAKEHELL Viscount Sheridan has been rendered blind. She cannot help but miss those dark brown eyes that scorched more than one innocent young lady's heart as he watched them from the shadows of a ball-room. Oh, my dear Viscount Sheridan, won't you come out into society again? Lady Society is issuing you a challenge. Do not hide from her, or else she will unearth those secrets you hold most dear.

Perchance there is a lady who might yet tempt your sightless eyes and convince you to live again. Would you not like a woman once more to warm your bed? A woman to tame your wicked heart?

LONDON, APRIL 1821

Using his silver lion's head cane, Cedric, Viscount Sheridan, rapped it harshly against the cobblestones of the winding path in his London townhouse garden as he tried to navigate his way to the fountain. All around him the world was a winter gray. Yet his other senses assured him it was spring. Sunlight warmed his face and arms where he'd rolled up his sleeves. A flower-scented breeze tickled his nose and tousled his hair. Cedric took seven measured steps, counting them in his head.

Seven steps to the center of the garden, then five steps to... He caught the tip of his boot on a raised stone, stumbled and collided with the ground. He stifled a cry as stones bit into his palms and the bones of his knees cracked.

Panting, every muscle tensed, he lay on the ground for a long moment, fighting off the waves of shame and the childish urge to whimper with the pain. His eyesight hadn't been the only thing he'd lost. It seemed sense and balance had abandoned him as well.

Finally he picked himself up, patted the ground around

himself to find his cane and rose unsteadily to his feet. He was a grown man of two and thirty—he could *and would* bear this pain as any well-bred gentleman was expected to.

It was a small mercy none of his servants were around to witness this moment of weakness.

Once more. Five steps to the fountain, he reminded himself, and taking care to lift his feet higher, he avoided any more raised stones. He should know this path by now, as he had walked it a hundred times. Yet he still couldn't see it as clearly in his head as he knew he should. When the tip of his cane rapped lightly on the stone fountain's base, he bent over and reached out to find the ledge and, with a great sigh of relief, sat down.

Every hour of every day, from the moment he rose for the day until he retired to bed, he lived in constant fear of toppling precious family heirlooms, embarrassing himself in front of his friends or family, or worse, causing further damage to his body. It was a cruel twist of fate to have once been a virile man afraid of nothing, and reduced to someone who woke each morning only to remember he was forever trapped in darkness.

Too often in the last few weeks, he'd sat at his desk, head buried in his hands, the heels of his palms pressed deep into his eyes as he tried to bring back the vision he desperately needed.

His despair was too strong, and he couldn't summon the will to care.

Thank God for this garden. Peace, quiet, no one to see

him in this state. Moments like this were a blessing. There were no social callers, no awkward visits from people who didn't understand the trials of being blind. Out in his garden, he could exist without worries, without anxiety. The fresh air, warm sun and the sounds of birds and insects made him feel alive again, as much as a broken man could. The temptation to remain outside forever was a strong one, but his hands burned from being scraped raw and he'd have to come inside to sleep and eat.

A bee hummed somewhere to his right, probably skimming the budding flowers. The twitter of birds in a nearby tree teased his ears, filling the silence with a delicate trill that was distinct and clear. He could make out every note, each singular melody and the changes in tempo and pitch as the birds talked to one another.

No more could he focus on the tiny details of sight, like the faces of his sisters and his friends as they laughed and talked, or the way wind would stir the trees into rippling waves of emerald in the summer, or the way a woman's mouth turned that perfect shade of red when kissed by a lover. Sounds, scents and touch were his only companions now. He clung to the sound of Audrey's delicate giggles, and the softness of Horatia's hand when she held his while guiding him around.

The light steps of a footman on gravel disturbed him from his thoughts. The sure-footed steps had to be Benjamin Abbot, one of the older footmen. He'd learned so much about his servants in the last few months. The maids by their voices and the sounds of their skirts, the footmen by their heavier steps. Each servant was unique. It was one of the things he'd learned to value most after losing his sight. He'd always had a good relationship with his servants before, but now he relied on them more than ever.

"There is a young lady here to see you, my lord."

"Oh?" Cedric didn't bother looking in Benjamin's direction. There seemed little point in looking at a person if one could not see them. "Did this lady give you a name?" he asked the footman.

"Miss Chessley. Baron Chessley's daughter," the footman replied.

Cedric drew in a sharp breath.

Anne is here? Why?

He'd been with many women over the years, seducing his way from one bed to the next. But not with Anne Chessley. She was different. She'd intrigued him, resisted him, and challenged him. A veritable ice maiden in her ivory tower, yet each time he caught her eye, for a brief second heat would flare, so bright and hot it made him hungry for her. She was a challenge, and he'd always been one for a good challenge.

Last year he'd courted her, but she hadn't let him near enough for even one kiss. He'd spent a fortune on sending lavish bouquets and had purchased opera box seats facing her father's box in order to watch her enjoy the music from across the theater. And yet she had remained unattainable. Always polite, but never truly open. After months of trying, Cedric had been forced to admit defeat. She would never surrender to him or his attempts at seduction.

And then he'd lost his sight. Any thought of marriage now was inconceivable. While his fortune was still a draw for some eligible ladies, he could no longer stomach the macabre dance of courtship. Not when all he heard were the rude whispers of the ladies behind their fans about his condition. He wanted no such revulsion or pity from his future wife.

Anne would certainly pity him, or be discomforted by his newfound clumsiness. She was too cold-hearted to care whether he could make it five feet without hurting himself or damaging something around him. He couldn't fathom what she'd be doing here of all places, not when she'd spent so much time avoiding him. Furthermore, she was not one for social calls and wouldn't dare pay one to him. Add to that the news he'd recently heard regarding her, and he couldn't imagine why she was here.

Last week when his friend Lucien and his sister Horatia had come by for their weekly visit, Cedric had learned that Baron Chessley, Anne's father, had died in his sleep. Anne was now a wealthy heiress and had no need of anyone, let alone Cedric. Which brought him back to that infernal question—*Why had she come?*

Was she so ravaged by the grief of losing her only living relative that she was coming to him for solace? He doubted it. What could he offer a woman like her? He was half a man, broken, damaged. A bloody fool.

He forced his face into a businesslike façade. He would treat her the same way he treated all the young ladies he came across since he'd lost his sight, with polite distance. His pride demanded he maintain the upper hand, especially with Anne. She must never know that he still desired her, still craved her with a madness that escaped logic.

Visions of her gray eyes played tricks on his mind. To remember her so vividly, the pale pink lips that curved in a smile only when she dropped her guard, and the way her nose crinkled when she disagreed with him. His chest constricted at the memories of their often passionate discussions on horses, their shared interest. It was the only way he'd ever gotten her to respond to him, by drawing her out through her strong opinions. The icy little hellion loved to argue, and he'd taken great delight in provoking her to blushes.

Damn. I've become a sentimental fool.

The footman coughed politely, reminding Cedric he was waiting.

"Please bring her to me," he instructed.

It was too much of a waste of time to find his way back inside now. Far easier to have her brought to him in the gardens instead. The weather was fine, and he knew Anne well enough to know that she enjoyed the outdoors.

The footman's steps retreated, and a minute later

Cedric picked up the sound of a lady's booted steps on the garden path. He heard her gasp when she came close enough to see him.

"My lord! You're bleeding!" Anne rushed over. Her scent hit him, an alluring scent of orchids that was uniquely hers. He sensed the warmth of her hands close to his own as she joined him at the fountain. She clasped his palms and gently touched his stinging skin. He'd become so used to the cuts and scrapes that he barely noticed them anymore.

She clasped his palms and gently touched his stinging hands. He repressed a shiver. Without sight, all he had left to make sense of the world were touch, taste and smell. Anne's touch lit a hint of fire beneath his skin.

"Bleeding?" he asked dumbly, too wrapped up with the sensation of silk skirts brushing his shins. His hurt hands long forgotten. Excitement burned in his veins, and that old urge to seduce rose to the surface. He couldn't recall a time when she'd been this close to him of her own accord.

"Yes, my lord. There are bits of gravel in your palms. Did you..." She hesitated to continue.

His need for her withered at the pity in her tone. "Did I fall? Yes," he answered curtly. He'd never needed pity, and he didn't want it now, certainly not from her. He puffed out his chest and scowled in her direction. An unsettling silence filled the air between them. Anne always had the power to put him on edge, make every muscle coil and tense. What expression was she wearing on that face of hers? Were those delicate brows he remembered arching above her lovely eyes with surprise, or set in a frown? Damnation, he wished he could see her.

"Would you let me help you?" Anne asked quietly.

"How?" Skepticism filled Cedric's tone.

Rather than reply she tugged her gloves off and grasped his hands, putting them into the cold, crisp water of the fountain, and her fingers gently rubbed and scrubbed at his stinging palms. Then she brought his hands back up.

"Do you have a handkerchief?" she asked.

"In my breast pocket," he said. He felt her hand delve into the pocket of his vest and retrieve it. The simple action was strangely erotic and sent his pulse fluttering. He was always the one to slide a hand under a lady's bodice, or skirt. It was quite a different experience to have a lady's hand moving under his clothes. He could feel the warmth of her skin close to his chest. With an inward grin, he relished the sensation of her soft hands invading his clothes.

When she found his handkerchief, she patted his hands dry and then held his palms up. Her warm breath glided over his skin in a soft pattern as she blew gently on his cuts to dry them.

"I don't think they will bleed further. You must take care not to do anything rough to them for a few days so you won't excite the cuts again."

Her scolding tone caught him off guard and shattered

the warm bubble of desire around him. "Thank you, ma'am," he replied stiffly, more from shock than anything. "Pardon my bluntness, but why have you come?" The burning question *why* still plagued him.

Anne was silent for a long while before speaking. When she did, her hands pulled away from his, severing their contact.

"I am sure you've heard about my father."

"I have," Cedric said softly. "He was a good man, and I do not say that about most men of my acquaintance. You have my deepest sympathies and condolences."

Pain lanced through him, sharp and sudden behind his ribs. *His own parents' coffins being lowered into twin graves. His two little sisters clutching his arms on either side, their cherubic faces stained with tears.* Those were memories he did not want, memories he fought every day to keep buried.

"Thank you." Her voice was steady, but he knew how strong Anne was and it made him proud of her. At the same time, he wanted to draw her close and whisper soft, sweet things in her ear, to comfort her.

That shocked him. Since when was he the sort of man to comfort? He was a rakehell, a seducer and rogue of the worst sort. Not one who cuddled a woman to his body.

"It is actually his death which has brought me to you."

"Oh? I can't imagine how…"

"If you forgive me for my bluntness, my lord, the truth of the matter is that I need to marry. My father's death has left me wealthy and unfortunately more of a target for the fortune hunters of the *ton* than I would have liked."

He didn't miss the tinge of desperation in her voice. As long as he'd known her, she'd always shied from the public eye, and the burden of being an heiress must have been a great one.

"And what has this to do with me?" Cedric asked. Surely she didn't think...it was too much to hope that she would ask him to court her again.

"I need a husband, and most of the eligible men seeking a bride are not what I would ever consider to be suitable matches. I came here...hoping that perhaps..." Her hands grasped his, and the action startled him, but he kept calm and gently held on to her.

What did she hope? His chest tightened. "Speak your mind, Miss Chessley," Cedric demanded, perhaps a little too strongly. Her grip on his hands loosened, and his hands dropped into his lap.

"Perhaps this was a mistake. I shouldn't have bothered you," Anne muttered apologetically. He heard her rise to leave.

Cedric stood with her and reached blindly in her direction, hoping to catch her wrist to halt her. Instead his hand curled around the flare of a womanly full hip. Rather than release her, he dug his fingers in, just hard enough to halt her escape. A startled gasp came from the sudden contact.

"TELL ME WHAT YOU CAME TO SAY, PLEASE," HE HALF-pleaded, not wanting her to go.

He'd spent so much time alone of late, which he'd thought he preferred given his condition. But Anne's company was welcome. It reminded him of better times, yet it left no sting of his lost sight. Rather it lit a fire in his blood, reminding him of the way he used to tease her and how she'd resisted him with her delightful verbal sparring.

He restrained himself from a grin when she did not try to escape his hold.

"I came to ask you if you would consider marriage...to me." The last two words were a breathless whisper so faint, he wondered if he'd imagined them.

"You want to marry me?"

He could have Anne at last! Yet he'd sworn to himself that marriage wasn't possible, that any woman who tied herself to him would never be happy with a damaged shell of a man. How could Anne think he would be a good choice? If she thought she could be his wife in name only, she was mistaken.

If he and Anne married, he would get her beneath him in a bed and find the heaven he knew awaited him there. If marriage was the only avenue in which he could find paradise, then he would have the banns read immediately. Still, if he knew Anne, which he did, there had to be a catch.

"Yes. Well...'want' is perhaps a strong word. But I would marry you if you asked me."

"Why me?" If she had her pick of fortune hunters and other young bucks, why would she settle for a blind, pathetic fool? It made little sense.

"Of all the men I've met, you have remained interested in me and have no desire to pursue me for my fortune since it is well known yours is far greater than mine. I am under no illusion of the true reason for your interest. My father's stallions would become yours, of course, should we marry. You would be free to breed your own mares with them. I thought perhaps that might entice you. I would be willing to work with you on the breeding, since it is a shared interest. I also believe we could grow to like each other well enough to get along. You have my father's approval as well as Emily's, and that assures me of your character."

Cedric laughed to himself. Even with his rakish reputation among the *ton* and rumors in the papers, her father had approved of him? They'd met often at Tattersalls to discuss fine horseflesh. He and the late baron had agreed on nearly everything, except politics, but those debates had been lively and well-argued on both sides over glasses of port at clubs like White's.

A deep pang struck him then at the sudden sense of loss of the baron. He'd let his blindness become a reason to wallow in his own darkness and hadn't even given much thought to how Anne must feel. Her father, a man she was very close to since she'd lost her mother so young.

And she came to me for protection from fortune hunters...

The thought made him feel warm in a place deep inside that had been left cold these many long months since he'd lost his sight.

"You would honestly marry me? I must warn you, Miss Chessley, I am no longer the charmer I once was. My life has become...complicated." The admission hurt him like a blow, but it was unavoidable. She had the right to know what she would face if she married him.

"I know, my lord. I had a favorite spaniel that went blind when I was a child. I know the hardships you face." Her voice was still a touch breathless.

"I don't think comparing me to a dog is quite helping your case, Miss Chessley." He laughed wryly before becoming more serious. "I don't respond well to pity, and if we married I would be your husband in full. I am sure you know what that means. Therefore, you should see yourself out."

A short gasp escaped her, but he couldn't tell if it was shock or outrage. Bloody hell, he couldn't read her, not the way he used to. A faint tremor moved through her, and he felt it through his hand that still rested possessively on her hip.

"I would offer to escort you to the door, but it takes me a while to find my way out of the gardens once I get here." Despite his telling her to leave, he didn't remove his hold on her.

Fight me, Anne. Don't go.

He hated telling her to leave, but he knew how it would be between them. She would remain icy, he would remain blind, and neither of them would ever figure out what to do with one another outside the bedroom. Such a concern might not have bothered him before, a part of him had always expected a marriage in name only, but since the happy marriages of his two close friends, he'd discovered he longed for more than sensual satisfaction with his wife, should he ever take one.

At first he'd brushed it off as sentimentality, but being surrounded by couples in love had altered his perceptions, and as he reviewed his childhood with more frequency since the accident, he remembered the easy relationship of his parents. He realized that a large part of him had always yearned for something similar. He wanted what his friends and parents had: love *and* friendship. He used to laugh about such things, as though they were the naïve aspirations of poets, but now he needed them.

"I am aware that you would be entitled to your rights as a husband. I would not deny you." It was stiffly and bravely delivered, and she still did not back away from him or demand he stop touching her.

Cedric's lips twitched. He had enough memory of her to know what expression accompanied that tone of voice. Her chin would be raised, her high cheekbones rosy with embarrassment and her lovely eyes flashing with unspoken indignation. His hand dropped from her hip, but he did not hear her leave. She remained close, the sound of her breath teasing his ears.

"You may agree to lie limp beneath me, but I do not want that in a wife. I desire a willing bedmate, something you made clear to me last spring that you would never be."

"People change," she answered.

"Perhaps, but a woman's nature often does not. You were always fashioned of ice, Miss Chessley, and I have no intention of worsening my already crumbling life by freezing to death in your bed. Simply evading fortune hunters is not enough for you to seek me out. Do you think me stupid as well as blind?"

He felt the air shift before the slap hit him full across his face. The attack sparked a fire of arousal in him rather than anger. Maybe he could melt her after all.

"How *dare* you speak like that!" Anne hissed.

"I apologize if the truth hurts, but I am weary of the pretense of civilities. Now, please leave or else I may spout further truths that may be upsetting to you."

"You ruthless cad!" Anne moved to strike him again, but he had the advantage of anticipating her reaction.

By luck alone, he caught her wrist and jerked her body against him. His other hand settled upon her shoulder and moved along to cup the nape of her neck. He held her still in his strong grip and moved gently toward her face. He was able to find her cheek and kiss a soft path to her lips. Once he found it, he abandoned all pretense of tenderness and ravaged her mouth.

She trembled in his embrace, her own tongue retreating from his at first. But he continued his campaign, rubbing his fingers on her neck in a soothing fashion until she relaxed against him. The swell of triumph he felt when her tongue slipped between his lips was glorious. And then Cedric withdrew, stepping back from her, his breath coming fast.

"If you can swear to respond like that to me in bed, then I will ask you to marry me." It was a challenge he didn't expect her to rise to, but he prayed she would. His desire for her, one he'd harbored for years, protecting the low banked fire, now sparked into a slowly building inferno. If only she could agree to open herself to him...

"I...can." Her husky, breathless response tugged at his baser side, his lower parts hardening with need. She continued to speak, unaware of the effect she was having on him. "What I mean to say is you kiss much better than I expected."

"You swear then? To respond in such a way each time I come to you?" Cedric pressed.

"I swear," Anne promised, but Cedric heard the hesitancy in her voice.

He gentled his hold on her and tried to soften his voice. "I will not ever force you, if that is your concern. But I will warn you my appetite for pleasure is voracious." He flashed her a smile he'd broken many hearts with and only wished he could see her reaction to it.

"I would rather handle your appetites, my lord, than suffer one more night at a ball having to dance with those fools who see me as no more than a pile of gold in a ball gown," Anne declared.

Cedric nearly laughed. There was the spitfire he remembered, the one who rose to every challenge he issued. Maybe it was only a feeble imagining that she'd come to him out of pity or the belief that he wouldn't press her for a full marital relationship now that he was blind. He was a betting man by nature, and he'd wager, given her response, that she loved to spar with him just as much as he liked to with her. Perhaps there was a chance for them after all.

"I suppose that settles it. I shall endeavor to do this properly then." Cedric reached out to find the edge of the fountain's base and used it as a steady force to get down on one knee. He reached out a hand in her direction.

"Please give me your hand, Miss Chessley." He gripped her offered hand in his own, feeling the faint edges of mild calluses, a hand belonging to a woman whose world involved horses. She wasn't wearing gloves. Strange, he hadn't noticed it until now.

"Miss Chessley, would you do me the grand honor of being my wife?" He smiled, the absurdity of the moment too amusing to remain bottled up. It was a tragedy he couldn't see her eyes. Would their gray depths sparkle with passion or be murky with uncertainty?

"Yes, my lord," Anne replied, breathless again.

Cedric wondered whether his smile had affected Anne. He rose with her help and searched for his cane. She put it in his hands, and he felt her grip tighten as he smiled again.

Had his smile affected her? Or was she genuinely happy he'd proposed? God, he wished he could see. Too long he'd relied on the language of the eyes. Now he was lost, a clumsy man with only his ears and hands to guide him.

"Excellent. When would you prefer to announce this?

I believe it is tradition to wait six months, until you are allowed to go into half-mourning."

A panicked hand latched on to his sleeve. "No! I wish to marry within the week. The season is in full swing, and a quick marriage will end the numerous assaults on Chessley Manor by the bachelors of London."

The pitch of her voice changed as she spoke of fortune hunters, and he wondered if that was the truth. Still, he would not question her if she was coming to him. The idea of being married held an appeal he hadn't thought possible before. He wouldn't be alone. Not anymore. Her voice would break through the darkness and keep him from falling into despair.

Still, there would be consequences. "You know the *ton* will have our heads over the scandal. They'll assume you're with child, or imagine worse motives for such haste."

"I didn't think you were the sort to fear scandal, my lord." Her challenging tone had him biting back another laugh. How well the lady knew him! They really would suit after all, he had faith now.

"Of course not. I thrive on it. I was unaware that you shared my...*lust* for attention." He wished he could have seen her face. Did she blush at his suggestive words?

"I may not *lust* for it, as you put it, but I don't fear it." Her tone suggested truth. He'd have heard her uneven breaths or a tremor in her voice had she been lying.

"You would prefer then that I procure a special license?"

"Yes, if it is not too much trouble," Anne said.

"Very well. I will write to you tomorrow."

"Thank you, my lord." Anne's hands tightened in his as she leaned forward and brushed her lips on his cheek in a ghost of a kiss. Passion fought with tenderness inside him at the unexpected contact. She remained close by. "Would you like me to guide you back to the house?"

It was he who hesitated this time. Dare he agree and admit his fear of stumbling? Or would refusing upset her? Damnation, he wished he understood women better. He'd lived with his sisters for years and was intelligent enough to admit he knew next to nothing about the feminine species or their complex and often unfathomable views of humankind. Perhaps it was wiser to accept her offer than to upset her. "Yes. That would be good of you."

Cedric was surprised when she tucked her arm in his and they proceeded along the cobblestoned path in silence. But it was not a rigid silence like he expected. Something between them had changed. He only wished he knew what it meant. But he would soon find out. They were to wed, after all. How odd that he was torn between dread and fascination.

❧ 2 ❧

"**I** think it only fitting that he's been deprived of sight, devil that he is. May he never fix his lecherous gaze on another virtuous woman ever again," Lord Upton announced to the men in the main card room of Berkley's, an elite gentlemen's club. There were several murmurs of agreement on this, but an equal number of disgruntled mutters.

Cedric entered the card room, fighting off the natural panic of being in a room where he felt intensely vulnerable. "Stow it, Upton. I'm blind, not deaf. Do not make me call you out."

His cane swung back and forth across the carpet as he navigated his way through the tables. He could not see Lord Upton's face, but the disquiet in the area of where he heard Upton's voice was telling. Cedric smiled and waited for his friend Ashton Lennox to join him.

"Cedric?"

He flinched at the sudden sound of his friend's voice. Ashton had a way of walking softly as a cat.

Although Cedric could no longer see, he remembered well enough how Ashton looked. Tall, pale blond hair and sharp blue eyes. Ashton was one of his closest friends and the one Cedric trusted most to help him survive without his sight. Ash had always been more patient than the other League members, and he needed that dependable patience to help him muddle through now. He could imagine the intense gaze his friend fixed on him at that moment. Even in a world of darkness, he still sensed when he was being watched.

"It's fine. Upton is a damned fool, that is all." He discreetly gripped Ashton's right arm and let Ashton lead him toward the private parlor that was reserved for him and his friends. Although his pride demanded he make his way on his own, reason reminded him that if he were to be so foolish as to walk without someone to guide him, he'd likely trip and give that bastard Lord Upton just what he wanted from Cedric, to be the laughingstock of the room.

Sleep with a man's daughter one time and don't marry her...he acts like I burned down his house.

Cedric's ears picked up on the sneer in Upton's voice, which seemed far too close for comfort. "Dueling with a blind man? His honor is not worth that foolish endeavor."

Cedric stiffened and cursed his remaining senses,

which had heighted in awareness since his loss of sight, especially his hearing.

"Pay him no heed," Ashton said coolly.

"Unfortunately, he's right. I'd have to have my second point my pistol in the right direction, and even then the shot would be unlikely." He let this slip in his usually sardonic tone, but the truth of it ate away at his insides.

That was perhaps one of the worst things about losing his sight and having his balance diminished. He could no longer ride, shoot, or hunt. He couldn't do *anything* he used to do. Even going to his gentlemen's club had become a nuisance. He felt exposed without one of his friends accompanying him. Over the past several months he'd learned to recognize men based on their voices and the way they walked, but it wasn't enough to feel secure when he was out and about in London. Every sense was heightened, yet his concern that he could be attacked remained just as high. Having his sight last December hadn't saved him from danger, and now he was even more vulnerable.

An assassin almost certainly hired by Sir Hugo Waverly had tried to kill him last Christmas. The assassin had almost succeeded, and it was because of this Cedric had lost his sight. Trapped in a burning cottage with his sister Horatia, he truly thought they were going to die. At the last moment, Lucien Russell, the Marquess of Rochester, had found them and dragged them both bodily from the burning building as flames leapt around them. The last thing Cedric remembered was the sound of a wood beam groaning as it broke from the ceiling and collapsed on his head, forcing him into this world of darkness.

The doctor who had seen to him had been unable to determine whether his condition would be permanent. But Cedric had accepted it as such after the first two months passed. Cedric had opened his eyes each morning to a slate of gray; every night he'd forgotten in his sleep that his eyes were sightless, and every morning he awoke anew to the agony of his loss.

At first he'd suffered from a stifling panic, but he'd forced himself to calm down with slow, deep breaths. What followed then was an aching sadness, a helplessness that made him furious and terrified. He was resigned to darkness and to living life at a slow pace, doing little with himself until yesterday when he'd received Anne in the garden.

It was Anne's visit that had him calling a meeting of his closest friends, known to most of London through the society papers as the League of Rogues. The League consisted of Godric, the Duke of Essex; his half brother, Jonathan St. Laurent; Lucien, the Marquess of Rochester; Charles, the Earl of Lonsdale; Ashton, Baron Lennox; and himself.

Cedric felt Ashton's muscles in his arm shift as Ashton opened the door to the private parlor. The rumble of familiar voices surrounded him as he and Ashton entered the room.

"Good to see you, Cedric," Godric said somewhere

to Cedric's left. Godric had somehow managed to leave the arms of his sweet wife, Emily, to join them at the club.

He remembered how Godric had convinced the League to abduct the poor woman last year when her uncle had embezzled money from Godric. She was meant to be a pawn in a larger game, only it turned out Emily was far better at moving the pieces. That abduction had landed Godric with a wife who had been up to the challenge of taming him. Cedric grinned. Nothing had been the same for the League since Emily had become a part of their lives.

"Is everyone here?" Cedric listened to the shuffle of boots and the rustle of clothing as the men took their seats nearby.

"All here," Lucien announced. That red-headed devil had recently married Cedric's sister, Horatia, even facing a duel with Cedric to do so. More than once it had occurred to him that his blindness might somehow be God's punishment for his stubbornness on the matter.

Cedric trusted these five men with his life. With the exception of Jonathan, they had survived countless close calls with death and been a party to many scandals in the *ton*. But above all they were friends, and it was as friends that he needed them the most now.

"What's this you said in your note about news?" Jonathan asked.

"Can someone pour me a scotch and push me toward a

chair?" he asked with a half-joking smile. His friends chuckled.

Ashton urged him a few steps forward, and Cedric's knees brushed the firm cushion of a chair. He took a seat and set his cane down on the floor.

"First, before we hear what Cedric has to say, I have some news of my own," Lucien said, his voice a little breathless with excitement. "Is it all right if I speak, Cedric?" His voice carried some secret weight, at least to Cedric's heightened hearing. What could make Lucien, one of the boldest men he'd ever known, become timid?

Cedric nodded.

"Horatia and I...well...we are expecting. The doctor confirmed it this morning."

"A baby?" Cedric sat up, elated at the thought. He then thought of Anne and himself. Would they someday be announcing such news? Was he ready to be a father? Instinct said no, but his heart still stirred at the thought.

"Yes. The doctor said she has been with child for two months now. We can expect the child in November." The pride and warmth in Lucien's tone was obvious.

Four months ago Cedric had been appalled and infuriated when his friend, a rakehell who could make Lucifer himself blush, and Cedric's sister had become lovers. It had felt like he'd lost his sister, a companion he'd relied on so much, and one of the two people in his life it was his duty to protect from rogues with wicked reputations. Now it was one of the most wonderful things in the world to know that his friend and sister were so in love and so happy with each other. Secretly, he'd feared that a marriage between them would put some distance between him and Lucien, but it hadn't.

Cedric and Lucien's friendship had been through a rough patch last December, but Cedric couldn't deny the truth. Lucien loved his sister with a depth Cedric hadn't thought possible. And soon Lucien would love the child who was on the way. Envy slithered inside Cedric, curling and twisting. He wanted a marriage like that, with love and children.

He sighed wearily. *Lord, I'm getting sentimental.* Time and circumstance had changed them all, it seemed.

The cheers and teasing commenced all around Cedric as the warmth of his friends cloaked him.

"Congratulations!" Charles and Ashton said from either side of Cedric.

"A baby Russell," Jonathan marveled with a devious chuckle. "Your mother must be pleased as punch, Lucien."

Cedric was unable to stop his grin. "I'm to be an uncle then?"

Lucien laughed. "Many times over, I hope."

Cedric glowered. "Have a care, man, that's my sister you married, not a broodmare."

"Very well, I'll let Horatia decide the number of children. But *you* will have to deal with my mother when she doesn't get her ten desired grandchildren."

"Now," Jonathan prompted. "Let us hear your news, Cedric."

"Oh...right. Well, Ashton and I have just come from the Doctors' Commons where I procured a special marriage license. I'm to be married within the week."

There was a spewing sound and brandy sprayed over Cedric's face.

"Bloody hell! Who did that?"

"Apologies," said Charles. "You just caught me off guard. Did I hear you correctly?"

Cedric removed his handkerchief from his pocket and mopped his face, trying not to scowl in Charles's direction.

"Married to *whom?*" Lucien asked, his tone echoing Charles's disbelief.

"Anne Chessley." He waited for any sort of reaction, but he hadn't expected the silence he met instead. What were they doing? Staring at him with gaping mouths or glancing at each other in concern? *Damn my eyes.* A chair creaked nearby as someone shifted in their seat.

"What? No congratulations?" Cedric tried to joke, but his grin faltered as the silenced continued.

Finally Ashton broke the quiet. "I think they are merely surprised as you gave up on courting Anne last year."

Lucien cut in. "And she is supposed to be in mourning for her father."

"Marriage next week seems extremely scandalous, even for gentlemen like us," Ashton added.

Godric spoke up, his tone gentle. "Ashton makes a fair point. Not that I care one whit about what society considers scandalous. Not when there are true injustices in the world. I am deuced glad to hear you are marrying Anne. I know Emily will be ecstatic to hear you and Anne finally settled down together. She was always convinced that you cared more about Anne than you let on."

"The only reason I'm not congratulating you, old boy, is because you've now evened the odds of sane men versus married men in this room." Charles's droll tone set Cedric's teeth on edge. "Ash, Jonathan and I will have to hold out against being leg-shackled."

Cedric snorted at this. Charles and marriage went as well together as...well...Charles and a convent full of nuns —which, in other words, was not well at all.

"Anyone else care to question my judgment in marrying Anne?" Cedric asked defensively.

"I am not questioning your judgment," Ashton replied, "but I am most curious as to how it came about. I agreed to take you to obtain a special license, but until now you've been close-lipped on the matter of why."

Cedric sighed. It was a question that had been plaguing him since Anne came to see him the day before. With any others he would not breathe a word of his true feelings, nor explain what had transpired with Anne the day before. But the League had different rules. They shared the darkest of secrets without a second thought, such was the depth of their trust in one another.

"As you know, Anne is now the heiress to her father's estate since he passed away. Apparently the young bucks and fortune hunters are already in relentless pursuit of her fortune. She sought me out and proposed a scheme of sorts."

"A scheme?" Godric sounded intrigued by Cedric's choice of words. The last time the League had involved themselves in a scheme, they'd taken part in a messy abduction, and Godric ended up married.

"Yes, she asked me to ask her to marry her."

"Hold on, you're telling me that Anne, the ice maiden, asked you to propose to her?" Charles didn't sound convinced.

"She's *not* an ice maiden," Cedric growled.

"Weren't you the one who named her that?" Charles reminded him.

Cedric clenched his fists. "I was mistaken. I expect all of you to respect my wish that she never be addressed that way in *or* out of her hearing again."

"Of course, old boy, whatever you say," Charles agreed.

"So finish the story," Jonathan prodded.

Cedric gave a little shrug. "It is that and nothing more. She suggested the scheme, and I agreed and got down on one knee and asked her to be my wife."

There was another interminable period of silence that seemed almost to deafen his sensitive eardrums as he waited for his friends to speak. Even the other conversations in the room had died down, as if the men in the room were straining to overhear what was going on in their little corner.

"But *why* did you agree to ask her?" Godric inquired, the only one brave enough to shatter the quiet.

He steeled himself and spoke, soft but firm. "Not one of you in this room can comprehend what it has been like for me. I cannot live as I used to, cannot pursue the life I once had. But when Anne came to me, I realized that she may be my one and only chance left to live."

The silence in the room now filled with tension. With that awful silence suffocating him, he started to speak. His friends had to understand why he'd agreed to Anne's offer.

"She has agreed to marry me despite all the things I cannot give her. I cannot praise her for her loveliness. I cannot take her to balls and dance with her. I cannot even go riding with her. That she has come to me over these other men seeking her hand, it lessens the sting of my current condition. I believe, given time, that we may be able to make ourselves decently happy together."

"Decently happy? Cedric, you deserve love, great love, not decent," Godric replied with surprisingly deep emotion. Lucien murmured his agreement with this.

Cedric shook his head. It was so easy for them to believe that. They had both been lucky to find women who loved them. He was not so fortunate. His past was shadowed with far too many regrets and poor decisions.

Fate held no such love for him, and decent was in itself a gift.

"It is kind that you think so, Godric, but I do not agree. I've hurt both my family and my friends too often of late and have been a selfish bastard most of my life." He held up a hand to silence the murmurs of disagreement. "I plan to marry Anne in a week, and I wish you all to attend." He let the invitation slip out a little more quietly, suddenly afraid that his friends would desert him.

"I shall be there," Ashton said, putting a hand on Cedric's shoulder.

"Horatia would have my guts for garters if we missed it." Lucien's reply made Cedric snort. His little sister would no doubt have Lucien trussed up in the finest clothes of her choosing and sitting on the first row of the church pew. *If only I could have my sight back for one moment to see that.*

Godric and Jonathan assured him they too would come.

Charles was the last to speak. With an exaggerated sigh he said, "I *suppose* I ought to go, if only to make sure you don't trip and knock out the archbishop. That sort of thing is likely to bring lightning down on us all, and Christ knows I've got enough bolts of wrath thrown at me every day."

A rough pat on the shoulder shook Cedric as Godric spoke. "In honor of your announcement, would I be able to tempt you to dine with us tonight? Emily will send

Anne an invitation as well. It would be good to have everyone together again."

"If you wish. Just send word to me when dinner is and I shall be there." Cedric fumbled for his cane where he'd set it down. Another hand touched his as it found the cane and pressed it into his palm.

"Thank you," Cedric said.

"You're welcome." Jonathan cleared his throat. "And how does Miss Audrey fare, if I might ask? I was told she and Lady Russell are currently in France?"

"Yes. They are somewhere near Nice the last I heard," Cedric said.

He had sent his youngest sister, Audrey, on a European tour with Lucien's mother just a few weeks after Lucien and Horatia married in early January. Audrey was eighteen and a pretty, vivacious girl. She'd managed to do well growing up without their parents, having only Cedric as her guardian. This year should have been her second season, but Cedric's blindness had left him unable to escort her to balls and parties, her lifeblood for entertainment. Audrey had been moping about for nearly two months, and he'd felt like he'd lamed a favorite horse. She needed to be out in the world, experiencing life, so he'd asked Lucien's mother to take Audrey abroad to Europe for half a year.

Next year would be soon enough to unleash Audrey onto the world. She was innocent and naïve, but also determined to get a husband, a deadly combination for her virtue and Cedric's nerves. Therefore, he had proposed her trip with the promise that as soon as she returned he would have a potential husband waiting for her. He would collect a smattering of men he approved of and would present them to her and let her choose.

It turned out Audrey's absence had been a blow to Cedric's social tendencies. He missed her morning chatter about the latest Parisian fashions over breakfast, missed her insistence that they go driving in Hyde Park in his phaeton so she might see the handsome bucks of London. He missed her hugs and the patter of her slippers on the stairs. He'd sworn long ago that his sisters were a damned nuisance, but he'd since eaten those words and enjoyed the pair of sisters he'd been gifted with and had stopped cursing his luck for having no brothers. Horatia and Audrey were everything to him, the only family he had left. Horatia's marriage and Audrey's trip had left him very alone in his townhouse.

"Well, I had best be off. Er...Ash, would you assist me to the carriage?" Asking for help wounded his already battered pride, but the embarrassment of asking his friends was lessening slowly. They did not offer pity, and once he realized this, he was thankful. They merely helped him, and that meant a thousand words he'd never say to them.

"Of course." Cedric felt Ashton's hand take his arm and guide him toward the door.

"I'll send word on dinner to everyone," Godric called out cheerfully before the parlor door swung open.

"Now, where shall we go?" Ashton asked Cedric politely. He never seemed to mind accompanying Cedric on his errands about London.

Cedric grinned. "To see my future bride."

3

A nne Chessley stood in the entryway of her townhouse on Regent Street. Her back and neck were tense as she fought to remain poised and cool, hoping to hide her racing heart and the creeping flush in her cheeks. Had it only been yesterday that she foolishly sought out Viscount Sheridan and convinced him to propose to her?

God, please don't let this be a mistake. What if he didn't come? What if he changed his mind and didn't go through with the wedding? Anne shoved the thoughts aside, though not easily.

How much difference one day can make, she thought. Since her father had passed the week before, sleep had eluded her, but last night...she'd drifted to sleep with thoughts of Cedric and that wicked kiss he'd given her. No, not given, *shared.* As much as it embarrassed her to admit it, she'd kissed him back.

Anne smoothed her black crepe gown over her hips and sighed. The ripples of the stiff fabric were an uncomfortable reminder of her mourning and her grief. Her father, Archibald Chessley, was dead, and she was alone in the world.

She was too logical not to be aware that part of her still denied he was dead. She had witnessed his lifeless body when she'd found him in his chair in the library, cold as marble, after a chambermaid had rushed to her bedroom to tell her he was gone.

The emptiness of her home had cut her deeply and driven her to action. She couldn't stand the silence anymore. A part of her still expected him to emerge from his study, cigar smoke wafting from him, or to have him join her outside and offer to go riding together in Hyde Park. It had just been the two of them since she was four when her mother, Julia, had died from pneumonia.

And mere days after his death, she'd been forced to endure suitor after suitor leaving their cards on silver trays, hoping she'd give them a chance to court her. All for her blasted inheritance. If they acted this way while she was still in mourning, the fortune hunters would become more determined to compromise her, even at the risk of scandal, in order to coerce her into marriage. Such a marriage was an unimaginable fate that she needed to avoid at all costs. She could only think of one person who wouldn't care about her money and whom she could stand to marry. Viscount Sheridan.

She smiled faintly. He was a tall, handsome gentleman with brown hair and warm brown eyes. A stubborn jaw and aquiline nose gave him a rebellious and imperious look, but his full, sensual lips revealed his humorous streak. She loved to watch him grin. His smiles always sent her pulse dancing and erased her rational thoughts.

She'd gone to him because she knew she could be honest with him, let him know the truth about why she needed to marry with haste. What she hadn't realized until last night, when she'd returned to an empty house, was how desperate and lonely she was. No more late-night conversations by the fire with her father, no morning breakfast chatter. Just deafening silence.

She assumed that a man like Cedric would not understand her wish to marry out of loneliness and it might not engender his sympathy. Yet he was the only man she could stand the thought of marrying. They shared a surprising number of interests, and could likely make a go of it, if he went through with it.

It was why rushing to him had seemed so natural. He always had something of interest to say, even when he wasn't trying to shock or seduce her. Being around him, she'd never felt alone.

But seeing him yesterday had been unexpectedly painful. He'd been sitting by the fountain, hands cut and bleeding, trousers and shirt dirty all along the front. It had been obvious he'd fallen shortly before she'd arrived. Seeing the blood on his hands and the almost casual way he'd forgotten about it jolted her heart. It seemed he'd grown used to falling, to getting hurt. No one should be in such constant pain that they grew accustomed to it like that.

Anne had wanted to wrap her arms about the wounded viscount's neck and comfort him, but she resisted. They knew so little of each other, and he didn't know her well enough to see the difference between pity and compassion. He would despise her if he thought she pitied him. She only desired to comfort a man who had been deeply hurt. She couldn't begin to imagine what he might have endured since he'd lost his sight.

It had been ages since she'd seen him. All the balls she attended, the dinner parties, were empty without him there. He'd closeted himself up in his house and no longer participated in life. It was as though he'd given up, and something about that made her chest tighten. A man like him should be experiencing life, not closeted at home. Perhaps if they married he could find some peace and she would ease the sting of her lonely heart by keeping him company, perhaps even easing him into some activities again.

Yes, I'll convince him to live again. Why that mattered so much, she didn't want to consider too deeply.

So here she stood, waiting for him to arrive so they could discuss the details of their new life together. But try as she might to focus on the future, her mind kept reliving their kiss from yesterday. In all of his seductions last spring he'd never kissed her. He'd teased and hinted about it, but she'd politely rebuffed him each time. Then yesterday he'd taken control and changed her life with one fiery meeting of their mouths. After that Anne knew she *would* marry him. The hunger tinged with desperation in his kiss sent her spiraling with mirrored longing. It was as though something ancient and soul deep had stirred to life, and she couldn't deny the urge to satisfy that hunger any longer.

It hadn't been her first kiss. Her first had been taken—stolen—by a man she despised. A man who still frightened her. And he'd stolen more than just a kiss. He'd taken something that she could never reclaim. At only eighteen years old, she'd lost any right to a marriage like her friends. Any potential bridegroom would have realized she was no longer a virgin, and the scandal it created would be unbearable.

She would have to tell Cedric, but not yet. Not until after they were married. It felt wrong to conceal such an important truth from him, but she couldn't risk losing his agreement to their union.

She'd learned firsthand that men had but one goal, to pleasure themselves, often at a woman's expense. But Cedric's kiss had promised something different. It had teased, then instructed and then encouraged her to seek her own pleasure from him. He'd then said that he would only marry her if she promised to respond to him like that. He wanted a willing bed partner, a willing lover.

To Anne that meant he wanted a woman who would seek her pleasure back and not expect the man to leave when he alone was satisfied. That kiss told her Cedric would be a generous lover, one who would care for her passion in return. As nervous as she was about her future wifely duties, somehow that kiss had rekindled a fire that had died when she was eighteen. That was why she had agreed to this.

Horse hooves pounded on the driveway and the clatter of carriage wheels jolted Anne out of her musings. Cedric was here. Her heart gave a traitorous flutter, and her hands trembled.

She hastened away from the door and ran up the stairs to the parlor, where she checked her appearance in the small framed looking glass. She studied her face with a frown. Her cheeks, too sallow from her grief in the past week, made her look exhausted to the point of ghoulish. With a muttered curse she pinched her cheeks, hoping to liven up her coloring. Then she smoothed her brown hair back, relieved to see the hints of gold still there when the sunlight hit it just right. Her hair made her passably pretty, as did her eyes, but she was nothing compared to the ladies she'd seen Cedric spend time with over the years. True beauties.

She sighed, her heart stinging. Then she froze.

What am I doing? He cannot even see me.

She could probably wear a cloth sack and he'd never know unless he touched her...

But he *would* touch her. The very thought of how he might do that made her body flush and suddenly she was a little dizzy. Taking a seat in a wingback chair in the parlor close to the front entrance, she waited. A minute or so later a footman announced Baron Lennox and Viscount Sheridan's arrival. As she had been expecting him, she'd given the footman orders to bring them to the parlor directly.

Lord Ashton Lennox entered first, his left arm dropping from Cedric's side as though neither man wanted her to see he'd been guiding Cedric like a child on leading strings. Anne rose at once and smiled at them as she approached. She took Cedric's outstretched hand and without a word led him to a chair.

"I am glad to see you are in good health, Lord Lennox," Anne remarked.

Ashton chuckled pleasantly. "Thank you. I ought to have made my apologies again for the nature of our last meeting." Anne had to admit, Lennox was quite dashing when he wasn't gazing at someone with that frightening intensity she so often saw him use. It was as though he was analyzing everyone and everything around him—for what purpose, she could only guess.

"I take it you have fully recovered?" Anne asked, thinking back to last December when she'd seen Ashton at Emily's house, bleeding from a gunshot. He'd been wounded while he and Godric had been at a house of ill-repute. Given the time of day, and the happily married status of the Duke of Essex, Anne suspected there was something more behind why the men had gone to the Midnight Garden midmorning, and it had nothing to do with bedding women.

It was an awkward thing to see Lennox again after she'd seen him bare-chested. Under other circumstances that might have been considered compromising. Thankfully, they'd been at the Duke of Essex's house and Emily wouldn't have breathed a word to anyone about what happened. Still, Anne wasn't going to forget seeing Ashton's bare, muscled chest, wound or no. It made her wonder what Cedric's bare chest would look like...

Heat crept into her cheeks. When Ashton raised a brow, she glanced away until he spoke.

"I have, thank you. May I offer my condolences on your father's passing?" Ashton was ever the gentleman, and Anne smiled warmly at him.

"Thank you. He is greatly missed. And how are you, Lord Sheridan?" Anne turned to Cedric, who had been silently facing her. His once vibrant and warm brown eyes were blank, but the rest of his face held the nuances of his expressions. He looked intense and focused with his brows knit together. She couldn't help but wonder what he was thinking about.

"I am well, and you?" he replied.

"Very well." Damn, this was all too formal. But what

had she expected? She had put so much effort into pushing him away the last few years that bridging that gap to form a friendship seemed almost impossible. She also feared that if she showed any warmth toward him he'd treat her motives with suspicion and not trust her when she asked for his help.

Cedric cleared his throat. "As my letter informed you, I have procured the special license and set a date at St. George's five days hence. Is that amenable to you? I do not wish to rush you if you need time to have a gown made or..." His voice trailed off.

It was clear he had no knowledge of a woman's requirements for a wedding. Fortunately for the both of them, she was going to wear a gown she already owned and did not desire any unnecessary amount of fanfare.

"A Saturday wedding will be lovely," Anne assured him.

The subtle lines of tension about his mouth relaxed. "Good. That is good. Oh, I mustn't forget. Godric has invited me to dine with him this evening, and I believe Emily will be sending you an invitation shortly. I hope you will consent to come."

She was surprised by his eagerness, though he quickly struggled to veil it in his expression.

"I will be happy to come, of course," she answered.

Emily St. Laurent, the Duchess of Essex, was Anne's close friend. When Anne had been eighteen, she'd had her come-out in London and met Emily's mother. The lovely Mrs. Parr had helped her enter society smoothly. Anne had vowed to return the favor for Mrs. Parr's daughter when Emily's parents had been lost at sea over a year ago.

Of course, Anne had little actual time introducing Emily to London because Godric, Cedric, and the other rogues he called his friends had abducted the poor girl on her second night coming out in London society.

None of that mattered now, however. Emily had tamed the darkly handsome Godric, and the two were so madly in love that Anne was often sad and jealous when she had to be around them. Admitting that wasn't something she was proud of, but it was the truth. She did envy her friend for her happiness, but she was also glad Emily was so blessed.

Tonight she could dine with them and enjoy the glow of her own upcoming wedding. She and Cedric may not be in love, but they seemed to share an equal eagerness for their marriage and that in itself was a pleasant surprise.

"Oh, Cedric, I've just realized I've left my riding gloves in the carriage. I will go and fetch them." Ashton rose quickly and departed the room, leaving Cedric and Anne alone.

"Did he just make up an excuse to abandon me?" Cedric started. Anne stifled an uncharacteristic giggle.

"I believe he did..."

"Does he think we're too stupid to realize he came in a coach and therefore has no need for riding gloves?" Cedric stood up as he spoke and held out a hand toward her. "May I sit with you?"

"Oh. I'm in a chair. If you wish, I could come to you on the settee?" Anne offered.

"I would like that." He sat back down and waited for her to join him.

Anne took a seat next to him and was startled when Cedric reached into his coat pocket for a small velvet box.

"This was one of my mother's favorite rings. I would like for it to be yours." He opened the box and Anne gasped. The ring was lovely. A stone was nestled there, a gem that seemed to change color in the light.

"It's beautiful! What gemstone is that?" Anne asked.

"It's a very rare gem found in Russia. It changes colors by reflecting whatever shades are closest to it. It reminded me of your eyes. I think I chose it for that reason rather than buy you a new ring. Do you like it?"

"Yes." Her voice was a little broken. She felt her eyes welling with tears. He'd remembered her gray eyes and the odd way they reflected colors. For some reason that alone put her on the verge of crying.

"Shall I put it on for you?" Cedric offered.

"Please." She put her hand on top of one of his and he took it, his thumb stroking the length of each of her fingers, as though counting them before he reached her ring finger. Then he plucked the ring from the velvet box and slid it on her finger. It fit perfectly, she noted with a shy happiness.

"I..." Cedric shrugged off his words and Anne had the feeling he wanted to say something more, but they were not friends, not lovers and not married. They were mere acquaintances, which felt enough like strangers for all intents and purposes, and she supposed he didn't feel comfortable speaking freely with her yet.

"Thank you for the ring, my lord."

"Anne, we're about to get married...please call me Cedric." The plaintive note in his voice made her agree.

She tried the name aloud. "Cedric." She'd said it often enough around Emily but never in Cedric's presence. She liked the sound of it almost as much as she liked the sound of her own name on his lips. It brought unbidden desires to her mind. Would he whisper her name hoarsely in the darkness as he came to claim her? Would he roar it like a lion? After her only experience of intimacy with a man, she'd been hurt and frightened, but now she was intrigued and excited. She was physically responding to the mere thought of Cedric bedding her.

Cedric seemed to reconsider his silence and opened his mouth to speak when a footman at the parlor door interrupted him.

"There's an invitation for you, madam, and I have a message for Lord Sheridan from Lord Lennox. He regrets that he must take the carriage and see to a personal matter immediately."

"He what?" The look of panic on Cedric's face was startling. Anne realized the dread he must have felt at being forced to travel the city alone. It must be dangerous too.

"Thank you, John. I'll take the message." Anne quickly rose and took the offered note and the footman left.

"Is everything all right?" Anne asked Cedric as he got to his feet. His eyes stared vaguely in the direction of the door, anxiety plain on his face.

"He left me..." Cedric's voice, although a low masculine timbre, still held the frightened waver of a little boy.

Anne's chest tightened at the sight of him, the mighty rake fallen so low. Rather than revel in Cedric's plight as she might have once, she felt only compassion. He'd agreed to rescue her from her situation, and it was only fair that she do the same for him. But she would have to do it in a manner that was less obvious. Anne knew enough about men to know that they hated being taken care of like children.

"If Lord Lennox does not return with your coach in a few hours, I would be most appreciative if you would accompany me in mine to the St. Laurent house for dinner. It would be most convenient. I don't wish to trouble my lady's maid to accompany me just for the brief duration of a carriage ride."

Cedric looked calmer, her suggestion working wonders on his anxiety. His shoulders, which had been bunched up tight, dropped back down and he took a deep breath.

"I would be delighted, but as you can see...I am not in my evening clothes. I need to return to my house to change."

"I do not take long to prepare. I could be ready in an

hour, and we could take my carriage to your house before we continue." Anne prayed he could hear the hope in her tone.

"That would be...acceptable," he answered after a moment.

"I appreciate that you can offer me an escort. Now would you care to wait here in the parlor while I go and get dressed for this evening?"

"Is that the proper thing? I must confess I'm dreadful at following the rules of propriety. I would much rather stand in your bedchamber listening to the sounds of silk rustling against your skin as you slip the gown on...but I am certain that you would not allow that." Cedric chuckled. "You might think I've faked my blindness these past few months just for that opportunity." His sensual lips were parted for his laughter, and Anne could feel herself blushing madly. Thank goodness he couldn't see her face.

"I've struck my fair lady speechless!" he teased as Anne scowled at him. His lady? Not yet. Lucky for him he could not see her, otherwise he would have realized he was in trouble.

"Are you always going to be so..." Anne trailed off, lacking a word that could encompass his behavior.

"Wicked?" he suggested with a cocky grin.

"Yes," Anne replied as she started to walk past him. Cedric's hand reached out and bumped her forearm before his hand anchored itself to her wrist.

"What are you doing?" Anne demanded as he reeled her into his embrace.

"I thought it was customary to seal an engagement with a kiss."

Anne's body flared treacherously to life at his words, but she resisted.

"You kissed me yesterday. Besides, kissing is only for the wedding," Anne argued, jerking against the steely muscled arms that locked around her waist, securing her against him.

"Only the wedding? I don't know who instructed you in the ways of desire, but they were either a fool or an idiot," Cedric said in a husky voice.

Anne stared up at his brown eyes focused distantly on her face, as though he knew instinctively how tall she was. He shifted one of his hands from her waist and let it slide up along the black crepe gown she wore. The heel of his palm brushed the side of her left breast and she shivered.

Cedric's eyes narrowed as he repeated the motion, moving his palm a few inches inward, stroking the crepe fabric only few inches away from the tip of her breast. To her mortified fascination her nipples hardened, as though desperate for his touch. Anne tried to pull away, but Cedric's intense look held her in place as his hand resumed its original path up her side and along her shoulder. His fingertips ran a slow line up her throat and along the line of her jaw to reach her chin.

Anne felt as though she was an uncharted foreign land.

Cedric's fingertips were memorizing the contours of her country for his own private map. When he discovered her lips he traced them, and then parted them with the pad of his thumb. Anne reacted without thinking and nipped him with her teeth.

"Bite me anywhere, anytime, my little hellion," he purred as his head descended toward hers.

Anne was only too aware that she was imprisoned by the strength of his arms. She was no tiny, delicate creature. Anne had a full figure with muscles and curves she'd often despised, but she'd never before taken for granted her natural strength. Being unable to escape Cedric was both infuriating and strangely arousing. He would never force her to his bed, he'd said, but it was obvious he wasn't about to sit idly by and wait for her to come to him. He took her by surprise and established his dominance over her like a stud stallion with a broodmare. She knew he would not stop until he'd mated his body to hers. The dark turn of her thoughts was obliterated by the meeting of their mouths.

Cedric tasted her gently for the first few seconds, as though learning the shape of her mouth, before he let loose his rough passion. He dug a hand into her hair, fisting his fingers in her coiffure, and tugged, forcing her head to fall back and leave her mouth and neck at his mercy.

Anne's hands were trapped at her sides, clenched into fists, then unclenched as Cedric's mouth sucked on her earlobe, then moved to the sensitive skin just beneath it. She fought off a shiver as tingles shot down the length of her spine as his lips moved in slow, hot kisses.

"Melt for me, love," he encouraged between breaths. Anne felt the instinctive need to obey, but her mind threw up a red flag in warning.

"Can't." Her voice was breathless as she fought the pleasure she could feel rising deep inside her.

"Yes, you can...be wicked with me, Anne."

Cedric's hands in her hair loosened and cupped her neck, holding her still so his mouth could wander back to hers.

"Open your mouth," he commanded before slanting his mouth over hers again. She refused to open, and he slid his fingers around her left breast and pinched her nipple sharply. The sensation shot a fierce desire straight to her womb. She gasped. Cedric swallowed the sound of her shock with a deep growl of satisfaction as his tongue invaded her newly opened lips.

Anne jerked in his grasp, but he refused to surrender his control of her. He kneaded her breast, cupping it, shaping it with his strong hand. Anne's knees buckled rebelliously.

Cedric released her as abruptly as he'd captured her. "I will tame you yet."

Anne pulled away, putting several feet of distance between them. Once they were married she would have to be careful; she couldn't allow him to paw at her and control her with her own passions. She'd vowed to come to his bed willingly, but now she feared she'd been too brave to assume she could manage it without losing herself. When Cedric kissed her it seemed to undo her from the inside out. When his lips meshed with hers she felt time rewind itself to that first night she'd seen him.

She'd been so young and foolish then, ready for love and marriage and a sweet life. Anne shook her head to clear it of sad memories and noticed Cedric flash her a mocking smile full of satisfaction.

"No doubt when we marry you think to take up the habit of hiding from me, Anne, but know this—I may be blind, but my other senses leave me quite capable of finding you. Each move you make I'll hear the rustle of your skirt, or catch the lingering scent of your perfume. I will make you mine all the more fiercely. Now go and change for dinner before I decide to scandalize you and follow you to your chambers."

Anne needed no second warning. She was out of the parlor and rushing up to her room in seconds, but she couldn't escape the echo of his laughter. They'd fought a battle of wills, and she only realized now that she had lost. Cedric was far more cunning than she'd assumed. He was not outwardly a scholarly type or a businessman, but he had a wealth of carnal knowledge that had put her at a disadvantage today.

I must always be on guard, she told herself.

As Anne dressed in the sanctuary of her bedchamber,

she selected a gown of russet brown that had golden embroidery on the puffed sleeves and hem. It was a gown more suited to autumn with its hues more pumpkin than like flowers, which fashion dictated during the spring. She knew she should have stayed in her mourning blacks, but the thought of a lovely evening wasted in that awful black crepe was an unpleasant one.

Her father wouldn't have wanted her to wear black for long; he'd never approved of the conventions of mourning.

Grief attends to itself in its own time, in its own way, her father had often said. *It neither expects nor desires formality.* The dinner at the St. Laurent townhouse was private in nature, and Anne felt confident that Emily would not demand she wear black.

After Anne dressed she called in her lady's maid, Imogene, who looked briefly startled at Anne's choice of gown, but knew better than to comment on it.

"What would you like for me to do with your hair?" Imogene asked as she eyed the tangled mess of Anne's coiffure. Anne blushed.

"Something loose perhaps?"

"That would be wise. Since I foresee much mussing in your future." Imogene winked. The pair, close in age, had been as close as servant and mistress could be for the last four years. Imogene teased her mercilessly whenever she thought she could get away with it.

"Is it that obvious?" Anne asked sullenly.

"That your fiancé sees through that wall of manners

you put up? Yes. The staff are most excited about your upcoming nuptials, if I may be so bold to say." Imogene smoothed a hand over her dark hair that was pulled back in a subdued but still fashionable knot before she set to work on Anne's hair.

"Bold, yes, but please continue. What do they say? About my decision." Anne was very close to her staff here; she'd known all of them since she was a child. And she was concerned that her haste in marriage might damage their opinion of her.

Imogene began pulling pins out of Anne's hair and started brushing it with a silver-backed comb. "Well, we know you're supposed to wait and all, but most of us have seen those vultures circling around the house, and none of us blame you one bit for speeding things up. You couldn't have chosen a better man. We ladies like the viscount. He's most appealing to the eye, with a fine pair of legs on him and a smile to melt butter..."

Imogene sighed dreamily, clearly performing for her benefit. Anne bit her lip to keep from laughing.

"And the young lads admire him for reasons I'd not like to say in front of your ladyship. The older men here recognize his influence and wealth. Your father could not have hoped for a better match, God rest his soul. The viscount will do well by you, treat you like the lady you are."

Imogene's hands worked their magic, twisting and twining until Anne's hair was gathered at the back to keep it out of her face, but the light brown waves still made a lovely fall of bright rich color loose enough that Cedric could still thread his fingers through it without ruining the pins holding her hair up.

"Thank you, Imogene, it's lovely as always." Anne patted Imogene's hand, which rested lightly on her right shoulder.

Imogene giggled. "Are you ready? I'm sure your young buck is eager to make off with you."

Anne laughed, despite the furious blush Imogene's words brought forth. "Imogene, I swear!"

CEDRIC COCKED HIS HEAD WHILE HE WAITED IN THE parlor, listening to the sound of Anne's laughter. It was light yet slightly husky, a laugh better heard in bed after her lover had pleasured her until she was limp and sated.

Cedric smiled. *Soon I will be that man.* The kiss he'd given her today had been unplanned, but no less satisfying. She shouldn't have bitten him. For some reason that had made him as hard as a marble statue, and it had taken all his strength to keep from throwing her onto the settee and showing her how much he liked to bite back. She wouldn't have fought him for very long, but she was still too resistant to him. She would have used his actions to paint him the villain.

It was better to wait, to seduce slowly. Being both parent and brother to his two sisters, he'd been exposed to the secrets of the feminine mind enough to know how Anne would react. Women were intelligent creatures, and they had to be courted and seduced properly to be won over and not merely subjugated.

Cedric ran a hand through his hair, enveloping himself in the brief memory of that last kiss. Her skin felt as smooth as satin, her hair soft as silk and her mouth—*God the taste!*—sweet, wet and unbelievably hot. He hoped that she would eventually put that mouth on other places, preferably below his waist. Sensation during lovemaking had intensified after losing his sight, and the thought of Anne's hot mouth around him there... An irrepressible grin twisted his lips at the thought.

Each kiss he took from her was rich in the promise of passion yet to come. He would woo her with whispered words, sensual caresses and drugging kisses until she was no longer able to resist him. He wanted her to beg for him, to need him as desperately as he needed her.

He had once thrived on his sexual conquests, and he'd had his share of mistresses over the years, but Anne was different. Winning her seemed a different level of achievement altogether. But it was going to be so much harder to win her over when he couldn't even see her. It was a challenge, but one he was willing to rise to.

He could track her without his sight. The scent of wild orchids left an impression in the air like the invisible essence of a fairy queen. And the sounds... His imagination dined on the whisper of her skirts on the carpets until it was as sweet to hear as a lover's gasp of pleasure, creating a vision in his mind of her raising those skirts just for him and baring milky smooth thighs virgin to his touch.

God, I've been too long without a woman, he thought glumly and shifted on the settee as his groin tightened and his trousers stretched.

Instead he focused on how he was going to murder Ashton for leaving him here. He'd make that blond-haired fiend pay. Ashton was supposed to protect him and guide him, not abandon him in a house with unfamiliar terrain. It had taken him weeks to learn the lay of his own house, count all the steps and memorize the floor plans and furniture arrangements.

Being at Anne's without his friend's guidance was frightening. He would never forgive the man for the terror he felt when the footman had announced Ashton's departure. The fear had practically immobilized him until Anne had spoken. Had it not been for her, he might have collapsed or lunged for the door and hurt himself again.

But Anne had assessed his panic and calmed him, distracted him. They were not even married, yet she already seemed to know how to cope with his condition. He sensed no pity, nor contempt or disgust in her tone when she spoke to him. Her reluctance to touch him or welcome his embrace had nothing at all to do with his blindness.

The same could not be said for his former mistress

Portia. Just three weeks after his accident he had returned to London and summoned her, hoping to banish his sorrows in the comfort of her body. Portia had come, eager for his company as well, but when he could not praise her beauty she'd grown bored. She seemed irritated at his clumsy touch. When he'd once been powerful and mastering over her body, he now touched tenderly, hesitantly, unsure of himself. The worst part of the evening had been when he'd tripped over the edge of an upturned carpet and fallen flat on his face. Pain had exploded in his body, and she had dared to laugh. Still, he had gotten up and tried to erase the moment with a wry joke at his own expense.

When he offered her a glass of wine he'd missed her outstretched hand and spilled it on her gown. She'd shrieked like the devil's own and slapped him. Unable to see her blow coming, he'd been unprepared for the sharpness of her hit and he'd stumbled back in surprise. This had only worsened his already teetering balance and sent him sprawling on the floor. He'd cracked his head on the baseboard of his bed and lay half-conscious at her feet, broken in every way that mattered.

And to add to his misery, she'd stood there and shouted at him. "Who could ever sleep with a broken excuse of a man like you? You can't even see your boots to put them on! I wouldn't let you bed me if you were the last man in all of England!" And then she'd gone. His valet had heard the commotion and rushed to his aid.

What sort of man am I? Portia had been right. He was as helpless as a babe. A man no longer. The truth of that was just as emotionally crippling as his blindness was physically. He'd wanted to die.

It was a thought he'd never spoken aloud to anyone and hadn't acted upon because too many people he loved would be hurt by such a coward's way out. Yet it didn't change his feelings, or the sense of desperation and helplessness that made him wish to end everything, the pain, the shame, all of it.

Until Anne. She had come to him, hiding her plea for marriage to him behind that cool bravado she'd always had. Her bravery had been the deciding factor for him. If she was willing to give married life a try, then so was he.

Besides, how hard could marriage be?

❧ 4 ❧

Emily St. Laurent lounged in the library of her London townhouse, a book in one hand and the other stroking her beloved foxhound Penelope. The dog was nearly ten months old and no longer the sweet pup she'd been when Emily had received her as a gift, but a proud grown-up dog.

When Emily had been abducted by Godric and his friends, Cedric had traveled to London and bought the puppy for her, hoping it would keep her at Godric's estate and dissuade her from running off.

It hadn't stopped her. She'd escaped anyway, taking the dog with her.

Penelope was her closest friend after Anne Chessley and Cedric's sisters. The dog let out a contented sigh as she rested her head on Emily's knee. Emily smiled and shut her eyes for a moment. The April sun was warm as it poured through the tall windows of the library, embracing her face.

"Emily." Goosebumps broke out over her skin at that deep voice.

She opened her eyes to find her husband towering over her where she lay on the couch.

"You're back!" Her cry of joy woke the sleeping hound.

Penelope barked excitedly, and Godric ran a hand over the dog's body with a rough pat and scratch. Penelope jumped from the couch and sat obediently at Godric's heels. He took a small treat from his pocket, and Penelope watched him intensely. Godric tossed the treat in the air. Penelope caught it and escaped to a far corner of the library, leaving Emily and Godric in peace.

"Now I've got you all to myself, darling." Godric slid her down on the couch so she lay upon her back. Then he sat on the couch's edge and leaned over her. He threaded his fingers in the loose waves of her hair and gazed into her eyes.

"Shouldn't you shut the door before...?" Her breathless whisper died as he began to unfasten his breeches and raise her dress.

"Before I ravish you? No one will disturb us," Godric promised with a wicked glint in his green eyes.

"You're an absolute fiend!" Emily moaned as he rained kisses down on her face and neck while his hands worked on her undergarments.

"And you wouldn't have me any other way." He bit her neck and Emily gasped as he plunged deep into her.

"How was the meeting?" Emily asked, causing Godric to grunt in annoyance.

"Clearly, I haven't distracted you enough, woman." He thrust in deeper and harder.

Any rational thoughts she might have had left exploded into fragments beyond her reach.

"More!" she demanded.

Her husband obliged with a devilish grin. "That's a far preferable response."

Once they were both sated, Godric nuzzled his wife's neck before speaking.

"Horatia is pregnant," he said in an oddly quiet voice. Emily cupped his chin and forced him to raise his head to look at her. His green eyes were full of wonder.

"She is?" Emily thought she felt something inside her stir to life. Was now the time?

"Lucien says the baby is due in November."

"That's wonderful!" She meant it to her very core. Horatia had suffered for so many years and Lucien had been so afraid of love that a baby, their baby, would be a miracle.

"Do you want children?" Godric asked. They were still connected, limbs entwined, noses almost touching.

"Yes, yes I do." She was suddenly shy, something that rarely happened when she was with Godric.

"I don't want to pressure you. I know you are young,

but I am much older and..." Godric trailed off uncertainly, his cheeks slightly ruddy.

"I had never thought I would want children so early, I am nineteen, but I guess...I guess we don't have to worry now." Emily caressed his cheek, feeling the light patch of afternoon stubble that lined his strong jaw.

His brows drew together in concern. "What do you mean?"

"I'm pregnant. At least I think I am. My monthly courses were due two weeks ago." Before she could say more, Godric was squeezing the life out of her and kissing her.

"Lord, I hope you're right," he breathed. "I hope it's a girl."

"You want a daughter? What about an heir?"

"We'll have dozens of children. I want a daughter first, so that I can spoil her rotten. Boys aren't nearly as much fun in that regard. They don't like being fussed over, but girls do. I want many daughters, you hear me?" Godric twined a lock of her hair around his finger and tugged it playfully. "I want them all to look just like you," he added in all seriousness. Emily blushed, pleased by Godric's sweet insistence.

"We'll have several of both. I have a feeling our sons will be incredibly troublesome, just like their father." Emily giggled as Godric, still inside her, hardened and he moved his hips against hers. Godric made love to her again, until their faces were once again gleaming with a sheen of light sweat.

After a time of pleasant silence and cuddling, Emily gently moved her loose-limbed husband off her so she could fix her clothes, then returned back to the subject she'd tried to speak about earlier.

"Other than Horatia's upcoming motherhood, what else has happened? I know something did because Cedric summoned your entire League, didn't he? What was it about?"

Godric rolled his eyes in mock exasperation. "You make us sound like a bloody war counsel, darling."

In some ways they were, given the troubles they faced with the elusive Hugo Waverley. Godric had told her much, but not everything, of their past with him, and such meetings always concerned her. "Well, what did he want?" She brushed a lock of dark hair back from his eyes and snuggled closer to him.

"He simply wanted to inform us that he's getting married."

"What? To whom?" Emily demanded, fearing for Anne. She knew Anne had been intrigued by Cedric for some time. She'd never said it, but for a woman who insisted Cedric's attentions were bothersome, she tended to ask a lot about him when he was absent. If Cedric married, it might hurt Anne's feelings, however guarded. Emily couldn't deny her secret wish to unite the two stubborn people.

"I'm not sure you'll believe me." Godric grinned sheep-ishly, like a lad caught stealing sweet meat pies from the kitchen.

"Who? Tell me or you will be sleeping in here tonight. *Without* me." She punched his chest lightly to show him she meant business. Godric wrapped his arms around her waist and tucked her into his side.

"He's going to marry Anne," he said finally.

"*My* Anne?"

Emily was flabbergasted when Godric nodded.

"Well, that's good isn't it?" She gazed at Godric, trying to gauge his reaction.

He appeared puzzled as he brushed some hair from his eyes. "I think so. They went about it quite oddly, but at least they're doing it."

"What do you mean, oddly?" Her fingers, which had curled in his shirt, tensed.

"Well, the way Cedric told it, she came to him and asked him to propose to her."

"How strange. Why?"

"You're asking a man, darling. I don't claim to be a scholar in the mysteries of women. Cedric told us she had become a target for fortune hunters and marrying him would put an end to it." Godric didn't seem to think there was anything more to it than that.

"How long until the wedding? She'll be out of mourning next April, and that would make a lovely time for—"

Godric interrupted Emily's marital musings. "Next week."

"Next *week?*" Emily squeaked. "But she can't! It's unheard of. You know how society can be on such matters, their penchant for cruelty. She'll be gossiped about for months! Her father barely dead and she's running off with one of the League of Rogues? I know we all know the truth, but the *ton* will make up whatever venomous stories it pleases."

"I have a feeling neither she nor Cedric cares about society. He's blind and she's been on the shelf for years."

Leave it to Godric to boil down two complex personalities so bluntly, she thought.

"You may be right, but shouldn't we at least caution them?"

"I won't. Damn the *ton*. Let them wag their chins. It will all be over when the next scandal sweeps through the assembly rooms. I'll stand by Cedric in St. George's next week no matter what. He needs this marriage, Emily. He's been broken since the accident, in spirit as well as body. But when he was telling us about his engagement, I heard hope in his voice for the first time. If a speedy marriage can cure him of his blue devils, then I'm all for it."

Emily rested her head on his shoulder, her fingers playing with the now crumpled cravat tied at her husband's neck. "You're right."

"Of course I am," Godric said imperiously. Emily pinched him in the arm and he yelped.

"You little..." He started to tickle her waist, Emily's greatest weakness, and she dissolved into a fit of giggles until she was gasping for mercy.

"Do you think they'll be happy, Godric?" Emily asked.

He ran a fingertip down her upturned little nose, and she couldn't help but admire the flush of life in his face and the glimmer of love in his bewitching green eyes. How had she been so blessed to have him fall in love with her?

"They may need some artful nudging. I believe you are the expert in that field, so I shall leave it to your careful ministrations." His hands stroked up and down her back, the intimate and tender gesture filling her with warmth.

"I am, am I? And just what artful nudging have I done lately?"

Godric smirked and slid her onto his lap. "I believe this will refresh your memory." He groaned in pleasure as she squirmed, feeling his erection beneath her bottom.

"You're of a particular single-mindedness today, aren't you, my love?"

"All this talk of babies and marriage has put me in the mood to make sure we do in fact get those babies." Godric captured his wife's mouth before she could reply. She knew they would spend the rest of the afternoon working on this newfound interest.

ANNE TOOK CEDRIC'S OFFERED HAND AS HE GUIDED HER into the coach. She watched in silent interest as he tapped the tip of his cane against the metal step that hung down from the door. He looked handsome in his black evening clothes, clean-shaven and brown hair tamed just enough to give the impression that he'd risen from bed after a night of rough play and combed his hands through it.

Once Cedric seemed certain the step was there, he raised a booted foot up and slowly lowered it down. This gave him confidence, and he reached out for the edges of the coach's open doorway.

"Here, let me help..." Anne began.

"I'm fine!" Cedric snapped as he climbed into the coach and felt around him for the seat. When he sat down directly next to her, he jabbed his cane on the roof to signal the driver to move.

"My lord, I don't think it's proper for you to sit so close to me."

"As I reminded you this afternoon, Anne, I don't do *proper*. Now would you please give me your hand? I should like very much to hold it." He demanded this so gruffly she was torn between refusing him flat out and laughing at his audacity.

"If you think I'll just give you any part of my body when you are in such a foul mood, you are gravely mistaken." Anne scooted as far away as possible, but Cedric soon crowded her.

He threw up an arm in front of her, resting his palm

flat on the wall next to her head, trapping her in the cage of his body. Anne's pulse raced as Cedric's face drew close to hers. His vacant brown eyes seemed so cold that she couldn't repress the shiver they drew from her.

"I should not have snapped at you," he said quietly, his warm breath fanning her face.

"Are you apologizing then?"

"It is as close to one as you will get. *Now, give me your hand.* Do not make me ask again or I shall simply do as I wish without asking permission."

"Why?" Anne dared to ask. Her breath hitched as he sought her left arm. Finding it, he slid his rough grip down to her wrist and pulled her hand into his lap.

"I should like to hold it, that is all. Surely you would permit such a chaste desire from your future husband?" He flashed a mocking smile in her direction as he surrounded her hand with both of his.

"Relax, Anne," he said calmly.

After a long minute she did, not even realizing she'd been so tense before. They rode in silence, listening to the clatter of the coach on the cobblestones before Cedric slid her glove off and began to stroke her hand. He drew long, lazy patterns on her bare skin and then turned her hand over to explore her palm, tracing her lifelines to the rapid pulse of the underside of her wrist. Then he did something she had not expected.

He raised her hand up and pressed his lips to her wrist. Anne watched in fascination as he flicked his tongue against her skin, his lips curving into an unconscious smile, the way one does when tasting something unexpectedly sweet and the pleasure of it catches the taster off guard.

CEDRIC THEN TOOK ONE OF HER FINGERS INTO HIS mouth, sucking it between his lips. Anne held in a whimper at the sudden flush of heat and the aching throb that came from within. The feel of his mouth hot and wet around her finger did something to her. Her tongue moved out to wet her lips just as Cedric's tongue circled her finger, teasing it, caressing it, and then he lightly nipped her.

"Oh!" Anne tried to jerk her hand back into her lap, but he did not let her go. Instead, he pulled her against him, his other arm banding around her waist.

"Ask me... Ask me to kiss you." He dipped his head with exquisite slowness.

When his nose brushed hers, his lips followed, sweeping against her slightly parted lips. "Ask me to end your resistance. Let me inside you."

Had Anne been thinking clearly she might have realized he meant more than something physical. But her mind was focused on the more literal images his words conjured. Cedric rising above her, propping himself on his arms as he buried himself deep between her legs. To her surprise the image was not as unwelcome as she feared it might be.

Her silence was answer enough. Cedric pushed her away from him so roughly that she fell back onto their shared seat with a startled gasp. For an instant she saw rage, disappointment and despair on his face before he schooled his features back into that ever mocking self-assurance. Cedric had let her retreat, but Anne worried that the smug look on his face promised future moments where she would not be allowed to do so.

His arrogance angered her. She wanted to scream, to hit him, to leave the coach and go home, but she squared her shoulders and said nothing. It was the only way she could show him that he hadn't affected her.

The trouble was he *had* affected her, very deeply. Some dark part of her wanted his mouth back on her fingers, and other places. She blushed, never more thankful he couldn't see her shame.

"Are you pleased to be dining with Emily tonight?" Cedric asked, as though he hadn't just made her speechless a minute before with that very mouth of his.

It also did not fail to stir her jealousy that he and Emily were so close. Despite their bond of friendship, it still hurt to think Emily knew Cedric better than she did. Though Anne had never encouraged his attentions before the accident, a part of her had hoped he would not give up. That he wanted her enough to continue to fight for her.

And Anne secretly wondered whether all of the men who'd abducted Emily had fallen in love with her to some degree. Their devotion to her was unshakeable, and rakes never devoted themselves to anyone without reason.

Cedric misinterpreted her silence. "You are not pleased then?"

"I'm sorry. I was woolgathering. Of course I am happy

to see Emily. I am just worried that she won't approve of my casting aside my mourning clothes for her dinner tonight." It was a lie. She wasn't worried about that at all, but he could never know her true reasons. Silly nonsense, to be jealous of her dear friend.

Cedric sat up straighter, as though her admission caught his attention. "You're not wearing black?"

"No. Somehow I felt it would make my father sad. He never approved of wearing mourning clothes for very long. He knows, wherever he is, that I..."

For a moment she could not speak; her throat constricted and her eyes burned. *I will not cry. I will not cry. I am not weak.* She repeated the mantra that had kept her from showing any strong emotion since her father died.

"That you miss him," Cedric finished for her.

"Yes." Anne wondered at the fact that he completed her sentence. Did he understand her so well? Or was she merely so transparent that even a blind man could see the depth of her grief?

"So, if you are not wearing black, what *are* you wearing, my dear?" Cedric grinned wickedly, but the affect put her strangely at ease, dispelling the tension of her heavy sadness.

"It is a simple satin gown, russet brown with a bit of an autumnal orange hue to it under the right light."

Cedric reached out, his hand settling on her thigh as he explored the feel of the satin beneath his fingers.

"I am glad you aren't wearing that awful black crepe

anymore. I despised the way it felt when I touched you. A woman's clothes should create pleasure when sliding against one's skin. It should entice her lover's touch."

Anne was bewitched by the spell his hand wove over her thigh, the slow exploring caress. So light that it did not disturb the satin, yet she still felt the heat of his skin sink through her gown, creating a heady anticipation deep in her womb.

His touch reminded her of her father's stable master, Harvey, as he worked with wild unbroken geldings. Harvey always gentled the wildest of the young horses with his soft whispers and feather-light touch.

Suspicion suddenly flooded Anne. Was Cedric planning to lull her into thinking she was safe and then pounce? Surely that was his plan. Just as she steeled herself to demand he cease touching her, he stopped of his own accord and set his hand back on his lap as though nothing had happened.

"I do not think Emily will mind you casting off your mourning blacks. Emily is a most understanding little creature. Sometimes I think she understands *too much.*" This last sentence was delivered in such a disgruntled mutter that Anne couldn't help but wonder what he meant, not that she would dare ask.

"I hope you are right," she murmured instead.

"You'll soon find out that I am often right. Do not be shocked by it." His tone was imperious, but she sensed the faintest hint of teasing behind it.

"I can't help it if I am shocked, my lord. Your arrogance is limitless after all," Anne retorted.

"As it should be," Cedric replied. Part of her wanted a nice vicious fight with him for his cheeky tone, but he wouldn't even give her that, the insufferable cad.

The coach came to a stop, and a footman dressed in the midnight blue and silver livery of the Duke of Essex opened the coach door on Cedric's side. Cedric took his cane, reached for the edges of the coach and felt for the step.

Anne noted that he was far more hesitant getting out than getting in. She couldn't help but wonder if he'd suffered a nasty fall from a coach recently. She could only image how painful that must have been, not to mention humiliating.

Anne's stomach twisted in unease. How often had he hurt himself since last December? The memory of finding him in his gardens, hands bloodied, was one that haunted her. Even as he tormented her with his kisses and caresses, she could not hold her usual indifference or fury at him like she could other men. Cedric had suffered like she had, and that fact bound them together now as kindred spirits.

"Are you coming?" Cedric called out, offering his hand.

She took it and let him help her down. Lifting her skirts, she walked with him toward the steps of the St. Laurent townhouse. To her dismay, he did not release her hand. It seemed he wished to embarrass her by such an obvious display of ownership of her person.

"My lord, you must release my hand," she whispered, tugging to free herself.

"Ashamed of me already, Anne?" Cedric replied rather loudly as the footman opened the door to the foyer for them. He did that so often, murmuring her name at the end of a question or a sentence, as though getting her used to the sound of him saying it. It had riled her before, but now she was growing accustomed to the honeyed way it rolled off his lips.

"You know I am not. A gentleman would let me take his elbow, and I could assist in guiding you to the door," she replied icily, but Cedric merely chuckled, as though her tone did not concern him at all.

"I'll not trip." He waved his cane in front of them, tapping the stones. "Relax, love. No one here tonight will judge us if we show outward affection for each other."

"Is that what you call this? I would call it enforced imprisonment of my hand," Anne hissed. But before she or Cedric could continue this line of conversation, Emily came out of the nearest room and hurried over with her husband, Godric, on her heels.

"Anne!" Emily hugged her tightly, her young face shining with excitement.

"It's so good to see you, Emily. Your Grace." Anne dipped into a slight curtsy in Godric's direction, even though one of her hands was still firmly clasped in Cedric's. Godric beamed at her and nodded in greeting.

"We are so glad that you could attend. Please, come

this way." Godric took Emily's arm and proceeded with Anne and Cedric back into the room from which they'd come.

From the multitude of bodies and voices, she realized that she and Cedric had arrived last. The Earl of Lonsdale was leaning against the mantel of the fireplace speaking to Godric's half brother, Jonathan St. Laurent. Lord Lennox sat on a couch conversing with Horatia, Viscountess of Rochester. Her husband, Lucien, stood behind the couch, hands resting on his wife's shoulders in a gesture both affectionate and protective. The intimacy they displayed made Anne's heart stir with envy and sadness.

Emily and Godric moved into the room, leaving Anne and Cedric standing in the doorway, exposed to the others. Anne moved instinctively closer to Cedric, her left arm brushing his, fingers tightening around his hand. She felt embarrassed and awkward being here in what was so obviously a strange sort of family built upon love, loyalty and friendship, none of which she had a claim to other than with Emily.

"What's the matter?" Cedric whispered, his concern touching her heart.

"I just... What if they don't like me? Your friends, I mean. They barely know me," Anne whispered back.

"You have Emily's friendship and approval, and what's more you have mine. If they don't treat you kindly, then they will answer to me."

"I didn't mean..." She didn't want to sound like she

expected him to choose her over his friends, should it come to that. She would never want him to make that choice.

"Please relax and lead me to a chair, will you?"

Anne got Cedric seated and then took a chair next to his.

"I believe congratulations are in order," Lord Ashton said. He smiled at her and the rest of the room followed suit in offering their excitement over the upcoming marriage.

Anne's fears about being found wanting by Cedric's friends seemed to be ill-founded. She finally relaxed, letting out a sigh of relief. Cedric must have heard this and put his arm around the back of her chair, cupping the nape of her neck. She was about to protest when his thumb and forefinger began to rub up and down the sides, massaging the tense knot of muscles there. The sensation was divine, and it seemed to melt every bone in her body.

"All will be well," he said, continuing to stroke her neck. Anne blushed when she noticed Emily watching her and Cedric with avid interest.

Emily led the group in the sitting room through polite small talk until the dinner bell rang. Everyone rose and headed for the dining room. Cedric offered his arm to Anne and she took it. It never ceased to amaze her how often they touched now. It seemed his body and hers were dancing in a slow spin around each other, and someday soon they would collide and never again be fully separate in some mysterious and primal way.

Anne's breath hitched in her throat at the thought. Even blind, Cedric was still a powerful, masculine force that could easily dominate and possess her. She blushed deeply as she was reminded all that power and handsome perfection was hers now. But as much as the prospect thrilled her, it also frightened her out of her wits. What if he found her wanting? What if he found no pleasure in her bed and sought it in the arms of another?

How am I to keep him if I cannot trust myself to surrender to him?

C edric was ignorant of his fiancée's thoughts as he walked with her to dinner. He let her body guide his, feeling the faint pull of her when he needed to alter his path. It was a skill he'd worked on when Ashton led him about while he first learned to survive with his condition. Fortunately, he was decently familiar with Godric's townhouse, but the nervousness that held his body made him more hesitant than usual.

He wanted to show Anne that he could still play the English gentleman, that he was not as helpless and hopeless as he felt. He sagged into his seat at the table with relief. His body seemed to naturally tense when he was up and about, as though some part of him expected to be injured somehow. Feeling more like himself, he reached out boldly to find his wine goblet...

Splunk!

His hand collided with the thin stem of the goblet, toppling it onto its side. He heard wine sluice over the table and the chatter around the table halted. Cedric, even blind, could sense every eye in the room fixed upon him. It was mortifying. The only relief was that he couldn't see the pity in their faces.

It was too much. He hated eating in front of others and this was why. Cedric shoved his seat back, which happened to hit a footman. The footman stumbled, dropping a replacement goblet, which shattered on the wooden floor close by. Cedric got to his feet and felt about for his cane, but it wasn't there.

"Cedric..." Godric said somewhere near his right, but Cedric shrugged off his friend's coaxing tone. With as much pride as he could muster, he walked in the direction of the door to leave the dining room. He didn't want to apologize; he didn't want to hear the pity in their voices. He needed solitude.

Charles called after him, "Cedric, really, it's fine," but Cedric had already reached the door and propelled himself out into the hall. Hands outstretched, he summoned a map of Godric's house in his head and made for the library—at least he hoped he was heading in that direction. Facing his friends was hard enough when he wasn't breaking costly crystal goblets. He'd been able to accept their help the first few months, but by now he should have mastered his hands and legs, no longer creating such accidents. It was shameful and he couldn't stand to receive any aid, not when he shouldn't need it any longer.

Cedric muttered a curse when he tripped over the threshold of the library. He knew it was the library by the thick, musty scent of a multitude of books. He'd never been one for reading, but he'd grown fond of libraries since he'd lost his sight. With a library he always knew where he was. Their unique aroma gave them away, and he felt comforted knowing exactly where he was in a house for a change.

"I wish I had my cane," he said to the book-filled room. He usually kept it close to him, but he'd been more preoccupied with Anne and had forgotten where he'd placed it. It took him a few minutes of blundering about before he stopped hitting bookshelves and found a deep-backed settee to slump into. He lay back and rubbed his eyes. A useless gesture, but it was a habit he couldn't break. Cedric took a few deep, measured breaths, but his hands were still shaking.

"Pull yourself together!" he hissed at himself.

There was a soft rap on the library door. Cedric didn't move. He heard slippered footsteps approaching him. The scent that teased his nose was flowery, but not the scent of wild orchids. It wasn't Anne.

"Cedric." Horatia sat down by him on the settee and laid her head on his shoulder as she used to do when she was a child. Brotherly instinct took over, and he wrapped his arms about her, pulling her close to him in a tight hug.

"Do you want to talk about it?"

"I have nothing much to say, my dear. I'm a pathetic creature who can't even dine with my friends. I'm sure Emily is devastated that I broke her fine crystal."

Horatia laughed. "She declared you did her a favor. She detested that crystal, and you gave her an excuse to dispose of the rest. She ordered the butler to have some footman take it all away after the meal is over. She seemed quite gleeful about it." Horatia's soft tone was full of amusement, and Cedric heard only truth in her voice. Still, Emily could just as easily have been putting on a show for his comfort when he later heard of it.

"And the others? How did they react?" he asked.

"They don't mind at all. We have all adjusted to what happened to you. Everyone but you, that is. What they mind is the way you think they won't accept you as you are now. None of us are perfect and none of us expect you to be either. You have to stop pitying yourself or I will get cross with you, and I do not want to be cross with my favorite brother."

"I'm your only brother," he cut in with a grin tugging at the corners of his mouth.

"A triviality," Horatia teased and kissed his cheek.

"Horatia..."

"Yes?"

"About your condition..."

"The baby?" Horatia's tone held a hint of embarrassed surprise.

"I just wanted to say, well, that I am overjoyed to be an uncle. And what's more, I am glad that you and Lucien are happy. I've been such a fool. I nearly got all of us killed because I could not believe that people could change. But we can. I know that now. I've changed, Anne has changed. It seems we've always been changing, but have never been aware of it until now."

"Is it true that Anne asked you to propose to her?"

He patted his sister's shoulder, a smile on his lips. "Yes. It was an odd surprise, but not an unwelcome one."

"Well, I certainly like her, as does Emily. But are you sure you will be happy with her? I thought she had no interest in you."

How he loved his sister. She was always thinking of him, even when she shouldn't have to.

"I thought so too at first. But something is different. She's become vulnerable since her father's death, and I couldn't refuse to play her white knight when she asked me to."

"But will she make you *happy*? Lucien worries she is too guarded to love anyone, but you deserve love, not just companionship."

It was the second time someone had told him that today, and he felt strangely warm inside and yet guilty. He didn't *deserve* love, none of the League did, but if it came and he could grasp it, he'd hold tight and never let go.

"Don't worry, Horatia. I have ways of melting her icy walls." Cedric grinned. "In fact, if you could tell Emily that

I am still dreadfully embarrassed and would like to take my meal in here, could you see to it that Anne brings my food?"

"I doubt that Anne would go along with a request more suited to a footman," Horatia cautioned.

"Tell Emily that I *insist* Anne brings it."

"And just what, dearest brother mine, are you planning to do when she does?"

"You are married to Lucien, sweetheart. I am sure that you have some idea how much fun sharing a meal can be."

"You devil!" His sister's indignant tone was marred by a smothered giggle. "Just do not rush her." Horatia rose from the settee. She placed a kiss on his forehead and departed. Cedric grinned. The evening could still be salvaged with a bit of help from edible seduction.

❦

ANNE SQUIRMED IN HER SEAT AS HORATIA RETURNED TO the dining room.

"Is everything well with him?" Ashton asked. All eyes fixed on her. Anne did not envy Cedric's sister having the attention of the room.

"He is a little embarrassed. He needs time to compose himself." Horatia took her seat next to Lucien before turning to Emily. "Would it be possible to send him a plate of food and someone for company? I think he isn't ready to face everyone, but I believe he does not wish to be alone either."

"Oh, certainly. I'd be happy to..." Emily started to rise, but Charles stopped her with an intense look. She plopped back down into her seat, her sweet face a picture of confusion.

"Why doesn't Miss Chessley go? I mean, it seems with the upcoming wedding that perhaps the affianced couple would enjoy some private time together. Unless, of course, the lady does not wish to be burdened with the company of an ill-tempered blind man."

It was a flat-out challenge. Anne frowned at those suddenly serious gray eyes. Now she saw the rogue in him, the seductive and dangerous man she'd had the fortune of avoiding since her coming out five years ago. It would take a strong woman to survive being the prey of that particular predator.

"I would be happy to share a private meal with Lord Sheridan." Anne rose from the table, causing all the men to jump to their feet. She followed a stunned Emily out of the dining room, who instructed a waiting footman to bring two plates to the library before she turned to Anne, hands on her hips and violet eyes filled with concern.

"You don't have to dine with him, really, Anne. Charles is being an imbecile."

"It's perfectly fine. I believe Lord Lonsdale is testing me. Despite the manner in which he delivered his opinion, I am honored to be the subject of his challenge because he demonstrated such loyalty to Lord Sheridan. I would not wish to marry a man who did not have good taste in friends."

She meant every word. As much as it irked her to have to prove herself, she was glad to think Cedric had so many people watching over him. The two fell in step, walking leisurely to the library in order to give the staff time to prepare and catch up.

"But still, Charles was far too rude, and I will not allow such impertinent behavior inside my house." Emily raised her chin angrily.

How far she has come, Anne thought with pride. To be such a young debutante and then a duchess half a year later, she played the part well and would only get better at it.

"Please don't trouble yourself on my account. I would much rather prove Lord Lonsdale wrong by showing my dedication to my fiancé."

"I still cannot believe you are marrying Cedric. I had my hopes, of course..." Emily trailed off when Anne stopped short beside her.

"What do you mean?"

"Well, for as long as I have known Cedric, he's asked me about you. Heavens, he *never* stopped until..." There was no need to finish the sentence. *Until the accident.*

"He...talked about me?" Anne whispered, her throat tight.

"He was so frustrated over your constant refusals to

see him, to even speak to him, that he was going mad. You were always on his mind, and still are, it would seem." Emily's soft voice was full of mystery, even knowledge about things Anne, even older than Emily, had yet to grasp.

Anne had the sudden urge to tell Emily everything, to spill out the secret she'd been keeping inside her guarded heart for so long, but she couldn't trust herself not to falter. Emily had so much to handle as a duchess that Anne did not want to burden her friend with her own emotional nonsense. She must find her own way to persevere.

Before the silence between them could stretch any further, Anne and Emily reached the library.

"He is in there?" she asked. Emily nodded just as the footman arrived with a silver tray and two plates of food.

"I left out any entrees that might pose problems for Lord Sheridan, such as the peas," the footman said discreetly to Emily.

"Thank you, Jim, I appreciate your consideration. Please take the meals inside and set up the main table."

"Yes, Your Grace." Jim bowed his head and entered the library. When the footman had left, Emily turned her attention back to Anne. "You really mean to marry him?"

"Yes." How many times would she have to defend her choice? Was it so impossible to think she actually wanted to marry Cedric?

"But will you be happy with him? Don't marry him

unless you can promise me that you will be happy."

"I will be happy. It may not be a happiness like yours, but I believe that marriage to Lord Sheridan will give me a sense of contentment I have not found before now."

Emily snorted. "Contentment? Oh, Anne, I do not think you know Cedric as well as you think. He won't be satisfied until he's seduced you to the point that you won't remember your name. He loves a challenge. It is what keeps him going, especially these days."

Anne smiled. "I am well aware of his love of challenges. I mean to give him one." With that she stepped into the library to find her fiancé.

Cedric was leaning back against a scarlet velvet settee with a dismal look on his face. Anne motioned for Jim to leave once he finished setting up the table.

"Is that you, Anne?" Cedric cocked his head to the side. Anne had the strangest feeling that he'd recognized her by her scent.

"Yes, my lord. I've had dinner brought for us." He seemed to hear her approach and held up a hand to stay her.

"I'm blind, not an invalid," he snapped as he got to his feet. He was lucky he could not see the hurt those words had caused her. Cedric reached the nearest chair and pulled it out for her. He couldn't see his error. Her plate was a good few feet away from that seat, but she reached over the table and slid her plate toward the seat he offered.

"Please sit," he said a little more cordially.

"Thank you." Anne slid into the seat offered. He pushed her in a few inches before he pulled his own chair back with caution and seated himself next to her. Anne watched as he slid his hands along the table's surface until his fingertips bumped into the edge of his own plate.

"Ahh, there we are," he said to himself and drew the plate toward himself before hunting for the silverware.

It struck Anne then that Cedric's loss of sight affected more than his vision. Every move he made was slow, measured, calculated to prevent injury to himself or damage to things around him. His muscles tensed and remained unbearably taut. His face seemed perpetually strained at the effort of reining in his movements.

She couldn't forget the man he used to be. A man of power and strength with a fearless swagger in his steps that was entirely gone now. His natural physical grace had been erased, like a stallion lamed. He would never regain the beautiful gait she'd once loved when she'd seen him dance. The fear of falling or striking something would forever mar his movements. Even now his face tightened with frustration as he floundered about for his silverware.

Anne spoke up with a gentle voice. "Six inches to your right." She then sipped her wine and felt a fleeting sense of victory when he found his spoon. He ran a cautious thumb over its rounded edge and then grinned in her direction.

"May not be the best utensil, a spoon, but it's easier to

work with than a fork." Cedric's casual remark made Anne choke on her wine.

"Beg pardon?"

"With a fork I spend half my meals trying to find the food and the rest trying to get it into my mouth. Spoons are easier to use. I prefer forks only when I'm eating something that requires it to be held in place for cutting."

Anne pictured Cedric trying to eat and finding each meal a source of constant frustration. It did not escape her notice now that he looked thinner, paler than he used to. Perhaps he wasn't getting enough food to eat because of how much trouble it was, or perhaps his melancholy spoiled his appetite.

What a tragedy it was that he lost the bloom of his manhood to the slow wasting away of his condition. Blindness alone was not his enemy, it was losing the little pleasures of one's life because they were now impossible to do.

It was no wonder he had jumped on her offer of marriage. He needed something, or someone, to focus on. Someone to break the despairing monotony of his current existence. Rather than feel good that she was offering him such a reprieve, Anne could not help but wonder if he was merely using her the way he would have used any woman who asked him to marry her. Emily might be wrong about Cedric still wanting her—she was such a romantic, after all.

Last year he'd been intent on seduction. The passion was there, the fire of his longing for her, even if only physical, and she'd been terrified of how she'd respond. But now his kisses, while just as hot, were tinged with desperation and it upset her. As selfish as it was, she wanted him to kiss her because he wanted to kiss *her*, not because he had to feed his rakish need for contact with a woman's body.

"I am sorry if my conversation is not to your liking," Cedric said.

"What?" Anne hadn't been listening and couldn't remember what he'd been speaking about. Cedric's head was turned in her direction, but his brown eyes were distant as always, and his usually sensual mouth was tightened into a grim line.

"Ah, I've lost the ability to entertain a beautiful woman, it seems. I regret that I am not the man I once was. We could be having a very different evening together." The ghost of his old smile flitted over his lips, as though he was reliving some of his more wicked moments with other ladies.

"I am not beautiful, my lord, but your compliment is kind. I am enjoying our evening now. Please do not think I find your ability to entertain as lacking in any way." Anne picked up her fork and began to slice the breast of her pheasant.

"You think you are not beautiful? Perhaps I'm not the only one who is blind in this room. To me you are a diamond." Cedric's tone had lost its gruff defensiveness and became silky.

Anne narrowed her eyes at him. Was he making fun of her? To compare her to a cold, sharp stone? Or was he trying to say she was costly? Neither of these comparisons was even remotely appealing.

"Again, I've said something wrong," Cedric mused as he glided his spoon toward the lumpy mass of what Anne hoped was a fattening meat pie. She wanted Cedric to eat more. His cheekbones were too gaunt and his eyes too hollow. How had she not noticed this before? Was her own self-absorption strong enough to blind her to his suffering?

"I'm sorry, my lord, I'm not in the best of moods for conversation."

"Is there nothing we might talk about?" Cedric asked with genuine hope in his voice.

He really did want to make things work between them, and for some reason it stung her with guilt, that she had trapped him into marriage without warning him that she would not be so easy to seduce or even befriend. *Have I wronged him already?* she wondered silently, but there was no easy answer. Anne was silent for a moment before a question sprung to her lips.

"Emily says you won your Arabian mares from a sheik in a game of whist. Is that true?" She couldn't contain the excitement in her voice. She wished very much to hear more about it.

"Emily told you about that, did she?" Cedric grinned

from ear to ear as he spooned a few big mouthfuls of pie into his mouth and swallowed.

"I would love to hear the full story, if you wouldn't mind sharing it with me." Anne felt a little shy, but she did very much wish to hear the tale.

"It is true I won the horses, but I shall tell you the *true* tale. I admit I rather censored the story with Emily. She was so innocent, and I didn't wish to frighten her with tales of my recklessness, not while she was Godric's captive."

"What parts did you leave out?" Anne leaned forward on her elbows, curiosity holding her in its thrall.

"Well, there was much more to the wager than a pair of horses and money. And the sheik was not actually a sheik but a very rich Arabian merchant who specialized in slavery."

"Slavery? Of people?"

His face darkened. "Oh yes. He was a charming but evil bastard. And powerful. The sort who has equally powerful friends who allowed him to get away with almost anything. Almost." A look of danger and wildness suddenly gave this conversation a new edge she hadn't anticipated.

"And what did you really wager with him?" Her question came out a little breathless.

Cedric smiled rakishly in her direction before replying. "His horses for my freedom."

6

"Charles! I want a private word with you immediately." The Duchess of Essex tapped her foot and pointed to the door. Charles rose from his chair, and the others at the table looked away in various directions. No one would save him from Emily's wrath, it seemed. *Cowards.*

He shouldn't have challenged Anne. He realized his mistake now. But if Emily was going to lecture him, he'd not make it easy for her.

"Today, if you please," Emily commanded.

With an exaggerated sigh, Charles followed her into the hallway, where she turned and punched him in the chest with a little balled fist. She moved to strike him again, but Charles blocked the blow with his forearm, acting so instinctively that he didn't even realize he'd moved. The pugilist in him always managed to rise to the surface, it seemed. He grabbed her delicate wrist before she could assault him a third time. He was so annoyed that she'd resorted to striking him that he kept her wrist locked in his grasp.

"What is it that has upset you, m'dear?" He tried to sound patient, but his voice was low in warning.

"You! Your behavior! How dare you say such things to Anne? She is my friend, and you are a *guest* in this household. I will not tolerate you threatening her, or holding my arm against my will like this!"

Charles uncurled his fingers and Emily snatched her wrist back, rubbing the reddened marks on her fair skin with a scowl.

"Apologies," he muttered. "But I did not threaten her."

"It certainly sounded as though you did. You challenged her about her choice to marry Cedric. To a woman in love, that *is* a threat."

"And how do you know she is in fact in love with him? I've seen no proof."

"Why do you care if she loves him or not?" Emily asked. Charles turned his face away, studying the blue and white patterned wallpaper as though the answer to her question lay there.

"Why do you care?" Emily repeated.

"Why? Damn it all, Emily, it's because of you." He regretted the words the moment he said them. Now he'd never hear the end of it.

Emily's eyes went wide. "What do you mean?"

"You changed everything, don't you see? Ever since we abducted, you nothing has been the same. We've lost what made us strong. You've singlehandedly crippled the League of Rogues. Godric is a fool for love, Lucien and Cedric fought a duel over a woman, Cedric is blind, Ashton is more melancholy than I've ever seen him, bloody Hugo Waverly seems to lurk behind every dark shadow trying to ruin us, and I...I can't seem to wake from this living nightmare of perpetual fear. We've been ruined...ruined by *you!*" He punctuated these sharp words by driving his fist against the wall.

Emily stepped back in alarm. Charles stopped and bent his forehead to the wall as he drew in a deep, steadying breath. He'd never hit a woman, would never a hit a woman, but sometimes punching a wall eased the tension in him.

"I've ruined you?" Emily's voice trembled, but Charles would not look her way, not for all the tea in China. He could not bear to see her cry, which was exactly the point he'd tried to make. The League of Rogues shouldn't be capable of being felled by a young woman's tears. They couldn't afford to have that weakness, not if they were to survive. The events that led to Cedric's blindness had been but a warning of what was yet to come. If only she knew Hugo the way he did...

"Everything is different. I expect things now, things I'd never dared to dream about before. What if my dreams fail? What if I do not deserve what I hunger for? Yes, I blame you for that." Out of the corner of his eye he saw Emily's hands move about her face, as though to dispel any evidence of her tears. Damnation. He didn't want to be talking to her about this—he didn't even want to be *thinking* about this.

Emily put her hand on his shoulder. "What do you dream about? What do you fear you'll never have?"

Charles shut his eyes. For a long moment, he considered not answering her and keeping his thoughts private, but Emily had this awful way of getting inside his head and making him want to bare his soul to her. "I want an end to my nightmares, and a woman who loves me so deeply that my heart will be fit to burst. Godric and Lucien have that...but what if I cannot? What if I don't deserve such a thing?" There it was. He wanted love. He was a fool and the angels would mock him for it.

"How could you ever think you don't deserve to be loved, Charles?"

"There are things about us even you don't know, Emily."

She waved the notion away. "Nonsense. Your heart is loyal and true, as are those of your friends. And if I have to take Ashton's fleet of ships and sail them to the ends of the earth to find someone who loves you, I will. You will have such joy that your heart won't be able to contain it, so it will overflow into everything and everyone around you. I know that this dream can become a reality, but it requires patience. Can you be patient for me?" Emily asked.

Charles's answer was to turn and pull her into him, hugging her tight. It never ceased to amaze him how she could turn him into a child. She made him feel safe, cared for, and yet she was a full decade younger than he was. Godric was a lucky man.

Drawing in a deep breath, he answered. "I can be patient...I can."

Emily tried to speak, but her voice was muffled by his waistcoat.

"Pardon?" he asked her as he pulled back.

With a little dramatic inhale of breath, she looked up at him. "Are you still angry with me?"

"I never could stay mad at you for long, m'dear," Charles said before he kissed her cheek and released her. "You go back into dinner. I'll be along shortly. I just need a minute."

She focused on the worried expression he wore on his face. "Are you sure?"

"Yes. On with you now." He shooed her away.

Once Charles was alone, he crept toward the partially open library door. Inside he saw Anne with her back to him. She was politely directing Cedric as to where to find his spoon. Their conversation was awkward for a time before she asked about Cedric's horses and his famous wager. Cedric grinned, happy to tell the story, and she leaned toward him with open curiosity. Charles saw no love yet between his friend and Anne, but he did see *hope*. Perhaps for the first time since Cedric had lost his sight.

Charles swallowed the tight lump in his throat, then backed away to avoid disturbing the occupants of the library.

He did not return to the dining hall, but instead sat down on the second-to-last step of the main staircase. Elbows on his knees, he buried his face in the shelter of his palms.

He did not look up immediately at the sound of boots coming down the stairs. A hand rested lightly on his right shoulder, and only then did he face the person who had stumbled upon him in his emotionally ravaged state. It was his newest servant, the lad Tom Linley.

"Everything all right, my lord?" Linley's eyes were filled with concern, his blond hair a mess of tangles beneath his flat cap.

Linley was an odd boy, quiet to the point of being timid. Charles suspected that the boy had seen serious abuse at the hands of a former master. But Linley always turned up whenever Charles felt the most alone. It was as though the lad had a sixth sense for when his master needed companionship.

Though he claimed he was twenty, Charles suspected he was much younger. Linley had been decently educated because his mother had been a lady's maid to the mother of an earl, and he raised his baby sister all on his own since his mother's death. With half the League either married or engaged, Linley had become indispensable to him, a companion so crucial to his daily life that he felt like a part of Charles's family, as much as any servant could.

"I'm fine, lad, truly. It has been a long day, that is all." Charles raked a hand through his hair and let out a shaky breath.

"It is true, my lord," Linley said after a quiet moment.

"What is?" he asked, perplexed.

"That you have a heart worthy of love. Her Grace is right. Someday a woman will love you, and you will be happy. It's the way of things."

"Don't tell me you are the romantic sort?" Charles teased and shoved the boy's shoulder. The boy flashed a rare grin, and Charles marveled at the change such a smile had on the boy's face. The worry and fear that often lurked there simply vanished.

"You ought to smile more, Linley. The ladies will be beating down your door," Charles advised. Linley blushed.

"No time for that, my lord. I already get far too much exercise chasing after you, if you take my meaning. That is a most grueling and consuming task in itself."

"Why, you cheeky little..." Charles reached over, feigning to strangle the lad, but they both burst into laughter. "I suppose it is. I can't seem to sit still for more than an hour's time. There's too much to do—women to bed, horses to race, men to box. Sleeping is for the dead."

Linley smiled again and a pleasant silence settled between them.

"I suppose I ought to return to dinner, otherwise Emily will send a search party for me, and I'll have to bear her scorn a second time." Charles got to his feet. "I shall send a footman to collect you when I wish to have the carriage pulled around."

As Charles walked back toward the dining hall, Tom Linley remained seated on the stairs. A smile, unguarded, curved his lips, then slowly dropped into a frown.

"YOU WAGERED YOUR FREEDOM AGAINST THE SHEIK'S horses?" Anne asked as Cedric paused to finish the last bit of his dinner.

He moved to stand. "Indeed."

"I don't believe you."

"It does not require your belief to be true," he said, passing her by.

"Aren't you going to tell me what really happened?"

"If you would join me on the settee, then I shall."

Anne rose to her feet as well and moved toward him. "And if I don't?" Anne returned cautiously. She had every intention of joining him, but wanted to see just how much he was up to the challenge of wooing her. Emily was right —Cedric needed a challenge to keep him interested.

"Then your curiosity must forever go unsatisfied." Cedric felt his way over to the settee and then seated himself. Anne was on the verge of smiling or snorting at his arrogance, she wasn't sure which.

"You believe my curiosity is that strong? Do you claim to know me so well?"

Cedric smirked. "Only a dimwitted fool would not desperately want to know how I escaped the clutches of an evil slave trader and returned victorious with a pair of the man's best horses. And you, my lovely diamond, are anything but a fool. You cannot resist knowing how I avoided a nasty fate, such as a eunuch for an Arab's harem."

As Cedric spoke, Anne drifted closer and closer to the settee until she surprised herself by sliding into the space left open next to him. Like a foal lured with the promise of sugar cubes, she waited eagerly for him to share the rest of his tale.

"A eunuch? Oh please, tell me the rest!" She didn't even realize she was tugging his sleeve like a spoiled child until he seized her. Cedric wrapped a possessive arm around her waist and dragged her onto his lap. Anne fought off the panic at their sudden proximity, but when his muscles tensed around her she ceased, giving up the fight.

"You really do love to humiliate me, don't you, Lord Sheridan?" She settled herself on his lap, then jerked violently after feeling a particularly stiff part of his anatomy directly beneath her.

"Christ, woman! Easy or I won't be able to demand my

marital rights." Cedric eyed her askance before adding, "Maybe that's what you want, you little hellion."

"Don't be ridiculous. I'm just not used to..." She waved a hand helplessly at his lap. "That thing making an appearance."

"You've a lot to learn about men. That *thing*, as you call it, will be making many appearances. And as my wife you'll be attending to it, just as I will be attending to your needs." He leaned close to her, his long brown eyelashes fanning out as his sightless eyes seemed to search in vain for a glimpse of her lips.

"Would you do something for me, Anne, darling?" he asked. He'd called her many endearments, but *Anne, darling* seemed to stir something deep inside her.

"That depends. Will it involve something I shall regret?"

"Just nibble your bottom lip for a brief moment."

"What? Why?"

"Please." His hands on her back moved slowly up and down in a soothing motion.

"Very well." Anne found herself doing as he asked, nibbling her lower lip and watching his responding smile, his blind gaze still lowered.

"Now, why did I just do that?" she asked as Cedric shut his eyes, an expression of pain and bliss all at once on his face.

"I wanted to picture you with pink, swollen lips, as though I'd just kissed you until you couldn't breathe. I could see it so clearly when I closed my eyes. Most women have faded in my mind, but not you. *Never* you."

Goosebumps broke out over Anne's skin. She bit her lip to stifle a wistful sigh that his words could ever be true. She was the only woman who wouldn't fade in this blind man's mind? It couldn't be possible, yet she wished it was. Trying to change the subject, she spoke again. "Was this a ruse to lure me onto your lap, or will you tell me the story? Perhaps there is no story to tell."

"Of course there is a story, my heart. I assure you that my desire to lure you into my embrace was entirely secondary in importance to satisfying your curiosity."

Anne's heart's tempo shot up when he called her *my heart*. She knew logically that he, like any rake, threw such sweet endearments out frequently and meant nothing by them. She couldn't help but wonder if each pet name he came up with would continue to move her until she was half in love with him.

Cedric nuzzled her cheek, moving down to her throat. Anne shifted on his lap as a wave of lust uncoiled in her belly. She could not give in to his seduction or lose her heart to him. It would devastate her when he would not be willing or able to love her back as she feared.

"So what happened?" she persisted.

Cedric sighed in disappointment. "You are very deter-mined this evening, aren't you?" He moved his face back, his unseeing eyes aimed several inches to the left of her face.

"I am when you tease me with a tale of Arab slave traders, horses and harems."

"Very well, I shall satisfy your curiosity. But know this, you will satisfy me when I come to you with my own desires."

Anne said nothing, forcing herself to regain control before any unbidden images of Cedric and his desires took hold of her focus.

"It was a warm evening in March of last year. Ashton and I were at Berkeley's for the night playing cards with a friend..."

⚜ 7 ⚜

L *ondon, March 1820*

Cigar smoke hung in hazy clouds near the ceiling of Berkeley's dimly lit card room. The majority of the men lounging in chairs about the card tables were in their mid to late thirties. The young sensible bucks of marrying age were enslaved at the dances of Almack's that evening. Only the most dangerous of men were left free to prowl tonight and seek their pleasures without worry of crossing the paths of society mamas and their marriage-minded daughters. Cedric, Ashton, and their friend James Fordyce, the Earl of Pembroke, chose a table near the main fireplace to play a few games of whist before heading to a pleasure haunt in a few hours.

Ashton spread the deck of cards out and shuffled them

while Cedric and James flagged down a club servant to bring three glasses of port.

"Thank God Letty did not expect me to accompany her to Almack's," James confessed to Cedric. James blew out a sigh of relief. Cedric chuckled at the relieved expression in the earl's eyes.

"Not a lover of the quadrilles, Pembroke?" Ashton asked.

James laughed. "When a man reaches twenty-eight, he shouldn't have to suffer escorting his sister to such events. I argue that it is a matter of principle to excuse myself from such abominable dances and pointless flirtations."

"Isn't your mother expecting you to choose a bride soon?" Cedric asked.

"Yes, but I don't want to marry just any chit. Any woman at Almack's tonight is not a woman I want to marry."

Cedric snorted. "Then my sisters are safe! What a relief that is."

"I would not wish to be there either," Ashton mused. "In fact, I feel quite guilty because I forced my brother into taking Joanna tonight. Rafe was not pleased, but when Thomasina and I pushed on him, he caved."

"It's been a few years since Joanna came out, hasn't it?" James asked, sipping his brandy.

"Yes, bless her heart, she'll be twenty-two in a month and no man has come around asking for her. I can't understand why. I've been most encouraging to any man who has even so much as asked for her to pass the salt at dinner engagements. But it's no use, not one man has shown he's even remotely interested." Ashton sighed and thumbed through his cards.

Cedric was only half listening to this—talk of marriage and sisters always put him on edge. He didn't like thinking of his own sisters marrying. Ashton's older sister, Thomasina, was already married with a passel of children, but Joanna was the baby of Ashton's family and her brother was apparently determined to see her wed.

"What? No suitors?" James exclaimed in surprise. "Joanna is such a lovely girl!"

Ashton shrugged. "Thomasina believes that she's too likeable, as a companion, not a woman. She has many men who admire her wit and humor, yet none of them so much as send a bouquet of flowers. Damned if I can figure out why. She has a sizeable dowry, and I've not hidden that fact from any man."

"Men are fools," Cedric announced grimly.

"So how is Letty?" Ashton inquired as he began to deal the deck between the three of them.

"Spoiled is what. Last week she told me that a genteel lady ought to own at least a dozen pairs of gloves. I dared to ask what was the use of so many gloves in the spring and she fairly bit my head off. She used some French words I've never even heard of..." James remarked with pensive amusement.

Cedric chuckled. "The fascination with fashion I once

believed to be restricted to the fairer sex, but unfortunately I've seen far too many dandies prowling the streets who were arrested by the splendid sight of themselves reflected in a shop's window glass. A bunch of popinjays, the lot of them." Cedric sipped his port as he eyed one such colorfully dressed dandy who was chatting with a foreign-looking gentleman who had just entered the room.

"I say, Pembroke, do you know that man there?" Cedric gestured to the foreigner.

"Freddy Poncenby?" James asked, shooting a scathing glance over his shoulder at the dandy who was waving his arms excitedly as he spoke. Poncenby was not a favorite of any gentleman at their table. He was a tad too cowardly, and there was a touch of weasel in him that Cedric didn't trust.

"No, the other gentleman."

"Oh! Why that's Samir Al Zahrani. He's from Nejd in Arabia."

"Al Zahrani?" Cedric eyed the man curiously. He was tall with deeply olive skin and a harsh but handsome face and form. Dark brows swept over a pair of black eyes that scanned the room with a militaristic precision that stirred Cedric's curiosity.

"I heard he is a wealthy merchant, which given the power struggles and political upheavals in that part of the world is quite a feat."

"A merchant of what?"

James, a seasoned rake who had little occasion to act

self-conscious of delicate matters, actually looked flustered.

"That depends on who you ask. Most people will tell you he deals in textiles, but I've heard that he runs another far more lucrative business on the side. Slave based." James uttered this last in a soft tone. Ashton and Cedric exchanged surprised looks.

"Slaves?" Ashton's tone was heavy with disapproval. Parliament had outlawed the slave trade over a decade before, though slavery was sadly still legal abroad, though not on English soil. As William Cowper had once said, "Slaves cannot breathe in England; if their lungs receive our air, that moment they are free. They touch our country, and their shackles fall. That's noble, and bespeaks a nation proud."

Sadly, not all within the nation held such nobility.

"Yes. I heard he has recently begun to offer his 'wares' at various brothels in London. But that isn't nearly as frightening as the rumors that he's come here to take our own English roses back to Nejd with him to fill his markets there. Rumor has it such a prize would be worth ten times what he makes elsewhere."

"What?" Cedric sat up straight in his chair. "That's nonsense, Pembroke. Someone would know if our ladies started vanishing, and that would raise an alarm." He slapped his cards down, momentarily losing interest in the game.

"It would be an act of war," Ashton agreed.

"It is the truth, I tell you. I heard several members of the House speaking about it last week. Out of session, of course. His father is a foreign emissary and a powerful merchant in his own right. If he did try such a bold move, he might even get away. It might take too long to rally the navy to chase him down. I've been keeping Letty on a short leash ever since that man made his presence known in London." James looked entirely too serious, as though he'd been giving the matter a great deal of thought.

Ashton leaned back in his chair and placed his cards face down on the table. "Be at ease, Pembroke. No doubt if such things were on his mind, he's been warned off by those very men you spoke of. Nothing like shining a light to chase away the shadows. And should Letty go missing and you need a fleet of ships, you'll have mine to hunt the man down."

"Thank you, Lennox," James replied.

"I think I should like to meet this man."

"Cedric..." Ashton warned. "We have enough enemies at the moment."

Cedric grinned. "Who said anything of enemies? Let's invite him to play whist." Cedric did love to play with fire, even at the risk of being burned. Cedric called out to Freddy and the foreigner. "Freddy, won't you and your friend join us for cards? We're about to indulge in a high-stakes game."

The foppish Freddy Poncenby, a man of only twenty-two, fairly ran to their table in excitement, the mysterious

Samir Al Zahrani on his heels. A pair of tall, dark-haired men flanked the trader on either side. Guards, Cedric assumed.

"I say, gents, what a top-notch idea! Have you met Mr. Samir Al Zahrani? Mr. Al Zahrani, this is Cedric Sheridan, Viscount Sheridan, James Fordyce, the Earl of Pembroke and Ashton Lennox, Baron Lennox."

"It is a pleasure, gentlemen." Al Zahrani's voice was a rich baritone, heavily accented, but his English was beyond reproach.

Cedric and the others rose from their card table and greeted him. Then with a little jerk of his head, Cedric indicated a door behind them.

"What do you say we move to a private room?"

With murmurs of agreement, the group moved to an enclosed chamber and closed the door. There would be no way they could be watched or overheard.

"Have a seat," Cedric offered with a devilish grin. When Ashton met his gaze he rolled his eyes, no doubt realizing the night was not going to end as peaceably as it had begun.

"Do you ever play whist, Mr. Al Zahrani?" Cedric eyed his target with a knowing smile. The idea of cleaning out a slave trader's pockets made his body tense with antici-pation. He detested slavery, and if robbing this fellow blind would put a dent in his pockets, he'd do it in a heartbeat.

"I have played a few times," Al Zahrani answered as he

took his seat next to Freddy. Ashton quickly collected the cards and reshuffled them before dealing them out.

The five men played three hands. Cedric played carelessly at first, losing two hands early on. As the game progressed, port was consumed liberally by all except Al Zahrani, who did not wish to indulge.

"I say, Al Zahrani, you wouldn't happen to have heard of a horse called Firestorm? I believe that's his English name," Cedric asked, his voice smooth and relaxed thanks to the port. Firestorm was a purebred Arabian stallion who was worth a fortune and rumored never to have left Arabia. Nor was the horse permitted to be bred with any foreign breed. No Englishman had been able to get his hands on any of his offspring.

"Firestorm? Indeed I have, Lord Sheridan. That horse belongs to my father. I have two mares that are one and three years old that were sired by him."

"Do you really?" Cedric sighed wistfully. "I would kill to see such a fine bit of horseflesh."

"I have them here in England, should you care to see them. It would be an honor." Al Zahrani offered this with an air of smug pride in his dark eyes. It was obvious he was the sort who loved to flaunt his possession of something others coveted.

"I just might," Cedric mused and resumed playing his hand.

After six more hands, James and Freddy declined to continue but remained to watch Ashton, Cedric and Al

Zahrani play for increasingly higher stakes. Cedric was flushed with the alcohol of the port and the excitement of the plan he was about to set in motion.

"I wager eight hundred pounds I can win this hand. No man ever beats me when I'm on a streak." Cedric slurred a little as he downed the last of his port and grinned at Al Zahrani. The Arab watched him speculatively, then gave a dark smile that Cedric ignored entirely.

"The thing about a streak is that it must inevitably end, my friend. Let us make a wager on something more valuable. How would my pair of mares suit you?" Al Zahrani tossed out casually.

Cedric pretended to consider the offer. "And my forfeit? Perhaps I send you my mistress for the duration of your stay in London? Lovely little bit of flesh she is. Knows her place, too. She'll treat you well on her back, like any woman should." He waited, seeing if Al Zahrani would take the bait.

"One of your women?" Al Zahrani, brooding, stroked the back of his cards, which lay on the table. He studied Cedric, as if realizing what was truly being insinuated by his offer. "While that intrigues me, I sense it would be no great loss to you."

With a huff Cedric reached for his drink again. "Two women then? I suppose I could find another quickly enough."

"Alas, no. If anything you are only proving my point.

Clearly my horses are worth more than a dozen of your English women."

"Well then, what would satisfy you?"

"I engage in a special sort of trade…and I would have great use of you as a servant in my house, to guard my precious wares."

"A viscount as a servant? Good God, man, you are bold! Just what is it that I would be guarding and for how long?" As he spoke, Al Zahrani's guards shifted on their feet by the door, making sure no one could enter or leave.

"You would be positioned as a guard for my female wares. Of course, you would need to be rendered harmless in order to ensure the females go untouched."

Cedric smirked. "Some sort of chastity belt, I take it?"

"I am afraid we are a little more…permanent with our solution to the problem."

Cedric heard a round of gulps from the other men at the table.

"You'd make me a eunuch, is that what you're saying? I mean, I do understand, women aren't nearly as valuable as a good horse, but still, a man's parts are *his* parts."

It was a bluff. Al Zahrani had to be counting on him backing down from such a wild proposition. Cedric felt a flash of panic at the thought of castration, for a number of reasons. As the last male heir to the title in his family, he had a duty to bear a son. And the thought of never again being able to bed a woman was a bleak notion. Despite his bluster aimed at luring Al Zahrani into this bet, he valued the company of a good woman more than a hundred of the finest horses.

"Do not tell me that you are afraid to lose? I thought Englishmen were fearless." Al Zahrani was still smiling, but darkness reflected in his eyes.

"Me, afraid? Why, that's absurd. I merely hesitate, as any decent man would when threatened with slavery and the removal of his manhood," Cedric retorted. There was a murmur of agreement from his friends. Poncenby noticeably cupped his hands over his groin.

"You do realize there is no slavery on English soil?" Ashton interjected. Cedric shot him a look. *Damn it, man, don't interfere.*

"It would not be slavery, and you would not be on English soil. As a matter of honor, you would willingly leave with me to my home country, and once there remain under my employ indefinitely."

Which was just a fancy way of saying the same thing.

"Well? Shall we agree to the terms and finish the hand?" Al Zahrani asked.

Cedric slanted his cards up from the table, eyeing his hand. "I'm not entirely sure my freedom is worth a pair of horses..." Cedric said.

"I can promise you, Lord Sheridan, the horses are worth the freedom of a hundred men, and even one viscount." Still, the man had that inherent smugness.

"Cedric, be wise about this," Ashton said softly.

Cedric met the gaze of his close friend and for a

moment he was fully sober, fully in command of himself.

"I'm as wise as the day I met you," Cedric replied, to which his friend almost burst out laughing. Ashton really should have learned by now to trust him on matters of risk.

The night Cedric and Ashton had first met was the night they had saved Charles from being drowned by Hugo Waverly. They'd been aided by Lucien and Godric, and that night the League had been formed. Cedric had been the calmest during that harrowing rescue, which no doubt had helped save Charles's life.

They had only failed in one thing that night. Another man had been the first to try and save Charles from Hugo, and he'd paid the price for his bravery. His death haunted the League still, and it was the reason Hugo had damned them all that night.

"Very well." Ashton laid his cards down, signaling his withdrawal.

"Then we have a wager, my lord?" Al Zahrani asked.

Cedric flashed him a mad grin. "We do."

Both men revealed their hands, and Cedric snickered in triumph. Everyone but Ashton exclaimed in wonder at Cedric's winning hand.

"When shall I come by and collect my mares?" Cedric asked with a satisfied smile, like a cat fattened on a canary.

Al Zahrani spat, throwing his cards down and leaping to his feet. "You cheated! There was no way I could have lost. It was a mathematical impossibility!"

Cedric scoffed. "Me a cheat? Nonsense. I played a decent hand of whist. Any Englishman could have done that." He crossed his arms over his chest and leaned back in his chair, not at all perturbed by the fury of the Arabian merchant.

"I will *not* give you my horses! I refuse!" Al Zahrani shouted with such loathing that poor Freddy Poncenby dove under the nearest card table for cover.

Ashton sighed at the sight of Freddy's green and white striped trousered bottom peeping out from under the table's edge.

"I played fair with you, Al Zahrani. Every man here saw the game. I won and you owe me your forfeit, lest your business associates in England learn of your unwillingness to honor a debt. Don't tell me *you* are the one who's afraid?" Cedric finally stood, but the action was a leisurely uncoiling of his strong, athletic frame. The others stepped back, giving Cedric and Al Zahrani plenty of room to handle themselves should they come to blows.

After an intense duel of stares, the merchant backed down. "So be it! I will have them sent to your residence in the morning. Enjoy them while you can. Justice ultimately arrives to men such as you. When that day comes, I will walk over your grave, have my horses back and laugh last," Al Zahrani declared.

"Don't flatter yourself. I've never expected to live long or peacefully. If you want revenge for an honest game of cards then you best get in line, because I've done much worse to much better men, and they have more of a right to kill me than you."

"This is not the end between us, Lord Sheridan."

"Yes it is. Either call me out or walk away with your heart still beating."

Al Zahrani glared at Cedric before leaving with his guards.

Once he was gone, Ashton and Cedric resumed their seats along with James.

"You chaps really play for keeps," the Earl of Pembroke muttered with a strained smile.

"Of course we do." Cedric shot him a devil-may-care grin.

"Er, Poncenby, you can come out now." Ashton nudged the tip of his Hessian boot against the striped rump of the cowering dandy. Freddy emerged, looking embarrassed, his face scarlet to the roots of his fashionably cut brown hair.

"Well if you will excuse me, I've had enough excitement for one night." Freddy bid the others adieu and practically sprinted for the door. There was a loud crash and shriek as a servant boy was run over by Freddy making his exit from Berkeley's.

Cedric smothered a laugh. What good luck to finally have two purebred Arabian mares with pedigrees worth a fortune! Now only if he could find a decent stallion to breed them with...

ANNE FOCUSED ON CEDRIC'S FACE, SECRETLY ENJOYING the wealth of emotions that flitted across his features as he told her the story. "You don't think the Arab will return for you, do you?"

Cedric smiled. "He left London shortly after he delivered the mares to me. He simply had to make a show of pride before he left, and I had to respond in kind. It is the way of things when the stakes are so high."

He showed more animation than she'd seen from him since he'd gone blind. For a brief few minutes he'd been the old Cedric again, the one who...

Anne shook her head, dispelling thoughts of the past, thoughts that stung too deeply.

"You men and your pride. Is there nothing else that matters to you?"

Cedric's deep laugh poured over her. "Oh, my dear, you bait me with your innocence by asking that."

"What do you mean?"

Cedric cupped her chin and tilted his head down in reply, finding her lips with ease. Anne stiffened as his tongue traced the seam of her lips. Her hands fisted against his chest, as she went rigid in his lap.

Cedric pulled his mouth away to whisper, "Don't forget what you promised, Anne. Don't turn to ice in my arms, love." He brushed his nose against her cheek. "Please, my heart, don't shut me out."

His coaxing words tugged her down the slope of desire. It was more than lust, more than carnal craving.

She might have been able to stop herself, to keep herself from surrendering, if he hadn't dipped his mouth to her neck and nipped her skin, following it with a slow, teasing lick. The sharp but light sting of his teeth sent a wave of pleasure through her. Anne lost control and melted in his lap.

Cedric growled low as she let herself go limp in his arms and trembled at his kisses. He reached out to the side of the settee, gauging the distance to the other side before he slowly tilted Anne back to lie beneath him. He slid her skirts upward, pushing them into a pool around her hips. Then he palmed her knees, before gently nudging them apart. She should have clamped her thighs together, but instead she threw her head back and let her knees fall apart.

Cedric stroked his hand along her inner thigh, then bent her leg up. She moved with him, understanding that she needed to offer a cradle for his trim hips. She dropped her other leg off the edge of the settee, giving him ample room to lower himself down between her thighs.

The intimacy of their position was unbearable. Her breasts rose and fell with her soft, rapid panting. Trapped beneath him, she was at his mercy and did not mind as much as she should have. It seemed only natural that her hands would fall on his shoulders and glide under the tight-fitting jacket, peeling it off his body. He shrugged the coat loose and it dropped to the floor. She couldn't find it in herself to care that they might actually... She blushed a little, unable to even think the words.

Right here in the library...

❦

CEDRIC BENT HIS HEAD, HIS LIPS SEEKING ANY PART OF Anne that he could reach. She gasped when he reached the soft swell of the tops of her breasts and rained kisses down upon them. He was eager to delve beneath her bodice, to taste the pearled tips of those nipples, but reminded himself to slow down—he wouldn't bed his future wife in the library of his friend's house...well, at least not a woman like Anne. She deserved far better than that for her first time.

He didn't want to rush their lovemaking, not when he knew it would hurt her. But he could give her a taste of what was yet to come. Cedric rolled his hips hard against hers, grinding his erection against the silk of her underpinnings. Anne arched off the settee with a startled moan, pressing herself against him.

Cedric's lips trailed back up her throat to her mouth to nibble on her bottom lip until she whimpered. She seemed entirely unaware of the little sounds she made. Her inner wanton woman was in full control, and not just of her. Each sound, each shift of her body wreaked havoc on his sanity. And then she spoke...

"Are...the Arabian mares here in London?" Her voice

was breathless, and Cedric rubbed himself harder against her, wanting her silent save for cries of pleasure. But he fought off a smile when she struggled again to repeat her question. His woman certainly did love horses.

"No. They're in Brighton." He nuzzled her neck before biting down hard without warning, like a lion holding his female still for mating. She gasped in surprise, her fingers digging into his shoulders clawing him, not to release her but to hold him to her body. Cedric felt ready to roar. He'd found her weakness, that smooth delicious neck. Every woman had a secret spot that would drive them wild, make them senseless. Men had fewer such spots, obviously, but as a rake, Cedric had learned early on that finding a woman's pleasure point was the key to success, both for her enjoyment and his own. Having found Anne's, he would be merciless.

"Brighton? Why Brighton?"

Damn, the woman still has enough sense to talk? I've been out of practice too long. Cedric sank his teeth into the skin between her neck and shoulder, his hands sliding along her sides, then up under her skirts to cup her bottom. He jerked her into him just as he rocked himself ferociously against her. Anne twitched and trembled with violent shivers, murmuring a startled exclamation he couldn't hear over the roaring of the blood in his ears. Damnation, the woman would be his undoing with her natural sensuality.

Never enough, I'll never get enough of her.

Cedric caught Anne's lips with his, invading the silken

recesses of her mouth, questing for her timid tongue.

Every touch, every stroke, each delicious sensation and taste was all he had in the darkness, but it was glorious. Anne was glorious. Experiencing such passion as this with her was different from anything he'd ever expected. How was it possible that it was better than even his darkest fantasies had promised?

Never enough... Cedric tensed with his own need to come as Anne climaxed beneath him. Caged in by his arms, she shook with the aftermath of the moment and then buried her face in the groove of his neck. The intimate gesture, the silent communication, warmed his entire body with something that had nothing to do with the physical pleasure he'd just experienced.

Her hot breath, coming out in tiny pants, only heightened the pain in his groin. He would have none of his own pleasure, not tonight. But this was progress. He'd achieved the feat of truly pleasuring her, something he was certain no man before him had ever accomplished. There was a primitive sense of satisfaction from knowing that he was her first in that regard.

Cedric eased his weight off her. "Are you all right, my heart?" He could feel her start to pull away, but he caught her waist and tugged her against him as they both sat up.

"I don't know. Is that how... Does it always..." Anne seemed unable to find the right words. He could only imagine the confusion she must have felt at experiencing a climax for the first time. *La petite mort* could be frightening but also exciting for a young lady who didn't know what to expect, or so he'd been told.

"If done properly, then yes. And I do believe I know what I am doing when it comes to this sort of thing." Cedric wished he could have seen her face. It was the one thing he'd loved most when in bed with a woman. There was something stunning about how a woman's face lit up with ecstasy and joy as she came apart in his arms.

I will never see such joy on Anne's face.

"What if someone had come upon us?" Anne asked, her body stiffening in his loose hold.

"They didn't. And even if they had, we are engaged, and in a week we will be man and wife and it will no longer matter. Besides, no one under this roof would judge us." Cedric brushed his knuckles over her cheek. Anne leaned away from his touch.

That one small action sliced his heart. Would she always pull away from him? He could not marry a woman who fought him at every turn. He wanted, no, he *needed* someone who would not shy away from his touch. Cedric dropped his hand with a heavy sigh and let go of her waist.

"You should go. I wish to be alone."

Anne didn't move.

"Please leave me," he said more loudly.

"Why?" Her surprise sounded genuine.

"Anne, stop. Your due diligence is appreciated, but you never wanted to be here with me. Just go back to the others. I would hate to further disgust you with my advances." Cedric rose from the settee and turned his back to where he believed her to be. He was still hard and it angered him that he wanted her so much even when he was as upset as this. He desperately wanted to bed a woman who hated his very touch, and touch was the one sense he most relied on now. The irony was almost laughable. Almost. His only advantage was to use her inexperience with passion to overwhelm her.

"You don't disgust me, Lord Sheridan," Anne insisted.

Cedric huffed. "You can't seem to escape me fast enough whenever I let you go."

"I merely can't abide the thought of intimacy before our wedding. I want to obey the rules, even though I know you are far past that point in your...experiences."

"Rules? We've broken most of the rules already. One more shouldn't bother you, Anne. That is how I know you don't want me. When two people desire each other they have trouble waiting. They don't go stiff in each other's arms or pull away from a devoted caress."

Cedric frowned, considering his options. It wasn't too late to call off the ceremony. They had a few days to undo the wedding preparations.

"I'm crying off, Miss Chessley." He no longer felt the desire to breathe her given name. He'd once loved that her name was one smooth syllable, so easily murmured like a lover's sigh after a moment of bliss. Now it brought him pain.

"Crying off?" Anne's voice rose sharply.

"Yes. I do not wish to burden you with a husband you don't desire, and I will not shackle myself to a wife who loathes my touch."

"You truly think I loathe you? Look at me!" Anne spun him forcibly to face her.

"I *can't* look at you. Surely you haven't forgotten that."

"I haven't, because you won't let me! You are constantly throwing it in my face, and your friends as well, reminding us of how worthless you think you've become. I do not wish to marry a man who has rebuilt his life around pity. It's infuriating, Cedric!" Anne jabbed a finger in his chest. Cedric couldn't help but grin at her fury.

"What could you possibly find so humorous?" she sputtered.

"You called me Cedr—" He was jerked down and Anne's mouth fastened fiercely on his, with a thrust of her tongue and a powerful hunger laced in the rhythm of her lips.

When she finally released him she poked him hard in the chest again.

"*Never* think that I do not desire you! And if you even *think* to cry off, I shall tell everyone in Mayfair that you've compromised me and you'll have no choice but to marry me. Emily will have Godric drag your body into St. George's by your feet if he has to!"

She spun on her heel and left, the dazed viscount smiling like a lad.

She desires me!

8

The White House in Soho Square was filled with the sounds of the rich and elegant seeking their pleasure. It was a night for devilry and revelry. The young bucks who'd been trapped at balls, parties and sandwiched in the crowds at Almack's since the beginning of the season in January were finally able to escape to less reputable locations and enjoy themselves freely in ways they could not with the eligible ladies under the watchful eyes of their mothers.

Even a few ladies who'd borne their husbands the required heirs were taking the night to slip away from their cold marriage beds, along with some adventurous widows scattered throughout the expensively furnished rooms of the most famous pleasure haunt in London.

Samir Al Zahrani exited the Skeleton Room, one of the more macabre themed areas within the establishment, his soul blackened with greed. The English provided him a perfect market to carry on his trade, both legal and otherwise, with discretion and near anonymity.

Even his father, one of the emissaries visiting London, was unaware of the full extent of Samir's business affairs. Willfully blind, was perhaps more accurate. His father was a man of honor and would have tried to stop him, but Samir knew his father was an old fool who did not recognize opportunity when it presented itself. While his father's business struggled, Samir's thrived, and soon he would surpass his father in both wealth and influence.

He moved through the house, admiring the array of mirrors and the other unusual additions to the mansion that entranced and enthralled its well-paying guests. His purse was fat with coins and banknotes from his most recent sale of exotic women to furnish the house. No slaves in England? Perhaps officially. But those who thought as he did had their quaint little ways around such naïve ideals, and to avoid unwanted scrutiny.

New inventory was in constant demand in the cleaner pleasure haunts. Wealthy men did not want to bed weary and worn middle-aged women. That was where he came in. Samir Al Zahrani traveled the world buying and sometimes stealing rare and exotic women, and occasionally men, to sell to the highest-paying customers. Such as the operators of the White House.

But Samir's business had little to do with his presence in England today. He'd lost a pair of his most precious assets here a year ago. Two mares sired by his father's famous Arabian racer, the one the English called Firestorm.

Samir had been cheated in a card game by a damned Englishman, Sheridan. He would pay for his arrogance and trickery. Samir had vowed to kill the viscount and take back his mares. But revenge would take time, so Samir had soothed his wounded pride for a time in France before coming back.

He'd considered hiring a few local lowlifes to murder Viscount Sheridan and make it look like a robbery. His own private guards could have handled such a thing, but this required more care. The last thing he needed was for Sheridan's death to be traced back to him or his country. That would be bad for business. Tonight, he'd left his guards at home and ventured the streets alone.

As he was on his way out of Soho Square, a coach rattled past him and stopped, blocking his path. The muted glow of the street lamps did not seem to penetrate the darkness that cloaked the black coach in his path. Samir felt his hackles rise, like a dog sensing a threat yet unseen. Perhaps he should have brought his guards after all...

"Get out of my way!" he snarled up at the driver perched on the coach's front, but the driver remained silent. The door of the coach opened and a well-manicured hand slid out from the inky depths, inviting Samir to come inside.

"You are Al Zahrani, the Arabian merchant, are you not?" The voice was thick with its arrogant presumption of being correct.

"Fortune favors you tonight. I am Al Zahrani," Samir growled. Did this Englishman just think the first dark-skinned man he passed by was the one he sought? He had survived battles in deserts beneath a sun so hot as to kill any man from this wet country. He did not fear one smug English aristocrat.

"We have a common enemy, you and I." The hand beckoned him again, but Samir hesitated.

"And what enemy would that be?"

"The man who stole your mares. Viscount Sheridan." The voice spoke Sheridan's name with such loathing that Samir smiled. His inquiries had reached the right people, it seemed.

"You too wish this man dead?"

"Someday. But first I want him to suffer, to be humiliated, to never know peace up until the moment of my choosing," the voice from the coach said. "Come into my coach and we will talk."

So, he'd met an ally—a dangerous one, but an ally nonetheless. *The enemy of my enemy…* Samir hesitated, then reassured himself that his curved blade still rested in the silk lining of his British-style coat. He stepped forward into the carriage.

It was almost pitch-black, but Samir could make out the tall form of another man across from him. A pale face with hair so dark it melted into the coach's grim interior gave the impression of a disembodied face gazing back at Samir.

"How long have you been back in London? Did you arrive with your father, Ramiz Al Zahrani?" the man asked. Samir had the distinct impression this man knew the answer to his own question. It was a test of honesty.

"Four days. How do you know my father?"

The man waved his hand. "I know quite a bit about him. A well-respected gentleman, welcomed in all London circles. He's a credit to his country."

Samir detected no falsity to that declaration, which begged the question why a man who valued his father would be here now talking to him about murder and revenge?

"And have you sought word of Sheridan since you arrived?" the man asked.

"I have been busy selling my wares."

"That is a matter which you and I will speak more of soon. I think that your business interests and mine might just find common ground."

He sensed the man was not referring to his legal facade.

"You have an interest in my business?" Samir's laugh was cold.

"I most certainly do. As I understand, you seek to take some of our stock back to your country. My sources' opinions vary as to the why of the matter—some say it's because of the exotic price they would fetch, others the prestige it would bring and how it might play in terms of power and influence. One acquaintance is convinced a wager is involved somehow."

Samir smiled. The man didn't just want him to know that he had information, he wanted him to know he had a number of people supplying him with it. It was an indirect means of laying out his credentials. Spymaster, perhaps? But Samir had his own means of learning about people. Answering a single question could speak volumes. "And what do *you* think?"

"The why is irrelevant to me," the man said simply. "I am here to help supply you with some produce. Say, Viscount Sheridan?"

Samir held his breath. Was this man serious? "You are suggesting I kidnap a viscount on English soil? That would be impossible."

The Englishman chuckled softly. "That is *exactly* what I'm suggesting, and it is my experience that few things are impossible, only difficult. If you want to succeed and escape the law, you need only to ask."

"He's still the same arrogant bastard he was. I believe I can handle him on my own."

The Englishman shook his head. He might have been smiling. "Much has changed since you've been gone. Did you even know that Sheridan has gone blind?"

The man shared this bit of news with such delight that

Samir had no remaining doubt that this man wanted Sheridan dead as well.

"Blind? I had not heard. That should make matters easier, however, not more difficult."

"Then you do not know the company he keeps. As long as Sheridan is in London, your quest for revenge will indeed be impossible. You also don't realize how little time you have. Next week he marries a wealthy heiress, the daughter of a recently deceased baron."

"And what has this to do with me?" Samir demanded.

"His bride has fine English-bred stallions that Sheridan intends to breed with the mares he stole from you."

Samir clenched his fists. His mares were meant for breeding only to other Arabians.

"And what is it you propose to do?" Samir asked through gritted teeth.

"Sheridan marries in five days. I have a man employed at the Sheridan house, and I have learned that Sheridan intends to honeymoon in Brighton. This is where he is keeping your horses. Conveniently, this would also keep him far from those who would protect him."

"What do you want from me in this plan of yours?"

"You have control of a ship?" They both knew that he meant Samir's slave ship.

"Yes. I have the services of a ship. The captain has orders from me to dock when and where I tell him."

"Excellent. Here is my plan."

Samir leaned forward to listen to the Englishman, a

satisfied smile on his lips. Viscount Sheridan and his lovely bride would soon be begging for death, long before Samir would grant them such a mercy.

🙰

HUGO WAVERLY WATCHED SAMIR AL ZAHRANI EXIT HIS private coach and continue on his way. A minute later, the coach door opened again and Daniel Sheffield ducked inside, seating himself across from Hugo.

Daniel was his best man. The quickest, quietest, and deadliest of all the spies Hugo was in charge of for His Majesty. The man was only in his midtwenties, yet he'd been on more missions than any spy in England.

Daniel swept off his hat. "Well, my lord? Did he take the bait?"

Settling back in his coach, he lifted his cane and rapped on the roof, signaling to his driver to return home. Then he set the cane across his lap, staring at the wolf-head handle. It was not his favorite cane, that one had been stolen long ago...by Sheridan. He and Essex had attacked Hugo and stolen the cane as a sort of college prank. The devils. Sheridan had dared to keep it as a trophy, a way of mocking Hugo whenever he had the chance.

"He'll do as I directed and abduct Sheridan and his bride. He'll set sail from Brighton, and that's when we shall have the might of His Majesty's navy ready to sink the ship."

Daniel nodded. "And during their valiant effort to sink a known slaver ship, they'll have killed Sheridan and his wife, not knowing the two were hostage on board."

"Exactly." Hugo rubbed his chin thoughtfully. Daniel understood the delicate nature of dealing with Samir Al Zahrani. His father, Ramiz, was truly a good man, one who would be horrified to discover his son was conducting such a trade under his very nose. Yet it was Ramiz's influence with the throne that kept his son safe from any obvious recriminations. Samir couldn't be brought to trial for his part in the slave trade, a practice Hugo detested on every level.

So why not let the foolish man believe Hugo was on his side, then strike when the man had done Hugo's dark deeds for him? But if Samir were to die in a tragic accident when his ship was sunk after ignoring orders to stop and present his cargo for inspection...well...that would be a pity. A smile curved his lips.

"Two birds and one stone. Or cannonball, rather," Daniel added. "What is my next assignment, my lord?"

"Watch Samir and watch Sheridan. Both are hotheaded fools. We need to make sure one does not incite the other to act before the time is right. The kidnapping needs to occur during their honeymoon at Brighton, not before. Sheridan has too many friends protecting him here."

Daniel nodded, no doubt remembering Hugo's last two plans unraveling due to this fact.

"I'll arrange the naval interference. The HMS *Ranger* should be docking there around the time we need Samir's vessel to be sunk."

Lifting his wolf-headed cane again, Hugo rapped the roof twice to stop the coach. It rocked to a halt on Curzon Street...where Sheridan lived. Daniel put his hat back on and slipped out of the vehicle like a wraith in the night.

If only you knew how closely you are being watched. How closely all *you rogues are being watched.* Inside every house he had a man watching, waiting, feeding him information. When the time was right the men would act, snuffing out any rogues who were left, one by one.

But that was the end game. Now he would enjoy the middle game, his one vice in life in an otherwise unshakeable career of service to his country.

I will avenge you, Peter. They will pay for the night they let you die. They will pay. Then you can rest. And maybe I can as well.

It was a vow carved into his heart, and he would see it through at any cost.

❧ 9 ❧

Cedric fingered the stack of cards Ashton had abandoned on the table. "You know, Ash, you are not my favorite friend at the moment."

Ashton chuckled. "You wound me, Cedric."

Cedric huffed and listened to the sounds of feminine chatter. Emily and Horatia were with Anne, all three ladies whispering by the small fire in the hearth. He could hear the logs pop and snap. While the spring was relatively warm, today had been cooler than most.

"What has Ash done to deserve your displeasure?" Jonathan asked, the newest to their League. His blond hair and green eyes, not to mention the familial resemblance to his older brother Godric, made him nothing short of a young Adonis. He was more reserved when out among the *ton* at social gatherings than the other members of the League. Having lived most of his life as a servant, he was still unsure of himself when it came to the upper class and trying to act as one of their equals. He hadn't been aware that he was Godric's half brother until last September.

"The scoundrel abandoned me at Anne's house. I had no carriage, no servants, no way to get home." Cedric reached out in Ashton's direction. "Let me find your face so I can draw your cork until you bleed."

Ashton chuckled. His chair creaked as he no doubt wanted to avoid Cedric's grasp.

"Jonathan, catch him and hold him still so I can get a decent blow to his jaw," Cedric commanded, but Jonathan merely laughed.

"I wouldn't dare get in the way of your fists. You might miss him and hit me."

"So, villain, why did you leave me?" Cedric asked Ashton more seriously.

"Because I thought you and Anne should have some time alone. I hadn't intended to leave you alone at her house, but when I went down to check on our coach, a runner delivered me a note from one of my business contacts. I assumed Anne would be able to see you home and to Godric's tonight without issue. Was I right?"

"Of course you were. That's what I dislike about you. You are *always* right. But come now, what was this business matter that sent you flying from Anne's home with such urgency?"

Ashton's voice darkened. "I've been running into

stone walls with my usual merchants who buy my shipping services. Today I found out the source of those walls."

"Was it a business competitor?" Jonathan speculated.

"It is *always* a business competitor with Ashton," Lucien cut in as he, Godric and Charles joined them in the evening room and drew up chairs around the lacquered card table.

"Though normally you are not this affected by the tactics of your competitors," Godric noted thoughtfully.

"Yes, well, that's because up till now all of my competitors have been men. This latest adversary happens to be a lady," Ashton declared with a mixture of irritation and exasperation.

"A woman? I should have known!" Charles sniggered like a schoolboy who'd pulled the best prank he'd ever conceived. "Better not be another banker's daughter. You're becoming too predictable, old man."

"Careful, pup!" Ashton's sharp tone drew the attention of the three ladies, who turned their heads in the direction of the rogues. In response, the rogues dropped their heads and drew in closer to better shield their conversation from the women.

"Who is this most aggravating lady?" Lucien asked. "Do I know her? Have I bedded her?"

"I don't believe you have, Lucien, which leaves a very short list of possibilities, I know." Ashton's tone was heavy with wry amusement. "It is Lady Rosalind Melbourne, the widow of the late Lord Melbourne, a distant cousin to the prime minister."

"Rosalind Melbourne... I know that name from somewhere." Godric pondered and then his face lit up. "Rosalind is the sister to those three Scots I tangled with in Edinburgh some years ago." He laughed heartily and smacked the table. "What a row that was. Broke half the furniture in that alehouse as I recall."

"Those brutes are Lady Melbourne's brothers?" Charles's eyes went wide in astonishment. "One of them actually landed a blow on me, which I've not let happen since."

Cedric cut in. "Hold on, what Scotsmen? I've never heard of this."

Jonathan smacked his knee and chuckled. "That's probably because they beat my brother to a pulp and their tempers make him look like a bloody angel. What were their names again, Godric?" Jonathan shot a devious grin at his brother.

"Brock, Brodie and Aiden Kincade. Barbarians, the lot of them. I heard their father passed away last year. Left them a castle somewhere up in the Highlands."

"And what of Rosalind? Is she a barbarian like her brothers?" As always, Lucien focused on the woman in the story. He was a reformed rake, but still a rake.

"Lady Melbourne is...refined to a degree, but she's also ruthless," Ashton said. "She's taking business from me, and I don't care for it."

"Finally, there is someone out there to make Ashton angry. I thought nothing ever affected you," Cedric said.

"Is she fair?" Jonathan asked.

"Unfortunately, yes," Ashton admitted. "But she doesn't seem to use it to her advantage, not that I have seen."

"Then seduce the woman. She's a widow, isn't she? Should be easy," Lucien suggested. Suddenly something struck Lucien in the back of the head and glanced off Cedric.

"Who threw that pillow?" Lucien demanded, turning around. "Horatia, behave yourself!"

"Why should I when you clearly aren't?" came her reply down by the fireplace. It was clear she'd been eavesdropping on the entire conversation.

"What was that for?" Godric asked.

Lucien harrumphed before turning back to his friends. "Horatia tends to chuck pillows at me when she's angry. I figure it could be worse, she could throw vases. So I keep the house well stocked with all sorts of soft projectiles to appease her vigilante needs to strike at me at will."

"You deserve it, Lucien," Horatia said over-loudly. "Suggesting seduction like that. How awful!"

"I'm sure I do, darling," Lucien called back over his shoulder. Another pillow smacked soundly into Jonathan.

"Why the devil did you duck, Lucien?" Jonathan muttered. "You're the cad, not I. I'm not up to taking a beating from your wife. You know, Cedric, I do believe I like your other sister better. At least she doesn't throw things whenever she fancies."

"Ha! Jonathan, you've never seen Audrey on days when she can't find the right bonnet," said Cedric. "Good God, the little sprite can tear down an entire house trying to find what she's looking for." The memory brought a smile to his lips. He missed her terribly. Hopefully she and Lucien's mother would return from their trip to the Continent soon.

Jonathan tossed the pillow over his shoulder, and it landed on the snoozing foxhound, Penelope. The dog let out a yip of surprise, then sniffed the pillow with suspicion.

Cedric cleared his throat. "Speaking of Audrey, I thought I should have a word with you, Jonathan. I promised her that I would have a husband waiting for her when she returned from her European tour."

"You, er...mean she wants to marry me?" Jonathan's voice rose up in the way a man's voice only could when threatened with marriage.

"She mentioned an *interest* in you. You do not have to accept, and I intend to have other prospects ready as well. I only want you to consider it if you know you could be a good husband to her."

"I am flattered, of course..." Jonathan managed. "But I shall have to think on it."

"No rush. She won't be back until June." Cedric wished he could have seen Jonathan's face. He could almost picture the young man's terror. Jonathan was as much of a rogue as his brother, but he did not have the same desire to pursue ladies of quality, at least not with any sense of permanence in mind.

"Cedric, permit me a question?" Godric asked in a low tone to prevent being overheard by the ladies.

"Ask away, old boy."

"Is Anne aware that you marked her during your... private dinner this evening?"

Cedric's face flushed. Dear God, he hadn't thought that everyone would see his rough love bites. He no longer thought much about what was visible and what wasn't.

"Are they that noticeable?" Cedric asked.

"It appears that either she fell on her fork or you had a nice couple of nibbles on her neck." Lucien's tone dripped with devious amusement. "Your lack of sight is making you a sloppy seducer, Cedric. I've never known you to leave a woman so clearly tumbled."

"I didn't tumble her..." *At least not fully,* he silently amended.

"So she did fall on her fork then?" Lucien supplied.

Cedric groaned, slapping his palm over his forehead in resignation.

"If she doesn't notice the marks, then I'm sure Emily and Horatia won't mention it," Godric attempted to reassure him. "Well, probably."

Ashton returned to a safer topic. "So things are going well between you?"

Cedric hesitated, too ashamed to admit how off balance he felt around his future wife. Seduction had never been a problem before. Now, though, he questioned his every move and wondered if he was moving things too fast or not fast enough.

"I am not sure if marriage is what she wants. *I* desire it, as foolish as that sounds, but she tries to keep her distance, as though she fears I'll wound her." Cedric let out his breath in a long sigh. "I cannot see how. I'm only capable of hurting myself these days."

"She may fear a wound of the heart, rather than that of the body," Godric suggested. "Emily fought me off in part because she believed that if she fell in love, I would eventually cease to want her and would move on to the next challenge. With any other woman I might have, but not Emily."

"A wound of the heart?" Cedric repeated curiously. "I suppose that would explain her guarded exterior. Is there no way I can convince her that I would not throw her over for another woman? I mean, I've had my fun as a rake, but my life has changed, and marriage is a serious business. I would not enter into that particular contract so lightly with just anyone."

"We know that, Cedric, but Anne does not. You must find a way to prove yourself. With women, actions speak loudest," Ashton advised. "A thousand delightful promises won't matter against one that she wished you'd kept and failed to. Do not assure her with words, show her that she is yours and you are hers and that no one shall come between you."

Cedric rested his hands on the lacquered table, feeling the cool surface beneath his fingers. "How on earth am I supposed to do that?"

"That is what you will have to figure out for yourself."

"You know, Ashton, one of these days a woman will so completely tie you up in emotional and physical knots that you'll be begging for *my* advice and I will gloatingly tell you to figure it out for yourself," Cedric said with a dark chuckle.

"Don't be silly, Ashton is far too composed and rational to fall prey to feminine wiles," Lucien teased.

Ashton cleared his throat uncomfortably. "Of course. No woman will ever get the upper hand with me."

Cedric chuckled. "Now you've doomed yourself."

ANNE WAS LISTENING TO EMILY AND HORATIA SHARE various wedding stories to amuse her.

"Godric was so nervous he told me he ruined three neck cloths on the way to the church. His valet almost wept." Emily shot a glance in her husband's direction and blushed when she saw him gazing back. Godric's face was a picture of love and devotion and it warmed her deep inside to see it.

"Lucien had to endure an hour-long lecture from his

mother before she would even let him go into the church. Apparently she had wanted her firstborn child's marriage to be normal. Instead, he was marrying me within a week of nearly dying from a duel. She was most upset she couldn't have a normal wedding ceremony. When Lucien finally got inside, Charles told me that Lucien was ready to fall on his knees and beg my eternal forgiveness. He didn't need it, of course, but I did so love to tease him about it after the wedding." Horatia clutched a pillow in her lap, an extra weapon to throw should Lucien voice his rakish advice too loudly again. Someone had to keep the reformed man in line.

"Have either of you met this Rosalind Melbourne?" Emily asked. Horatia shook her head but Anne nodded.

"She is Lord Melbourne's widow. I hear she is quite the businesswoman, but she tends to avoid most social events. She is Scottish and doesn't always feel welcome in London circles, I think. Which is a pity. She is a lovely woman, and quite friendly."

Emily straightened in her seat. "You have met her personally, Anne? Could you arrange for me to meet her?"

"I suppose. Why the sudden interest in Lady Melbourne?"

Emily smiled. "I've never seen Ashton's feathers ruffled before. And a woman capable of doing that to a man like him intrigues me. Ashton certainly needs his feathers ruffled."

"I could certainly agree with that. Even when he was

wounded from that gunshot, he maintained a disturbing level of civility while your husband tried to stem the flow of his blood. Lord Lennox's self-control is unnatural."

"So you will introduce me to this Lady Melbourne?" Emily was almost vibrating with energy.

"Of course. I believe she likes to attend the opera. We could arrange for all of us to go and I will introduce you if she is there."

"Oh, I do love the opera." Horatia smiled, her warm eyes so much like her brother's, lit with joy at the prospect of an evening of musical delight.

"Lady Rochester," Anne began.

"Anne, please call me Horatia. We are to be sisters soon. I want no titles to stand between us."

Anne shyly corrected herself. "Horatia."

As an only child, she'd never known the joy of having siblings. To be openly claimed by Cedric's family now that her father was gone strangely made her want to weep. "Does your brother enjoy the opera as well?"

Anne knew so little of Cedric. Truly knew him, that is. She knew his mannerisms, his way of charming those around him, and what was officially recorded about him. She'd made it the purpose of her first season out to know him, but as a man he was still a mystery. What color did he favor, what was his favorite dinner dish? Did he enjoy the opera? There was much that she wished to know, and her eagerness for this surprised her.

"Cedric isn't much interested in the arts, but opera

seems to be the one exception. He rents a box in Covent Garden," Horatia said. "He hasn't gone since..." Her voice trailed off; there was no need to finish her sentence. "But I think he should go. Opera is more about music than the scenes and actors."

"That is true," Emily agreed. "It is settled then. We must convince Cedric to attend the opera. You must ask him, Anne."

"Me? Why me?"

"He might feel flattered that you wish to be seen with him in public."

"I'm marrying him, there is nothing more public than that," Anne argued.

"Yes, but a night at Covent Garden with him will make him believe you aren't ashamed of him."

"I'm not ashamed..."

"*We* know that, but men can be such fickle and sensitive creatures, despite their bravado. Show him how you feel," Emily encouraged. "Words have little meaning to men. They don't want verbal reassurances. They want kisses in the rain, long tight embraces, and quiet afternoons shared together."

Horatia smiled knowingly at her. "Emily's right, Anne. Cedric feels that he's a burden to everyone, but if you can entice him to take you to the opera, he will feel wanted, desired." Even as Horatia said it Anne's mind flashed back to the library, where Cedric believed she did not want him. Could his sense of self-worth and desirability be that damaged? She'd half believed he meant only to play her right into his arms, but she now knew the sad truth. He really did believe himself undesirable, that no woman would have him.

The question that Anne faced was whether she could entice him into her arms long enough to reinforce his self-worth, while not throwing her own heart into the mix. To prove he was desirable would expose her to the greatest heartbreak she would ever know. Was she strong enough to withstand such a tearing of that part of her she'd protected all these years?

The last person she'd dared to love had died a week ago. Anne wished that she wasn't so afraid of love, but it was terrifying. To love someone so completely meant you gave them the key to your soul, and with that they held the greatest power over you. Her father had been the only person she'd dared to trust with that key. He hadn't disappointed her in that, but his death had been all the more painful because of her love for him.

"Go on, Anne, ask him," Emily encouraged.

Anne looked over her shoulder to catch a glimpse of Cedric at the card table. Surrounded by his friends he looked healthier, happier, as though their good spirits had revived him somewhat. Anne suddenly wished she could do that for him, make him smile and relax enough to just be himself and be happy.

Anne rose and started toward the men still deep in conversation. The soft rumble of their voices was like summer thunder after a light storm. It was a peaceful sound, the low murmurs, but her presence now halted it.

"Lord Sheridan," she began, her voice almost cracking with tension. She tried to ignore the weight of the five masculine stares. Cedric was directly in front of her, his back mere inches away, and the sudden proximity of him brought flashes of their passionate moment in the library. He turned his head toward her.

"What is it, Anne?" His tone was not irritated like she expected but patient. Without thinking she laid a hand on his shoulder, feeling the steel of the muscles beneath her palm.

"Your sister said you rent a box at Covent Garden."

Cedric's brows rose in surprise. "I do."

"Would it be possible... I should like to see the opera that is playing tomorrow night."

"You wish to have me loan the box to you?" There was a deadness in his tone built from his assumption that she would attend the opera without him.

"No, no. I wish for *you* to escort me." She squeezed his shoulder a little, hoping it would encourage him.

"You do?"

"Of course."

"Dinner, too?" Cedric suggested hopefully.

"That would be lovely," she answered in all sincerity, and was rewarded with Cedric's smile. He covered her hand with his.

"Then consider it done, my dear." He returned her squeeze and then dropped his hand back to the table.

"You realize Emily and Horatia will wish to go to the opera too," Godric groaned.

"We ought to make a night of it, all of us," Charles suggested with a respectful glance in Anne's direction. Anne thought she saw him nod to her in approval.

"Would that bother you?" Cedric asked Anne quietly as his friends broke out into conversation again regarding this new development.

"I had thought some time alone with you to be my goal, but this is nice too." Anne's fingers brushed over his shoulder as she spoke. She was growing fonder of the moments they had alone, but being included among the League and their families was wonderful as well. However, it was better to be around them in this instance because they couldn't be alone, and he couldn't woo her with his kisses. She was succumbing to his patient and gentle seductions for better or worse.

"Don't worry, Anne. Even in a crowd I can still find ways to be alone with you." And though she suspected he meant to sound rakish, the words and his tone were instead boyishly charming.

"Thank you." She bent to whisper in his ear and to her own surprise found herself brushing her lips on his cheek in the lightest of kisses. It was highly improper to kiss him in front of others, but it was becoming easier to act foolishly when Cedric was around.

Cupping her cheek with his warm, strong palm, Cedric caressed her bottom lip with the pad of his thumb before he dropped his hand again. It seemed he was afraid to touch her for too long.

"You should return to the ladies. I wouldn't wish to bore you with our talk of business."

Anne harrumphed as ladylike as possible. "I highly doubt you were discussing business. And I'll have you know I am the one who spent the last two years managing my father's investments through his solicitor."

"Hear, hear, Miss Chessley." Ashton chuckled and raised his glass of brandy to her.

"Why you little..." Cedric caught his bride-to-be about the waist and pulled her onto his lap. Anne gave an outraged little squawk but it was a playful one.

"Oh dear, you'd best release her, Cedric," Lucien warned with a half laugh. "Horatia looks ready to hurl another pillow."

"Very well." Cedric let Anne fight her way out of his embrace, but not without swatting her backside as she left. She glared at him over her shoulder, only to remember he couldn't see.

"THINGS BETWEEN YOU AND ANNE ARE BETTER THAN I expected," Godric said in obvious relief.

"I think she's warming up to me," Cedric boasted.

Lucien sniggered. "I'm not so sure. I think your friendly pat just now set you back a week in your wooing."

"There's always the carriage ride home, I suppose." Cedric sighed dramatically, to which his friends laughed.

"Are we really all going to the opera?" Jonathan asked. There was a hopefulness in his tone that made Cedric's heart tighten. Having only recently discovered he was a legitimate brother to a duke and not a servant as he'd been raised meant he still held a certain caution that hadn't been present before. Jonathan had not been ill-treated, but he had not lived the lavish life Godric had either. Events they took for granted he still looked upon as grand adventures.

"Of course we are," Godric assured him.

"Which opera are we seeing, anyway?" Charles asked. He had never been one for theater, but he wouldn't miss out on a group event that promised to be a night of hilarity at the expense of his married friends.

"I believe the current opera is Gioachino Rossini's latest work, *Matilde di Shabran*," Ashton said.

Lucien quirked a brow at the usually business-minded baron. "I didn't know you kept abreast of the latest operas."

"We all have our little indulgences."

"Of course, but most of us satisfy that in the beds of lovely women...er, wives," Lucien corrected when Cedric coughed a warning.

"You are lucky that I already shot you for that," Cedric retorted.

"Thank you for that polite reminder." Dueling with Lucien over Horatia's honor had been one of the darkest days the League had ever seen, but Cedric had a bad feeling more were still on the horizon.

❧ 10 ❧

The following evening Anne took Cedric's offered arm and allowed him to escort her through the throng of people gathered in the foyer of Covent Garden's Royal Opera House. The strong scents of unwashed bodies and groups of low-necklined Cyprian ladies clinging to the men were an unwelcome sight, but Covent Garden was a blend of middle and upper classes that couldn't be avoided.

"God's teeth," Cedric muttered as a buxom woman fell against him, laughing raucously. He shoved her to the side with his lion's head cane.

"You are lucky, my lord, that you cannot see. The sight is most unpleasant," Anne confided to her escort. Cedric responded with a grunt of agreement and let her lead him in the direction of the stairs that would take them to his box.

A tall, fair-haired man blocked their path to the stairs. She froze like a rabbit caught in a snare. She'd never forget that man, or his pale eyes. The very sight of him chilled her blood.

Crispin Andrews.

He was the last man on earth she wanted to see. Her stomach churned and she tried to remember to breathe.

Not here. Not now... The man's gaze swept over the crowd and stilled when it settled on Anne.

"What is it, Anne?" Cedric asked when she dug her nails into his arm. Before she could reply Crispin was upon them.

"Miss Chessley, how good it is to see you. I was sorry to hear about your father. You have my condolences, of course." Those cold eyes studied her from tip to toe with such a familiarity that she thought she might toss up her accounts right there in front of everyone.

He waited for her to say something, to be polite and respond. What she wanted to do was strike out at him, render his beautiful face with the mark of the devil to warn women away from him. But she couldn't. She summoned that icy veneer she'd built the last two years. It had never been about keeping people like Cedric out, but about protecting herself from this one man.

Anne composed her face in a mask of politeness. "Thank you, Mr. Andrews. Have you met Lord Sheridan?"

Crispin shifted his gaze to Cedric, a smirk lifting the

corner of what some ladies believed was a handsome mouth. Anne knew only too well what that mouth was capable of and it wasn't good.

"I believe our paths have crossed on occasion. It has been a few years though. Last time was at a ball, I believe. You were in the company of a most attractive widow," Crispin replied. His casual tone was in stark contrast to the predatory sweep of his eyes over Anne's body once again. That knowing gaze of his was a blatant reminder that he remembered what had transpired between them. To him it had been enjoyable. To her it had been a nightmare.

"I must say it is a surprise to see you out and about, Miss Chessley. I thought, given the depth of your feelings toward your father, you would wish to honor his memory for the full length of the mourning period."

Anne flinched at the implication, her grip on her reticule hard enough that she thought she might tear the fabric.

Cedric gallantly rescued her. "I'm afraid that is my fault. You see, I all but demanded my fiancée accompany me to the opera. She wished to remain home in seclusion, but you know of my reputation. I hold little love for societal obligations such as mourning."

"Fiancée? Why, Miss Chessley, I had no idea you would be seeking a husband after...oh, but I'm sorry, I shouldn't speak so frankly of such matters." The incredulity in

Crispin's voice cut Anne to the core. It was obvious he hadn't thought her capable of securing such a man for matrimony, not after what he'd done to her. Crispin raised an eyebrow at Anne, as though he thought her situation was amusing. Her hatred for this vile creature continued to grow.

"We are to be wed this Saturday," Cedric continued, oblivious to the silent war between Crispin and Anne.

"Are you? How...blessed you must feel, Lord Sheridan. To have the wealth of Anne's...spirit under your command." Crispin spoke in Cedric's direction, but his eyes were still locked on Anne's face. "I haven't seen the announcement in the papers. When did you post the banns?"

"We didn't. We are marrying under a special license." Cedric's tone became frigid, heightened by his aggressive lean forward. Blind as he was, he seemed to sense the threat that Crispin presented and was ready to protect her. The anger and hatred she felt for Crispin lessened in the wake of Cedric's protectiveness over her. Cedric was inching toward Crispin, his head at a slight angle, as though carefully listening...or perhaps hunting him.

Crispin paused, shooting Anne a wicked smile before continuing. "Then you have my congratulations on the upcoming nuptials. Should I be offering congratulations on anything *else*, Miss Chessley?"

Before Crispin could utter another word Cedric

lunged, slamming the aristocrat up against the gilded wall, his cane pressed across Crispin's throat like a blade.

"Cedric, let him go!" Anne begged, tugging on his shoulders. Crispin's face began to turn purple.

"Have a care, sir. I may not be bothered by such slanderous tones, but that is my future *wife* you have insulted." Cedric finished with a primal growl.

Anne, desperate to prevent Cedric from harming Crispin and causing more trouble, wrapped her arms around Cedric and pulled. Cedric released the man, dropping him like a sack of flour. He spun on Anne, gripping her wrist, then swiped his cane like a scythe along the carpets, shooing people out of his way as she led him up the stairs and into his opera box. Despite his haste and anger, he didn't so much as stumble the entire way. The door banged shut hard enough that the frame rattled.

The curtains around the box's edge were not yet open, which meant Anne and Cedric had stepped into darkness. He pushed her against the wall with the warmth of the velvet curtains on her left side and Cedric's body in front of her. His cane clattered to the floor and his hands cupped her face, fingers tunneling into her hair. Rather than kiss her, as she expected, he held her to him, resting his chin on the top of her head. His breathing was ragged and his distant brown eyes clouded with emotional storms.

"Calm me down, Anne. Tell me there is nothing between you and Andrews. He made it sound as though you and he were more than acquainted." His plea was hoarse with desperation.

"He means less than nothing to me. He is a ruthless cad, and if I never lay eyes on him again, it would be too soon." Anne placed her hands around his wrists, rubbing her fingers back and forth over his skin. She hadn't meant to speak so truthfully, it had just slipped out. Her barriers seemed to crumble when it came to Cedric.

"I wanted to kill him. I could not see, of course, but something about his tone... I wanted to..." Cedric's dark confession would have shocked her, but she knew Crispin and despised him. She placed her fingertips against Cedric's lips, letting him know he didn't need to say another word.

"We're here now. You and me. *Together*. Let's sit down and enjoy the rest of the evening."

Cedric's hands on her face tightened, as though he feared she would vanish. He loosened his grasp and bent to retrieve his cane. Anne helped him to his seat, then pushed the curtains out of the way. An uncomfortable silence lingered in the air.

"I hope I did not embarrass you down there," he said after a long moment, his face turned away from her.

"You didn't. Mr. Andrews is the last man on earth I would ever be concerned about. Your instincts were correct. He was not civil tonight, and therefore your reaction did not have to be either."

Anne did not miss his sigh of relief. She wished she

could tell Cedric how she really felt. How seeing him nearly strangle Crispin over her honor had made her eyes sting with tears and her heart tighten with affection. She didn't want Cedric to hurt anyone, but it had made her feel a little better seeing the man who'd caused her so many sleepless nights suffer. Anne opened her mouth, wanting to say more, but as she looked out on the gallery below she caught sight of someone she recognized.

"Oh, there is Lord Lonsdale." Anne watched the golden-haired earl chase a pretty Cyprian in a scarlet gown through a row of empty seats. The woman squealed as she fled from the lusty earl's pursuit, in full sight of the growing audience.

"Do I even wish to know what Charles is up to?" Cedric's voice was more relaxed and a little bemused.

"He seems to be pursuing a lady about the gallery. And there they go...behind the green baize curtains of the stage." Anne found herself giggling as Charles and his latest lady love were promptly shoved back off the stage and into the rowdy masses milling about in the bottom part of the theater. Rather than run off, he simply put the woman on his lap and started to kiss her. Good heavens, that man was incorrigible.

She smiled, unable to contain how happy she was in that moment. To sit with Cedric and discuss his friends, from a place of intimacy rather than as the outsider she'd always been.

This might work between us after all...

CEDRIC LISTENED TO THE CROWDS GATHERING IN THE theater, the aroma of beer, bodies and oranges permeating his senses. He could picture the way the candles fringed the stage's edge like fairy lights, dancing attendance upon the performers who would fill the stage. People would still talk, even as the candles and lamps in the gallery were snuffed out and the orchestra stirred to life. Cedric remembered what a sensual joy it was to share the experience in a beautiful woman's company.

"Anne," he whispered as he held his left hand palm up.

He expected her to ask him what he wanted. But she never said a word. The warm weight of her hand, fine-boned but strong as her fingers curled around his made Cedric's heartbeat jolt into a quick canter. Was he pathetic for enjoying this simple touch, this strangely peaceful moment? In the past he had taken women to his opera box, seduced and pleasured them in the midst of mighty arias. Why did those moments seem less erotic now than the mere weight of Anne's palm in the darkness? Cedric savored the anticipation, the intake of breath before the first note sounded and the opera began.

Cedric let his eyes close, embracing the gray abyss as the music washed over him. He was fairly good with Italian, but it was a trickier thing to listen to it when being sung in an opera. He tried to imagine the actors, tried to envision the story. Ashton had read to him the summary of the plot earlier that day so he could be prepared for this evening.

There was a cold, woman-hating man Corradino, who by virtue of a pact with the father of the young and beautiful Matilde was in charge of Matilde's fate. Cedric listened to the deep, rich voice of Corradino as he swore to marry Matilde off, having not yet seen her beauty for himself. As a man who'd sworn himself free of the influence of women, Corradino saw the glorious beauty of a raging Matilde as she quarreled with Corradino's formerly betrothed, a jealous countess.

Anne was his Matilde, the stubborn, quarrelsome woman who inflamed him with desire at first sight. She did not know this, and did not have any idea how much he had wanted her when she had been in the delicate blush of her coming out two years ago.

But he did not bed innocents because at the time he could not bear to bed a woman who might fall in love with him. It always happened that way. As he roared his release and came inside an innocent woman, she would purr and sigh and gaze at him with love-stricken eyes, expecting that a proposal was but a heartbeat away.

But Anne, God how he'd wanted her that first night he'd met her. His desire had been so dangerous that he'd sought out a lovely young widow he knew and lured her into an alcove off the main dancing room at Almack's to ease his aching body. He'd taken the willing widow fast and hard, a grinding of hips and rough play against a wall.

Even afterward, he'd only found a momentary respite from his desire for Anne. His eyes sought her out in the dancing hall but he dared not speak to her, dared not acknowledge what his body wanted from hers.

I wanted you then. Now I want you more than ever, he thought, not chancing a pointless blind gaze in her direction. He had kept away from her, but the acquisition of the Arabians had changed things. It gave him a reason to pursue her, and so he had.

But how cold she'd been! Mocking smiles and a body that did not respond to his heated looks or suggestive words. He'd all but given up, resigned to a life without this woman who fascinated him like no other.

And then she'd come to him, begged him to rescue her. He no longer cared that she was in need of his name, not his heart. He would take Anne any way he could have her. Even if he could only hold her hand right now, just like this.

❦

THE AUDIENCE BROKE INTO APPLAUSE AND THE EMERALD curtains dropped down, covering the stage from view.

"That was wonderful," Anne admitted.

"I found the story to be most captivating," Cedric replied.

"Do you know it?" She hadn't thought he'd studied operas, only attended them.

"I had Ashton read me the summary so I might have something to picture in my mind. Is Matilde as beautiful to Corradino as she sounds?" Cedric asked, his lips lifting into the ghost of a smile.

"Yes. She is very beautiful. I believe Corradino's reaction to her is what is so enchanting. He sees only her, wants only her. It would be something, to be desired like that." Anne ended with a sigh and looked toward the stage bereft of the lively actors.

Cedric lifted her hand and brushed his lips on her open palm, making her shiver. She turned back to him, entranced by the sight of his mouth exploring her hand. He licked the center of her palm, and the spike of his tongue sparked the place between her thighs to life, awaiting something she kept refusing herself. But come Saturday, she knew that she could not keep Cedric barred from her bedchamber. And at that moment, she didn't want to keep him out.

"Drop the box curtains, Anne. Let me kiss you senseless. I need to taste the sweet innocence of your mouth and feel the weight of your body in my arms." Anne was halfway ready to let him, but the door to their box swung open. A shaft of light broke through and lit up Cedric's irritated face.

"Emily!" Anne pulled her hand free of Cedric's mouth as Emily and Godric came in.

"I hope we are not intruding," Godric apologized as he registered the disapproving scowl on Cedric's face.

"Not at all, Your Grace," Anne assured Godric.

"You bloody well are," Cedric grumbled, though only Anne heard him.

"Splendid! Have you both enjoyed the show?" Emily asked, alight with her natural mischief.

"Yes. Lord Sheridan and I were just talking about the story," Anne said.

"And about to make our own," Cedric said, again too soft for the others to hear.

Her smile widened as she reflected on the moment she and Cedric had shared before they'd been interrupted. She'd felt like Matilde, if only for a few seconds.

"Now, Anne, wasn't there someone you saw earlier that you said I should like to meet?" Emily's tone dropped as she spoke.

Anne leapt up. Of course! The reason that she'd come to the opera tonight was to introduce Anne to Lady Rosalind Melbourne.

"I'd quite forgotten," Anne replied and turned to Cedric. "Emily and I shall only be a moment. We must go and speak with someone."

"Do you wish for me to accompany you?"

Anne felt her chest clench at the hope in his voice. If it wasn't for Emily's need to scheme and spy, Anne would have insisted Cedric come along.

"Stay and keep Godric company," Emily jumped in. "I promise to return your lady to you before you know it, Cedric." While Cedric still looked disappointed, he seemed less hurt. Emily had that effect on people.

"I will be back soon," Anne promised before she let Emily steer her out into the hallway behind the boxes. As they descended the stairs, there was no evidence of the struggle between Cedric and Crispin to be seen. Anne wondered vaguely where Crispin had gone. Hopefully far, far away.

Anne and Emily did not meander down the hall twittering about the latest gossip as women were wont to do at the opera. Rather, Emily strode through the throngs of people with an expectant gleam in her eyes. A tracker on the prowl.

"Let me know the moment you spot Lady Melbourne," Emily commanded.

Anne looked from one end of the theater to the other and spotted their quarry. But Lady Melbourne wasn't alone.

Oh dear...

"Well, I have found her. But I do believe she would rather not be disturbed."

"Whatever do you mean?" Emily scanned the crowd and then realized what she had meant. She covered her mouth with her hands. "Is that her? The woman whom Ashton is escorting into that dark alcove?"

"Yes." Anne didn't know whether she ought to leave the lady and lord alone, or whether to run to Lady Melbourne's rescue. Lord Lennox had a particularly punishing expression on his face. Anne was not sure she could properly assess his intentions. Could a man be both angered and intrigued by a woman at the same time?

"Oh dear, I suppose I shan't have the fortune of meeting her this evening. I must confess, I've never seen

Ashton look so..." Emily failed to supply a word and waved a hand in the air.

"Confused?" Anne offered.

"Befuddled. And furious. Do you think she needs us to interfere?"

Anne watched the couple as they disappeared from sight. "You don't think he might physically harm her, do you?"

Emily giggled. "Ashton? Lord no, he would never... At least, not physically," she amended thoughtfully. "Her business might be in danger though. We ought to warn her of that, but not tonight."

"One can't help but wonder what is going on between them," Anne mused long after she could no longer see any evidence of Lady Melbourne or Lord Lennox in the theater.

What could the mysterious baron be up to?

❦

ASHTON'S PATIENCE WAS ON A RAZOR'S EDGE. WITH ONE hand on Lady Rosalind Melbourne's arm, he'd seized the opportunity to tow her into the seclusion of a nearby alcove. He feared what he might do now that he had her here.

Every muscle was tense, every sense heightened with excitement and, to be honest, arousal. It made no sense. He was furious with the lady. Anger and arousal had never gone hand in hand with him before, so why did he want to push this particular woman up against a wall and ravish her until she couldn't remember her name?

"I must speak with you, madam," he said, his tone dark and full of warning.

Rosalind struggled against his grip, and to his surprise Ashton found her difficult to hold down. With a rebellious toss of her head, her raven-hued locks flew loose over one shoulder. That didn't help with the problem of his rising desire. This Scottish hellion needed a good bedding to tame that wildness. He wanted it to be his bed she fell into.

Damnation! Gain control, Lennox. This is business. Now is not the time to let passion rule you.

"We have nothing to say to each other. Now release me." Rosalind refused to look at him. She kept her pointed chin aimed away from him. Her resistance was charming.

Charming? What the bloody hell was he thinking? He never liked it when people refused to do as he asked. He did not take no as an acceptable response. In the world of shipping he was as relentless as he was calculating and precise, something his competitors respected, even if they loathed him for it.

"Oh my dear, on that count you are mistaken. We have *much* to discuss." Ashton's free hand caught her chin and forced her to face him. She blinked in surprise, her eyes luminous in the shadows.

"You've been a naughty girl."

The rich timbre of his voice caused her to pale. Frightened a little, perhaps? Good. Why did the idea of catching her like this, of holding her captive, heat his blood? Was this how Godric had felt when dominating his darling Emily? Was that why his friend half lost his mind wherever Emily was concerned?

I cannot be feeling that. Certainly not for this woman.

The thought, chilling as it was, couldn't penetrate his predatory urge to settle the matter between them.

"I don't know what you mean." The hesitancy in her tone told him everything he needed to know.

"Is there any particular reason that you've been stealing my merchant shipping contracts? Or will you merely claim it is just business?"

Rosalind tried to pull her face away, but Ashton backed her into the corner of the alcove. He knew his encroaching stance was predatory, like an animal ready to attack. Her lovely eyes widened and she tried to back away, but couldn't. He had her trapped against the wall, exactly where he wanted her...

⚜

"WELL? ANSWER ME." ASHTON SLID HIS HAND DOWN her neck. His fingers shaped themselves around the column of her throat, and Rosalind felt a twinge of fear. But rather than throttle her, he caressed her. Her skin broke out into gooseflesh as a sense of anticipation began to rise in her body. Rosalind knew of Ashton's reputation. He was more than capable of compromising her. But here? Would he dare?

They'd crossed paths once before. Last December they had engaged in a bidding war for a shipping line. She'd conceded to him only because of her curiosity regarding how he'd wounded his arm. In exchange for the truth, she had relented and let him win his bid for the shipping line.

But she hadn't agreed to relinquish her other interests. Her late husband's business was important to her, her means of remaining independent. If he thought for one moment she would abandon it because he had the same interests, he was very much mistaken.

"I have just as much right to go after those contracts as you do," she argued.

His gaze leapt from her eyes to her lips. "If you wanted to get my attention, pet, I assure you that you have it."

"I'm not your *pet*," Rosalind snapped.

He crowded her even farther against the wall, pressing his body against hers with a low chuckle.

"You will be. I've bent many a woman to my will using her own desires against her. You will be no different." Ashton pressed his hips forward just enough to make it clear that she could not easily wriggle out.

"It is business, nothing more." Why did she have to sound so breathless?

"Poppycock." He used that same dangerously rough

voice against her. The usually silly word sounded strangely erotic on his lips.

"It's true."

"Liar."

"How *dare* you call me a liar!" Rosalind hissed in outrage. The blackguard had the nerve to grin at her. Her Scottish temper flared and the natural cadence of her tongue slipped. "Ya bloody galoot!" She broke free of his grasp and smacked a balled fist against his chest.

He grunted at the blow, surprised by her strength no doubt, then glanced down at her fist on his chest. He raised his face to meet her eyes, and quirked one pale brow in challenge. "You've not done this 'business' to any other shipping line. Only mine."

She raised her own dark brow right back. "How would you know that?"

"It is my business to know such things."

"Been spying on me, have you?" She hated that she couldn't keep herself from sounding like a Scot, rather than the English lady she'd fought so hard to become.

"You admit it then?" He still had his hand on her neck, his elegant fingers stroking her skin, even as she tried to break free of his hold.

"Of course I don't. I merely wish to know how you came to such a *stupid* conclusion."

Ashton's hand on her throat tightened, ever so slightly. A whisper of a threat.

"I met with the other line owners this afternoon.

According to them, only I seem to be suffering the effects of your Scottish temper."

Rosalind blushed out of fury rather than embarrassment. She dug her fingers into the big-boned wrist so close to her neck and tried to remove it. For a moment it seemed she would succeed, and Ashton looked at her in surprise before redoubling his efforts to hold her in place.

"What did you hope to gain by your schemes?" Ashton asked. "I was willing to stay out of your way if you kept away from mine. But here you are, tugging at the tiger's tail, and you ask me *why* you are on the verge of being bitten?"

"Are you threatening me, Lord Lennox?" Rosalind demanded. Surely he would back down. Surely he would leave her be now that he had made his displeasure known.

"Indeed I am, Lady Melbourne. And I fear you won't like my method of punishment."

"I've heard of your tricks, Lord Lennox. You won't break my company. My finances are secure. I have few debts and all my contracts are ironclad. Your 'punishment' would be a waste of time." Rosalind was confident that she had him there. There was nothing he could devise that would scare her in the least.

Until he kissed her. *Hard.*

Rosalind tried to fight him off, but the fierce baron was made of stone for all of her struggles. It was like trying to shift a boulder. A very nice, warm, masculine boulder...

So the baron wants to play that game, does he?

Rosalind would fight fire with fire. He intended to throw her off her senses and replace reason with lust? Did he think her resolve so weak? Every woman could expect such shocking behavior from a man. But had he ever considered how *he* might react if faced by an equally determined woman?

She met him kiss for kiss, leaning in until her body was flush to his. She would not deny it was pleasurable, but she couldn't afford to think about that, not now. There was a battle afoot and she was going to win!

When he wedged his thigh between her legs and started bunching her skirts up around her hips, she bit his lower lip. Already he was raising the stakes. His fingers dug into the bared skin of her thighs as he lifted her right leg to lock around his hip. The taste of blood and brandy shared by their mouths was a catalyst for Rosalind's arousal.

She'd always preferred things a bit wild, but her late husband had been far too old and sweet to ever give her what she'd craved. Not like this man who pinned her to the wall. He set fire to her very blood with his hard kisses and rough hands. But it was a tool, a weapon at his disposal, and one he was not afraid to use.

Forcing a hand between their tightly pressed bodies, she clawed a path down his tailored shirt and waistcoat to cup the bulge of his arousal that jabbed her stomach. She squeezed it, expecting him to cry out. Instead there came a throaty growl as he rubbed himself against the palm of her hand like a tame jungle cat.

"God, what you do to me," he moaned before he thrust his tongue deep into her mouth. Something in the gruff way he'd spoken those words made her body burst into flames. She captured his mouth, kissing him back just as ruthlessly. The war continued.

Rosalind writhed against him, trying to get closer, to ease the building ache inside her. An ache she'd thought she'd never feel again for any man. She had cared for the late Lord Melbourne, but there hadn't been love. And certainly not lust such as this. If only they had met under other circumstances. But it was time to put an end to this.

"You call this a punishment?" she challenged, fighting her desire to smile. His panting and shaking body was all she needed to know he was losing control of himself. The careful, controlled Baron Lennox was about to unleash that dark side he thought he hid so well.

She suspected they were a pair cut from the same cloth. Dark, hungry desires covered by cool, demure behavior in polite society. And she wanted to see how far she could push him. If she could break him the way he was trying to break her.

"You little minx," Ashton snarled and slammed her back against the wall with such force that she momentarily couldn't breathe. Her heartbeat spiked again and she gripped the back of his neck, hauling his head down to hers for another kiss.

"Is that the best you can do?" she taunted him.

"What makes you think you've seen my best?"

Before Rosalind could react, he penetrated her lacy underpinnings with a hand and cupped her mound. She gasped in disbelief. This was an act of desperation, but one that might just undo her.

Despite the rough plundering of his tongue in her mouth, the fingers between her legs were gentle. They probed her growing wetness, spreading the slick honey of her core about. Her late husband had never touched her like this. He'd taken her body calmly, careful not to hurt her, but he had never truly pleasured her either.

Ashton's touch was such sweet agony by comparison. His sensual play bathed her in fire. The ache was intense, painful even. This man was her competitor. He was ruthless and a notorious rake. Yet at that moment all Rosalind felt was the pleasure of being desired, seduced, and kissed with wild abandon. She'd never been an object of desire before, and this moment strengthened the last remnants of her feminine confidence.

ASHTON DID NOT KNOW HOW TO RESPOND TO Rosalind's eager reciprocation. Giving in, succumbing, even fainting he was accustomed to, but Rosalind had instead fought back with equal ferocity, matching him play for play. In the end, he'd struck where he knew she would be most vulnerable, and it seemed to be paying off.

He slid a finger into Rosalind's sheath, groaning with strained pleasure at the suction and warmth. Her inner walls latched onto his finger, and Ashton could barely control himself. The mere thought of himself inside her, rather than his finger, had him gasping for breath.

"Your body wants me, Rosalind...wants me buried in you to the hilt. Feel that?" He inserted a second finger inside her. Rosalind whimpered, her head falling back and her hands clenching and unclenching on his shoulders, like a cat kneading with its paws.

"Oh, it does, my lord. But do you think yours doesn't want me as well?" Her hand grabbed his arousal, making it even tighter against his breeches. Her hand moved and his eyes nearly rolled back in his head with a mix of pain and pleasure. Where had she learned to...?

Before he had time to realize what was happening, the little woman had gripped his shoulders and slammed him against the wall. Her mouth was on his, that sweet taste exploding on his tongue again.

I should push her away. I'm too close, too... Oh, to hell with it! I want to be bad again...

Ashton curled his arms around her body, using the wall behind him as support. With each rub of her hand, he felt his body respond, that tightness in his breeches almost unbearable.

"Wouldn't you like to pin me down in bed, Lord

Lennox? See my hair flared against a pillow? Tame that Scot's temper of mine?" she murmured. A bolt of hot arousal shot straight to his cock as she licked the shell of his ear. He groaned helplessly, the image she'd painted too damned perfect to ignore. Then she moaned and gasped as though he were bedding her, again and again. Another moment of this and he'd—

"Rosalind!" He hissed her name as his body went rigid and pleasure exploded through him. His shaft jerked beneath him and he sagged back against the wall.

He looked down at his breeches. *Oh no...*

The little Scottish hellion stepped back. At first he thought it might be in shock or regret, but no. Instead she smiled at her work and gave a husky laugh. "Well, now, at least my skirts cover my minor disgrace. I wish you the best of luck in dealing with yours, my lord." With a taunting smile, she pulled off one of her black gloves and dropped it between them on the ground.

Disposing of the garment that had touched his member, or was it perhaps some sort of challenge? Still smirking, she smoothed her skirts and left the alcove.

Stuck alone in the alcove to fight off his irritation, Ashton could only glare at Lady Melbourne as she disappeared into the heavy crowds preparing for the opera's second act. How the hell had a woman gotten the upper hand against him? There was no way he could step outside in this condition. He'd have to wait until the opera had ended and the crowds had dispersed.

Ashton slapped an open hand against the wall behind him and breathed in deeply. Then he glanced down at the glove, and with a vengeful delight, he retrieved it off the floor, tucking it securely into his coat pocket. He would find a way to return it to her when the circumstances ruled in his favor. Once he finished this little game.

Little minx. I'll get you for this.

❧ 11 ❧

The small white card propped against the vanity mirror spelled out Anne's fate in delicate script.

You are cordially invited to Chessley Manor
for a wedding breakfast to celebrate the marriage of
Lady Anne Isabelle Chessley to
Lord Cedric Alexander Sheridan.

"Am I truly doing this?" she asked aloud.

Emily stood behind Anne, her beautiful figure highlighted in a pale blue silk bridesmaid's gown. "Anne, you are in a wedding dress waiting for a carriage to take you to St. George's. Either this is some elaborate prank you've dreamed up to shock all of London, or you are doing this."

Anne fidgeted, her hands running over her silver silk

gown trimmed with Honiton lace on the bodice, sleeves and hem. The door to Anne's bedchamber opened and Horatia peeked inside. Both she and Emily were wearing lovely matching gowns with small tulle veils.

"Emily, our carriage is here. Cedric and the men have departed for the church. It is our turn." Horatia flashed a radiant smile in Anne's direction.

"So soon? All right, I'm ready." Emily's hands settled the wreath of roses and orange flowers over Anne's thin veil and secured it with a few hairpins. Once satisfied, she kissed Anne's cheek and left the room. Horatia lingered, however.

"I just wanted to say thank you, Anne."

"What for?"

Cedric's sister clasped her hands together in front of her, eyes bright with unshed tears. "My brother is the best of men. He has had to raise two sisters, mourned the loss of our parents and now his sight. The world has taken so much from him, and I fear he has so much left to lose. But with you by his side, he won't face the world alone. I am not sure you can understand my point of view, as you have no siblings. When I married Lucien and Audrey was sent away to Europe...I feared for him. He was so terribly alone."

"But he isn't anymore." Anne wished her eyes weren't burning. It felt foolish to want to cry. "I may not know what it is to love a sibling or suffer when they suffer, but solitude is something I do understand. Today I will pledge myself to your brother so that neither of us shall be alone ever again. We will survive together." Anne had barely finished speaking before Horatia clasped her in a fierce embrace.

"Thank you, sister." Horatia wiped a tear from her cheek and kissed Anne before she left the bedchamber. Anne took a deep breath, but a knock at her door startled her. She gathered her skirts and opened the door to find the Duke of Essex waiting there.

"Pardon me, madam, I thought perhaps I could escort you to the church? Cedric told me that you have no male family members to give you away." At this point Godric flushed, but he bravely continued. "It would be my honor to do so, if you wish." It was a bashful, bumbling, uncertain side of the man that Anne had never seen before. No wonder Emily was hopelessly in love with him. Beneath that stern countenance he was a man of deep emotions.

"You would do this for me?"

"You are a part of Cedric's world now and therefore a part of mine. I want nothing more than to see you properly given away to my friend. Besides, no one should ride to their wedding alone." Godric extended his arm to her. Anne linked her hand through his arm and let him escort her to the carriage.

Anne had expected her journey to St. George's to be a lonely one. But the charming duke sitting across from her made the trip entertaining, and far less worrisome. They arrived at the church in no time at all. Godric got down first and offered her his hand. She lifted her skirts out of the way and stepped down.

Ahead of her, the doors opened and inside she saw hundreds of curious onlookers, as well as members of the families of Cedric's closest friends. There didn't seem to be an empty seat available.

Fear sliced through Anne and she froze, unable to take another step. Godric turned her toward him.

"Anne, listen to me. Look straight to the front of the church. Find him. He's waiting for you." Godric turned her back to the cavernous opening and there he was. Cedric shifted restlessly, as though feeling her eyes on him.

"Look at him, only at him. It is just you and Cedric today. No one else is in that church. Walk to him and him alone." Godric squeezed her hand, and she found she was walking with him down the aisle. Her feet moved of their own accord, bringing her closer and closer to her destiny.

Look only at him. She did exactly that. Ashton stood at Cedric's side and leaned over to whisper in Cedric's ear. Whatever Ashton said seemed to banish the shadows on Cedric's face, replaced by a grin layered with relief. Anne felt her lips curving to mirror his.

We can do this, she encouraged herself silently.

The closer she moved the more she admired the man she was about to marry. He stood tall and proud in a dark blue frock coat. The white waistcoat snuggly fit his athletic frame, as did his light ivory trousers. Even his

192

cravat was perfectly set. It was simple and light, not the awkward multiple-ruffled creations most men wore. It was just like him. No illusions, no games. He dressed the way the world should see him, a man with strength and will. He was no daintily clad aristocrat. He was simply Cedric, and he was everything she'd ever dreamed of in her heart since she was a young girl.

Anne would later marvel that she didn't recall the music or even the face of the clergyman who joined them together. All that her mind and heart had focused on was the feel of Cedric's warm hand joining hers as they exchanged vows and wedding bands.

There was something powerful, something wondrous about the knowledge that what they'd done today no man could tear asunder. After being proclaimed man and wife Cedric brushed a chaste but lingering kiss on her cheek, and the tenderness of it made Anne light-headed.

"Shall we go, lady wife?" Cedric's face was mockingly serious.

Anne laughed as he broke into a teasing chuckle. "Lead on, fearless husband," she replied and took his arm.

They walked past the endless aisles of well-wishers and gawkers to the wedding carriage outside. Orchids and roses had been threaded onto delicate netting on its sides, and the glossy-coated bays snorted and stamped impatiently. Cedric caught Anne's hand to help her as she climbed into the carriage. She turned to him, taking his arm to aid him. For once he did not recoil from the offer.

He was barely seated before Charles and Lucien shouted a cheer and the crowd pelted them with rice. Cedric laughed and tucked Anne into his side, shielding her from the raining pellets. Cedric then pulled out a blue velvet coin pouch and tossed its contents into the air. Children scrambled forward to collect the shiny treasures as they rolled and clinked against the stone steps of the church.

"Let's be off," Cedric hollered to the carriage driver. The horses lurched into motion, and Cedric settled back into the seat and kept one arm about Anne's waist.

"I'm simply famished. How about you?" he asked.

"Oh yes. It's funny, I couldn't stomach a thing this morning. But now I'm starving," Anne admitted.

"I had a similar attack of panic myself. Got halfway through a scone before I realized I wouldn't be able to eat another bite. I am so relieved this is all over..." He paused speculatively. "I doubt that was the most romantic thing to say, was it?"

Anne laid her head against his shoulder. "I agree. It wasn't. But I shall confess I share the sentiment. When Godric and I arrived at the church doors I almost ran away. Can you imagine? The sight of all of those people staring at me..."

"However did you make it down the aisle?" Cedric's soft tone did not conceal his concern.

"I saw you waiting for me. After that, nothing else mattered." Anne inwardly chided herself for saying something so foolish and sentimental. It made her look like a pathetic romantic. She shut her eyes, wishing she could take the words back. When she opened her eyes, Cedric's face was an inch from hers. He surrounded her face with his white-gloved hands and leaned his forehead against hers.

"I love that about you."

"Love what?" Anne's gaze fell to his sensual lips, so close to hers.

"That deep down you aren't cold. You are an inferno, a blaze that consumes me."

"I'm not a—" she began, but Cedric possessed her mouth in a slow, tantalizing kiss. One to erase all those that came before it. She felt fresh and new, the blushing bride she ought to have been years ago. When their lips finally parted, she couldn't remember a thing about their conversation.

"What were we talking about?"

Cedric brushed his lips back and forth over hers in a feathery caress. "I'll be damned if I can remember." His remark left them both laughing.

The carriage stopped at Chessley Manor, where the wedding breakfast was to be held. In the brief span of time she'd been gone the servants had turned the manor into a living garden.

"I smell flowers, lots of them," Cedric observed, his head turning like a hound catching a familiar scent.

"My housekeeper has outdone herself."

Anne and Cedric entered the morning room to find the food all laid out. Exquisite silver trays laden with viands and lobster salad were among the delicacies. In the center of the large table a lavishly decorated cake was waiting to be devoured.

"Are we alone, Anne?" Cedric asked. The guests were still en route from the church, and the servants had scattered at the sight of the newlywed couple entering the morning room.

"We are."

"Excellent. Lead me to the cake." He peeled off his white gloves and pocketed them. Anne did as he asked, curious to see what he wanted. "Now dip a finger into the icing."

"What?"

"Please." Despite the blankness of his eyes, heat simmered in his expression.

"Fine, although I don't know what you'd want me to ruin our cake for." Anne dipped her finger into a discreet place near the base of the cake where she hoped no one would notice. A dollop of white icing coated her finger.

Before she could stop him, Cedric captured her hand and took her finger into his mouth, sucking on it. She felt the heated glide of his tongue. A moan escaped her lips.

"Shall I do that again?" he offered in a husky tone.

"No," she said, regretting it the instant his face fell. He couldn't see her, couldn't know that she meant to return the favor. She took his hand and carefully ran his own index finger along the same path she'd put her own and covered it with frosting. His body went rigid as she brought his hand to her mouth. Anne licked the icing from his finger, relishing the taste of sugar on his skin. The combination was nothing short of sinful. She could get used to such a decadent taste. And from the look on Cedric's face, she sensed he wanted to do more than lick her back.

"Like I said, lady wife. Inferno."

CHARLES MUTTERED TO HIMSELF AS HE EXAMINED TWO suspicious grooves in the frosting on his slice of wedding cake. "I say, I believe someone had a taste of this before I did."

"Just eat it," Cedric said gruffly as he used a spoon on his own slice. Dear, sweet Anne had brought him a spoon, remembering his aversion to sharper utensils.

"Righto, old boy." Charles dug into the rich cake and had a bite before speaking again. "I didn't believe you actually meant to go through with this, you know. But somewhere between the ring exchange and the vows it occurred to me that you genuinely care for your wife."

"Of course I care for her."

"I mean you *truly* care. I think you may be in danger of falling in love with her." *Falling in love* was uttered with all of the excitement of a doctor discovering an outbreak of plague.

Cedric found Charles's shoulder and jostled it in a brotherly fashion. "Well don't become joyous on my account."

All around them the Chessley morning room was filled with guests eating and chattering. Cedric had done his obligatory duty of greeting guests and enduring the numerous toasts to everyone's health before he could finally escape. He'd hunkered down in the corner out of the way, where Charles had joined him.

Charles changed the subject. "Have you and Anne given any thought to what you plan to do with the manor?"

"I haven't yet reached a decision. It is a lovely place, but I wonder if Anne will want to keep it after losing her father. Why do you ask?"

"Well, I escorted Jonathan to Drummond's Bank yesterday, and he was set on securing a loan to buy a town-house of his own. I believe he means to set himself up and start a life. I imagine that he's grown tired of being shuffled between Godric and Ashton's homes."

"You think he means to start settling down? At his age?" Cedric hadn't really thought it possible. He and his friends had only just started to want to settle down themselves. Jonathan was almost a decade their junior.

"Perhaps he's taken a serious interest in your offer of

Audrey. If he obtains the loan by next week, he can begin preparing a lovely little nest for a bride."

The comment would have sent him into a protective rage a few months ago, but now Cedric seriously considered it. "Do you think so? I should talk about it with Anne tonight."

"Aren't you more interested in activities that *don't* involve talking?"

"Careful, Charles," Cedric warned, but his tone was teasing.

"Do you think you will suit each other then?"

"With time, yes. But I believe I will have to introduce her to passion slowly. She's likely to be overwhelmed by it. Being untouched, she will have pain and discomfort the first time. God, I would wish that pain on myself a thousand times over if it would spare her."

"You've become soft-hearted, Cedric." There was love in Charles's chastisement that only the deepest of friendships could produce.

"If I have, let me never harden my heart again."

"Cheers to that," Charles commended before he sobered. "Oh, you'd best rescue your wife. Lady Dalrumple and her sister seem to be talking her into oblivion."

"What? Lead me over, will you?" Cedric latched onto Charles's arm as the pair threaded their way through the guests. Cedric knew when they'd reached their destination because Lady Dalrumple's shrill voice threatened to shatter his eardrums.

"*You!* Lord Sheridan, have done a *very* reckless thing. I was just *telling* your wife—"

"I beg your pardon?" Cedric cut into her screeching.

"*Marriage* within a *week* of Lord Chessley's death? It is *unheard* of!"

"Unheard of!" Lady Dalrumple's sister chimed in.

"I'm most sorry you feel that way, Lady Dalrumple. I admit I have a fondness for setting new trends in society," Cedric replied, pasting a charming smile on his face. "No doubt by next season it will be all the rage within the ton."

"Such *impudence!*" Lady Dalrumple turned her attentions back to Anne. "Have you no *shame,* Lady Sheridan? You have *spit* upon the ethics of *genteel* society and I will not *stand* for it. Know this, I shall take it upon myself to *singlehandedly* turn you out of *polite* society altogether!"

Cedric heard Anne's breath hitch. His own fury rose in a violent tempest. Grasping the thin threads of control, he resumed his polite demeanor.

"That is not the least bit distressing to me," Cedric said with a smirk. "In fact, I would consider it a favor if your influence could achieve such a Herculean task. My wife and I have much more entertaining things to do with ourselves than attend balls and galas. Now I believe I should escort you from our home. It would not do to have your reputation sullied by your presence here." Cedric released his hold on Charles and with luck he found the feeble form of Lady Dalrumple's arm.

"Come, madam, I'll see you to the door," he said loudly.

As he started to drag the stuttering matron along, he prayed he would not run into anything. As for the lady...

Lady Dalrumple suddenly squawked in pain.

"Oh, so sorry. Always thought this door was too narrow." Cedric's mocking apology earned a snicker from Charles.

"Why you—oomph!" Lady Dalrumple's reply was cut short when Cedric's boot caused her to stumble. His free hand found the door latch and he swung the door open.

"Ahh, here's the door. Have a lovely day, madam, and please do not come again. Ta!" Cedric practically shoved her through the doorway as her sister ran after her.

"You cannot live without the benefits of society, Lord Sheridan!" Lady Dalrumple shouted.

"Actually we can, and will do so most happily. Now if you'll excuse me I wish to go and ravish my wife." Cedric slammed the door and sighed, leaning against the stout oak for support. Then he caught the scent of wild orchids teasing the air.

"Anne?" The sound of satin skirts glided over the floor in his direction. Before he could say a word, his body was enveloped by hers. She buried her face in the crook of his neck and wrapped her arms about him.

"Are you terribly upset with me?" Anne asked.

Cedric was genuinely puzzled. "Why on earth would I be upset?"

"I came to you with this early marriage scheme, and now you've made powerful enemies."

"Powerful enemies? Darling, please. Lady Dalrumple is but an irritating gnat. She buzzes and annoys, but is entirely harmless. I'm not even sure how she got an invitation. However, if you believe you feel indebted to me in some fashion, I would be delighted to give you a few ideas as to how to make it up to me."

"Why do I suspect that this will involve a ravishing of my person?" Anne laughed. Cedric reveled in the delight of feeling her body shake with laughter. He settled his hands on her hips, holding her against him as he pressed his lips against her forehead.

"I would beg a kiss, lady wife."

"Just one?"

"A long one, preferably," he clarified.

"Very well." Anne's hands slid up his back, tracing his muscles and the slopes of his shoulder blades as she rose up on tiptoe to kiss him.

As their lips met Cedric closed his eyes, sinking deeper into that gray he could never escape. But when he held Anne, when he kissed her like this, he could almost feel his sight return. A tingling seemed to spread through him, and for a brief second he thought he saw stars. Anne deepened the kiss, and he readily surrendered all that he was to her gentle sweetness. As much as he loved dominating her senses, he loved it more when she did more than simply react to him, when she acted as though she wanted him just as much as he wanted her. Their lips parted with a soft pop, and Anne sighed dreamily.

"Do we have to return to the breakfast?" Cedric murmured in the hollow of her throat as he trailed kisses along her skin. He delighted in how her body responded.

"We must. It would be quite inappropriate, even for us, if we disappeared from our own wedding breakfast. Especially after throwing out a guest, gnat or no."

Cedric groaned in defeat and reluctantly let Anne pull out of his arms. The loss of her warmth felt like a gaping hole in his chest.

"Very well." Cedric took Anne's arm and they returned to the morning room.

⚜

THE LAST OF THE GUESTS FINALLY LEFT SOMETIME AFTER four in the afternoon. Anne and Cedric collapsed in exhaustion in the parlor. Anne's head itched terribly from the veil and wreath, and at last she allowed herself to take it off. As she plucked pins out of her coiffure, she watched Cedric settle back against the couch next to her.

"I say, we did a bang-up job, my heart. What do you think?"

"Excluding the unpleasantness of Lady Dalrumple, I would certainly agree." She eased the wreath from her hair and set it down on the floor. Next came the veil, and Anne let the lace float to the floor before she sighed with relief. Its weight no longer burdened her head, and the beginnings of a nasty headache faded before they could take root.

"Everything all right?" Cedric asked.

"Yes. I finally got rid of that veil and wreath."

"Come here," Cedric said.

"Why?" Anne was too tired to fight him off if he decided to finally ravish her.

"Please, come here."

He opened his arms, and the gesture struck her as sweet. It made her feel needed, and not just in the ways of the flesh. She hesitated for only a moment. The second she was close enough, Cedric gripped her waist and pulled her onto his lap. He adjusted his body so he lounged back along the length of the couch. He pulled Anne's body to lie on top of his, her back to his chest. Anne rested her hands on his thighs and moved softly as his hands settled on her shoulders, rubbing the tension out and kneading the stressful spots away.

"Let your head fall back."

Anne obeyed willingly, her head finding a perfect place on his shoulder to rest.

"That feels like heaven." Anne felt like a purring cat, content to let her master stroke and massage her forever.

"Who knew my wife would be so easily seduced?" Cedric chuckled, his warm breath fanning her right ear in a pleasant sort of way.

Anne's eyelids felt heavy. "Today was lovely, wasn't it?" She fought to stay awake, but she failed.

"I'm just relieved it was not a disaster," he said.

She slipped into sleep, letting his touch envelop her with warmth.

ONCE ANNE WENT LIMP IN HIS ARMS, CEDRIC KNEW SHE was completely at his mercy. Rather than take advantage of this as the old Cedric would have, he felt compelled to protect her instead. Cedric continued his gentle ministrations until Anne's breathing deepened into the slow, soft pattern of sleep. He wanted to stay there with her body wrapped in his, but their position wasn't ideal for his comfort if he wished to rest as well.

"Time for bed," he whispered, not that his bride could hear him. He eased her off him and then got up to open the parlor door. He summoned a maid to turn down her bed and retrieve Anne's nightgown from her packed trunk. There was no way that he would be taking her to his townhouse on Curzon Street tonight.

Cedric had spent a lot of time in the last few days acquainting himself with the layout of Chessley Manor. It proved to be useful now as he scooped Anne up into his arms and began a careful journey down the hall to her room. With some assistance from the maid and a couple of softly spoken warnings, he set Anne down on the freshly washed sheets.

"Shall I undress her?" the maid offered.

"Yes, thank you. I daresay I would do it myself, but I don't wish to wake her by trying." Cedric took a chair by the empty fireplace and listened to the rustle of fabric as the maid prepared Anne for sleep.

"She's ready, my lord," the maid whispered and quietly saw herself out.

Cedric found his way back to the bed and took off his boots, frock coat and waistcoat. When he got down to just his trousers he felt good enough to relax, but not enough to shock Anne if she woke to find herself under the covers with him.

Small steps, he reminded himself. He slid Anne under the counterpane of the bed, pausing as she stirred and muttered something unintelligible.

"Rest now." He stroked her hair back from her face and then got into bed with her, tucking her body into his. She nestled deeply into his arms and sighed like a tired babe. The feel of her against him was wonderful, heavenly. In all of his years of chasing and bedding women, he'd finally caught the one he never wanted to let go.

ANNE WOKE EARLY IN THE MORNING, THE DAWN'S PALE light only a drab gray presence behind the curtains. Although the bed was empty, she had the strangest notion that it hadn't been a short while ago. Blinking and delicately yawning, she stretched her limbs and got up.

She then realized she was still in her own home, her bedchamber at Chessley Manor. She had never made it to Cedric's townhouse last night after the long celebration. What had happened? Surely the man hadn't wanted to be deprived of his wedding night? Anne vaguely recalled easing into Cedric's lap in the parlor and getting drowsy beneath his gentle touch. After that, her memory faded. Where was her husband now?

Husband. It was such an odd word, and it had forced its way into her daily vocabulary now.

"Madam?" A young upstairs maid poked her head inside Anne's bedchamber.

"Come in, Nellie."

The maid bore a tray of tea and scones that smelled delicious. Anne's stomach rumbled in agreement.

"His lordship thought you might be hungry."

"I am." Her stomach made another impatient noise as Nellie set the tray down on the bed.

"Nellie, is my husband still here?"

"He just left ten minutes ago. He instructed me to tell you that he has made preparations for a departure to Brighton in a few hours. I've already packed all of your best clothes. His lordship said anything else you need can be bought in Brighton later."

Anne took a sip of tea and tried to remain calm. They were leaving so soon? The thought of leaving her life here behind, even just for a month-long honeymoon, was frightening. It would be just her and Cedric at his estate.

It wasn't that she didn't want this private time with him, but she was afraid they still knew so little about each other. Above all things, Anne loathed awkward silences.

"You've already packed everything?" Anne asked Nellie, though she already knew the answer.

"Yes, madam. Oh! I plum forgot, his lordship left this for you." Nellie handed Anne a small blue velvet box. Anne took it and opened it with a small amount of trepidation. Inside was a beautiful garnet stone surrounded by a ring of tiny diamonds. There was no chain, only a heavy satin ribbon with a metal clasp at the back.

"What's this?" Anne asked Nellie.

"He told me to tell you that he thought you would like to wear it when you choose to remove the ring he gave you. He knows you love to ride and a ring would snag on your gloves. He feared if that happened you might be tempted to remove it often and it might get lost. Do you wish me to help you put it on?"

"Oh yes, please do."

Anne marveled at the striking burgundy of the garnet and the subtle shimmer of the elegant diamonds. She had never been one for expensive jewels, but this simple yet sizeable piece seemed made just for her. How could he know she would love it? Treasure it as she had never done for other jewels, save the ring he'd given her that had belonged to his mother?

Nellie sighed dreamily. "His lordship has fine taste."

"He does, doesn't he? I only wish I knew what gift I

could give him." She knew a box of fine cigars or engraved snuffboxes would not have the same effect. She wanted to get him something wonderful, something he would never wish to be without. But what gift could measure up to that impossible standard?

Anne spent the remainder of the morning seeing to the household and the servants before she left for Brighton. The housekeeper had things well in hand, and Anne knew she could rest easily during their time away. Anne was tidying up her study when she heard the clatter of hooves and wheels outside. She scampered down the stairs like a puppy, surprised to find herself eager to see Cedric. They almost collided in the entryway.

"Darling, there you are," Cedric grunted as he held on to her to keep her from pitching them both to the ground. With an arm twined about her waist, he bent his head down carefully to place a tender kiss on her forehead.

The gesture was sweet, domestic, entirely unlike Cedric's usual kisses, but no less endearing. She had never known there could be more than one type of kiss, and now she wanted them all, several hundred of each and every kind.

Cedric grinned. "You were in a hurry."

"I was running and heard the horses. I wanted to see you—" She never got to finish. Cedric's lips claimed hers in a silencing possession. There was amusement in this kiss, yet there was a slow burning fire that built behind that teasing, like a second glass of scotch with its rich warmth.

"I'm sorry I ran into you," she mumbled between kisses.

"Never apologize for having childlike exuberance. I find it charming. I didn't want to marry a graceful swanlike creature. I wanted a woman who would go bounding in meadows and walking through forests trails with me."

"You make me sound like a faithful hound," Anne mused sarcastically.

"Nonsense. I make the dogs sleep out in the stables. You, however, belong with me, always. What say you to that?" Cedric pinched at her bottom, and Anne punched his chest with a balled fist.

"You're incorrigible."

"I'm a rogue, my heart, you'd best get used to it."

Anne allowed Cedric to usher her outside and into the waiting coach. She bid farewell to the manor and to the only home she'd ever known. Ahead of her lay unknown horizons.

DAMN THAT FOOL ENGLISHMAN. I'LL HANDLE THIS IN THE *manner I wish.*

Samir Al Zahrani had followed the Sheridan coach at a distance down the well-traveled road to Brighton. But as the couple's coach had taken the lesser-populated country roads toward the estate, Samir had been forced to drop back out of sight, lest Sheridan's driver realize they were being trailed. Using the road's natural underbrush as cover, he was able to guide his horse through the forest at the edge of the trail and avoid being observed.

When at last the carriage turned onto the drive that led to the massive country house of Rushton Steading, Samir flicked his reins against his beast's neck, steering him farther into the forest.

The Englishman, Sir Hugo Waverly... Yes, Samir had done his own research and discovered who the man was, or at least rumored to be. He had advised him to wait for the perfect moment and then snatch Sheridan and his bride from the house and take them to the port.

But Samir had no intention of following Waverly's instructions. If he took Sheridan and his wife ahead of schedule, he could have his ship leave port early. His men were back in town, waiting for instructions. It would have been too conspicuous to bring them along while he was still learning his enemy's lands and discerning how protected Sheridan was from attack.

Glancing up at the skies, Samir frowned. Thick storm clouds were building on the horizon, and a cold wind was starting to gather strength.

English weather. He sneered. Icy, wet and suffocating. It would be a relief to get what he came for and depart for home.

I shall suffer this weather tonight, but not for much longer.

He dismounted from his horse and started walking it through the woods, slowing as he approached the distant house. He'd likely have to bide his time, but he would do what was necessary to retrieve his horses from the Sheridan stables and, more importantly, exact his revenge.

❧ 12 ❧

Anne had developed a painful habit of handwringing by the time she and Cedric arrived at the Sheridan estate on the outskirts of Brighton. Rushton Steading, the vast ancestral home of the Sheridan family, was intimidating. The estate was mainly wooded areas where dark copses of trees hunkered down at the road's edge like silent sentinels. Anne drew in a shocked breath as their traveling coach rounded the nearest outcropping of forest and her new world opened up before her. The house itself was a grand mansion made of white stone, a bright beacon amidst the heavy emerald backdrop.

"Do you like it?" Cedric's voice was soft against her neck as he breathed in her scent.

Anne couldn't help but admire the multi-windowed edifice. "I've never seen anything so beautiful. I can see why you've favored hunting and riding, Cedric—this land is built for such activities."

"My father and I spent many hours in those woods with rifles and hounds." Cedric's voice was rough as emotion rippled through his words.

Anne frowned at her own callousness. To bring up his past had to be painful, both to be reminded of his lost loved ones and lost sight.

"What's the matter, Anne? You've grown tense," Cedric observed.

Only then did Anne realize he'd moved up behind her and wrapped her in his arms. He was constantly offering her comfort, and all she had ever offered him was cool indifference. Anne took a deep breath before she spoke.

"I am sorry for pushing you away," she confessed.

Cedric's hands, which had been stroking her waist, stilled at her words.

"You need never apologize to me about protecting yourself." Cedric dipped his head to nuzzle her neck.

"Are you angry that we did not share a bed last night?" Anne asked, gazing at his full lips.

"Don't be silly, my heart. Besides, I did share your bed, even if we only slept and nothing more."

"You *were* there! I thought perhaps I'd dreamt that you'd stayed."

"You shall expect me tonight then." Cedric's hands slid along her ribs, tightening possessively. Anne shook with anticipation, her breath quickening. Tonight she would give herself to him, let him unleash her inner desires. She'd waited so long for this, for someone to trust. She only prayed that he wouldn't be furious when he discovered she wasn't untouched. More than ever she regretted that one night with Crispin. Not that she'd been given a choice.

The coach pulled up to the steps of the mansion, and a footman rushed out to meet them.

"Welcome, my lord, my lady." The young footman offered a hand to Anne and she stepped down.

Anne was careful to give Cedric time and room to get out on his own, but she and the footman stood ready to catch him.

"Is that you, Hartley?" Cedric asked as he emerged from the coach.

"It is, my lord," Hartley replied with a slight Irish lilt, grinning as his master clapped him on the shoulder.

"How is the household?" Cedric slid Anne's arm through his and started up the steps, his cane tapping the stones.

"Mr. Bodwin is happy to have you home, of course. Mrs. Pickwick, however, has been tearing through the house in a panic, concerned that Lady Sheridan won't be pleased with the state of the house."

"Me?" Anne gasped.

"Don't worry, my heart. The head housekeeper tends to have these episodes of panic, regardless of circumstance. You'll find my butler, Mr. Bodwin, much more to your liking. He's a calm soul compared to our esteemed Mrs. Pickwick."

Anne felt suddenly shy as Cedric ushered her into her new home. The hall was full of servants, all lined up and ready to meet her. Anne could barely keep all of their names straight, but Mr. Bodwin and Mrs. Pickwick stood out as the more elderly and experienced of them.

"My lord, would you prefer to dine in your chambers or in the dining hall?" Mrs. Pickwick asked.

"My chambers, please. See that you provide for two. My wife will be joining me."

"Of course, my lord." Mrs. Pickwick seemed greatly relieved at the announcement of their intent to dine upstairs. "Here are some letters arrived from London with the afternoon's post." She held out a packet of letters and set them in Cedric's outstretched hand.

"Come, let me take you upstairs, Anne. I can offer you a tour of the place tomorrow. Tonight we shall eat, rest and settle in." The grin on Cedric's face was more one of boyish charm than devilish. Anne laughed in response.

"You weren't joking when you spoke of appetites."

"I never joke about the desires of my body."

Anne took Cedric's offered arm and let him lead her up the grand staircase to an ornately decorated bedchamber. Blue silks and cream walls gave the room a soft, sensual appeal. The colors and feel of the room surprised Anne. She had expected burgundy reds and dark wood, something that matched the passion she'd tasted in his arms.

"Have a seat, love." Cedric sat her down in a tall armchair near the fireplace, and it became obvious to Anne how comfortable he was here.

"Oh, I need a minute to freshen up."

"Ahh, of course." Cedric gestured. "That way, my heart."

⚮

ANNE'S STEPS RETREATED, AND CEDRIC SMACKED THE stack of letters in his palm. Far too many for him to want to bother with. After all, tonight was his real wedding night. *Wedding* night. He chuckled.

I'm a lucky devil.

He and Anne would finally have a chance to explore all of her hidden passions.

"My lord, will you be needing anything?" Thomas Pennyworth, another footman, asked from near the doorway.

"Thomas? Why not read me a few of these while I wait for my wife."

My wife. He smiled. What a wonderful word that was now to say.

Thomas took the stack of letters from Cedric, and there was a soft rustling of papers.

"The first is from a Mr. Crispin Andrews."

The name hit Cedric like a blow. He was about to tell Thomas to burn the letter, but Thomas began speaking.

"My Dearest Anne. It was such a pleasure seeing you again at the theater. Write to me soon, we've much to plan now that you've settled yourself in such a comfortable position. I believe congratulations may be in order for both of us. Crispin."

Cedric's heart froze. The letter hadn't been meant for him at all. He found it difficult to breathe, because the tone suggested something... Surely it couldn't have meant...

Dearest Anne?

We've much to plan?

What the devil did Andrews mean by that?

"Thomas," Cedric cut in. "That will be all. Please hand me the letters."

Thomas walked over and placed the letters in his outstretched hand, then retreated to the doorway.

"I'll fetch dinner for you, my lord." The footman's steps receded, leaving Cedric time to think, to worry.

A few minutes later Thomas returned with dinner.

Already Cedric could smell beef stew, pheasant and bread pudding in the air.

"Thank you, Thomas," he said before the footman could say a word. "You may leave once you've set up the table." Cedric's mind was still churning over the letter and what it meant. Anne had sworn to him that she despised Crispin, so why was she receiving such a letter? What could she and Andrews have to *plan*? Should he ask Anne directly? Or would she hide the truth and deny it...if only he knew what *it* was.

Light, feminine steps warned him of Anne's approach. He shoved the stack of letters Thomas had given him into the cushions of his chair by the fireplace.

⟨⟩❦⟨⟩

ANNE GLANCED AT THE YOUNG FOOTMAN LINGERING IN the doorway, his eyes on Cedric, who was sitting stiffly in his chair by the fire, an odd look on his face. The footman, Thomas he'd been called, was auburn-haired and around her age. He realized she was looking at him and dropped his head, smiling shyly as he ducked out of the room.

"How are you able to do that? Tell the difference between Hartley and Thomas?" Anne poured two glasses of red wine and placed one in Cedric's hand.

"How do I do what?"

"Know which person you are addressing when they haven't spoken. I could understand if you recognized the voices, but Hartley did not even say a word when we got out of the coach. How did you know it wasn't Thomas?"

"Ahh, well that's simple. I just started calling them all Hartley. Simplifies things you know." Cedric chuckled, the tension in his shoulders seeming to relax. Whatever had been worrying him before seemed to have faded somewhat. He was chasing shadows, nothing more.

"You're joking!" Anne gasped.

"I am." He laughed, but there was genuine pride in his tone as he leaned back in his chair. Anne followed the movement, admiring the fine legs that stretched out and crossed at the ankles. Cedric was simply beautiful to behold.

"With women I can often identify them by scent. With men it's either their voices or their movements. Sean Hartley has a slight limp from a horse kicking him a year ago. I can detect the difference in his movement."

"And how do you recognize me?" Anne asked, her heart stilling as she waited for his answer.

"Come over and I will tell you." Cedric cut a mocking leer at her, and she couldn't help but laugh at his teasing. She did as he asked and allowed him to settle her on his lap. She was still unaccustomed to his touch.

Cedric stroked her lower back in a soft circular pattern, like a father soothing a troubled child. "Do I frighten you, Anne?"

"I'm not afraid." It was a lie, and they both knew it.

"You sit there so still, barely breathing, like a rabbit in the underbrush. I don't wish to startle you and send you running." The earnest look on his face was heartrending.

"Is that how you truly see me?" Anne's voice shook as he traced an intricate pattern along the line of her collarbone. Heat flooded her body at such a feather-light caress.

"Are you asking if I see you as a frightened rabbit?" There was a sweet amusement in his tone. "Anne, Anne, my lovely but perplexing bride. I see you as so many things, but a frightened rabbit isn't one of them. You are more like a skittish colt, yet to learn its master's touch."

"A skittish colt?" Anne stifled a laugh. His sense of humor had always been so like her own. She found herself relaxing. "I believe I may have married the only man in England who would compare his wife to a horse."

"That's not true. Many a man has called his wife a broodmare," Cedric argued, his sightless eyes warming to a rich cinnamon.

"Is that supposed to win me over, Cedric?" Anne cupped his face when he broke into the most charming smile, one that melted her from the inside out.

"I love it when you say my name." He purred low and deep like a jungle cat.

"Didn't any of your past lovers call you Cedric?"

Cedric's brow furrowed, as though talk of the past wounded him. Anne brushed the back of her hand over his brow, wanting to smooth his worry away. He leaned into her touch, his eyelashes fanning across his cheeks.

"Most of them preferred to call me Sheridan. I suspect they loved to remind themselves of my title. I feel that I spent all those years bedding women for their bodies and they bedded me for my title. A fair trade, I suppose. I hope someday, with you..." He paused to turn and press a kiss into her right palm. "That we shall simply be Anne and Cedric. No titles, no distance between us."

Anne breathed a fervent prayer that someday he might

see her the same, as just Anne. She tucked her head into his shoulder, and he cradled her against his chest.

"I've turned melancholy on you, love. I swear I did not mean to."

"Never apologize for being honest about yourself or your past. I want only the truth between us." But despite his words, there was a sudden coolness to his face, one she recognized when he was trying to pull away from her emotionally. He'd done it so often when he thought she wouldn't marry him, or care about him.

"The truth... I agree."

There was a deadness in his tone that made Anne's stomach roll with unease.

"Anne, what is the true nature of your relationship with Crispin Andrews?"

"Cedric..." she began. Not now. She didn't want this conversation. It was too soon. "I haven't asked you about all of the women you've bedded before you married me."

"We promised each other honesty. Please don't insult me by lying now. It was clear you and he have a history."

Anne's throat constricted, but she knew he was right. She had to tell him. He deserved the truth.

"It was two years ago at Almack's, that night we first met."

"You met Crispin there as well, if I recall correctly."

"I was already acquainted with him, but it was the first time we were together unchaperoned. I was given permission by the matrons to waltz, and he asked me for the honor of escorting me to the floor for my first dance." Anne drew in a deep breath at the unsettling memory of that night. The hunger she had for one man and being held in the arms of another.

"I saw you dancing with him that night." Cedric's tone held midnight rage, an all-consuming emptiness that made Anne pull back.

"I saw *you* as well. You went off with Mrs. Thornton, that beautiful young widow all the men were courting that year." Her comment was just as accusing as his had been.

"Ahh, yes. Mrs. Thornton. I'm sure you know by now that I bedded her." His tone was increasingly callous, like he was goading her somehow.

"There was no bed involved. I *saw* you. You had her pinned to the wall in the antechamber to the dancing hall."

Anne withheld a gasp as his fingers dug deep into her hips, barring escape or retreat.

"Did you now?" His tone was dark, sarcastic, cutting. "You are a fine one to judge such things, *Dearest Anne*." Her name was so cold on his tongue, like a gypsy's curse, rather than a soft lover's murmur. She half expected to see Cedric's eyes crystallize into ice as he stared hard at her.

"Tell me, Anne, did you let Crispin have you? Is that your dirty little secret you've been keeping from me? The man you supposedly despised dared to send *you* a letter of congratulations. Called you his dearest Anne and said that you and he have much to plan. Tell me, what are you planning, *wife?*" Such cruelty hung in his words that Anne barely recognized him as the man she'd married only the day before.

Anne bit her tongue, tasting blood. He grimaced at her silence.

"Speak, damn you! Tell me my suspicions aren't true. That nothing ever happened between you!" The hurt in his eyes filled her with a choking fear and dread. He'd somehow uncovered the truth, at least part of it. She had to tell him, explain everything about that night.

"He was the only man before you—"

"All this time you've played the sensitive virgin. But Crispin had you that night and now you're only telling me when it's too late to undo this disaster. So, was that your plan? You've ensnared a wealthy, titled man in matrimony, and he can't escape. Bravo. Is he waiting to drink champagne with you at some cozy little inn after you abandon me in my darkest hour?"

Without a hint of warning, Cedric flung her off his lap. Anne hit the ground with a hard thump.

She reached for his knee, wanting to touch him, but he slapped her hand away. The brief contact stung as much as if he'd slapped her in the face.

"That's not what happened! Please, let me explain! I had no choice!" Anne's eyes were burning, and barely restrained hysteria rattled her senses.

"There is nothing to explain. I thought I could ask you for the truth and not become upset. But blood and hell—

fire, I'm not all right with any of this! Using me as a front while you and your lover make your plans!"

"No!"

"My name will *not* be dragged through the mud. Get out! For the love of God, get the bloody hell out of here!" he bellowed. Anne stumbled to her feet, limping as her bruised hip throbbed in protest.

"You have to understand about Crispin. He made me —" Foolishly she reached for him again, and the second her hands made contact with his calf he kicked out, narrowly missing her as she lunged away from him.

"Get out or I will *make* you."

Anne had never heard a clearer threat. His brown eyes had become dead, and his fists were clenched at his sides. Waves of anger rolled off him, warning Anne that she was in danger if she stayed. But still she was desperate to reach him through that fog of pain at her betrayal.

"Please..."

"I have never struck a woman before now. Do not make me lower myself to such an act tonight, not when you've already rendered me so broken."

He took a menacing step in her direction, and fear spiked within Anne's body. She turned and fled, and the ripping of her dress slashed the spreading silence between them. Anne fled through the hallway and down the grand marble stairs until she reached the front door. A confused footman opened it for her, and she rushed past him into the night.

She didn't think, she just kept going. Fresh air, if she could only get a few breaths of it, she could calm down, think... He hadn't let her explain, tell him what Crispin had done. He'd simply assumed he'd been her lover.

Surely tomorrow, when she had a chance to come to him after he'd calmed down, she could explain from the beginning. She knew Cedric, *knew* in her bones that if he understood she'd been raped, that he couldn't be mad with her. But tonight his pride was blinding him to the truth and he wasn't able to listen.

The gloom of night had swallowed the estate until only twilight bathed the landscape. Scarce patches of moonlight illuminated a path in the darkness. All Anne wanted at that moment was to never see another living soul again. She wasn't sure how long she walked, but she kept sight of the house from where she was. It was cold outside and thick storm clouds passed across the sky, occasionally blocking out the moon.

As she reached the trees, an unearthed root caught the tip of her slipper and she stumbled. Her arms flew out as she pitched forward onto the ground. She lay there, panting, hurting, dazed. And then she saw it, a shadow that detached itself from a tree. Not a shadow, a *man*.

"My lady, I didn't expect to find you such easy prey." The man chuckled, drawing closer, his steps nearly silent on the forest ground.

"Who are you?"

"A man who seeks justice. And revenge." Moonlight

glinted off his teeth as he smiled. There was a hint of an accent in his voice, barely there, but one she didn't recognize.

Every instinct in Anne screamed at her to move. Scrambling to her feet, she tried to run, but he grabbed her arm and shoved her face-first into the nearest tree. She flung herself back trying to break free, knocking the man off balance as she turned to face him. She couldn't make out his features in the darkness, except for the glint of his awful, knowing smile.

"I'd planned only to watch you tonight," he said with a laugh, "but who am I to resist what fate offers me."

She swung a fist at him, but the blow only glanced off his cheek.

"My lady?" A nearby shout brought the man up short. Someone was calling for her, searching for her. She nearly wept with relief. It was the footman, Hartley.

"Over here!" she shouted, but the shadow of a man lunged for her once more. He blocked her path back to the house, which left her few options of escape. Running fast, she headed toward the lake behind the house.

A hand curled around her shoulder, halting her. "Got you, little English bitch—"

There was a sharp crack and a burst of searing agony in her head just as they reached the top of a hill. Below her rocks and tree roots scattered the ground. There was nothing to break her fall. A soft grunt came from behind her and another blow, then stars fell behind her eyelids.

❧ 13 ❧

Sean Hartley, the footman, heard the crash from one floor below in the dining hall where he was polishing silver. The echo of shouting rumbled through the manor. It was not the kind of shouting he'd expected to hear on a honeymoon. This was all fury and rage. Sean got to his feet and headed for the dining hall doors. Viscount or not, no man would be hurting Lady Sheridan, not if Sean could help it. Raised by a single mother, he respected women and their defenselessness against the all too often violent temperaments of men. He would protect Lady Sheridan, even against his own master, consequences be damned.

"Hartley!" Lord Sheridan bellowed. "Get up here!"

Sean dropped the spoon in his hand and ran for the stairs. He passed Lady Sheridan on his way up. She appeared distraught. He paused to follow her, but his master shouted again. With a growl he turned back and continued on his way.

Lord Sheridan was in a fine fury. Pacing his room like a caged beast, he kept kicking the scattered and broken china cross the floor. The ivory shards were like crushed pieces of a broken dream, never to be mended, never to be used again.

"Here, my lord," Sean said from the doorway. Lord Sheridan spun in his direction.

"Prepare my traveling coach at once. Have the team ready within half an hour and pack me a valise. I am off for London."

"Of course. Shall I have a maid pack Lady Sheridan's things?" Sean asked carefully.

"That woman is not welcome here. Tomorrow I want her to be returned to Chessley Manor. But be quiet about it. I don't want a hint of scandal until I can arrange for an annulment."

Sean frowned, but did not argue with his master. He hoped whatever had divided the new couple was temporary. Perhaps a few days apart would cool the fires of their argument. Sean slipped out of his master's room and headed back downstairs to the servants' quarters. He roused the coach driver, Taylor Higgins, a young man of Sean's age.

"What is it, Sean?" Taylor grumbled, barely awake.

"Lord Sheridan wants his coach ready to leave within a half hour."

"You've got to be bloody joking." Taylor crawled out of bed and dressed, muttering all the while about crazy viscounts.

Sean didn't linger—he had a funny feeling in his gut. He woke Cedric's valet and sent him up to pack a valise and then turned his attention back to his increasing concern. He had a bad feeling about Lady Sheridan.

The viscountess's new rooms were empty. Her trunk had not yet even been opened. Sean's frown deepened. As he came back down the stairs, he noticed a footman staring out into the darkness.

"What is it, Henry?" he asked the other footman.

"It's Lady Sheridan. She was crying and rushed outside just a little while ago now. I didn't see where she went, only that she's gone. Should one of us go after her?" Henry bit his lower lip, continuing to stare out into the gloom.

"Yes. I'll go. Stay here." Sean brushed through the doorway past Henry.

He reached the forest across the road from Rushton Steading just as clouds obscured the sliver of the moon. He could barely see anything, but something compelled him to head toward the woods. The image of Lady Sheridan's tearstained face as she had passed him on the stairs flashed through his mind.

Then a scream tore through the night.

"God in heaven!" Sean broke into a run, his speed slower since his accident. But he kept a steady pace as he began to search the woods around the property. Far behind him he heard the commotion of horses and the arrival of Sheridan's coach, but Sean never turned back. He had to find Lady Sheridan.

"Lady Sheridan?" he shouted.

"Here!" The distant cry echoed off the trees, making it impossible for him to locate her.

Sean thought more than once that he saw fresh footprints, but in the darkness he wasn't positive. Thunder snarled and growled above him like a wolf hungry to devour the earth, but Sean's instincts kept him going. He prayed it wouldn't rain. It would be that much more dangerous and hard to find his mistress. Something was terribly wrong, and he wouldn't rest until he found Lady Sheridan.

Soon he was shivering and cursing the rising wind. He wouldn't be able to last much longer out in the dark.

And that's when he saw her.

Bathed in a momentary flash of lightning, she looked small and frail. She was lying halfway in the shallows of the lake, her clothes soaked clear through.

When Sean reached her, his first fear was that she was dead. Her face, too patrician to be called lovely, was drawn tight. Her lips were parted as though her last breath had escaped long ago. Blood oozed near her temple. He glanced up the small hill, seeing the myriad rocks and tree roots that could have been the cause of her injury.

He bent his knees and slid one arm behind Lady Sheridan's back and the other under her knees to scoop her up into his arms. At the close and sudden contact of her body to his, she stirred.

"Cedric... Please forgive me..." she murmured softly before her head lolled back onto Sean's shoulder.

"Hold on, my lady. I am taking you home," Sean soothed in a gruff tone. He only prayed he wouldn't be too late.

❦

CEDRIC COLLAPSED INTO THE BED OF THE FIRST INN HIS coach reached early in the morning. He was exhausted, upset and shaking all over. How had everything gone from bliss to a nightmare in mere minutes? All because of one damnable letter.

My wife doesn't love me. She's using me.

The thoughts kept running through his mind over and over, the words of that letter echoing in his mind. *"Dearest Anne...we've much to plan..."*

Anne had betrayed him. She'd married him, given him hope for a happy life, when she was in love with another man. Crispin Andrews. Her reaction when he said the name had been enough to tell him everything. She and Crispin were lovers.

She didn't want me to know, which is why she panicked when we met him at the theater that night. It all made sense now. *I've been such a fool. Anne would never have wanted someone like me. I'm a broken man. I've lost her forever. No. I never had her to begin with.*

He had hung such hopes and dreams on their union, but all was over now. The darkness around him was as oppressive as ever, perhaps more so. He wanted to die, to end the pain, the loneliness. Something had always held him back before, his sisters, his friends. But without Anne he was empty as a barren sea. His pain was deep, vast and lifeless. His future was no better.

"Oh, Anne, how could you!" He cursed and rolled over onto his stomach, face buried in his pillow. Still he wondered where she was at that moment. Was she packing her things and writing a love letter to her beloved? A violent rage swelled in him.

I should have killed him that night at the opera. He snarled at the thought of getting his hands around Crispin's neck a second time.

The sound of distant thunder caught Cedric's attention. The wooden walls of the inn vibrated with the fury of nature. The patter of heavy rain was a siren's call to the broken-hearted viscount. Cedric struggled to his feet and felt his way across the floor to the window. The latch gave way to his fumbling hands and the glass panes fell open.

Rain lashed across his face, the cold sting a welcome sensation after the numbing ache of Anne's loss. Thunder shook the earth around him, but Cedric felt only rain, saw only darkness. He stood there, letting the storm assault him until it calmed into a lulling drizzle.

"Cedric!" A voice far away echoed like that of a bleating lamb.

A chill set deep into his bones. "Anne?"

"Cedric!" The cry turned deeper, became rougher.

Cedric shook his head, wanting to clear his muddled thoughts. Anne was gone. He was alone. There was no one seeking him, no one wanting him. Fatigued, he crumpled against the window ledge, knees buckling beneath him. A crash, a shout, and then strong arms lifted him up, helping him to his bed.

"What in God's name are you doing?" a familiar voice demanded.

Cedric remained limp and unmoving as rough hands removed his soaked clothes and tucked him into the warmth of the dry bed.

"Bloody fool," the voice muttered.

Cedric finally recognized his friend's voice. "Ash?"

"Of course it's me. Who did you think I was?"

Cedric would have smiled if he'd had any strength. He was clearly in trouble if Ashton had grown upset with him. His friend's concern and anger was a soothing balm to his wounded heart.

"What are you doing, Cedric? You'll make yourself sick standing in the rain like that. Why are you here, of all places? And where is Anne?"

Cedric winced at the mention of her name.

"Gone," was all he could get out.

"Gone?" Ashton echoed.

"What are you doing here, Ash?" Cedric heard his friend shuffling about the room. The crackle and pop of fresh logs on the fire brought warmth to Cedric's body.

"I was on my way to see you, actually."

"During my honeymoon?"

"Yes. Unfortunately, the business that brought me to you is urgent."

"It is always business with you." Cedric's tone was gentler than he'd meant for it to be. Had Charles been right? Was he getting too soft?

"I had a rather unpleasant afternoon at Berkley's today."

"And what has this to do with me?"

"Everything, I'm afraid. Here, have a drink." Ashton placed a hipflask into Cedric's hands.

"That bad?"

"Yes. Drink."

Cedric swallowed the whiskey and coughed before handing it back to Ashton.

"Best tell me quick."

"It's about Anne and Crispin Andrews." Ashton sounded hesitant.

Cedric laughed bitterly. "Too late. I already know the truth. She all but confessed to having an affair with him."

"What? She actually confirmed this? Or have you merely jumped to a conclusion in that reckless way of yours?"

It was a curse to be so well known by one's friends, Cedric decided.

"She received a letter from him, mistakenly addressed to me. A congratulatory note layered with hints among other things as to their relationship. She admitted to sleeping with him. She didn't say much else before..."

"Before you stormed out without waiting for an explanation? Cedric, you are one of my closet friends, but sometimes I could strangle you for your rashness." His friend's anger radiated out from every syllable.

"Why all the judgment? What do you know that I don't? I have a damned letter proving their relationship!"

Ashton sighed. "It's a long story, but to start with, Anne is innocent of whatever horrible things you accused her of. She and Crispin are not lovers."

"And just how did you learn that?"

"From Crispin himself, when he admitted to forcing himself on her a few years ago."

"What?"

"You heard me, Cedric. He raped her the night you met her at Almack's."

The floor gave way beneath Cedric.

No...

❦

SEAN AND MR. BODWIN WATCHED THE ELDERLY DOCTOR assess Lady Sheridan's condition. She had a nasty head wound and a dislocated shoulder, likely from falling down the steep hill to the lake where Sean had found her. The doctor's eyes narrowed as he motioned for Sean to step forward. He handed the lad a thick piece of leather.

"Put this between her teeth. If she's conscious when I set the arm right, she's liable to bite clear through her tongue."

Sean opened Lady Sheridan's mouth and slipped the leather in. She was still unconscious, still that ghastly pale shade. Sean watched Mr. Bodwin as the doctor took hold of Anne's arm, lifted it slowly, rotated and then popped it back into place. Lady Sheridan's eyes flew open, and she let out a scream that nearly made Sean's ears bleed. The leather strap dropped onto her chest. She started panting, gasping for breath as her eyes fixed on her arm and then flashed up to the doctor.

"A thousand pardons, madam. I had hoped you would remain unconscious for that." The doctor then set a sling for her and began wrapping it around her neck and shoulder. Lady Sheridan, finding no comfort in the doctor's rough handling, turned her gaze toward Sean and Mr. Bodwin.

Sean couldn't help it—he took her uninjured hand in his and began speaking softly to her, though he doubted what he said made any sense. She sighed in exhaustion as her lashes dropped back onto her porcelain cheeks.

As Sean watched Lady Sheridan sleep, he thought it a

strange but wondrous thing that he knew he would die to protect her, and yet she'd only been his mistress for a day.

ANNE WAS UNAWARE OF HER NEWFOUND PROTECTOR. She was locked in a shadowy world where dreams commanded her attention. She saw Cedric's cruel lips and sightless eyes, seemingly lifeless, but the hurt was there all the same. The flight from his bedchamber. The blur of candle wall sconces. The moonlight-bathed forest, the reaching blackness and pain. The endless, unbearable, soul-wrenching pain of loss.

Cedric. Crispin. Her awful secret. It had cost her everything. One stupid, foolish mistake with the wrong man and she'd been robbed of the one thing that had come to matter most to her.

My dear heart, my beloved. She loved him. But that was no surprise. She'd always loved him, from that first glimpse of his name in her copy of *Debrett's Peerage* when she was just seventeen. He'd been but a silly young woman's daydream then. She'd never imagined she'd grow to love him as much as she did now. She'd loved him up to the moment he'd thrown her from his embrace in fury.

If you'd only let me tell you...if only you knew the truth.

LONDON, APRIL 1819

Anne's fingers dug into her father's arm as he led her into the main dancing room of Almack's Assembly Rooms.

"Chin up, Anne. You are an intelligent, lovely woman. The daughter of a baron. It is your right to be in the best of society," her father assured her with his usual confidence. He had the large, gruff appearance of a formidable bear, but deep down he was all sweetness.

"I know, Papa. But what if the Lady Patronesses do not give me leave to waltz tonight? I shall be mortified." Anne confessed this in a shaky whisper as her father led her past the milling grounds in the hall.

"I've already spoken to them. You are allowed to waltz. Indeed, the ladies all seemed quite impressed with you." Her father smiled down upon her, his natural warmth and affection soothing Anne's most immediate fears.

"What would I ever do without you, Papa?" she asked.

He grinned cheekily. "You'd marry a man who loves horses almost as much as he loves you and you'd have a hundred beautiful children."

She giggled. "A hundred? Papa, there's not nearly enough time for that many children. I shall promise you... six or seven?"

"That is an acceptable number I suppose."

Anne voiced yet another fear. "Papa, what if no one wants to dance with me?" At eighteen she was well into womanhood but had no life beyond finishing school until tonight.

"You fret too much, sweetheart," said Baron Chessley. "You are like your mother in that. Be bold. Take what you want in life. Never walk away from it."

"Be bold." Anne repeated the words with conviction.

At that moment the nearest wall of people parted to reveal a group of tall, impossibly handsome men standing near the dancing couples. There were five men in total, but it was one in particular who held her interest. He had his back to her, but he turned his head to the side as he spoke, presenting a fine aristocratic profile. His broad shoulders tapered to a trim waist and long, fine legs. Anne blushed as she realized that she was assessing him like a stallion. His brown hair had currents of deep auburn buried in the dark chestnut. Anne found her hands twining in her skirts as she imagined her fingers tangled in those silky strands. Anne crept closer, wanting to know what had made this man laugh.

"And so I said to him, 'You wouldn't know a cart horse from a racehorse.' The bloody fool called me out for his honor. I told him he owed *me* a debt of honor for enduring his awful assessment of English-bred racers."

Anne understood little of what the brown-haired man had just said, but it was obvious he took his horses seriously. She added that bit of knowledge to an ever-growing list of facts about this enticing stranger.

"Well, well, Cedric, it seems you've drawn a rabbit to

your fox den," a red-haired man murmured as he scanned Anne up and down with open familiarity that heated her blood.

The man, Cedric, spun about to face her, and that is when Anne knew she was completely and utterly lost. The music faded to a soft hum, and the candlelight at the edges of the assembly room flickered into darkness. All light, all life ceased to exist outside that moment when Cedric met her gaze. His brown eyes were as warm as cinnamon. He crossed his arms over his chest to stare down at her and swept those penetrating eyes of his over her form. He seemed to find her pleasing enough to offer a genuinely charming smile.

"And just who might you be, kitten?" he teased.

Anne's body fairly burst into flames at the way his sensual voice poured over her. She was aware that he was being far too forward with her, but she was helpless to resist the subtle quirk of his full lips when he smiled again.

"I'm Anne Chessley." She was lucky she didn't stutter.

"Baron Chessley's daughter?"

"Yes." She continued to gaze at him, completely enraptured.

"It's a pleasure, Anne, darling." He stole her Christian name and adorned it with a seductive endearment like he had every right in the world to do so. Cedric's smile was wide, like a cat eyeing a bowl of crème. He scooped up her right hand and raised it to his lips, brushing a faint but heated kiss to her knuckles, and all the while his gaze was fixed on hers.

"I am Viscount Sheridan." The name sent her reeling. *This* was the young viscount she'd studied fervently in *Debrett's?* The one whose name she'd heard mentioned in whispers by other young ladies. How he kissed like a dream and danced like a prince. She'd convinced herself he must be a fair-haired, fine-boned aristocrat prone to meticulous studies in a cozy library. She'd never been more wrong. Cedric was all vitality, all masculinity, and pure raw seduction.

"I am pleased to make your acquaintance, my lord," she answered, notably breathless. The men flanking Cedric exchanged secret smiles, as though her reaction was something they were all too familiar with.

Cedric shouldered his friends out of the way to ease her shyness. "Are you enjoying the season, Anne?"

"Oh yes, my lord. It is my first. Tonight I am debuting." All her hope and eagerness for a wonderful first night out filled her face and voice. At this announcement, Cedric's gaze darkened. Somehow her answer had changed him.

"Are you indeed?" The sudden coolness of his words confused her. Was it wrong to have admitted such a thing?

The red-haired man nudged Cedric encouragingly. "Ask her to dance. Go on, she's a sweet little creature, there's no harm in dancing with her."

Cedric flashed an impatient look at his friend before returning his focus to her.

"Would you like..." Cedric began, but Anne's father joined them with another man at his side.

"Anne, sweetheart, I've brought Mr. Andrews. You remember... Oh, why good evening, Lord Sheridan." Her father smiled warmly at Cedric, who returned it with equal affection.

"I've just had the pleasure of meeting your daughter."

"Excellent!" Baron Chessley turned to Mr. Andrews, a fair-haired young man a few years older than Anne.

"My lord, may I present Mr. Crispin Andrews? He is the son of a business associate of mine."

Cedric inclined his head toward Crispin, but Anne was already feeling the ebb of his passion. Something had ruined the seductive flirtation he had begun only moments before.

"I understand you've been given permission to waltz, Miss Chessley? Your father gave his consent that I should have the privilege and honor of escorting you." The admittedly attractive Mr. Andrews was already sweeping her away from Cedric and his friends. One of Cedric's friends bent to whisper in his ear, but Cedric brushed him away and stalked off. Anne lost sight of him as the crowds swirled around her preparing for a waltz.

"Lovely night," Crispin commented.

Anne smiled. It was too much to hope that she'd have a moment alone with Cedric. Here was a perfectly suitable gentleman who seemed genuinely interested in her, and she would be impolite to refuse him her attention. Unfortunately, she found him polite but rather conceited. He was attractive, she knew, but neither his features nor his voice could move her the way Cedric Sheridan's had.

"Yes," she answered, distracted as she found Cedric again. But now he wasn't alone. A lovely woman with fiery hair leaned provocatively on Cedric's arm as he whispered against her neck in a secluded alcove. Regret and hurt dueled for supremacy as she watched the man she hungered for leave the assembly rooms with another woman.

He isn't yours, she reminded herself.

But I want him to be.

"Do not waste your time on a man like Sheridan, Miss Chessley. He's only interested in experienced women such as Mrs. Thornton." Crispin's comment brought her attention back to her dancing partner.

"*Mrs.* Thornton?"

"The lovely widow that Sheridan has just escorted out."

Pain lanced through her at the thought.

"Ex...excuse me." Anne tore from his arms and narrowly escaped the dance floor without being bowled over by waltzing couples. Some wicked demon in her mind urged her to seek Cedric out, to see for herself if he was in another woman's embrace.

I shouldn't care, I don't truly know him, but I'd hoped...

Maybe Crispin was exaggerating, or had misread Cedric's intentions and the pair weren't actually lovers.

Anne followed their path and found herself in a darkened antechamber, just off the main assembly room. Strains of music hung in the air, the muted notes ghostly, haunting. There was a murmur, a gasp, and the curtains at the far end of the room were flung back.

Anne ducked behind a small alcove in the corner by the door and watched as Mrs. Thornton ran from a laughing Cedric, who was trailing her in eager pursuit. He caught her about the waist and pulled her back against his chest. She sighed as Cedric nibbled her ear, his hands coming up to cup her breasts. His fingers worked at the laces, loosening the front of Mrs. Thornton's gown to free one breast into his waiting hand. Without hesitation, Cedric pushed the woman against the wall, bracing her legs apart with his thighs. He dragged her skirts up, shoved her petticoats aside and caressed her between the legs.

Anne's body broke out into a sweat. Her womb clenched. She wanted to be there, facing the wall, as Cedric primed her body, not Mrs. Thornton's.

"Please, my lord, please. Take me hard." Cedric pinched the peak of her breast before fumbling with the front of his breeches.

"Hard is my specialty," he grunted and pulled her hips out for his entrance.

Anne watched in horrified fascination as Cedric took

Mrs. Thornton against the wall. It seemed both violent and sensual somehow, like a soft kiss merged with riding a horse at full gallop. When it was over the lovers fixed their clothes and made their separate exits.

Anne crumpled to the floor, chest heaving. She couldn't possibly love a man who would flirt with her and then take another woman in the next room.

If I don't love him, then why does it hurt so?

A voice disturbed her weeping. "I warned you, Miss Chessley."

Crispin Andrews emerged from the doorway. His eyes glowed like mercury. "He would never respect you. He would never realize the beauty of a woman like you. But I do."

Crispin was upon her before she could properly react. Their bodies fell to the floor. Anne's cry of pain was swallowed by Crispin's mouth. He seemed to have grown six pairs of hands, because her skirts were suddenly around her waist and his body was descending on hers.

"Mr. Andrews! No!" She put her hands on his chest, pushing ineffectively.

"Yes, touch me," he encouraged gruffly as he dragged her drawers down and released himself.

"Stop! Please!"

"Just give me a few minutes and I swear to you you'll change your mind." Crispin forced his mouth down on her and Anne couldn't stop him, he was too strong. Crispin thrust into her without warning, and pain sliced through her lower body.

The moment barely lasted beyond a few thrusts of his hips. Afterward Crispin stumbled to his feet, fixed his trousers, and then walked off, leaving Anne disheveled, confused and hurting. Blood coated her inner thighs and Anne nearly screamed.

Why is there blood? Deep between her thighs, everything felt tender, bruised, torn.

Had Crispin wounded something inside her? Anne tried to rein in her panic, comparing her moment with Mrs. Thornton's. Mrs. Thornton seemed to have enjoyed the intimacy, crying out and moaning. But Anne? She'd only had pain and the steady friction between her legs that had left her ashamed, disgusted and hurting. She had felt no pleasure at all.

Perhaps it wasn't in her to love. Maybe she had no heart for physical passion. The sobering thought chilled her very soul. Perhaps she wasn't made for lovemaking...

Am I a woman made of ice? she wondered in her daze. *No, I am not. But I won't ever know what it feels to be loved as that other woman had tonight...*

Anne got to her feet, fixed her gown with trembling fingers and fought off a new wave of tears. Something precious had been lost tonight, and it was more than just the innocence of her body. She'd been robbed of the innocence of her heart.

❧ 14 ❧

Cedric struggled to breathe. "You mean the night I met her she was raped?"

"The way Andrews told it, he pounced on her in an empty room. He didn't give Anne a chance to fight or flee." Despite the calm way in which he spoke, anger laced Ashton's words.

Cedric's fists were clenched so tight his hands were going numb. "How did you learn of this, Ash?"

"He saw me having a drink, and he was already foxed. He demanded that I congratulate him, of all things. He either did not realize who I was to you or mistook me for someone else. Andrews claimed that soon he would have a hold over your fortune once he said that your firstborn was actually his. He planned to blackmail you both. Said he knew Anne would do anything to keep her secret from you, or, failing that, you would pay for his silence about your wife's past."

"The bloody fool addressed the letter to me," Cedric said. His plan must have been made half out of a bottle to begin with.

"Dearest Anne, we have plans to make..."

Her reaction that night to Crispin in the theater hadn't been about concealing her old lover, but hiding from the man who had hurt her, violated her. Stolen her innocence.

If I ever find him again, blind or not, there will be a duel. I'll pin a bell over his black heart if I have to.

Cedric struggled to remain calm. Dread and grim terror swept through him. He'd lost Anne forever because he'd refused to listen to her explanation. But he had been so enraged, would he even have believed her? Would he have been as foolish as the rest of the *ton* and believe a scoundrel's word over hers?

He'd accused her of the worst sort of betrayal, but it was he who'd betrayed her.

"Cedric...what have you done?" Ash demanded quietly.

"She tried to tell me...but I wouldn't listen. That letter, I'd read so much into it. Invented a story that suited my own self-pity and thought the worst of a woman who had never for a moment thought to do me harm. I lost my temper and shouted at her to leave my house. I threw her out when she was at her most vulnerable." A shudder wracked his body. "Ash, if I am at risk of earning a place in the fires of hell, it's certainly for what I did tonight, above all my other sins."

"Where is she now?"

"Quite possibly on her way to London. I gave instructions to have her delivered back to her father's house in the morning. I was planning to stay here for a few days. Couldn't bear the thought of staying at Rushton until she was gone."

"I just came from the main road to London. Because of the storm, no coaches were traveling the road. She didn't pass me." Ash started moving about the room, gathering Cedric's clothes.

"Then she must still be at Rushton Steading."

"Good. Get dressed. We leave immediately. We'll have to ride since the coaches can't get through the mud." Ash started shoving clothes into Cedric's hands and went to call for a pair of fresh horses.

"Ash..."Cedric hissed. "You know I haven't ridden a horse since the accident."

"Bloody hell, man. You'll ride behind me on my horse."

In a matter of minutes, Cedric and Ashton were mounting a sturdy beast in the pouring rain. Cedric clung to Ashton's waist, his friend's body the only lighthouse in the storm around them and the darkness he could never escape.

Ashton spurred the horse into a mad pace, one that would surely wear the beast down in minutes, but Ashton refused the creature any second of rest. The horse kept its breakneck pace for nearly half an hour before Cedric's home was in sight. Cedric couldn't see it, but he could smell the thickening forest and hear the slowing tempo of the horse's hooves on the gravel walk leading up to the manor steps.

Mr. Bodwin's voice cut through the pattering of rain upon stone. "My lord! Thank God you've returned. I was going to send a rider out, but no one knew where Taylor took you."

He'd never heard Bodwin's tone so pitched with panic. "Bodwin, what's happened?"

"It's her ladyship. She's had an accident..."

Cedric was already barging up the steps, using Ashton's arm for support, but his rain-and-mud-slicked boots skidded on the marble and he nearly fell. Ashton's arms caught him and kept him on his feet.

"Where is she?" Cedric demanded.

"Her room. Sean Hartley is with her. He won't leave her side, my lord. He found her hurt by the lake. He said you'd quarreled with her and that it was your fault."

"Mine?" There was, perhaps some truth to that, but to hear such an accusation from the staff...

"He quite boldly said he was going to have a word with you. I told him you wouldn't tolerate that behavior in this house. I tried to have him escorted from the room, but her ladyship won't let go of his hand and—"

"Hartley can go soak his head while he seeks another employer. No man stands between me and my wife."

Cedric didn't care that he sounded like an ogre. All that mattered was getting to Anne.

"What happened to her? You said he found her by the lake?" Ashton interjected.

"As far as we can tell, she fell at the top of the north hill and landed by the shore on the lake. Sean knows the truth of it, I suspect."

Cedric was barely listening as Ashton helped him hurry up the stairs to the room he'd chosen for her. Almost wrenching the door from its frame, he burst into Anne's quarters.

"Anne?" he called out. A hard body blocked his path.

"She'll not be seeing the likes of you, my lord. Not today." Sean's Irish voice, rich with insolence, put Cedric in a rage.

"Get out of my way, Sean." He tried to shove the footman out of his path. The damned man was as immoveable as a bloody mountain.

"No, my lord. You can sack me if you like, but I'm not leaving. And you're not coming in."

Ashton tried to calm things down. "Why don't we take this discussion outside, so as not to disturb the lady?"

"I'm not leaving her," Sean and Cedric declared at the same time.

"Fine. We remain here. But no more shouting." Ashton took his usually diplomatic tone. "Now, Mr. Hartley, your loyalty is commendable, but this is Lord Sheridan's wife. You will let him see her."

Cedric felt Sean reluctantly step aside.

"We've also been told that you can best explain what tragedy befell Anne."

"I can," Sean answered in a standoffish tone.

"Please." Cedric added his own gruff plea.

"She ran down the stairs past me after *you* shouted at her and called for me. After I left your chamber and woke your driver, Henry told me she had gone outside. It took me ages to find her. She'd run into the forest and tripped. Dislocated her shoulder and struck her head on a tree. She was barely hanging on to life when I found her. I carried her back myself, and Mr. Bodwin summoned the doctor."

Cedric sank to his knees at Anne's bedside, his hands searching blindly for her. When his fingers came into contact with a sling he winced.

"Anne, I'm here, love, wake up." His words fell on deaf ears as his wife didn't stir.

He stroked her hand and turned his head to speak again. "What's happened to her? Why won't she wake?"

"The doctor gave her something for the pain and to help her sleep," Sean explained.

"What did the doctor say?" Ashton asked Sean.

"He said the shoulder had been disjointed but that was put into place and will heal in time. It's the head injury that worried him. She's been slipping in and out of consciousness, and he fears she might have suffered damage to the brain."

"What sort of damage?" Cedric's voice was barely audible. He felt like a lad again, losing his parents, enduring the test of becoming the man of his house at the cost of what he loved most.

"She's been unresponsive to our questions whenever she has her lucid moments. The doctor thinks she has suffered memory problems."

Unresponsive. The word was as devastating as an axe blow to his neck. Cedric moved to sit on the bed and spoke to his footman.

"Can she be moved?"

"Sir?"

"Can I hold her in my arms?"

"I don't think you deserve that, given your treatment of her," Sean replied.

"Now see here!" Cedric hissed. "I've always liked you, Hartley, but if you continue to defy me I won't just sack you. I'll see to it you have no references, and no hope for future employment. Do I make myself clear?" Cedric's anger was foreign and strange. He'd never threatened a servant before. It had always been his way to aid those who were not blessed with the same privileges he was.

Perhaps it was because at this moment Hartley was being the man Cedric wasn't. The man Cedric should have been all along. Loyal. Trusting. Brave. The man who had cast Anne out had been none of those things.

"Oh, I understand, my lord. But the lady's life and safety matter more to me than your bloody English pride, or references," the footman snapped back.

Ashton, as always, knew when to intervene.

"Hartley, I can assure you that no harm will befall Anne. There has been a grave misunderstanding. A letter had been sent, filled with lies and slander that your master unfortunately had reason to believe. Lord Sheridan now knows the truth of the matter and of Anne's innocence. She is safe with him, and you cannot imagine the guilt that he feels, which you are not helping. Now, can she be moved?"

Sean still seemed reluctant. "Yes."

Cedric drew Anne into his arms and buried his face in her hair. Her orchid scent was faint, as though mirroring Anne's fading life force. He whispered soft words of love and prayers for her to forgive him, hoping to coax her into fighting for survival.

"Please, my heart, fight for life. *Please*." The depths of his wretched despair brought a rawness to his voice that had never been there before. Part of him expected her to move, to stir and open her eyes. But when Anne continued to lie motionless in his embrace it shattered his last bastion of hope.

Immense, wracking sobs scraped his throat and burned his lungs. Never in his life had his grief been so great. Not even the loss of his parents had wrought such intense suffering. This time, he had brought it upon himself.

Cedric needed time to grieve, to cope with the loss of his last hope.

WARMTH. SOOTHING SOFTNESS IN A DARK COCOON OF safety. Rivers of gentle heat poured over her skin. Pinpricks of sudden coolness disturbed the embrace of that dark heat. Points of pressure smoothed away the sting of those cold spots. A continuous rumble of noise in the distance tickled her senses. She wanted to slide back into the darkness, but something in those sounds disturbed her, upset her. Blinding white light seared her face, her eyes, bringing with it a sense of body again.

What happened? The voice in her mind spoke; it was familiar, but no name emerged from the gloom of her terrible lethargy. The deep sounds that had been teasing her ears paused. She fought to speak with the maker of the words...yes. Someone had been speaking to her. She now fought to create words of her own.

"Help..."

She hoped the other person could understand her plea. Something warm and firm drifted over her mouth, then her eyelids, enticing her to respond. Icy coolness trickled between her lips, a liquid filling her mouth, easing a discomfort she hadn't realized she'd been suffering.

"Drink up. Good girl." The words had meaning now. An action, an offering of praise. For some reason she felt like smiling at that, but the effort required was too great.

"Please open your eyes. Just allow me one more

glimpse of heaven." The words brought equal amounts of warmth and pain to her.

Must try. Another struggle, less effort to speak. Her eyes cracked open, revealing a blurry world. As she batted against her heavy lashes, things finally settled into focus.

A crowd of men were ringed around her bed. A grim elderly man was studying her every move. A young footman stood by a wall to her right. Wariness was etched in his handsome face, as was a strange intensity. A tall ash-blond-haired man rested one shoulder against the left bedpost of her bed. He was elegantly attired, and his bright blue gaze was mesmerizing, but even he could not hold her attention when pitted against the man who crouched by her side of the bed. This man meant something more. Much more.

Something clenched tight in her chest as she studied his strong patrician features, the cultured appearance of a gentleman mixed with the casualness of a man who could have anything he wanted just by raising a brow. He was so beautiful it hurt. But she dared not look away, especially when she noticed something in him was flawed, or rather missing.

There was a strange vacantness in the brown depths of his eyes. A flash of pain lanced through her as she looked into them, like the wooded forests of an ancient land. A memory? She knew the man who held her hand so fiercely now was vastly different from the owner of those cinnamon brown eyes in that single memory.

"Anne, sweetheart, how are you feeling?" The sightless man spoke, his voice a gentle rumble that vibrated with concern. His face bore such a look of pain that she wondered if he should not be abed instead of she.

"Who are you?" She should know the answer. It was scratching at the back of her mind. Her question sent the room into a state of silent chaos built on shuffling steps, heavy sighs and furtive glances.

The elderly man approached her again. "I feared this might happen."

The rest of the men waited silently as he asked a series of questions she vaguely knew the answers to. What year was it? What country was she in? Those came naturally, but who she was and who the men around her were did not rise to the surface.

"Well, I must say, I am amazed at how well you are handling your condition," the elderly doctor said. "Most women in your place would be terrified, I would think."

"I see no point in that," said Anne. "Simply tell me what I must do to become better."

The old man smiled and nodded, explaining to her what might best assist her, much of it involving rest. When the doctor and the footman finally departed and the blond man agreed to see them out, she suddenly felt anxious about being alone with the blind man who still clutched her hand.

"What a fine pair we make." He muttered the words so softly she almost missed it.

"Who are you?" she asked again.

"I am Cedric Sheridan, Viscount Sheridan. Most importantly, I am your husband."

"Husband?" The word felt foreign on her tongue. "How long have we been married?"

"Barely a few days."

"Oh." The relief that swept through her was immense.

"You don't like me then?" His wry tone made her flinch. That hadn't been her intent.

"It isn't that. I was worried we'd been married for some time and that all of my memories of you were gone."

"We've known each other for years, Anne."

"Anne. Is that my name?" A ghost of memory flittered past a vacant window in her mind. *Anne, darling.* Someone had called her that once, she was sure of it.

"You are Anne Chessley, daughter of the late Baron Chessley."

"Late... He no longer lives?" The words trembled from her lips.

"He died just over a week ago."

Something inside her broke. A wall of strength she hadn't realized she'd still been holding on to. A father she could not even remember was dead.

"Did I miss him?" Tears welled in her eyes at the thought of the faceless man who was no longer in her life.

The viscount was there for her, securing her in his arms as if she'd been molded from the same body as he. The achingly perfect feel of being nestled in his embrace was terrifying. She knew nothing of herself except that she had always been strong, and yet in this man's arms she felt vulnerable. The last vestiges of her strength were gone and she was unable to pull away, unable to put distance between them.

When the tears started to soak his waistcoat, she found herself mumbling an apology in the groove of his neck and shoulder. Lips, warm and comforting, touched the crown of her hair as he shushed her and rocked her body in slow motions. Her tense shoulders eased as a wave of exhaustion, emotional rather than physical, took over.

"I wish I could remember you," she breathed against his neck.

"I think you would hate me if you could remember, Anne. It is my fault that this happened to you. If not for my callous nature and frail pride, you would be safe and we would be enjoying the delights of a newly married couple. Instead..." The viscount sounded confused as to whether he should be angry at himself or disappointed.

She stroked his cheek, wanting to return the warmth he'd given her. He pulled away, as though her touch had burned him.

"Don't! I don't deserve your comfort."

Anne felt a sudden fierce protectiveness toward him and wrapped her unbound arm firmly around his neck, locking herself against him. Her sling made it cumbersome, but the embrace was so important to her. She desperately needed to remain attached to him, even as he sought to push her away.

"Offering love and comfort is never about whether the receiver deserves it."

"Love?" Cedric's eyes widened in surprise. "Do you love me?"

Anne frowned as she considered this. "I must have. I can't imagine I would have married anyone unless I did." She was secure in her belief there. Love was vital for marriage, at least for her.

"How can you know that if you cannot even remember your name?" His skepticism cut her more sharply than she'd expected.

"I suppose I know it the way I know I do not like pickled eggs or salmon. It's instinctive, too deep to be removed from my mind." Loving him felt that way, bone deep, carved into the essence of her soul. "Do you love me?" The words were out of her mouth before she had a chance to think.

Her husband, the familiar stranger, merely flashed a charming smile.

"Well? Do you?"

"How about I tell you a story instead, Anne. Two years ago a man was at a ball with his closest friends. He knew that he had all he thought he could ever want from life: money, property, titles, companions tried and true. But there was an emptiness inside him, vast as the sea and ravaged by the winds of suffering and solitude. He laughed at others who claimed to love, or to be in love. But in fact he was jealous of them. On that night, surrounded by dancers, a young woman came to him. Against all propriety, all decency, she proceeded to gawk at him like a darling baby chick just out of its shell."

"Do not tell me I am this baby chick." She cut in with a tentative but teasing smile.

Cedric ignored her and continued speaking.

"When the man turned around and found her before him, all the world seemed to fade from existence. The very spark of life flickered like a flame in his body against the force of her presence. He responded as any man would when presented with such beauty and innocence. He flirted with her, promised her passion with his gaze. But when he learned just how innocent she truly was, he feared he would taint her with his presence. He forced himself back, to become cool, distant. But his friends encouraged him to try to win her, unworthy though he was. One dance was all this man wanted, all he could ever hope to deserve. One waltz and he could walk away with the memory of her body in his arms, a memory that could sustain him the remainder of his lonely life."

"And did they dance?" Anne was enthralled with his words, the emotions within her stirring as memories battled valiantly toward the light of her conscious mind.

"No. Another took her from him. The man reacted badly. Anger and jealousy raging inside him. He found another woman, someone easy to please and agreeable. He made that woman his, however briefly, instead of the one he yearned for. It was a mistake he would forever regret. But the woman he truly cared for gave him another chance. She *saved* him."

Anne winced as flashes of memories, sights and sensations plagued her. A beauty laughing as she demanded harsh love from the familiar stranger, and the tearing and rending of her own innocence at the fumbling hands of another man. Hurt, jealousy, despair. She could barely breathe.

"I've upset you. For that I am truly sorry." Cedric looked ashen, as though her reaction caused him more pain than she realized.

"No. I am glad you told me." Her arms dropped from around his neck, her body sagging in defeat. The truth lay between them now, an insurmountable obstacle that rendered her immobile.

"Would you like me to leave you alone to rest?"

Anne had never felt such confusion before. How could she want to drag him back into her arms and demand that he hold her for eternity, yet also never want to see him again? The conflicting emotions made no sense and only served to destroy the temporary reprieve of her aching head.

"Yes. I think it would be best if you left...for now."

She watched him untangle himself from her body with a cold detachment. But her heart flared to life when he eased her back into the mountain of pillows and tucked her sheets up to her chin, as though she were a precious child he only sought to care for.

"Rest now. If you have need of anything, this cord by the bed will summon the servants."

What if I have need of you?

"Goodnight, Cedric." His name on her lips seemed to bring her a measure of peace, but her throat tightened all the same as she fought off the urge to cry.

"Good night, Anne, darling." His response seemed so natural, so right, that Anne had to fight the desire to call him back to her that instant. It was the hardest thing she had done yet, to let Cedric Sheridan walk out of her bedroom door.

The solitude of her room was punishing, but she needed it. There was much to think about, much to understand about herself and her husband before she could figure out what she should do about the future, *their future...if they had one.*

❧ 15 ❧

C edric slumped heavily in his chair at breakfast the following morning. He'd barely slept last night. Regret and remorse had beat about him incessantly, resulting in a rather nasty headache, causing pinpricks of light in his otherwise sightless vision, as if to mock him as well as inflict pain. The soft click of the dining room door alerted him that he was no longer alone.

"How was last night?" Ashton's asked in a soft voice.

Cedric almost smiled. When he'd first become blind, people often raised their voices at him, as though his hearing had been destroyed and not his sight. Yet the sense most improved after the accident had been his hearing, by a fair margin. He heard even the smallest, lightest sounds now.

There was the low whir of a bumblebee as it butted against the dining room window behind him. There were the creaks in the old manor house, each groan of wood and protest of stone like an elderly man's weary sighs. Without any visual vibrancy, Cedric saw the world in a way he never had before.

"Dreadful," Cedric said, answering his friend's question. "She didn't remember her father, or that he'd passed away so recently. When I mentioned it she burst into tears as if it had just happened. Then she claimed she must have loved me if she married me and I couldn't say it back. I told her the truth about what happened the night we first met. After that she sent me away." Cedric's hands fumbled about for his morning tea, and he cursed when he spilled it.

"Ah. It does appear that you stepped in it, then. Rather deeply." Ashton placed a gentle hand on Cedric's shoulder, keeping him in his chair so he could not rise. "I will get you another cup."

"Thank you," he grumbled. "Did you sleep well?"

"Very well, all things considered. Some problems back in London to consider."

"Care to elaborate, Ash?"

"It is of no real consequence. I am merely having trouble with Lady Melbourne."

"Still?" Cedric couldn't believe his friend had failed to deal with her as he did with his other rivals. She should have been neutralized by now.

"I warned her against any further meddling, but she seems intent to rebel against my command to stay out of my affairs. I've never met a woman more ruthless. If I wasn't so furious, I'd have to admit I almost admire her for challenging me."

"Imagine that. There exists a woman in this world who does not buy into the famous Lennox charm nor surrender herself to your demands." Cedric meant the last part only in jest, but Ashton's tea cup rattled sharply.

"What have you heard?"

Cedric was puzzled by his tone. What nerve had he struck? "Nothing. Only that it is a rare man who will not back down to you and a rarer woman still."

"You make it sound like she's as rare as a unicorn."

"Rarer. You should marry her before she returns to the land of fairy stories."

"Certainly not." Ashton's tone was far too cold. Cedric sighed as he realized his old friend was concealing his true emotions.

"Why not?" Cedric was unhappy and at such times had an inclination to poke at his friend until he too was upset. Misery does so love company.

"I cannot marry a woman I cannot trust to come to heel. My wife must be ready to agree to whatever course of action I deem best. Without such trust, empires and dynasties collapse. As do businesses. Also, Lady Melbourne seems to delight in provoking me."

Cedric toyed with his cup on the table. "You do not seem to have learned anything after abducting Emily last year."

Ashton huffed indignantly. "I don't know what you mean."

"All women tend to do as they please, and often it is our meddling which makes matters worse. If Godric had told Emily that he loved her sooner, she might have been safer that night at my townhouse. Instead, they quarreled and she was kidnapped right from under our noses. And if I had let Anne explain herself..." The words darkened Cedric's spirits even further, to the point where he couldn't finish his own thought.

Ashton's only response was a grunt as he sat down next to Cedric.

"Have you seen Anne this morning?"

"I haven't. I was thinking of bringing breakfast to her. The doctor advised that she be under constant supervision. If her memory starts to return, it could be painful."

"May I offer some advice?" Ashton posed carefully.

"I suppose."

"Take this time with her, just as she is. Woo her properly. Let this be the courtship neither of you had. Should her memory return, she may not find the past weighs as heavy on her opinion of you."

"Woo my wife? What a novel idea." Cedric smiled wryly. "I hope it is possible, for both our sakes."

"Passion is always possible when two hearts are willing."

"Always? What about with Lady Melbourne?" Cedric's lips twitched as he continued to tease his friend.

"She is, as you say, from the land of fairy stories, and therefore not subject to the laws of our reality," Ashton replied.

"Are you planning on staying at Rushton Steading with us or do you have matters to *handle?*" Cedric accompanied the word *handle* by forming a woman's curves with his hands.

Ashton grunted at Cedric's jest. "I would not wish to overstay my welcome, Cedric. Tell me to go if that is your wish."

Cedric sat up straighter in his chair, all teasing gone. "It is not. I would welcome your company. In fact, you would help keep me sane while my world crumbles around me."

He meant it. At that very moment, everything around him seemed on the verge of collapse, and he was terrified of being alone when it happened.

"Then I remain here." Ashton's voice was full of genuine warmth, born of years of deep affection.

Cedric could breathe again, so long as Ashton stayed here and kept him sane.

"Excellent. If the weather permits, we could fish in the lake today." Cedric hoped that Ashton would agree. He needed to get outside for a bit, but he couldn't do so alone, unless he wanted to end up drowned at the bottom of the lake. It would be easy to take a footman with him, but it wasn't the same. Nothing could replace the reassuring comfort of a trusted friend by his side in a gently rocking boat, poles suspended above the water.

"I would like that," Ashton admitted. "My mind certainly needs clearing after Lady Melbourne. She has put me in a black mood."

"Shall we meet in the main hall in half an hour?"

"That would give you time to see to Anne's breakfast."

"Yes, I must make sure she has everything she needs." Cedric jumped on the excuse to see her, even if she didn't want to see him.

The two men parted ways outside the dining room. Cedric climbed the main stairs, thankful to be home again. His body knew this house as well as he knew himself. That awkwardness he often felt in London where there were more people, more dangers for a man who couldn't see, weren't present here at this house. In addition, he was becoming more sure of his body and his movements and far less clumsy. He knew where the stairs were, the location of each room he frequently used. Rushton Steading was a safe place.

It had been years since he'd spent more than a few days here. The past decade had been full of womanizing, horse racing and other such occupations that rakes engaged in, all in London of course. Leaving Rushton empty for so long had left him empty as well. The cool feel of the stair banister beneath his hand brought delightful memories of him sliding down it as a boy.

Lord, how he'd missed this place. It was *home*. Rushton

Steading had always been home. Horatia and Audrey had toddled up these stairs in leading strings. He had scampered about the grounds collecting frogs and tadpoles to torture his tutors.

The halls still carried the ghostly scent of his mother's perfume. Cedric expected to hear his father's booming laugh from the library at any minute. He had been blessed to have parents who married for love and had deeply loved their children. There was nothing more wonderful, more special than a parent's love for their child and that child's love in return. And Cedric had loved his parents with all of his heart.

It never failed to escape his mind that he had been luckier than his sisters. Neither of them had really known their parents as he had. They'd been children when their parents died in a carriage accident. Horatia had also been hurt in the crash. To this day she did not speak of the accident and Cedric did not press her to.

It was hard for him to forget how fortunate he was. His friend Godric hadn't been so lucky. Godric's mother had passed away in childbirth, and her loss had driven Godric's father into dark periods filled with brutal rages. Compared to Godric's suffering, Cedric had lived a veritable fairytale. It was what he wanted with Anne, to have a life together built on love and trust.

Surely it isn't too late for us?

Cedric's hands closed around the doorknob to Anne's bedchamber. He'd started to twist the knob when the door suddenly gave way. He stumbled as he plunged forward and fell unexpectedly. He expected pain. It always came after the fall. But there was no pain. Only the soft, firm body that cushioned his fall. A sudden gasp filled his ears as the body jerked beneath him and the familiar scent of orchids exploded around him in an intoxicating rush.

"Anne!" Cedric fought to climb off her, panicked that he'd crushed her. But Anne's struggles under him only locked their bodies more tightly together. Cedric desperately tried to dampen his sudden arousal, but the sounds she made and her squirming made it impossible.

"Anne, darling, please stop that...I can't see where to... I'm trying to..." Cedric muttered in exasperation until Anne went limp beneath him. Biting back a groan as his body responded enthusiastically to this new position, he tried to focus. The press of her bosom against his chest and the cadence of her panting breaths were not helpful in the least as he sought to restore his self-control.

I must be a bloody cad for wanting her like this. He couldn't deny it, however. Cedric wanted to take her right there on the damned floor, even after all she'd been through in the past few weeks.

Anne's next words caught him completely off guard. "I remember that. You calling me *Anne, darling.*" It was barely a whisper, but he knew what he heard. Anne placed her hands on his shoulders. Cedric wished he could see her face, but his memory of it was all he had left.

"I liked it when you called me that." Her confession was charming in its shyness.

"Damn," he cursed to himself.

There was no escaping his desire after that. He dropped his head and found her lips. Anne's hands fluttered against his neck before settling on his back. Pleasure coursed through him when her fingers dug into his shoulder blades, drawing him closer to her. He wanted more, wanted to taste all of her, but the tremulous quiver in her lips and the hesitancy of her touch turned to tension. His aching need for her plunged him into icy awareness. He couldn't have her, not yet.

"What's wrong?" Her warm breath fanned against his throat.

"It seems we've taken two steps forward and one step back." He gathered his wits, which had been like the scattered soldiers of a defeated army. Battle-bruised and weary, his wits rallied together weakly and he climbed off her.

"I'm sorry, Cedric. I would not resist you if wish to assert your marital rights. I am ready to do my duty." Cedric helped her to rise to her feet and cupped her face in his palms.

"Duty? If you remember nothing else about me, remember this. I want you desperately, I crave you like the air in my lungs. But I will *never* take what you won't willingly give me."

"But I just said that—"

Cedric silenced her with a finger to her lips.

"You offered no resistance. I want mutual passion, mutual desire."

He placed a feather-light kiss on her forehead and stepped back.

"I have arranged for your breakfast to be brought up. Ash and I will be leaving soon."

"Leaving?"

Cedric was startled when Anne's hands clutched his waistcoat, clinging to him.

"We aren't going far. The lake is close by, and we'll fish for a few hours."

"Fish? Oh, I thought that you were leaving me alone here."

Cedric warmed at the relief in her voice.

"I wouldn't dream of abandoning you, darling. I want you too much for that." Cedric held her hips close to him, letting her feel his still throbbing erection. It was a bit evil he supposed, to enjoy her shocked gasp, but he did.

"I thought I could control myself. But I can't wait much longer. Soon we will come together as man and wife. But I want you to want it as much as I do." He paused when she went rigid. "Don't fear. I will make sure you want me."

He teased the corner of her mouth with one last kiss. When she leaned into him eagerly, he withdrew and left her alone.

❧ 16 ❧

Anne put a hand to her lips. The taste and feel of Cedric's mouth still lingered pleasantly. She was torn between running after him and running far away. Although she could not remember him, or anything about herself, she was positive that she desired him. Her body responded with liquid fire to his touch, his kiss, even his voice. Cedric's every action toward her screamed of the primal mating of bodies and souls. Would it be so bad to give in to her desires? They were husband and wife, after all.

She could give in, but she decided that she would not let him be aware of such an intention. Not yet. Anne had her pride like anyone else, and Cedric's story had raised some questions she needed answered first. She was, however, fascinated with the idea of Cedric fully dominating her with that tender but exciting passion.

"My lady?" A voice broke through her thoughts. It was the young footman, Sean Hartley. He waited patiently at the edge of the doorway.

"Come in, Hartley. I am told that I owe you my life. I wanted to offer my gratitude to you."

Hartley blushed and cast his eyes to the ground. "'Twas no trouble, my lady. I am glad you are recovering."

"I seem to have no memory, except for tiny flashes, but beyond that I feel much better. My shoulder only aches a little."

Hartley looked mildly concerned at her words, his brows knitting together. Then he began to fish about his trouser pockets before withdrawing something. It was a beautiful garnet stone surrounded by tiny diamonds. Rather than being affixed to a chain, it was threaded through a black satin ribbon.

"I had to remove it when the doctor was seeing to your shoulder. I wanted to give it back to you in person because of what it means to you."

Anne drew closer, curiosity and bewilderment filling her at the sight of the lovely gem. "What is it?"

"I am told it was your wedding present from his lordship."

"A necklace?" Something about that stirred a longing inside her. Light caught the red garnet, and ruby spots of light danced on the wall behind her.

"I heard from your lady's maid that his lordship believed you would often take off the ring he gave you while riding so that it would not ruin your gloves. He wished for you to have this to wear in its place."

Anne felt the briefest flash, the pang of wanting to return such thoughtfulness. Had she given him something in return for such a beautiful gift? With a sinking feeling, she sensed she hadn't, and the thought filled her with shame. A man like Cedric deserved something wonderful. While she was recovering, she would put her mind toward that.

"Hartley, would you be so kind as to help me put it on?"

Hartley fixed the clasp at the ends of the ribbon and the garnet fell against Anne's collarbone as it if had always belonged there.

"Is Brighton very far from here?"

"About half an hour by coach." Hartley kept his head bowed in respect, eyes fixed on the floor.

"You need not look down when speaking to me, Hartley." Her voice was gentle as she tried to coax him out of his determined shyness.

"You are my mistress and the Viscountess Sheridan." His tone implied that was all there was to the matter.

Anne frowned with mild irritation. She didn't want her servants refusing to meet her gaze.

"And you do as your mistress commands?"

"Always."

"Then whenever you address me I should like you to

look me in the eye. Is that understood?" Anne planted her hands on her hips and waited.

"Yes, my lady." Hartley met her gaze. His shy blush made him utterly charming. Anne had no doubt that he was a rogue in the making if there ever was one.

"Now, about Brighton. I should like to go. Would you summon the coach for me?"

Hartley's expression turned grim and resolute. "I was given orders to keep you here on the estate. The doctor does not wish you to be far from the house should your memory return. There could be a chance of pain in such a case."

"The doctor?" Anne heaved a sigh. "Am I allowed to do anything?"

"I am sorry. The doctor and his lordship are merely concerned with your well-being." Sean's crestfallen gaze made her regret her somewhat petulant response.

"But not my happiness it seems," Anne muttered. "Will Lord Sheridan be gone a long time?"

"I am not sure. He has not been out on the lake since the accident," Hartley replied.

"What happened to him? Did I know him before..." Anne could not bear to finish.

"It's not my place to say, my lady."

One more mystery about my life, Anne thought. She tried to remember, shutting her eyes and focusing on Cedric and his sightless brown eyes. But nothing happened, except twinges of pain right behind her temples.

"Is the lake very far? The one where my husband is fishing?"

"Only a quarter mile." Hartley's eagerness showed his relief to discuss something else.

"Then take me there at once."

Hartley blinked in shock. "You wish to fish?"

"Heavens no. I would, however, like to swim." Her arm was still in a sling, but she'd practiced moving it this morning, and the pain had been surprisingly limited. A bit of light exercise might assist her recovery, if she took care to do it gently.

Anne stifled a laugh at Hartley's sputtering protests as she had him lead the way. He scrambled forward, knowing, as any man in his position, that she would not be deterred from this mission. Anne caught up with him in the hallway and marched alongside him, not at all like a well-bred genteel creature she knew she ought to be. Her father had always told her to move with purpose, even if one had no purpose at all.

The sudden recollection caught her breath in her chest. *Her father.* That brief memory seared her heart. She bit her lip. It was as though memories of him were hiding behind a thin gossamer veil, one she could make out faint shapes behind, but not fully see.

I mustn't push myself. I should take it slow. She breathed out and put her mind to those few memories which were coming back, the ones of her father, the way he would offer advice over warmed brandy glasses in the evening before the fire in their drawing room. The way Cedric would call her *Anne, darling.* And his kisses. Those burned through the barriers in her mind. A man who did that to her was no stranger; it was why she trusted him whenever he told her anything of her past. She had trusted him then, and she would continue to do so. Her body wouldn't lie to her, she knew it.

It was easy to forget her sadness once they reached the outdoors. The day was sunny, and no remains of the storm from the previous night lingered. It was a perfect April day, the trees heavy with emerald canopies and the wild-flowers a vibrant multicolored blanket on the fields leading to the lake.

Far out in the water Anne could make out the distant shape of a small fishing boat. It was a brown speck on the dark waters of the lake. Fishing would be good today, Anne knew. Rain always churned up the waters and made it impossibly murky, just the sort of environment fish preferred, as did fishermen. The hooks could be thrown in with shiny lures and the disturbed silt from the lake bottom would blur the fish's vision, making it far easier for the creature to mistake a lure for prey.

For once, Anne was thankful of her husband's blindness. He would not be able to see her when she stripped off her clothes and dove into the lake. Although she couldn't remember much about Cedric, she had a feeling he would be furious at her actions for a multitude of reasons.

"Hartley, please turn your back. I shall call if I need you."

"Yes, my lady." Hartley spun and walked into the nearest pool of shade to wait.

Once she was satisfied the young footman would not be turning around, she started undoing the buttons of her gown and sliding her slippers off. She placed her clothes in a neat pile on a dry patch of grass several feet away from the lake's edge and dropped the sling on top of them. Clad in only her chemise, she headed toward the water.

⚜

CEDRIC HELD THE FISHING POLE LOOSE IN ONE HAND, while his other trailed lazy patterns on the water's surface. Tiny fish came up to investigate, nibbling hopefully at the tips of his fingers. The heavy storm had mucked up the water and the fish were bold in their movements.

"I miss this, you know," Cedric admitted to his friend.

Ashton gave a low chuckle. "Miss what?"

"This." Cedric waved a hand about in the air, gesturing to the world around them. "I miss spending time with you, and the others. We haven't done something like this in years."

"It has been a long time, hasn't it?" There was a pensive tone to Ashton's voice, a note of sadness in it that made Cedric's heart tighten. "It seems the day the five of us forged our bond, that it was also the death knell for our old lives. Boyhood passed and we had to move forward to become the men we are."

"Not all of us moved forward that day." Cedric couldn't help but remember the life that was lost that night they'd saved Charles from drowning.

Ashton's voice turned somber. "No, not all of us."

Cedric sighed in agreement. Ashton had always been the one among them to see the truth, even the darker truths about them all.

"I was just thinking how strange it was that none of us have been indulging in our usual whims. Well, everyone except Charles, of course."

"What do you mean?" Cedric sat up a little straighter.

"Take Godric, for instance. Ordinarily he would be knee-deep in trouble with some arrogant mistress of his. Lucien would be at the Midnight Garden doing Lord-knows-what. And you would be at Tattersalls or the races, betting on horses at all hours of the day."

Cedric quickly saw the point of this discussion. "And you would be living in your office, eyes fixed to your investment figures the entire day."

"Exactly. Yet here we are, you and I, enjoying a day of fishing. It is like we are boys again, or rather not boys so much as we are regaining the essence of our younger selves." Ashton's voice was rough with emotion. "Forgive me, Cedric. I speak nonsense."

"No. You are right. Things are changing. We can't go back to the men we used to be. Nor even the boys we once were. So where does that leave us? The only route is forward, but what lies ahead?" Cedric voiced the question he knew was plaguing Ashton's heart.

"What indeed."

"I, for one, blame Emily. That little scamp has gotten the lot of us into this mess. Of course, I have to thank her as well. If not for sweet Em, then I would not have Anne." The thought of an Anne-less world sent a shudder through him.

"I too find it most amusing. Abducting her was the most foolish and yet somehow the wisest thing we ever did. I dare not think who Godric would be with today without her, or Lucien for that matter. He was getting darker, you know, in his desires. I was starting to worry." Ashton's admission caught Cedric off guard.

"What? I had no idea he was..."

"Oh yes. He was getting fonder and fonder of multiple partners. He was finding no satisfaction in bed play anymore. Men like him can burn out, and without love to fuel their passion, they fade away. Horatia's love for him saved his soul. He won't ever grow weary of her, I think. Love like theirs doesn't fade."

"It better not," Cedric grumbled. The thought of his best friend leaving his sister to bed other women put a sour taste in his mouth. He didn't want to think Lucien was capable of it, but he knew the man only too well. But thus far, his sister and his friend seemed lost in each other, and with the baby on the way, Cedric felt their world was looking up.

"Oh dear..." Ashton's voice was sharp with surprise.

"What?" Cedric sat up so abruptly the boat rocked from side to side, and cool water lapped up over the edges, soaking his shins. "What is it, Ash?"

"You must promise not to get angry."

Cedric growled low in his throat. "Ash..."

"It's your wife."

Cedric's heart lurched and panic seized him. "What about her?"

"She's swimming in the other side of the lake."

"Swimming?" he echoed, as his brain tried to decide if this was bad news or not.

"In nothing but her chemise. I highly doubt the doctor would want her to reinjure her shoulder." Ashton added this last comment as an amused afterthought.

Cedric fumbled for an oar and shoved it into Ashton's lap. "Row! Now!" he bellowed.

✨ 17 ✨

C lad only in her chemise, Anne headed toward the water. She felt rather wicked, being so scantily clad, but this was her property now, by virtue of marriage, and she wanted to do this. Only her husband had the power to stop her from doing as she wished, and he was far off on the other side of the lake. The thought almost made her laugh. He would be furious no doubt, but rather than scare her, the idea instead amused her.

It had been awhile since she'd indulged in such improper behavior of swimming in her underclothes. Even though she remembered little of her past, she couldn't deny how freeing the water felt lapping at her bare legs. As she pushed deeper into the cold lake, a memory surfaced.

Frolicking in the shallows of a similar lake, an older man watching her, an indulgent smile on his kind face. She laughed, a child's laugh, happy to play while her father remained close.

The pain of seeing that man's face for only a moment cut deep.

Papa. He had been dead only a week before she rushed to the altar? What had motivated her to do such a thing? Why had she married Cedric? And furthermore, why had Cedric agreed to it? No doubt the scandal of it would be the talk of the *ton* for the next decade. Anne placed a hand on her stomach, wanting to ease the creeping dread that settled there.

Focusing back on her desire to swim, she tiptoed farther out until she was waist deep, the chill of the water a stark contrast to the warmth of the air. It would take her ages to coax herself out fully at this rate. There was no other option but to plunge in. She dunked herself under and gasped at the sheer iciness of the water.

Soon the cold water felt good against the hot burn of her healing shoulder. She used her good arm to paddle out a bit farther and kicked her legs. This was her element, the physical pleasure of knowing one's body and understanding how it worked.

She stretched her limbs, feeling the muscles strain and work—it felt so good. Anne wasn't a thin woman. She was curvaceous with a bit of natural strength that tended to make gown fittings irritating when the dressmaker muttered about how she bulged in the wrong places. Her body wasn't perceived to be beautiful, not by the standards of the *ton*, but she'd stopped caring about such things long ago. That much she was sure of.

Anne swam far out into the lake, momentarily forgetting to keep her eye on Cedric's fishing boat. It wasn't until she had dived deep a few times before she noticed the fishing boat had pulled up onto the shore and a scowling viscount stood at the bank's edge glaring in her direction.

Cedric tapped his booted foot in the soggy grass, creating an odd squelching sound. Anne stifled a giggle as she read the look in his sightless gaze. He was promising her punishment for her wanton recklessness. Farther back, Lord Lennox was conversing with Hartley, both keeping their backs to her. Anne went as still as possible, using her legs and good arm to tread water.

"I know you are there, Anne. Come out at once. You should not be risking yourself, not with your shoulder." He punctuated this with a jab of his index finger at the ground near his feet, as though to make her heel like a spaniel.

"I'm not coming out with you there," she responded, trying to keep from laughing at her sudden need to play the imp.

"I cannot see you and the others aren't looking."

"No," she stoutly refused. The clenching of his fists told her that once she was within his reach she'd be in trouble—what sort of trouble she was unsure, but she doubted he'd hurt her.

"Go in after her, Cedric," Ashton hollered over his shoulder.

Anne gasped at the forwardness of his suggestion. She was nearly naked and the idea of Cedric catching her swimming in nothing but her chemise was exciting, and a tad frightening.

"Please, Anne. I haven't swum since I lost my sight."

"Since when does one need to see in order to swim?" His admission managed to calm her a little and she tried to tease him. She was afraid and so was he, even if their fears were different.

"Please do not make me drag you out. It will be unpleasant for us both."

"Cedric, wait." Anne wanted more than anything to connect with him, to uncover the reasons that had made her marry him. "Why don't you come out into the shallows, join me for a minute. If you don't, I might be tempted to stay here and grow a tail. Would you like that, husband? To have to come and find me in my underwater grotto?" *Trust me,* she urged.

"No."

Now he was the one refusing to cooperate. What an amusing situation they found themselves in.

"Do you plan on hiding in a shell for the rest of your life, husband? Come into the water as high as your waist, get reacquainted with it."

"She has a point, Cedric," Ashton cut in.

"You may return with Hartley back to the manor," Cedric said, his voice a little gruff.

"Very well. Come find me this evening." Ashton turned and walked away with the footman.

"Are you truly going to make me come in after you?" Cedric knelt down to pull off his boots and roll up his trousers.

"Most definitely."

Anne's eyes fixed on Cedric's muscled calves as he began to gingerly walk into the water. He got in knee-deep before he paused and tilted his head, as though listening for any sign of her. Anne had the sudden feeling he was hunting her. She held her breath and drifted farther back, but a startled fish splashed by her shoulder. Cedric lunged for her and toppled into the water. His cry of alarm startled her. She swam for him, catching him about the waist as he flailed in panic.

"Put your feet down. It's shallow here," she urged.

"I know." He suddenly stood and grasped her body, hauling her to him. A hunter victorious, he smiled and curled his arms around her back, hugging her.

Cedric relaxed. He was blinking rapidly, water streaming in rivulets down his face as he clung to her. As his breathing began to slow he bent his head, resting his chin on the top of her head.

"You'll be the death of me, Anne," he murmured. The warmth of his breath against her temple made her skin break out into goose bumps.

Trembling, she stroked his cheek, watching his empty brown eyes fix on something distant. The vast emptiness there was starkly beautiful, like a tragic hero from an opera. He called to her, begged for her to fill him with love and light.

"Why do I trust you?" she whispered. "I should be terrified that I remember so little of my life, yet thoughts of you ease my fears. Why?"

Cedric was silent for a moment. His large hands spanned her back, making her feel small in a way she'd never felt before.

"From the moment I met you, you captivated me. You were clever, but also sweet and innocent. Then that innocence was ripped from you and you remained strong and alone. I saw myself in you, a kindred spirit. We bear our burdens and fight to keep those we love happy and safe. It was inevitable that I would want you, desire you the way I do."

She combed fingers through his wet hair, brushing it out of his eyes. "What was our wedding like?"

He gave a boyish smile. "Perfect. You were the loveliest bride to grace St. George's."

"Flattery from a blind man?" she teased. "I wonder if that's reliable."

"I knew how you would look, and then I held you in my arms, your scent, your touch. You were perfect. We were both happy."

"Were?"

"We quarreled a few days ago. I left and you fled into the night. That's how you came to be wounded." Cedric massaged her shoulder and sighed.

Anne pressed her body into his, molding herself against him, and he moaned. "Can't we forget all of that? Can we not start over?"

"Darling, I'm doing my best not to ravish you senseless at this moment. It would be unfair to you in your condition. I will not have you remember me as a monster." Cedric's valiant and honorable words were somewhat diminished by the insistent press of his arousal against her hip beneath the water.

"Have we made love before?" She wanted him to say yes. It would explain her body's recognition of his, her desire whenever he touched her.

"We've come close. In the library of Godric's townhouse."

A flicker of memory overtook her. *A couch, two bodies tangled on it, teeth sinking into her neck as she climaxed around his fingers.* Anne shuddered in Cedric's arms.

"I think I remember that, or at least my body does." It never ceased to amaze her how easy it was to be so open and honest with him.

Cedric responded with a honey-rich laugh. "I would hope so, you little hellion. It was quite the experience for both of us. I've never had such pleasure watching a woman come apart in my arms."

Anne was thankful he could not see her blush. Despite

her body's initial warmth, the cold water was starting to settle into her skin. Cedric's hands ran the length of her arms as he tried to warm her.

"I believe we've had enough swimming for the day. Shall we go?" It wasn't so much a question as a politely phrased command. She didn't mind, however, because she was getting colder by the minute.

"Yes, let's get inside." Anne guided him out of the water and tugged him to a halt by her pile of clothes. He put on his boots and waited patiently as she drew her gown over her body, ignoring the discomfort of her wet skin sticking to the fabric. Once she donned her slippers and fastened her garnet necklace about her neck she took his hand. They walked back to the house in amiable silence, until the shrieking of the housekeeper sliced through the air.

"Never in all my years!" The elderly woman paused to poke Cedric with the cane he'd left at the manor. "Swimming without someone to watch over you? And in your clothes, no less?"

Anne waited for Cedric to berate the housekeeper for her treatment of him, but the viscount merely smiled.

"We're fine. Send someone to light my bedroom fire and bring something to eat in an hour."

The housekeeper scoffed loudly and walked off. Cedric wrapped an arm about Anne's waist, tucking her into his side and kissing the crown of her hair. The teasing and affectionate gestures he so often did without a second thought made her melt inside. Was this love, or something close to it? She hoped it was with all of her heart. In this new world where she was so alone and her memories so dim, the thought of being loved was her oasis in the desert.

"I can feel you thinking. What is it?" Cedric asked as they ascended the stairs.

Anne nibbled her lip, debating on what to tell him.

Cedric patted her waist. "Come, sweetheart, talk to me."

"I want to be happy, and I feel that maybe we will be. Do you think me very foolish?"

"To hope for happiness? Never, my heart, never."

"How do you always do that to me?" she whispered, her voice shaking with emotions she was afraid to let out.

Cedric's face lined with concern. "Do what?"

"Make me feel strong, even when I feel the weakest I have ever been."

The corners of his eyes wrinkled into fine lines as he smiled. "We are kindred spirits. You make me whole again. When I am with you, Anne, the darkness in my eyes ceases to penetrate my soul."

Anne's own eyes suddenly burned with tears. What a tragedy for him, to know the life he loved had been changed forever. There were so many things he could no longer do. The thought that she could help him was a powerful one, a wonderful one.

Cedric led her into his room. It was dark, the curtains

pulled over the window, making Anne feel that it was evening rather than midday.

Evening. Such an intimate hour of the day. She couldn't help but imagine that he might finally take her to bed, despite his insistence he would not until she was better. He pulled a cord and a maid appeared immediately. Her eyes widened as she took in the soaked clothes of her master and mistress.

"Molly, would you be so kind as to fetch Anne's night-gown and have a footman prepare a bath here in my chamber?"

Anne blushed as Cedric tugged her toward his dressing room. A large metal tub awaited her behind a screen, big enough for two people.

"Wait here." Cedric went around the other side of the screen to change his clothes.

Through the dim light Anne could only hear the rustle of fabric, the whisper of it on skin. Her body began to ache. One peek, she promised herself, and leaned around the edge of the screen. Cedric had stripped every bit of clothing off, with his back to her as he shuffled through a collection of clean shirts, his hands rubbing the cloth between his thumb and forefinger as though measuring the quality of the textures.

Anne, however, could not keep her eyes off his hips and buttocks. The sculpted flesh looked hard and trim. She had the sudden urge to dig her fingers into it, to urge him to take her body now, and to hell with waiting. Anne made an involuntary sound as he spun around, revealing his front. That male part of him was there before her eyes and she swallowed hard. He was incredibly large. *Too* large.

Her thighs clenched together. *That would never fit.*

"Everything all right, darling?" he called out, unaware she could see him.

Anne ducked behind the screen and responded. "Yes, I was just cold." A blatant lie. Her body was hot enough to warm the entire lake.

More soft rustling, the sound of bare feet and then Cedric came around the screen in a loose shirt and snug trousers. His feet, Anne noticed with fascination, were large and beautiful. She'd never thought feet could be lovely, but his were. The feet of an athletic man. He padded over to her and kissed her forehead.

Anne was overcome. This beautiful, seductive man was all hers. How did she come to deserve him?

"A hot bath and warm meal will do you good. How is your shoulder? I want the doctor to come and put a new sling on as soon as you are done here."

"It aches a little, but otherwise it's fine. The doctor set the shoulder well."

"Thank heavens for that." Cedric sighed against her cheek before kissing her lightly.

A few minutes later Anne was stripping off her clothes and easing into the steaming bath. Cedric remained close by, and although he could not see her, Anne felt exposed and vulnerable nonetheless.

"Feeling better?" Cedric asked as he knelt by the tub, his hands coasting along the outer rim, moving slowly toward her upper body as though he was trying to find her.

"Immensely." Anne rubbed her sore neck. It ached occasionally, probably from her accident. The second she shut her eyes, Cedric's hands descended on her shoulders from behind. She was about to protest, but he shushed her and began a relaxing massage. The intimacy of the moment felt blindingly familiar. A splash of memory, white lace and the smell of roses and orange flowers, and Cedric's healing hands.

"You are so wonderful at that," she said drowsily. He rubbed a knot out of her shoulder and answered with a throaty laugh before kissing her neck.

"Are you tired?"

"A little," she admitted, balling a fist against her yawning mouth. "But it's only the afternoon and I can't sleep yet."

"I want you to sleep, Anne. You need to rest to get well. Shall I have Hartley bring you a sleeping draught?" He started to rise, but she stopped him with a hand on his arm.

Anne sat up, exposing herself to his blind gaze, water sloshing over the sides of the tub. "No."

"Easy, easy. I would not force it on you. I know better than that."

Anne sensed his comment came from a past experience, but she couldn't seem to remember the details.

"May I suggest another method?" Cedric was grinning as his hands on her shoulders slid down to the pebbled nipples of her wet breasts.

She gasped, startled by his boldness. He pulled her down and pressed her toward him so she lay back in the tub. He kissed her throat, nibbling at the sensitive spot below her ear that sent a flurry of pleasurable chills down her spine.

"Is this acceptable, Anne?" he whispered as he caressed and cupped her breasts. Anne nodded, sighing as one of his hands glided over her ribs and down her belly to the apex of her thighs. The sensation of his hands on her body, the tender way he manipulated her, stroking, caressing, leaving a fire in the way of each brushing touch, was nothing short of erotic. Every part of her was attuned to his touch, like a pianoforte's keys warmed by the player's hands, ready to create music.

His voice was silky as a spider's web and evanescent as midnight as he pressed onward, entering her folds with a gentle finger. "And this? May I touch you here?" She'd never thought she'd want a man to touch her there, to enter her body, even with his fingers, but with Cedric it wasn't enough, she wanted to connect to him every way she could.

He played with her, stroking, flicking, advancing, then withdrawing. His finger was large, and her body clasped tight around it, and when she unconsciously clenched her inner muscles around him, he answered her with a low animal growl. The sound vibrated across her body and she arched her hips up, trying to push his finger deeper.

"Yes, touch me, *please*." Desperation and hunger for him gnawed at her bone deep.

"Let me kiss you, Anne, darling. Surrender yourself to me." His voice was hypnotic. Each word made her want to agree to anything he asked.

Cedric took her lips with his, his mouth teasing and seductive. His tongue thrust inside at the same time he slid two fingers into her, filling her. Anne arched in the tub, water slapping over the sides. Cedric deepened the kiss further, his fingers increased their steady rhythm, and Anne moved her hips, trying to satisfy the need for something she couldn't vocalize. When Cedric's thumb passed over her bundle of nerves she whimpered in pleasure. He repeated the action, still pumping his fingers, and in a matter of seconds she was panting and white-knuckled, clinging to the tub's edge.

"Not yet, my heart, I wish to exhaust you properly."

Cedric backed off on his movements and resumed his leisurely caresses.

She snared one of his wrists and forced it back down between her legs. "Please, Cedric. I need you."

"You need me?" Shock layered his tone, and it made her ache to think he couldn't believe her.

"More than anything."

Cedric groaned as though her words had undone him. He captured her mouth with his and began his stroking again. Anne's body shot straight back to that heightened awareness and craving for pleasure. In moments she shattered beneath his touch, aftershocks of pleasure rippling through her, making her feel weak and heavy like a mountain of immovable stones. His harsh breath against her ear told her he had been aroused as much as she was. They were connecting, even if it was in small steps.

We can do this. We can make this marriage work and be happy together.

She had to make it work. The thought of losing Cedric, or giving him up, was impossible.

❧ 18 ❧

Cedric kissed Anne's forehead, taking pride in having weakened his woman's resolve. He felt like a conqueror of old, having taken his woman and sated her. He'd denied his own in return, but there had been a wonderful heat inside him at feeling her come apart in his arms. She was far less inhibited than before. He had to fight off the waves of lust that demanded he claim her completely.

He stole another kiss from her lips. "I love it when you melt into me like that." He nipped her bottom lip, feeling playful and yet relaxed. Anne responded with a fatigued sigh and slid lower into the tub, no doubt too exhausted to stay upright.

"I think it's time we got out you of there, love."

"So soon?"

Cedric lifted her to her feet and began to dry her off. Anne didn't even feign a protest. He took his time, drying every lickable inch of her. When he returned her to his bed, he helped her don her nightgown and reset the sling for her arm. Exhaustion claimed Anne, and she put up no resistance when he tucked her into his bed. He stroked back her hair and joined her beneath the sheets, tucking her into his side.

"My darling Anne," he said, and for the thousandth time he wished he could see her. Did her guard relax in her sleep?

Anne burrowed against him, her hands balled up and tucked against his ribs, her head resting in the crook between his arm and chest. Cedric couldn't believe how full his life felt at that moment. How much he loved holding this woman close, her familiar scent all around him, knowing she was his, now and always.

Cedric dozed on and off for the next half hour until Hartley arrived with soup and tea. Reluctant to leave Anne's side, he eased out of the bed and woke her up with a smattering of kisses.

"Food is here, and I have things to attend to. If you need me, send Hartley to fetch me."

Anne rolled over onto her back, cupping his face in her hand, stealing a final kiss. The fact that she had initiated the moment stole his breath. He wanted nothing more than to topple her back into bed and make love to her until neither of them could walk.

"May I go to Brighton in a few days?"

Cedric frowned. "Only if you feel up to it. Hartley must go with you. I don't wish for you to be alone and unprotected."

"Unprotected? Is there a reason I should be concerned?"

Cedric felt Anne sit up and catch hold of his arms.

"It may be nothing, but do you remember last Christmas when I lost my sight?"

"I'm sorry, I don't."

"Well, the accident was not so much an accident, but rather an attempt on my life, and that of my sister. Ashton was also shot by someone last year, and we believe it is all connected. He's no doubt been watching all of us, but since your accident, I worry that you might be weakened for a time. If noticed, he might take advantage of that weakness somehow."

"But who would want to kill you?"

Cedric laughed, but there was no humor in it. "Plenty of men want me dead, but few would ever attempt it. And only one man has vowed to kill me and the other members of the League. Hugo Waverly."

"Sir Hugo Waverly? I know that name. Somehow I know it."

Cedric's hands curled into fists. "Yes. He swore to see us all dead, and his attempt on Horatia's life also resulted in my blindness."

"How?"

"A fire had been set in the gardener's cottage, and as I was being rescued a beam fell on me. The impact blinded me and turned me into this clumsy, stumbling creature."

"Oh, Cedric." Anne's voice was impossibly soft. He flinched as her hands wound around his neck, but he relaxed when she began to kiss his jaw and cheeks. His arms circled around her waist, holding her briefly against him before he released her.

"So you will promise me you will take Hartley with you whenever you leave this house? Even on my land you may not be safe. Waverly's hired assassin stole Horatia from her own bedchamber." He'd almost lost his best friend and his sister to that monster. He would not lose Anne too. Even now he had himself questioning whether her injuries had truly been from an accidental fall, or if something far more sinister had been interrupted.

Anne patted his chest with a tender hand. "I promise. I'm no fool. And I don't want you to ever worry about me."

"Thank heavens for that. It seems most of the women in my life are determined to gray my hair before I reach forty." He curled his hand around hers and brought it to his mouth for a kiss. "I really must go. Get some rest, my heart."

Cedric left Anne and went hunting for Ashton. He found his friend in the library after making inquiries to a passing footman.

"Ash?" Cedric entered the library, listening for the familiar crinkle of a newspaper being folded. Ashton was nothing if not a creature of habit.

"On the settee," Ash supplied.

Cedric navigated the room, avoiding chairs and book-shelves to find his friend.

"How fares your lady?" Ashton asked, his usually serious tone now sprinkled with a hint of amusement.

Cedric grinned in spite of himself. "Resting after a bath." After such a powerful climax Anne would need to rest for a few hours.

"I'm glad to hear it. I was worried that you two might have quarreled after the lake."

"Nonsense. I'm blind. She has no memory. It's practically impossible to find anything decent to quarrel about."

"Good, good." Ash sounded oddly distracted. Cedric cocked his head, pondering his friend's tone. There was something amiss, and it bothered him that he could not read Ashton's face the way he used to.

"You have never been one to hide your concerns, Ash. Pray, what weighs so heavily on your mind?"

"It's about Waverly."

"Hugo?" To think he'd just been warning Anne about the man.

"Is there any other Waverly who causes us so much grief?"

"Well, what about him?" Cedric patted around until he

found a wingback chair facing the settee. "You haven't had word about him, have you?"

"No, but we should be doing something about him. The attack on you and Lucien during Christmas, and the bullet that tore through my arm were not accidents."

"Of course, but we cannot prove Waverly was behind them," Cedric reminded him.

"I think the drowned cat at Charles's house was a clear enough signature, don't you?"

Cedric frowned. That had indeed made things clear, not only of the architect, but the motives behind his actions. Hugo's intent was destruction, but his motivation was revenge. It seemed the League's past sins were at last coming back to haunt them.

"I know, I know. But no one outside the League would understand." Cedric slumped back in his chair as though the weight of decades of worry had settled on his shoulders. "I just warned Anne not to leave the residence unattended because of him. What would you advise we do, other than be vigilant?"

"That is the problem. I haven't the faintest idea."

Ashton was as much of a strategist as Cedric, and to not have any idea how to handle a situation was unsettling.

"I've been preoccupied of late, and Waverly's involvement in these attacks has been so concealed that I have had little to go on in the way of evidence. One cannot go to a magistrate purely with one's instincts and vague connections. To make matters worse, Waverly has left London again. I believe he is preparing for whatever he has planned next."

"If only we knew which one of us he means to target." Cedric let out an exasperated sigh.

"Unfortunately, there is no way to know. I always believed that Charles would be his true target, but it seems he means to do away with all of us."

"Over what happened to Peter? That sin isn't on our hands alone."

"No, but he holds us responsible."

"What the devil is wrong with that man that he can't let his grudges go?" Cedric muttered.

"You know it's more than that. It has everything to do with Charles's and Hugo's fathers. There was much bad blood between them. Our interference on Charles's behalf put us on the funeral pyre with him. And losing Peter in the river only gave him more wood to burn." Ashton shifted in his chair as though restless.

"I would not change a second of that night. I would dive in after Charles again."

"As would I. But I wish..." A long moment of tense silence followed as both men were plagued by dark memories of how they had saved one, but failed another.

"How is Charles?" Cedric hadn't spent much time with him in recent months. The man was far too fond of pulling pranks in the hopes of lightening Cedric's mood, which almost always backfired.

Ashton sighed. "He still has the nightmares, but he's been better recently. That doesn't stop me from worrying about him, though."

"You think you can cure him of his nightmares?"

"No. At least, not anytime soon. And at the moment I am much too busy trying to deal with Lady Melbourne."

"Again we return to Lady Melbourne. Anne told me the night of the opera that you disappeared to a dark alcove with her." Cedric enjoyed the responding sputter of shock from his usually collected friend.

"And what did you *do* with Lady Melbourne in said alcove, hmm?"

"I...we...that is to say..." Ashton, always so eloquent in speech, was entirely at a loss for words.

"Oh, quite. I'm sure you and she enjoyed...whatever it was." Cedric couldn't stop the grin that spread across his face.

Ashton recovered himself and properly responded. "I was negotiating with her."

"Negotiating? Is that what they are calling it nowadays?" Cedric was fighting every urge to laugh.

"I thought a bit of physical persuasion was the wisest course of action," Ashton argued, but there was a breathless tone to his voice. If Cedric didn't know better, he'd swear the man was embarrassed about something. "She has a bit more...fight in her than I realized. I have to find a way to stop her antics from destroying my shipping lines. Extreme measures may be necessary."

Cedric sobered slightly. "You always were the coldest seducer of us all."

It was the truth. Ashton had been the only one among the five original members of the League who never lost control, who never let his passions rule him. In the wake of his calculating seductions he'd left countless victims. Almost all of his conquests had been related to his successes in the business world. One night he would bed an opera singer who was mistress to a shipyard owner. The next night he was pinning the daughter of a banker to a wall just off an assembly hall, persuading her to reveal her father's secrets. Ashton could be completely ruthless.

"Yes, well, a leopard cannot change its spots," Ashton muttered.

Cedric crossed his arms over his chest. "Are you so sure? Godric and Lucien have proved that saying false."

Ashton was silent a long while.

"Some men are fated to be fortunate. I don't count myself among them."

"Damn the Fates, Ash. Make your own luck. Look at me and Anne. Against all odds we are stumbling our way toward happiness. Who's to say you can't do the same?"

Ashton let out a loud, amused laugh. "Marriage suits you, Cedric. It truly does. Now, off you go. Find that wife of yours and give Lucien some competition on the begetting of heirs."

It was Cedric's turn to laugh. "Only you could phrase that so indelicately as to make me sound like a prized stud." Cedric got to his feet, retrieved his cane and headed for the door. It was time to go to his study and have his steward assist him with some letters. Then, once he finished his business, he would find his wife and surrender his self-control. He wanted to make love to her, regardless of whether she remembered him; he wanted to love her, to seduce her into loving him. If that made him a villain, then so be it. He was a rogue, after all.

❦

ANNE'S MAID FINISHED FASTENING HER GOLD-COLORED day gown and threaded a few more pins into the tumble of curls atop her head.

"There you are, milady. It looks lovely."

"Thank you, Becca."

"Will you be needing anything else?" the woman asked, her cap-covered head bowed respectfully.

"Actually, I was wondering if I might be shown to the library. I shall wait there until dinner."

Becca bobbed a curtsy and led Anne down the stairs and to the library.

The room was beautiful. Gilded chairs and tables were littered with books, but the books, she noted, were layered with dust. There was a distinct impression of someone having been here once, a long time ago.

Someone who loved to read. Anne caught the cover of the nearest heavy tome and turned it over. The gilt lettering read *A History of the English Monarchy.* Anne knew that Cedric had never opened this book, and it wasn't like he'd opened any of the others. He hadn't been one for reading, even before the accident.

This quiet scene glowing in the afternoon sun felt like a memorial to someone long gone. Could it be that Cedric's parents had nestled in these very chairs, turning pages with interest? Anne's throat constricted at the thought of Cedric leaving the books out. Had he been unable to put them away? Did he want to feel that his parents might come back at any moment? Or was it merely that he never came to this room and the servants didn't have the heart to put them away?

"If you are looking for something to read, Lady Sheridan, might I suggest this?"

Anne turned to find herself face-to-face with the tall, pale-haired Lord Lennox. She took the small volume he held out to her.

"*Lady Briana and the Troubled Viscount?*" Was the title his way of communicating with her?

"Cedric is one of the finest men I have ever known," Lord Lennox said.

Anne was bespelled by the light in his vivid blue eyes. In a sudden flash, she pictured Ashton bare-chested with a bloody shoulder wound, his features etched with lines of excruciating pain. Anne's head spun and she wavered on her feet. Ashton caught her by the waist, steadying her.

"Is everything all right, Lady Sheridan?"

"I saw you...covered in blood. Why did I see you bleeding?" She clutched at his waistcoat for support while she fought off a wave of nausea.

Ashton looked at her curiously. "You saw me covered in blood?"

"Yes... Your chest was bare, and your shoulder was... wounded," she added with a flush of heat in embarrassment. She ought never to have admitted to having seen him half-naked.

"It's a memory and nothing more, Lady Sheridan," Ashton soothed. "Last December you came to visit your friend, Emily Parr, now the Duchess of Essex. I believe Cedric told you I'd been shot last year. Godric was tending to my shoulder and you came in upon us. I am sorry the memory has upset you."

Anne blinked in surprise as the memory sharpened and everything came back about that particular day. She remembered Emily, her good friend. Godric, the brooding and handsome Duke of Essex. They weren't blank titles any more. They were friends she remembered. If only the rest would come back. Anne's racing heart settled and her shoulders slumped in relief.

"Thank God. I was worried I might be suffering from visions." She rubbed a hand along her forehead.

"Do you remember anything else?"

Anne gave a shake of her head. "It's all a blur. I wish I could."

"Do you remember the night you first met Cedric at Almack's?"

Anne started to say no, but Ashton cupped her chin and had her look at him. "*Think hard. I was there. There was a waltz starting. Cedric turned to face you...*" The smooth narration of Ashton's voice poured through her, seeking out dark spots in her mind, bathing them in pools of shimmering memory.

"He smiled at me and I felt..."

Ashton focused on her even harder. "Imagine him there, turning to see you for the first time. The look he gave you. The smile. What did you feel?"

She surrendered to his eyes and spoke what her heart remembered, even though her mind insisted the memory was gone. "I felt that everything I'd ever known to be true wasn't anymore. That my existence began in the curve of his smile, and the first breath in my lungs was rooted in the gleam of his eyes. My heart was his."

Ashton released her chin and placed his palm on her cheek. He brushed his knuckles along her cheekbone, soothing and tender. It was only then Anne realized tears were streaming down her cheeks and he was wiping them away.

"I didn't mean to make you cry, Lady Sheridan."

Anne sniffled and wiped her face with the heel of her hand.

"I remember it now." Something in Ashton's insistence of her thinking about that night had brought a fleet of memories back into her mind—her father, Cedric, Emily. So much of who she was had returned, and her head was pounding with the ache of it all.

"Are you feeling unwell?" Ashton inquired with some concern.

"I just need some fresh air." Anne struggled past him to get free of the library and the onslaught of memories. But escape from her emotions was impossible. She stopped herself short from crashing into her husband, who had just come around the corner a few feet away from the library.

"There you are, my heart. I'd recognize that scent anywhere."

Anne threw herself against him, wrapping her arms around his waist. She buried her face in his chest, taking in the scent of him, the aroma of leather, stables and sandalwood.

"Is something wrong? Have you been crying?"

"I remember the night we met," she answered.

"God in heaven... No wonder you're in tears. I'm so sorry. I wish I could take those memories back. Of Andrews hurting you, or myself and that other woman." He held her close, banding his arms about her.

"Cedric, please, listen to me. It's not those things I was remembering. I was remembering what it felt like to see you that first time. How much I cared for you..."

"Cared? As in past tense?" His hands stiffened just the slightest bit.

"I still care."

"And that made you cry?"

Anne burrowed herself deeper into him. "Yes and no."

His chuckle shook his chest, the sensation against her face delightful, comforting. "It has to be one or the other. Which is it?"

"Cedric, nothing is ever that simple when discussing love."

His grip loosened, but he pulled her closer, the embrace far softer.

"Loving me makes you weep?"

"In a wonderful way." She tried to tease him, but it still came out watery. "But you mustn't let it encourage your sense of self-importance."

"Well, we both know how well-endowed that is." He pressed his hips against hers, just enough for her to feel the bulge in his trousers.

"*Husband.*" A laugh escaped her lips. She adored his natural inclination to be playful. It always eased her moods.

"Well, dry your eyes, love. I've decided to spend the day with you. What would you like to do?"

"Could we spend it in the stables?"

"What on earth for?"

Anne repressed a giggle at the perturbed expression on

his face. "I want you to finally show me your Arabian mares."

"Of course. Your memory must be returning if you remember that obsession. And here I was thinking I'd get you alone in a pile of hay and have my way with you." Cedric nuzzled her neck.

"Perhaps you shall," she replied.

❧ 19 ❧

The skies were once again heavy with black clouds, the bellies of which hung low enough to touch the distant horizon. Anne gazed at the ominous sight as the gloom of the coming storm settled around her and Cedric. The air was filled with the rich scent of late-blooming flowers and of rain yet to come. Her skin tingled as a warm breeze swirled and eddied about her. The stables were just ahead, the musty aroma of hay and polished leather teased her, reminding her of a past that was still somewhat hazy.

Cedric swung his lion-headed cane back and forth over the gravel path as they walked toward the wide double door entrance of the stables.

"How many horses do you have?"

He flashed an indulgent smile. "You mean how many do *we* have? They are yours now as well. And we have fourteen, including my four dappled grays for my private coaches."

"And the Arabians? What are their names?" Anne's hand tightened on his arm as they reached the stable doors.

Cedric paused, sweeping his cane over the threshold to determine if he had clear access before he ushered her inside.

"Their sire was the famous Firestorm. The two mares I have are called Winter's Heart and Autumn's Flame. I've been calling them Heart and Flame."

Anne held her breath in excitement as Cedric counted the stalls, his cane tapping lightly on each stall door they passed. Inquisitive equine faces poked out of the wooden enclosures.

Cedric set his cane against one particular stall door. "Ahh, this should be Winter's Heart."

A snowy white mare stuck her head out, her nose brushing Cedric's palm. He flinched at the sudden contact, then relaxed as the mare nibbled his fingers.

Anne peered into the stall to get a better look at the mare. "I can't believe it. She's pure white. Not even a hint of gray." She'd never seen such a magnificent creature before. The breeding which must have gone into Winter's Heart was unimaginable. No wonder the Arabian merchant had threatened Cedric's life. Losing these two horses must have cost him his very soul.

"Oh, Cedric, she's beautiful." Anne trailed a hand up

Heart's neck. The horse's large eyes were onyx pools reflecting her face. With an impatient huff and a heavy stamp, Heart shifted and nudged Cedric's shoulder. With a grin he dug into his pocket and retrieved a lump of sugar. Heart took it daintily from his palm and munched it in the most ladylike manner Anne had ever seen. Anne smothered a giggle.

Cedric heard her and snorted. "Heart is my well-behaved lady. Flame, on the other hand..." He pointed to a stall two doors down where a stunning red chestnut mare was watching them, ears flicked forward in their direction.

"Flame is my little hellion. All fire and spirit."

Anne blinked as a whisper of a memory flitted past. Cedric's voice calling her "little hellion" and speaking of her as an "inferno." A blush crept across her cheeks. Anne focused on the second mare, laughing as Flame nipped Cedric's arm to get at the hidden lumps of sugar.

Anne listened with delighted fascination as Cedric told her tales of his youth. His love for his parents, his sisters, and his horses was evident from his tone and the expressions of joy on his face. He looked livelier than she'd seen him in months. How she remembered his darkness of the heart before now, she couldn't say. But she knew this man; this happy man was the one she'd loved, still loved. It was this Cedric she had married. Anne's heart clenched as he looked toward her. It was almost as if he could see her.

I wish I could give you my sight. I wish I was the one who suffered in your place.

"Well, shall we head in?" Cedric felt about for his cane just as thunder shattered the silence. A deluge of rain crashed down over the stables a moment later.

"Perhaps we ought to wait," Cedric suggested.

"'Tis only rain."

Cedric tightened his grip on her. "Where there is thunder there is lightning and I do not wish to brave that risk, not with your injuries."

"Very well. What are we to do?"

"There is an empty stall at the back. We can rest there until the storm passes."

Cedric led her back down the row of stalls. It was to be her and Cedric alone in a warm, hay-filled stall. So much could happen before the storm passed.

Cedric hailed one of the grooms, and the man produced several clean blankets for them before he disappeared into the tack room and firmly shut the door. Anne watched Cedric set his cane down and spread the blankets out on the clean bed of hay.

"Come and sit." His tone was soothing, a temptation she couldn't refuse.

Once Anne was seated comfortably in the center of the large woolen blankets, he eased down beside her.

Cedric brushed his hand over the blanket, looking away from her. "I used to hate coming here. After the accident, that is. It reminded me of how much I'd lost. It is a funny thing, to at last have your heart's desire yet never be able to enjoy it."

Anne's throat tightened as she saw the look of bewilderment on his face.

"But coming here with you..." He paused, searching for her hand, then lacing their fingers together. "It made the loss of riding less painful."

"What do you mean?"

Cedric raked a hand through his hair. "Being with you...it's like seeing the world again when I thought I'd be trapped in darkness forever. I didn't have to ride the horses today to feel happy. Simply being here, touching them and talking to them, it made me feel a joy I'd thought lost forever. I owe that to you, Anne. I owe you everything. Name your heart's desire and I will see that you get it. It's the least I can do for giving me a piece of my life back."

Cedric raised her hand to his lips, feathering kisses over her knuckles and on the inside of her palm as he waited for her answer.

"I want only you. All of you." Where such boldness came from she had no idea, but the time was here and waiting would only threaten her chances of being happy. She kissed his hand, wanting him to feel the depth of her love.

Cedric's empty eyes seemed to darken. His lips parted, and he released her hands carefully, a guarded gesture.

"Anne, I have little self-control left in me. Do not test it. I don't want to force you to do anything."

"I'm not testing you. I meant what I said. Don't you

know that? I want *you*." She held his hand to her chest, hoping he'd understand what she meant.

He surprised her by withdrawing and standing. He moved to the stall door, feeling for the handle and pulling it shut. Then he drew a shaky breath and turned to face her. The privacy of that moment, the two of them closed away from the rest of the world, captured Anne in its solemnity. They were on the edge of a cliff together and the slightest breeze could send them careening down.

"Do you trust me?" he asked. A glimmer flashed in his gaze, a light she'd not seen since before he'd gone blind.

"With every breath. With my entire soul."

Cedric leaned back against the stall door. She'd forgotten the confidence and power he used to have before he'd lost his sight. He'd been a force of nature, a whirlwind of passion. Now he was a muted storm, a quiet rain, and she was still hopelessly in love with him.

"Have you ever seen someone train a young gelding?"

"Yes..." Anne recalled her father's master groom spending several hours in a solitary stall stroking every inch of the gelding's body so that the horse became familiar with the groom's touch and being handled.

Cedric stepped forward, a hint of his grace and confidence echoing in the strong steps. There was nothing in this stall he could hurt himself if he fell upon it. Here, he was a master of his surroundings and he knew it.

"By experiencing the comfort and pleasure of the

groom's touch, the gelding learns to trust him, and the groom is able to saddle him and ride him."

Cedric's mouth transfixed Anne so much at first that she didn't even notice he'd moved until he was kneeling at her feet. His fingers sought the laces of her slippers, undoing them. She didn't stop him. To her surprise, she lifted her foot to allow him to ease it off.

"You see, horses are like people. Their trust must be earned." Her other slipper joined the first on the floor a few feet away.

"Have you ever tamed a gelding?" Anne asked him. Her body quivered as Cedric moved around to sit behind her. His fingers slowly puzzled through the complicated hooks on the back of the gown. Her breath hitched with each gentle tug as he pulled the gown close to loosen the tension and unfasten each hook.

"I have tamed one. When he was older he turned out to be my best racer. Most men think taming a horse means breaking its spirit."

"But not you?" Anne shut her eyes, savoring the slide of Cedric's hands along her shoulders as he peeled the gown down off her body. She lifted herself up to rid her body of the now cumbersome muslin fabric.

"Taming a creature is not about ending a creature's wildness. Taming is about harnessing the spirit, so that the creature can reach its full potential."

Anne held her breath, expecting him to start removing her chemise, but instead he moved back to her front and slid a palm up her calf until he found the ties of her garter on her outer thigh. Fascinated by the dexterity and gentleness of his hands, Anne eased back into the bed of hay, content to let him undress her. Outside the whisper of rain against wood beat a steady rhythm. Her heart settled into a matching tempo as she surrendered into Cedric's slow seduction.

Cedric rolled her second stocking off, and his hands returned to her bare legs. He set them apart, merely stroking her inner thighs. His palms rasped softly over her sensitive skin, making her impossibly aware of his strength and roughness.

"You have no idea how you feel to me. Your skin is soft, like satin. I've never known that beauty could exist in the mere act of touching you." His husky purr had her legs trembling. Her reaction seemed to please him. Never had anyone touched her like this, like she was precious, delicate and desirable.

Cedric pressed on with his exploration, his hands working to clear a path through her petticoats. She shifted restlessly, uneasy with her building desire.

"Easy, darling."

Anne fought to remain calm as he pooled her skirts around her waist. A surge of panic struggled up inside her when his fingers stroked her bare hips. She was open and exposed. Even if he couldn't see her, he could still touch her.

"Someone might see us." Her words weren't meant to deter, merely caution.

"No one will. My grooms know when to stay away."

"Then they know that we are—?"

Cedric leaned forward and pressed a kiss to her mouth, silencing her. As his lips moved over hers, Anne forgot her worries and melted to that velvet heat. She moaned in protest as he broke away from her, but it was only so he could remove her chemise.

Before she could stop him he had settled atop her, one leg sliding between hers to press down on the sensitive, aching apex of her thighs. He swallowed her moan of shock with another kiss. She was completely nude and vulnerable beneath him, and yet he was still fully clothed. There was something sinfully wanton about this, but Anne couldn't summon the will to care.

The smooth fabric of his waistcoat and the rough cloth of his trousers teased her senses and spread heat throughout her body. Cedric's hands were everywhere, guiding over her hips, sweeping possessively over her bottom, exploring the dark triangle of curls between her legs, and kneading the heavy mounds of her breasts. The constant petting and stroking was taming her, the way he'd no doubt meant to do.

"I wish I could see you, Anne. It breaks me inside not to be able to." Cedric's voice was rough and uneven as he placed kisses on her forehead.

Anne nuzzled his throat as she began to slide his coat

off his shoulders. "You see me. You always have. It's I who has been blind."

Cedric trembled. "All this time you have been right in front of me, and I couldn't see you. But you are *mine* now."

She smiled and nibbled his ear. "That I am."

Cedric groaned and found her breast with his mouth. He laved her nipple with his tongue before drawing it into his mouth. Anne arched up, desperate for the pleasure he was giving her.

Everything with Cedric felt pure, vibrant. Each lick of his tongue, each nibble on her skin by his questing teeth made her gasp with pleasure. Places all over her body were aching and feverish. She wanted things she didn't understand.

"Please, Cedric, I need you."

"Not yet, love, there is so much I wish to do." He kissed his way down past her navel and was tasting her between her legs before she could even comprehend what he was doing. Anne raised her head, seeing him there, feasting on her. His broad shoulders kept her open and vulnerable.

"Oh Lord," she moaned. His soft lips burned her skin, making her writhe helplessly.

"You taste divine. Like cinnamon and cream." He drew his tongue along her center, and Anne couldn't stop the scream that ripped from her throat as devastating pleasure exploded through her. He wrapped his arms around her thighs, raising them to throw her knees over his shoulders, the new angle offering him better access.

He thrust his tongue deep into her, a taste of the powerful possession yet to come. When Anne thought she couldn't stand another second, he drew the bundle of nerves peeping from beneath her hood into his mouth and sucked, hard.

She lost the last vestiges of her control to a wildfire of pleasure and panic. When she shouted his name, everything else vanished. The world seemed to drop out from underneath her. Raw, sinful ecstasy like she'd never imagined consumed her. In that single instant she was swallowed by more than passion. Erotic magic wove a spell around her as sensations rioted her senses. One minute she'd been clinging to her control like the reins of a bucking stallion and the next she was flying. She was engulfed in a roaring wave as she fell back into her body.

Vaguely she became aware of Cedric shedding his clothes. Anne fought feebly to sit up but he settled over her, his wicked mouth wild and hungry as he kissed a searing path from her stomach back up to her mouth. She laid a palm flat on his chest, feeling the muscles tense and shift, revealing the frantic beat of his heart. She'd never been this close to anyone before, physical or emotionally. Feeling that rushing heartbeat, wild as her own, seemed to tie them together, forge an unbreakable bond between them.

"Touch me. Touch me everywhere," he encouraged in a

soft growl and settled himself between her legs. She swept her hands over his back, his arms, his abdomen, memorizing the grooves of his muscles and the power of his body beneath her touch.

The massive and insistent press of his arousal rubbed against her, the delicious friction blurring her vision. Anne wound her arms around his neck, the irritating ache of her shoulder forgotten for the time being. All that mattered was letting Cedric inside her. She wanted him to lay siege to the emptiness she'd struggled with for so long.

His hands gripped her hips, his eyes hooded as he drew back from her. "Tell me you can take me, Anne. Please." The raw need in his voice had her shifting restlessly, urging him to fill her.

"Yes, I'm ready. Hurry." She'd barely gotten the plea out before Cedric thrust inside. They shared a moan as he thrust again and finally sheathed himself.

"You're so tight, my heart, you feel... God if you only knew!" Cedric hissed and began to rock against her. His motions were reverent, admiring, so at odds with the desperate man who'd pushed into her moments before.

"Why did you slow down?" Anne panted.

"Do you think me to be an impatient man?" Cedric chuckled and lowered his head to her breast, suckling a sensitive nipple.

"But I need you to..." Anne's voice died as he bit the tight bud playfully.

The feel of skin sliding across glistening skin melded

with the rhythmic rustling of their bodies on the blanket-covered hay. The heavy wool of the blankets created an enticing sensation against her back and bottom as Cedric rode her, his thrusts shallow and teasing. Frustration lapped at her and a growing tide of need swelled within her core. He slid one hand down between their bodies, his thumb finding the hard knot of nerves in her mound. He circled it, rubbed it until Anne began to thrash. It was the oddest sensation, the slow, shallow strokes of his shaft mixed with the quick play of her bud.

"Come for me, darling," he breathed against her lips.

She came in a quick wave of pleasure and melted beneath him, but Cedric left her no time to recover. He withdrew from her, ignored her cry of disappointment and urged her to roll over onto her stomach. She rested in the bed of hay, propping her body up on her good forearm, allowing Cedric to raise her hips into the air.

"What are you doing?" Anne was half shocked and half fascinated as he caressed every inch of her from behind. The heat of his palms sliding over her skin made her shiver, and her need for him reawakened.

"I'm going to mount you. Take you just like this." He kissed a path from her bottom up along her spine to her neck. He cupped her sex possessively, pressing the heel of his palm against her, the pressure exquisite. She reacted out of sheer instinct, pushing her bottom backward, seeking him, needing him deep inside her. She'd orgasmed only moments before, and already she was craving him again.

"I've dreamed of this, of you and I together." His voice was soft and dark like a starless winter night.

But Anne had long since lost control of speech. She merely panted as he took her hips and guided himself to her wet entrance. He took her in one powerful jab. She arched her back in shock as he seemed to go deep enough to touch her womb. Ecstasy streaked through her as she gave herself up to him.

CEDRIC CURSED AND PULLED OUT BEFORE PLUNGING back in. His hips pistoned against the cushion of her backside. He'd never favored willowy fey-like women, preferring a woman closer to his size. Anne was a perfect match —her muscled body with elegant lines and rich curves was the most erotic thing he'd ever felt beneath him. She met his energy with her own, and he was relieved and excited. He'd feared taking her like this would upset her, but now he was unable to regret his actions.

To finally have her in the way he'd craved for years, it was too much, the pleasure too intense. Every instinct screamed with animal intent, to bind her to him forever. Now he had made her his, as much as any man could possess a woman. Men so often deluded themselves into believing they controlled the fairer sex, whether in bed or marriage. But the truth was that they could no sooner catch hold of a woman than they could harness the wind. And Anne was certainly a gale force he'd never wished to tame, only embrace its intensity.

"More!" Anne's desperate gasp nearly made him smile, but he could barely control himself as it was.

All his concentration was required to ride her over the edge of bliss before he could allow his own release. He slowed briefly, then dropped over her, covering her back with his chest. His arms encased her shoulders, his fingers lacing through hers as he resumed the wild thrusting from behind.

She tossed her head back, her dark tresses spilling to one side of her face, leaving her neck vulnerable. He sought her weak spot with his teeth and bit down. That was all it took. She clamped down around his shaft as she gave an uninhibited cry of sensual excitement, drawing him deeper, as though to keep him inside her. His own climax unleashed along with a hoarse cry from his own lips.

Anne collapsed onto her stomach beneath him. Too weak, he remained on top of her, unable to move away for a time. When he finally managed to, Anne cuddled against him. He took several deep breaths, shocked at the miracle he'd experienced.

For a few brief seconds he swore he'd glimpsed Anne, seen her curves bared to him.

Nonsense. How could that be? His imagination must

have taken over, blurring the lines between fantasy and reality. The sensations and ecstasy of making love to her had been unlike any he'd had before with any other woman.

"Did I hurt you?" His voice was soft, but his breath was still ragged.

"No...I believe I enjoyed the roughness."

He knew her well enough to hear the blush in her tone. He absolutely adored that she could admit what she liked about their lovemaking. It was a good sign that their relationship, their trust, was healing.

"I didn't mean to get carried away," he admitted. "I blame it on the surroundings. The sounds and smells here make a man forget he's not a beast. I swear I didn't mean to treat you like a broodmare."

He was completely baffled when his remark was answered by a girlish giggle, quite unlike Anne, or at least the Anne he thought he knew. Could it be there was still a young girl inside her, that her icy walls were finally vanishing enough that she would someday be soft and sweet with him?

Anne's hands settled on his chest, fingers tracing invisible patterns. "If that is how you treat broodmares, then by all means, let's come to the stables more often." She paused, suddenly reflective. "I suppose I am proving to be the worst sort of wife. I am behaving more like a mistress. I ought to scold you and lie limp next time, shouldn't I?"

"Don't you dare!" Cedric's response was half-teasing,

half-serious. "I enjoy your brazen behavior. Having one's wife behave like a hussy in her husband's bed is most satisfying." He lifted one of her hands to his mouth and pressed tiny kisses to her knuckles.

"Hussy?" Anne gasped of mock outrage. "If I had a riding crop, I would switch that pretty behind of yours." Again he could hear that hint of a barely there laugh.

Cedric tugged her body over his and cupped her bottom, clenching one cheek. "If we're speaking of punishments, my lovely wife, then I'll be happy to dole out spankings when required." He swatted her bottom and he knew by the hiss that escaped her that there would be a fresh pool of heat between her legs.

"How dare you!" she chastised, but he lifted her hips up and impaled her on his newly hardened erection.

Anne's breasts rubbed against him, the rasp of her tight nipples a sinfully decadent sensation. She arched her back, her body moving upright against his. Cedric used his hands on her hips to guide her to the right angle and the right rhythm. Once Anne settled into a slow rocking, he sought her breasts. He thumbed her nipples and pinched until her body jerked. Cedric knew she was close to coming yet again. Their ride ended in a delicious cacophony of mingled cries and heavy grunts. His wife wilted onto his chest, their bodies still locked together. The weight of her on him was strangely soothing, a physical reminder that he was no longer alone.

"That was...that was so..." Anne's words traveled across his chest and up his neck to his ears in a ticklish pattern.

"Breathtaking. Perfect. Stunning," he supplied. "Don't take this the wrong way, Anne, darling, but I hope that we made a baby."

"The future Viscount Sheridan conceived in the stables? Even for you that is too scandalous."

"Nonsense, Christ was born in a manager, wasn't he? It is little different here."

"I highly doubt any child of ours would have such high morals. He'll be a devil for sure. I'll give birth to a little pagan with a wicked streak."

"And we'll both spoil the child, won't we?" He laughed, delighted at the idea of a little boy running rampant over their hearts.

"Then I'll pray our first child is a girl. She will have to have more of me in her and therefore will be more sensible and manageable." Anne's warm breath fanned across his neck as she kissed his throat.

Cedric chuckled. "Manageable?" Humor filled him as he stroked Anne's back. "You have met my sisters, have you not? Sheridan women are notorious for their inability to be managed. If I have even one daughter, she'll be spoiled worse than any boy we have. Audrey will tell you that I'm dreadful at saying no to them."

"So I shall be the parent who enforces the rules then while you sneak them sweets behind my back? Very well, I shall contrive for sons only."

Anne was giggling again and Cedric was tempted to spank her just for the passion it would arouse, but even he was too tired to do much more than lie in their makeshift bed and hold on to his dear, precious wife.

Soon Anne was sleeping, her even breaths against him unbearably sweet. Cedric coaxed her sated body off him and reached around her to pull the blankets over them both. The storm outside continued, as though the clouds and rain were determined to keep them in the stables. Never in Cedric's life had he ever been thankful for rain. Until now.

20

Icy, *clawing darkness. Choking, suffocating blackness. No air.*

Charles couldn't breathe. Ropes cut into his wrists and his ankles, immobilizing him. Struggling, the burn of his lungs as air couldn't get to him. He was going to die in the river, drowned, swallowed by eternal darkness...

"Help!" The hoarse shout ripped from his throat. "Help me! Please!" It died in a frantic whimper as water filled his lungs.

Suddenly a hand touched his face. "It's all right, my lord. You are safe. Wake up," a voice soothed in a whisper close to his ear. Charles's body spasmed and sweat beaded on his forehead and drenched his clothes.

"Take a deep breath, my lord. It is only a dream. You must wake now."

He drew in another breath and then let it out in a slow exhale. Air, not water, filled his lungs. The nightmare evaporated into the darkness.

He was safe.

"Thank you," he said to whoever had been there. His body went limp as exhaustion claimed him again.

He drifted in and out of sleep for a few hours before he had the strength to get up. He wasn't alone. Tom Linley was sprawled out on an armchair close to Charles's bed, fast asleep. His face was strained with worry, and Charles's heart ached for the young man.

The lad was good company, and a strong boy who wasn't afraid to do the right thing, even when it was the harder path to choose. Charles respected a man like that. It had been a refreshing change of pace to have the lad accompany him about town, and with his list of unwed friends growing ever shorter, a welcomed one.

Tom had had a hard life, losing his mother and raising his baby sister on his own. Charles had found the boy working at Berkley's and convinced him to abandon his job there to work for Charles. The look on his housekeeper's face when he'd brought Tom's baby sister Katherine home with them, however, had been quite amusing.

"A babe? Here? My lord..." The plump woman had begun to protest, but little Katherine had let out a hearty cry and his housekeeper had huffed and reached for the baby. "Give her here, I've got some milk I can heat up for the wee one."

A room had been provided below stairs for Linley and his sister, and the servants had seemed to take to both the lad and the babe instantly.

Charles had to admit that having a baby around was... interesting. He hadn't realized how much he'd missed being around children sometimes. He'd helped raise his own sister, Ella, who was over a decade younger than him. Despite his personal aversion to marriage and wives, he had no qualms with children or infants.

The only problem with the babe under his roof was that the upstairs maids, ones he'd often stolen a kiss or two from when the mood took him and if they happened to be smiling back at him, had changed. Now they would rush to the baby's room to hush it if it cried, rather than rush to him if he crooked a finger.

All the more reason for him and Linley to visit Charles's usual haunts in pursuit of pleasure.

Sitting up in bed, Charles shoved his covers back and swung his feet over the side. He was still half-dressed in his trousers and white lawn shirt.

Damnation, another late night with too much to drink. Too little and he couldn't sleep at all. Too much and the dreams he had invariably took him back to those dark waters, darker deeds, and lost friends.

He combed his fingers through his hair, sighed and tilted his head back, fighting to wake up. His heartbeat had finally calmed after the last remnants of his dream settled like tea leaves at the bottom of a cup.

He glanced over his shoulder, surprised he hadn't disturbed the lad in the chair. Charles had intended to hire the lad as a valet, but the boy had proved himself indispensable as a companion about town. A master of clothing, he selected things Charles himself would have chosen, their fashion sense so closely matched in quality.

Charles considered what to do the rest of the evening. He couldn't go back to sleep. He shouldn't have slept in the middle of the day to begin with, but after that bout of drinking at the club that afternoon he'd ended up in bed around four o'clock.

Avery Russell, one of Lucien's younger brothers, had invited him to the Dandy Club tonight, and not simply for drinks and gambling. Avery was a spy. It was a well-kept secret about Lucien's family. Only the League had ever been allowed more than the most basic of details as to his line of work.

More than once, Charles had found himself a participant in one of Avery's missions to gain information, preferably when it required plying a person with drink, gambling, or women to loosen their lips. As Avery had explained it once, Charles was not the sort of man one would ever suspect to be engaging in espionage, and was therefore the perfect person to do the questioning.

Even Cedric's youngest sister, Audrey, had aided him a time or two by questioning the wives or mistresses of particular targets over tea. The little scamp had a knack for befriending any woman and getting them to talk, especially when it came to their husbands or lovers. She probably heard more gossip than *The Quizzing Glass Gazette*.

Charles walked over to the nightstand and splashed water from a small porcelain basin on his face to wake up before he laid out a pair of trousers, shirt, waistcoat and overcoat on the bed. Once he was dressed, he shook Linley's shoulder to rouse him.

"Come on, lad, we're off to the Dandy Club."

Linley rubbed his fists against his eyes, blinking wearily. "What time is it?"

"A little after eight." Charles tugged on the edges of his coat, smoothing it down. "I think tonight we should go see about finding you a woman. You are certainly old enough."

"My lord!" The young man made a choking noise. "My job is to accompany you, not join you in your pleasures."

Charles faced him and cupped his palms on Linley's shoulders. "I will hear no more arguments. I plan to bed several women tonight, and I will not be doing so alone." He drew a perverse satisfaction from the flash of panic in the boy's eyes. It reminded him of several of his friends back at college, especially Peter...

The thought threatened to darken his mood, so he rallied back with added enthusiasm. "You need a woman, lad. It's time, especially if you wish to keep up with me. I give you full permission to chase skirts while we're about town."

Linley's jaw gaped, but he didn't utter another word of protest.

Charles strode to the door, eager for his night of revelry to begin. "Fetch your coat and let's be off."

The Dandy Club was a gambling hell well known for the army officers and soldiers who haunted its halls, seeking pleasures and thrills that eased the memories of the battlefield. Charles was at home among their tortured souls. He had his own horrors and nightmares to wrestle with. Oil lamps bathed the rooms in a rich gold, exposing the scenes of debauchery and gambling. Charles scanned the crowds, seeking familiar faces. At his side Linley was doing the same, brows knit in consternation.

What a green lad the boy was!

"My lord! What a pleasant surprise." A lovely woman in a red satin gown sauntered over. Her wealth of dark hair tangled down her neck as though she'd been recently tumbled.

"Mrs. Hollingberry, how are you?" He brushed a lingering kiss on the inside of her wrist, causing Mrs. Hollingberry's brown eyes to gleam.

"Are you here alone, my lord?" She claimed his arm before he could respond and did not spare a glance at Linley, who trailed behind.

"I cannot be alone if I am with you." Charles chuckled, relishing the thought of bending the lusty widow over the nearest surface.

Her grip on his arm tightened. "And would you *like* to be with me?"

Charles freed his arm, then curled it around the widow's waist, tugging her against his side so that he could lean down to whisper in her ear.

"It would be my dearest wish"—he paused, listening to the hitch in her breath—"to make you scream with pleasure." He didn't miss the sudden rise in her breasts as they strained against her tight bodice.

"I shall find us a room." The eager widow tugged him away from the hazard tables and toward a hall that led to an empty billiard room.

"Tell your boy to wait outside, unless he wants to watch." Mrs. Hollingberry cupped Charles's erection, applying just the right amount of pressure.

Desire flooded through him. Base, pure instinct. Nothing more than the need to fuck and then be done, but it still called to him. He knew it didn't feel this way for Godric or Lucien—they'd spoke often enough of the differences of bedding a woman they loved versus those they'd bedded in the past. But Charles feared that sort of emotion. Better to find satisfaction with women like Mrs. Hollingberry than to run the risk of falling in love.

"Here, lad, find a woman of your own." Charles tossed a heavy coin purse at Linley, then dragged the *giggling* widow into the private room and slammed the door.

The second he was alone with Mrs. Hollingberry, he prowled toward her. She gave a delighted shriek as he caught her and lifted her up to set her on the bed. It was an easy thing to ruche up her skirts around her waist. The skin of her thighs was smooth as he spread his palms up her legs. The widow wriggled closer to him, curling her legs around his waist and reaching for the front of his trousers.

"How do you want it?" he asked. "Hard and fast?"

"Oh yes," she agreed, palming his now freed erection with her slender hands. "You do that so well."

He groaned at her firm, knowing touch and shifted closer. Soon he was tangled around her, shoving deep into her body. But it wasn't the same. He found his satisfaction, just as she did hers, but it was...*shallow*. A flash of momentary lust, quickly extinguished.

He withdrew from her and fixed his clothes before helping the lady with hers. She gave him a wry smile, stroking his chest. She still sat on the edge of the bed leaning back a little on one hand.

"You were always a good bed partner, my lord."

"I sense that there is more to your statement." Charles clenched his teeth and stared down at her.

Mrs. Hollingberry met him with a level stare. Her fine features, usually so attractive, seemed more calculating tonight, but not in a way that concerned him. Rather he was puzzled. Usually when he bedded a woman like her, they wouldn't be able to think, let alone look at him like that.

"You seemed distant tonight."

"I suppose I am," he admitted. His mind had wandered quite far from the moment of pleasure.

"And what could consume the mind of the Earl of Lonsdale and make him melancholy?" Mrs. Hollingberry's eyes glittered as she continued to study him in open curiosity. Her sudden scrutiny made Charles's skin itch. Why did this feel familiar?

"I'm sure I have no idea," he replied with a wry chuckle. It wasn't the truth though. For the past few months he'd been coasting along, like a skiff adrift at sea, carried by full winds, but now rudderless. Helpless and at the mercy of the winds of change. If only he could find some sense of control or direction, he might not feel so damned weak.

"Well, this was fun, my dear, but I have the strangest urge to drink myself under the nearest table." He flung the door open and found Linley staring at him.

"Have we finished, my lord?" Linley's disposition was cold and professional, and altogether unlike himself.

"Well, yes."

"Very well, I'll be outside with the coach when you're ready." He stalked down the hall and vanished in the crowds in an instant.

"What the devil has gotten into him?" Linley had never shown any sign of a temper before now.

"Perhaps the woman he approached spurned him?" Mrs. Hollingberry said, joining Charles at the door, watching the crowd. "Shame. If he had waited, I might have given him a turn. Handsome boy, that."

"I think I really do need that drink. Goodnight, Mrs. Hollingberry."

Charles kissed her hand and headed straight for the nearest hazard table, where he hailed a servant for drinks.

Perhaps the widow was right. Charles made seduction look easy, and even with a purse full of coins at his disposal, some charm and care was needed to woo a woman here. He imagined such a rejection would not have been handled tactfully, either.

Poor lad. Charles hadn't even thought to advise him beforehand. No wonder he was in such a rush to get out.

Two hours had passed by the time Charles had drunk himself beneath a card table.

"Looks like you need a hand, Lonsdale." James Fordyce, the Earl of Pembroke reached under the table and offered a hand to him. Charles gripped the hand and allowed himself to be hauled up on his feet. His vision cart-wheeled and he blinked rapidly, trying to get a steady fix on the man's face.

"Ready to go home, Lonsdale?" Pembroke asked.

"Suppose I ought to. Bloody hell, what a night."

Pembroke slid one arm around Charles's waist, supporting him outside to hail a hackney to get him home. Linley emerged from the shadows of a nearby mew and joined Pembroke in supporting Charles by ducking under Charles's left arm.

"There you are, lad," Charles greeted the boy.

Linley's disapproving scowl cut across him as the boy spoke to Pembroke. "How deep into his cups did he get tonight?"

Charles's friend laughed. "Enough to swim to France, I imagine, but he'll be fine on the morrow."

"You know, Pembroke, you're a good sort...good fellow," Charles mumbled.

Pembroke laughed. "Thank you, Lonsdale. You're not too bad yourself."

"No, I'm not, I'm a damned fool and a coward." Charles's words slurred as he stumbled over an uneven cobblestone. Pembroke lifted him up a little, and Charles's stomach roiled violently, but Linley helped catch him before he fell face down on the street.

Pembroke hailed a waiting hackney and assisted Linley with getting Charles inside, gave the driver his address and slipped the driver a handful of coins. As the hackney jerked forward, Charles slumped back against the seat, fighting off a wave of nausea.

"Won't be long before we're home, my lord. Then you can sleep it off."

It didn't surprise Charles that Linley knew exactly how unwell he felt. The boy had a talent for knowing what his master was feeling. He hoped the lad hadn't been too embarrassed by whatever had transpired at the club. He hadn't meant to upset the boy.

Charles was barely coherent by the time the hackney stopped in front of his townhouse. The driver hauled him to the door, muttering all the while about drunken louts.

"My lord, are you able to walk?" Linley's voice cut through the heavy fog of Charles's inebriation.

"Ah." He winced as the world spun around him when he attempted to put his feet one in front of the other. "Linley, be a good lad, make the floor stop moving, will you?"

He thought he heard a little chortle from his servant before a polite reply came out. "Of course, my lord, shouldn't be too hard to accomplish that."

Charles's legs gave out at the bottom step of the stairs and he sank to the ground, chuckling a little.

"My lord, how much have you had to drink?"

"Only a moderad...motorate... More than enough, I suppose. Take me to the servants' quarters. There is a spare room. I'll sleep there."

Linley hesitated but finally helped him to his feet again, taking him to the servants' quarters. Charles's sight kept blurring until he was gently shoved toward a narrow bed.

"I'm sorry about tonight, Tom. I'll teach you everything you need to know next time to woo a lady. On my honor." He slapped one hand over his heart, but Linley huffed.

"Wool-headed fool," Linley muttered. "Get yourself killed being that deep in your cups without me to watch your back."

"Right you are." Charles laughed as he collapsed onto the bed. "Can't be too careful. Danger around every corner, lad. Promise to teach you to box first thing on the morrow."

"Don't need lessons, my lord. I know how to fight better than you, I'd wager."

That almost woke Charles up with laughter. "Ha! I was taught by the best pugill...puggle...boxers in London."

"Aye. And you're a right terror to witness inside the ring. But there's a difference between fighting for sport and fighting to survive, my lord. Now, get some rest."

The boy was still muttering about Charles's foolishness as darkness and sleep closed in on him.

❧

JONATHAN ST. LAURENT FINGERED THE TWO FOLDED sheets of a letter and the blob of melted wax he'd broken. Ashton's instructions had been written in a code the League had invented years ago, one he'd only become privy to when Godric had asked him to join their ranks last September.

It was an honor he would never forget. So many years he'd watched his half brother and the other lords from a distance. Now he was one of them, no longer a valet, not from below stairs or the wrong side of the blankets, but a true legitimate son of a duke, even if his mother had been a lady's maid to the duchess. His father had married

Jonathan's mother legally, albeit secretly, after Godric's mother had died in childbirth, along with a sibling Godric would never have the chance to know.

Learning of his birthright had changed Jonathan. Many young men at his age would have been demanding their inheritance and spending all of their time gambling and wenching, living life to excess. Not so for him. The temptation had been there at first...but those desires had quickly faded. There had been too much at stake. Emily Parr, Godric's wife, had been in grave danger. The League had rallied together to save her. Jonathan had joined them, and the foolish need to act out with his new money and power had nearly vanished overnight. In its place, a desire to protect those he cared about had become his priority.

That was how he'd ended up outside a dockside pub called the Devil's Eye, running a secret mission for Ashton. The baron had his fingertips in nearly every major bit of business in London, but his primary ones involved shipping. The Lennox lines were a sturdy fleet of merchant ships that Ashton had recently expanded by acquiring a competitor's business. Ashton's letter had mentioned possible activity connected to Hugo Waverly on a docked ship called the *Maiden Fair*. Jonathan was to track any sailors who came ashore and eavesdrop on their conversations.

Ashton's letter had mentioned that Waverly was seen visiting this vessel, rumored to be connected to the underground slave trade. Given what the League had told him about this man, it seemed the kind of disreputable affair he'd be involved in.

The door to the tavern crashed open and three drunken louts in sailor togs stumbled in, laughing and shoving one another. Jonathan stepped into the shadows and stole a mug from a passing barmaid's tray. Rather than scold him, she halted, her lips forming a kissable moue shape. An invitation. One he would have gladly accepted before last Christmas. But no, he still had the taste of a certain little young lady on his lips. A lady who had made her interest in him abundantly clear.

"I finish my shift in an hour," the maid said, looking hopeful.

"Alas, I cannot. But it flatters me, for you are quite lovely." He captured her free hand and pressed a kiss to her skin, slipping her a coin for the drink he'd taken.

Damn! He wanted so badly to bed a woman, but after Audrey Sheridan's reckless abandon toward him, he could imagine no other. If he wished to have a lady like Audrey be his wife, he could no longer chase skirts in taverns. The one thing he'd learned from his brother and Lucien in the last few months was that loyalty to one's wife was not only expected, but desired.

Charles kept insisting he was too young to crave what Godric and Emily had, but Jonathan craved it all the same. Audrey, the feisty little chit, was a warm wind on a cold day and just as wild. Like taming the winds, no sooner could he do that than tame the young lady. But he wanted to be with her for the wild ride she'd no doubt give him.

Jonathan turned his attention back to the sailors. The *Maiden Fair* was the last ship to come into port, and these three men looked ready to fall deep into their cups. The briny odor of the sea clung to their clothes. He crept closer, tracking them as they settled down on the stools by the bar counter.

"So then I says, 'Whatcha gonna do in Brighton? Ain't nuffin there but stodgy tight-breeches, and no wenches to visit,'" the old sailor boomed out in a voice natural for storytelling. The men on either side of him hooted in laughter.

"And what did he say to that?" one of the other men asked as he removed his gray woolen cap and mopped his sweaty face.

The man banged his mug down on the counter, sloshing its murky contents over the sides and onto the scuffed wood. "He says, 'Ain't no business of yours, but I've been hired to get an English gent and his new wife and that's where they'll be.'"

"Wot?" The man on the right blinked. "Ee ain't serious, is he? You don' mean…"

"More…*cargo?*" the third man finished.

"Aye."

The one with the gray cap shook his head. "That's more trouble than we're paid for."

The old one sucked his teeth. "Is he daft? We're short

on crew as it is, and half the ones showin' up tonight are green."

"Ee says we're all getting paid double for the trouble."

The three men shared significant looks before they lowered their heads together, voices dropping low. There was no mention of Waverly, but something about the three men bothered him.

He couldn't have misheard them, could he? Cargo? That might have simply been some sort of slang for passengers, he supposed, but their tone and concern suggested otherwise. Was their captain planning on nabbing an English gentleman and his wife? That wasn't good. He couldn't sit by and let that happen. And if there was a connection to Waverley, there was always the chance this concerned the League.

This was going to be a long night. He splashed a bit of ale on his clothes and ruffled up his cravat and coat, then stumbled over and took a seat next to the sailors, calling for more ale. Having caught their attention, he gave them a friendly grin.

"Evening." He nodded and pointed at the barmaid. "Lovely little chit, eh?"

"That she is," the storyteller agreed.

"A lovely round of pints for my lovely new friends." Jonathan winked at the maid and then leaned in toward the trio conspiratorially. "Let's toast to lovely ladies, eh? I couldn't help but overhear you are bound for the *Maiden Fair*. I've just paid for passage on the ship. I'm happy to buy rounds for you gents who will be sharing the trip with me."

That seemed to warm the men up. After several rounds the sailors were spilling more than their ale, and what they had to say was both very interesting and not good at all.

He caught the maid's attention. "Sweetheart, I need to leave a note for you to deliver." Pressing a few coins into the girl's hand, he waited for her to return with a slip of parchment and a quill. As the sailors burst into a lewd song, Jonathan scratched a message. Then he handed the letter to the maid and whispered the address to her. After that he followed the sailors, who were now making their way back to the docks.

Jonathan sighed. *So much for going back to my home to my own bed tonight.*

❧❦❧

GODRIC CRADLED EMILY IN HIS ARMS, KISSING HER always delectable lips.

"What about dinner?" she managed to ask.

"To hell with dinner, I have what I want, darling." He pinned her against the settee in their drawing room, one hand coasting up her leg as he slid her skirts up to her waist. In the low candlelight she was lovely, so lovely.

Her face flushed as she panted, and those violet eyes he adored sparkled. Emily was so beautiful it sometimes hurt to look at her. His chest ached and yet turned soft and warm around his heart.

"I love you, Godric," she breathed against his lips. Each time she said those words, it undid him. He groaned and slid his hand toward the apex of her thighs.

An anxious rap of knuckles on the door made them both jerk up, glancing toward the entrance of the drawing room.

"My apologies." A footman stood there, unable to hide his blush. "This was just delivered. It's from Mr. St. Laurent. The boy who left it was told to say it was urgent."

Godric pulled Emily's skirts down and climbed off the settee. He took the letter from the footman. "Thank you, Nelson."

The man vanished down the hall toward the servants' quarters. Godric broke the wax seal, unfolded the sheet of parchment and read over the note.

"What is it?" Emily leaned over the back of the settee, arms braced as she studied him.

His heart pounded with building dread.

"Jonathan's aboard a ship associated with Waverly headed for Brighton. Lord knows how he pulled that off. He'll likely be there in a few days. I have to ride to Brighton immediately." He didn't want to frighten Emily. With the babe inside her, he felt more protective of her than ever.

"Godric," she warned in a tone that brooked no argument. "You aren't telling me everything, are you?"

"It seems Jonathan overheard of a plot by some sailors who've been hired to abduct someone—possibly Cedric and Anne. I have to warn them. I must get Charles and go." He turned to leave, but Emily had locked her arms around him from behind.

"I shall go with you."

He looked down at her over his shoulder. "Em. It's going to be dangerous."

"We've survived danger before," she reminded him.

"And I nearly lost you, have you forgotten? I haven't." He hated how hoarse his voice became but memories of Emily on a bed, barely breathing, left him hollow and terrified.

"This isn't the same, Godric. I'm not the one in danger," she persisted. "Anne is as much my friend as Cedric is yours."

"Yes, but now there are the three of us to consider. I don't want to worry about our babe." He turned and placed a hand over her still flat stomach. Every dream he'd buried was contained in this one strong-willed female. He would not lose her or the child. More than ever he understood what had driven his father to abusive rage and melancholy after he'd lost his beloved wife. Godric knew without Emily he would be lost.

"I'll be safe." Emily touched her stomach. "We'll both be safe."

Godric was tempted to argue, but there wasn't time.

"If you come, you'll do what I say, for the safety of you and the child."

"Of course." Emily lifted her skirts and dashed up the stairs, calling out for Libba, her lady's maid. Godric summoned a footman to have his coach brought around and a groom to ready the horses. They would need to contact Charles and Lucien at once and ride immediately for Brighton.

"Ready?" Emily called out as she came down the stairs. She wore a pair of breeches and a loose-fitting shirt and coat.

"What is that you're wearing?" Godric demanded.

"What's wrong?" Emily spun around, glancing down at herself.

He waved a hand at her. "You are wearing men's clothing."

"Oh, that, yes. Much better suited for an adventure, don't you think?"

"Adventure?" Godric groaned in annoyance, but there wasn't time to argue.

"Indeed. Let's go."

He took her arm and helped her down to the waiting coach. He prayed they wouldn't be too late.

❦

HAD IT ONLY BEEN TWO WEEKS SINCE ANNE HAD married Cedric? How was it even possible that she could know such happiness in such a short time? Life with Cedric had settled into a perfect rhythm. They did so much together: dining, playing, lovemaking. Long conversations would end wrapped in one another's arms, forgetting what they had even been talking about. Each day brought new discoveries as they explored each other's bodies and souls. It was almost inconceivable to believe she could be this happy.

Anne lounged back in Cedric's bed. *Their bed.* She'd ceased sleeping in her own chamber. She surveyed the mess they'd made of the bedroom this time. Clothes hung from every surface. She giggled. They'd been a little too enthusiastic in their latest bout of lovemaking. Cedric lay sprawled out on his stomach, naked and uncaring. His eyes were closed, one arm tucked under his pillow, the other curled around her waist.

"What are you laughing about?" His voice was heavy with sleep.

"Us. I'm afraid your valet will be distressed at the new mess we've made."

"A few wrinkled shirts and trousers won't distress the fellow. He is glad to see me happy."

Anne rested one of her palms over his arm about her waist. "And before the accident? You were unhappy then?"

Cedric's sigh told her everything. "Somewhat. Ever since my parents died...it has been hard. I was close to them. There was so much love in our house. My parents were a love match, you see. To lose the life they brought to..." Cedric was unable to continue.

"We don't have to talk about this."

Cedric looked toward her. "No. I need to. It's why you affect me, Anne. What I feel for you, it's what my father felt for my mother. Love matches are rare in our world. What I mean to say is that you are mine, Anne. My love match. I need you, all of you, forever."

He sat up in the bed and tugged her close, so their hips touched and he could curl his arms around her.

"I want children, lots of them. I want us to sit at afternoon tea years from now, surrounded by laughter and grandchildren. I want to be with you when we are old, when life has finally given us peace. These last few weeks have been such a gift." He rubbed his hands on her back, their loving touch so full of gentleness that Anne couldn't resist leaning into him for a kiss. Cedric moved in at the same time she did, embracing her in his arms. Their mouths met, brushing lightly, then shifted into a deeper, lingering kiss that left her weak. With a smothered laugh, she fell back as he tipped her back on the bed and settled into the cradle of her hips.

Anne nuzzled his cheek, and the shadow of stubble on his chin scraping over her skin made her shiver. "I think I love you more than I did before. Is that possible? It's like falling in love with you all over again."

Cedric kissed the corners of her mouth, urging her lips

into a smile. "I could spend the rest of my life like that, waking up and falling in love with you."

Anne arched her hips, encouraging him to enter her. Cedric possessed her mouth and slid into her welcoming heat. With each gentle thrust, they seemed to merge further until they moved in perfect rhythm. One second she was a solitary creature, and the next she was a part of something bigger, something mysterious she couldn't explain. Every impossible dream she'd ever had seemed suddenly within reach. With Cedric at her side, she could do anything.

His warm mouth settled over her breast, and his teeth scraped her aching nipple, making her shove her hips hard into his. What had begun so sweet and sensual now turned raw and primal. Anne had to have him buried inside her, to feel him reaching her soul. When their pace became too fast, Cedric slowed it and Anne thrashed her head wildly, desperate for release.

"Please, Cedric!" she almost wept, needing to climax.

He gasped and fought off his own release as he panted against her neck.

"You've ruined me for every other woman, Anne. I'm yours, always."

His words caused a burst of stars and light inside the core of her being. She couldn't resist the explosion of pleasure and love as her orgasm spread through her. His own harsh cry of release softened as he came deep inside her. It was she this time who wished they had created a life. It only seemed right that such love, such joy would leave a miracle like a child in its wake.

Cedric rolled off her and tucked her in against him, pulling the sheets high above their bodies.

"I love you, Anne." He kissed the tip of her nose and sighed.

"And I love you." They didn't need any other words.

⚜

ANNE PAUSED BEFORE A DRESSMAKER'S SHOP ON THE Steine not too far away from Donaldson's Library. Everywhere around them were people in colorful clothes. Shop windows decorated the sides of the streets and crowds moved in throngs. Many flocked to Brighton to visit the sea, others to ride through the picturesque streets in their barouches and make a social display. Anne found it all amusing and oddly delightful to watch.

"What do you think about me buying some new gowns?" she asked.

Cedric smiled. "Only so long as they are brightly colored."

Thank heavens we didn't stay in London. My lack of proper mourning attire would scandalize everyone. Anne peered closely into the window, studying the fabric reflections and the styles.

"Well if you wish to go in, I'll wait outside."

Before Anne could reply, Ashton joined them outside the shop.

"Cedric, I'm off to Donaldson's if you'd like to accompany me."

Anne smiled, relief sweeping through her at Ashton's thoughtfulness. She didn't like Cedric to be on his own when they were away from the house. He wasn't familiar with the streets, and he could easily get turned around, hurt or lost, set upon by footpads—even hit by a coach. The fears of what could happen to him were almost endless, and difficult to put out of mind.

"You should go, Cedric. Keep Lord Lennox out of trouble. I'll join you at the library." Anne stood up on tiptoe and brushed a kiss on his cheek.

"Are you sure?"

"Quite sure."

Anne turned back to the shop when the two men departed.

"Excuse me. I don't mean to be presumptuous, but are you Viscountess Sheridan?" A buxom lady with a cheery face and dark hair smiled down at her.

Anne blinked. "I am."

"I'm terribly sorry to be so forward. I am Lady Pickering, wife of Sir Edward Pickering. We live not too far from you and your husband. I've been meaning to send you a letter, to invite you to dine with us tonight. I apologize for the late notice, but I couldn't resist now that I've happened to meet you."

"It's a pleasure, Lady Pickering. I am ashamed that I haven't thought to write to you myself. Cedric has spoken at length about you both. My husband and I would be delighted to attend your dinner."

"Wonderful! Edward will be so pleased." Lady Pickering joined her at the shop window. "Lovely aren't they? The modiste here is so much better than those in London. Are you going in? I'd love to join you. I need a few gowns myself." Lady Pickering's eyes swept over the window display of fine fabrics and stylish hats.

There was something about the woman that felt warm, motherly even, something Anne had little experience with but had always longed for.

"If you'd like," Anne said. "I would love the company."

Lady Pickering clapped her gloved hands together. "Splendid! Shall we?"

Anne followed the woman into the shop, and the modiste and her assistant met them at the door. They took turns getting their measurements and then were provided with some plates of various styles to consider.

"May I speak frankly with you?" Lady Pickering's tone was cautious as they sat next to each other on a settee and thumbed through the fashion plates.

Anne glanced at the woman, a little concerned, but she nodded.

"I've heard the news about your father, and your marriage only a week after his passing." Lady Pickering toyed with a blue ribbon on her sleeve as she spoke. "I'm not at all sure how to say this."

Anne's stomach clenched. "Please, Lady Pickering, speak your mind."

Her cheeks reddened. "Well, Lady Sheridan, the former one that is, was a dear, dear friend of mine. When she died, it quite broke my heart, you see. We were friends since our youth and our husbands were friends as well. Losing them was devastating, not only to Edward and me, but to everyone who knew them. The Sheridan family is well-respected and loved. The boy—pardon me." She cleared her throat. "Viscount Sheridan is just as dear to me, like a son in many ways. He may be a bit of a rogue, but he is a good man, and he deserves a wife who loves him."

Anne gave a sigh of relief. Reaching out, she covered Lady Pickering's hand with her own.

"I love my husband to distraction. Despite the unorthodox start to our union, I love him more each passing day than I ever believed possible."

Lady Pickering smiled, though it was tinged with sadness.

"That was all I wanted to know. Now, about dinner, what would his lordship prefer to eat? I will happily alter the menu since I suspect some foods must be difficult for him."

Surprise flickered through Anne at the woman's astuteness. There were plenty of foods that made dining difficult for Cedric, but Lady Pickering was thoughtful enough to realize this. It only made Anne adore her all the more.

"Anything eaten easily by spoon is preferable," she answered, though in truth he'd found it less and less trying to manage a knife and fork as of late.

"That shouldn't be too difficult." Lady Pickering handed the plates back to the modiste, gesturing her interest in some of the styles. Anne did the same.

After an hour, the ladies had ordered several excellent gowns. Anne didn't want to leave Lady Pickering, who was perusing a few hats on display in a window at the milliner's shop next door, but she felt it was time to rejoin Cedric.

"Lady Pickering, I hate to leave, but I must find my husband."

The other woman laughed. "Of course, my dear. Off you go. Dinner is at eight."

"Thank you!" Anne bid her goodbye and crossed the busy street toward Donaldson's Library.

<hr />

SAMIR AL ZAHRANI MOUNTED HIS HORSE AND TROTTED down one of the main streets of Brighton. He muttered a string of curses at his black luck these past few days.

He'd learned where his prized horses were being kept, right alongside inferior English nags. But he could not retrieve them both alone. He'd also missed an opportunity to take Sheridan's wife in the woods by the lake. The house had been full of servants after that.

But today was the first day the couple had left the sanctuary and gone into Brighton, and he'd sensed a fresh opportunity. Soon his ship would arrive and he could leave this wretched isle. But first he had to acquire what he came for.

Foolish Englishmen and their pride, thinking they could not be attacked in a crowded city. What little they knew...

Sheridan and a companion with light blond hair had separated from Sheridan's wife, leaving her vulnerable. Exposed.

If I can kill her, it will leave Sheridan on unsteady ground.

He waited. In time, Lady Sheridan exited a dressmaker's shop and waved goodbye to an older matron before crossing the street. Samir kicked his heels into his horse's sides and the beast jolted forward...

A BLACK STALLION RUSHED AT ANNE FROM THE SIDE AS she crossed the road. The horse reared and Anne screamed, stumbling to the ground.

The horse calmed and the rider, a handsome, olive-skinned man with dark hair and darker eyes slid from the saddle to help her to her feet.

"A thousand pardons. You crossed so quickly in front

of me, I did not see you." His gaze ran the length of her body. "You're not injured, I trust?"

Flustered and smarting from her fall, Anne hastily shook her head. "No, no, I'm fine. Thank you." She tried to tug free of his hold on her waist. "Please, sir, let me go."

For a moment she feared that he had no such intention. But her fall had attracted the attention of a number of people who were also coming to check and see if she had been injured.

His hands dropped. "Again, my apologies. It has been some time since I've been in the presence of a lovely woman. It has made my manners lax." The gleam in his eyes now made her uncomfortable.

"Excuse me." She darted around him and back into the street. It was rude, she knew, but something about him... she didn't want to stay. She forced her ill thoughts off with a shrug, convincing herself it was nonsense.

Donaldson's Library was a timber-boarded building, freshly painted in white. A large verandah overlooked part of the circulating library. A group of ladies gathered like brightly colored birds in a small flock, gossiping beneath the verandah. Anne avoided them. Their chatter no doubt would lead to trouble later in the two popular Brighton assembly rooms, the Castle Inn and the Old Ship Inn.

Thank heavens Cedric wasn't one for balls and dancing anymore. Although, Anne had to admit she wished she could have danced with him, just once. Their first opportunity had been lost, and in the years she'd known him, they'd never had a chance to make up for it.

She entered the spacious rooms of Donaldson's Library, trying not to think about how she wanted one silly quadrille or a waltz with her husband. Though he grew more confident in his step each day, she knew he'd fret about falling or stepping on her toes in a public gathering. The *ton* could be a cruel bunch when they thought they could prey on a weak party. Her nose stung a little with a rush of emotions. The sadness, the disappointment. Such a small thing to desire, yet its very unattainability only made her want it more.

The library shelves were filled. The spines gleamed in the light that cut through the windows. She paused at a nearby reading table, resting her palms on the gleaming wooden surface to slow her breath. A few young ladies walked past, books in their arms, whispering with little smiles.

"Did you see that gentleman? The blind one?" the taller of the two ladies asked her friend.

Every muscle in Anne's body tensed. They had to be talking about Cedric. What were the odds of another blind man in a library in Brighton? Were they going to laugh at him? If they did, so help them... Her husband had survived enough and didn't deserve to endure any mockery of his condition.

The other woman blushed and ducked her head, her

bonnet hiding her face from view. "Such a handsome man."

"Wasn't he? And his friend, the blond-haired gentleman..." She sighed wistfully. "But I could not possibly ask to be introduced to a stranger. Such a pity." The ladies disappeared around a back row of bookshelves.

Anne relaxed, collected herself, and hastened the way the ladies had come. She found her husband and his friend seated in a pair of chairs by a reading table. Cedric leaned forward, his forearms resting on his knees as he spoke to Ashton. When she came into view, Ashton looked to her, then back to Cedric. Cedric continued to speak, unaware of her approach behind him.

"It's a new world, Ash. Believe me, marriage is surprisingly wonderful. Are you sure you don't want to give it a go?"

Ashton's lips twitched as he put a finger to his lips to indicate Anne should remain silent. She paused a few feet away, holding her breath.

"And what exactly is so wonderful about it? I admit, I'm quite intrigued by your newfound eagerness." Ashton flashed her a wink, and she fought to contain a giggle.

Cedric leaned back in his chair, lacing his fingers behind his head.

"There's nothing better than having the most beautiful creature in your bed at any time you please. Much better than a mistress. And I'm sure my wife would agree— access to me at all times is a benefit of leg-shackledom."

Cedric's smug tone sparked a reaction in Anne that was half amusement, half exasperation.

"Wouldn't you agree, lady wife?" Cedric chuckled and turned his head in her direction.

"Oh! You beastly man." Anne laughed and rushed over to him, swatting his shoulder with a gloved hand. When he tugged her over to his chair and onto his lap, she squeaked in surprise. "You knew I was there the whole time, didn't you?"

Cedric nodded, that playful grin making her melt. She adored the way he unleashed that smile on her without holding back.

"Your scent, remember?" He nuzzled her cheek. "It gives you away."

For a long moment, she surrendered to his embrace, loving the feel of his arms around her, cuddling her close to him.

An old woman with a bonnet covered in wilting ostrich feathers gasped at them as she rounded a bookshelf and spied Anne on Cedric's lap, his arms wrapped around her.

"This is a *library*," she said, clearly scandalized.

"Pardon me, madam," Cedric replied politely. "But my wife and I require some privacy. Sod off."

The old woman bristled and thumped the top of her parasol on the wooden floor.

"How dare you, sirrah!" she blustered and left.

"Oh dear," Ashton said, laughing. "That was Lady Beach, you know. One of Prinny's acquaintances."

Cedric snorted and hugged Anne even closer. "Lady Beach be damned. I want to hold my wife."

Anne glanced about, making sure no one else was watching them before she kissed Cedric's cheek. It was something she hadn't yet tired of, this delightful ability to touch him, kiss him, whenever she wanted. The man had been right about the benefits of marriage.

"How was your dress shopping, love?"

"Fine, thank you. Lady Pickering was there. We are invited to dine tonight at their house. Is that all right? She's such a dear. I didn't want to refuse her."

"Lady Pickering," Cedric mused. "Second mother if I ever had one. Always trying to fatten me up."

Anne sobered. "Yes, well, she's right to. You've grown too slender, husband. I don't like it. If I must become a meddlesome, bothersome wife to take care of you, then I shall."

"If telling me to eat more is your idea of being bother-some, then I adore you even more." Cedric began to nibble on her ear, and Anne shivered. Desire blasted through her like bolt of lightning.

"Well, I shall leave you two to peruse Donaldson's a bit," said Ashton. "A ship of mine just came into port and I need to check on it. Shall I meet you back at the house after dinner this evening?"

Anne sat up. "I'm sure Lady Pickering would love for

you to join us."

Ashton waved a hand. "She is a wonderful woman, but I'm afraid I must see to business and it may take more time than expected. Send Lady Pickering my regards."

As Ashton departed, something inside her sighed a little. Lord Lennox was an enigma. He always seemed to be alone, save for the other members of the League.

"What's the matter, Anne? I can hear you thinking." Cedric jostled her a little in his arms to get her attention.

"I'm worried about Lord Lennox. He seems so lonely at times. So focused on his work."

Cedric's blank eyes betrayed no emotion, but his smile wilted a little.

"Ash is a very complex man. You know what they say, still waters run deep."

"Have you known him all your life?" Anne had to admit the League of Rogues had always fascinated her. Five wealthy, powerful noblemen who eschewed society's formalities and made vices their mistresses. It should have been a topic she'd avoided to contemplate, yet she couldn't resist. But she felt her knowledge of their pasts and relationships was likely based on rumor and *The Quizzing Glass Gazette* more than truth.

"We met at Cambridge. I had seen him around the grounds of Magdalene College, but we hadn't been formally introduced. He and Lucien were friends, and Godric and I were friends. We were two separate pairs, if that makes sense," he chuckled.

"What about Charles? How did you all finally meet, and where does he come in?"

Cedric's expression shuttered closed, and Anne didn't press him.

"There was one night, in the late fall, Godric and I were sneaking back to our rooms. We saw someone drowning in the river and a friend of ours, Peter Wellsley, was trying to save him. Two other men, I later found out they were Ashton and Lucien, joined Godric and I as we dove into the river to save the drowning man, which was Charles, and assist Peter. Charles had been bound hand and foot, and Peter helped me cut him loose. We saved Charles, but Peter...he didn't make it. He stayed beneath the water too long trying to hold Charles up. The loss was a great one to all of us. Peter was one of Charles's dearest friends, and one the rest of us knew well. After that night, we five became inseparable. Bonds of grief can do that."

Little puzzles pieces seem to slide into place for Anne. "Charles is the key that holds you all together?"

For a moment Cedric said nothing, as if matters couldn't be so easily summed up as that. "At first. But over time each of us formed close ties to one another. There is nothing like knowing a man who has fought through hell and back beside you to solidify a bond."

Cedric's cheeks were a little ruddy with embarrassment, but she loved him for it. Loved the way he loved his friends. Not many men, or women, could boast of such a close connection.

"And Mr. St. Laurent? Godric's brother?"

"Jonathan?" Cedric chuckled. "He is a welcome addition to our number. That reminds me." His tone turned serious. "Anne, how would you feel about selling your father's house in London? Jonathan is interested in settling down and is considering courting Audrey, at least according to Ashton. I gave him my blessing and thought we might help him out a bit." Cedric paused, then took a deep breath before continuing. "I thought, perhaps, if you agreed, we might sell it to Jonathan. I would love to see that house filled with love and children, but if you wish to keep it, we will. The choice is yours."

Anne's eyes stung. Her father...in the past few weeks she had been so happy that she'd almost forgotten. And it moved her that Cedric would ask her what she wanted to do. Once they married, all of her property had become his. He could have sold the home without asking her, but he hadn't.

It was a tempting thought, to keep the house. But it was better to let it go. If it went to Jonathan, and perhaps Audrey, they would see the house frequently enough, and it was as he'd said—it would be filled with love and children.

"If Mr. St. Laurent is interested, then we should. I will trust you to see to the arrangements."

"Excellent. I can have Ashton write him a letter and, if he's amenable to it, we can get my solicitor to draw up the paperwork."

"Thank you." She meant it. To show him, she leaned into him, curling her arms around his neck and kissing him thoroughly, despite the public nature of where they were. He groaned at her assertive kiss and returned it, but all too soon had to pull them apart.

"I wish we could continue this, my heart, but Lady Beach will not be our last unwelcome spectator if we do not go home at once. Some enterprising scamp might start selling tickets."

She couldn't help but giggle as she climbed off his lap.

"Then by all means, husband, summon a coach."

"As you wish." His lips curved into that smile that had won her heart the very first time she'd seen him. Only this time, it was even brighter because it was full of love. For a moment she was unexpectedly afraid.

What if I were to lose him now? My heart is too tightly bound to his. If he were to go, so would I. If any other woman would have told Anne she'd felt that way about a man, Anne would have thought she was being melodramatic, but now she understood. A deeper connection was forged by two hearts and it could not be easily broken.

She slipped her arm in his as they left Donaldson's Library. Swallowing hard, she tried to think about something else. The dinner tonight. That would be wonderful and fun. Yes, the dinner. Everything would be fine. If only something inside her didn't keep worrying that she was going to lose Cedric forever.

❧ 22 ❧

"Well, that wasn't a complete disaster, was it?" Cedric chuckled as he climbed into his coach across from Anne.

Anne grinned. "No, it wasn't. You did wonderfully." She held something in her arms, something Cedric could not see. It was a surprise for him, one she and Lady Pickering were quite excited about. They had managed to smuggle it all the way to the coach without Cedric suspecting anything.

"Why don't you come sit by me, lady wife?" he suggested with a brow raised in that rakish way of his.

It took all her self-control not to giggle. It had been a long while since she'd given something to someone she cared about. Her heart beat faster as she finally spoke.

"All right." She joined him on his side of the enclosed coach and let him pull her against his side. When he leaned in closer, he froze, nostrils flaring. His eyes widened, then narrowed.

"I smell..." He paused, sniffed, then his hands moved from her waist to her arms. When he encountered the bundle she cradled to her bosom, he stiffened.

"Anne, are you...is that a *dog*?" He tilted his head to one side. The deep rumble of his voice stirred the creature awake. The puppy in her arms stretched, yawned and licked Cedric's fingers, which had brushed against the pup's wet nose.

"Lady Pickering's favorite King Charles spaniel had a litter two months ago. She thought we might like one. She said your mother loved King Charles spaniels." Anne prayed he wasn't upset. Cedric had given her so much and she wanted to give something to him in return. He couldn't go hunting and a large dog wouldn't have been happy in the house. A smaller spaniel was perfect. The dog would be a companion to Cedric, one who could follow him and keep him in good spirits.

"Did you know that I bought Emily a dog?" Cedric's lips hinted at a barely there smile.

"Why...er...yes. I remember she told me about her foxhound, Penelope." She paused. "I swear my intentions are entirely different."

Cedric's rich laugh warmed her. "If you got me a dog to keep me from escaping you, I would take that as a compliment, my dear. Now, show me the little scamp." He opened his hands and Anne passed along the sleepy bundle. It had woken during their discussion and wriggled in Cedric's arms as he took it. Watching him cuddle the white and cinnamon-brown pup to his chest filled Anne with such love.

"My mother's last spaniel before she died was an energetic chap. Forrest was his name. I always liked the little fellow. What do you think, love? Does he look like a Forrest?" Cedric ruffled the dog's ears with a playful smile. Even though he could not see the dog, he was evidently enthralled with the pup already.

"Yes, he looks like a Forrest." She covered her mouth with a gloved hand. To be so happy...she couldn't believe it. Wherever her father was, she hoped he could see that she was all right, that she'd found her place in the world at this man's side.

"When we get home, this little chap is going to a basket to sleep and you, lady wife, will be seeing to your duties in our bed."

The cheek of such words would have enraged her had any other man said them, but when they came from Cedric it lit her blood and made her body yearn.

"If I see to my duties, then you must see to yours." She couldn't resist teasing him.

His rakehell grin sent her pulse into a mad gallop. The coach stopped, and when the footman came to open the doors, Anne smiled when she recognized Sean Hartley.

"Sean? That you?" Cedric held out the dog to him. "Take little Forrest here and put him in a basket in your chambers. I'll take charge of him in the morning. My wife and I will be occupied the rest of the night."

"Of course, my lord." Sean took the dog with a smile and stroked its ears. He gave a quick glance to Anne and she returned a nod, encouraging him to do as he was bid.

As she and Cedric entered the house they found the servants were scarce, as though sensing the need for privacy for their master and mistress.

"Take me to the drawing room," Cedric commanded.

Anne slipped her hand into his and led him. He used his cane to sweep across the carpets. Anne pushed the door open, revealing the rich Tudor decorations and the plush red settee facing a black marble fireplace. Wooden beams, intricately carved, curved up in fluted shapes over the molded ceilings. Red damask drapes covered the tall windows, and moonlight peeped through the thin slits of the mostly closed curtains. Despite the fact that no fire was lit, the room felt cozy, even if it was dark.

Cedric began to lead her, as though he knew the whereabouts of the room's furniture by heart. He stopped in front of the settee and turned her to face away from him.

"It is dark, isn't it?" he asked. His tone was soft, low and dangerously seductive.

Anne swallowed before replying. "Yes, quite dark."

"Good. I want you to close your eyes. I'm going to make love to you and I want you to feel it as I do, with sensations and sounds, but no sight."

"But—"

"Close your eyes." The dark command from him flooded her belly with welcome heat. "You and I will share the darkness together. Feel it, embrace it." He slid one hand around her waist to cover her stomach. His large powerful grip was firm and possessive, and the heavy warm breath against her ear was thick with forbidden carnality.

"Lift your left leg and place your foot on the cushion of the settee," he murmured before he kissed the shell of her ear, then nibbled on the lobe.

Anne, lulled into his seductive spell, leaned back against his body as she raised her leg. She had to tug her skirts up to her knees to do so, which seemed to be exactly what her husband desired.

His palm remained on her stomach, holding her against him, while his other hand settled on her knee, then began to glide over her stockings and peel her skirts even higher up to her waist. He stroked her bare inner left thigh, which with her leg propped up, gave him easy access to her. It was a struggle to keep her eyes closed as he touched her. There, in the darkness, they were together, and every sense was heightened.

"Breathe with me." Cedric's fingers had reached the apex of her thighs. He parted the undergarments and stroked the wet lips of her sex.

Anne breathed in, feeling him do the same behind her. One of his fingers slipped between the slick folds of her mound and penetrated her. Her hips jerked against his hand and she whimpered in erotic delight.

"Hold your skirts up," he whispered. Her hands, which had been fairly useless, latched onto the white crepe and sarsnet slip. The black wreaths on the bottom of her skirt whispered as she dug her fingers into the silk.

"Cedric," she murmured as he continued to thrust that single finger into her, playing with her body as though reveling in his power to torture her with pleasure.

He rocked his hips into her from behind. "What do you feel?" The hard pressure of his arousal dug into her lower back.

"You," she groaned.

His deep laugh made her quiver around his teasing, tormenting finger.

"Besides me, little hellion. What else do you feel?"

She focused on breathing as her body began to dance toward a climax.

"My blood is pumping, hard. I can feel my heartbeat everywhere," she confessed. "And my breath, I can't get enough. I need you."

He nipped her neck and slid a second finger inside her, curling the tips of his fingers and brushing over some secret spot deep inside her that made stars dart behind her closed lids.

"Let go, darling. I'm here to catch you." He coaxed her into the explosion of her release, and she couldn't even scream.

He had barely touched her, yet this time she seemed connected to him on a level she hadn't thought possible. Her eyes were still closed and all she had were sensations. The rough pads of his fingers, the warm breath on her neck, the hard body pinning her back against it. The roar of blood in her ears as her climax continued long afterward. This was how it felt for him, when they came together. Pure sensation. There was so much she wanted to say, but couldn't seem to find the words. Her eyes flew open.

He withdrew his fingers from her body and slipped them between his lips, sucking them. Her thighs quivered with longing as she watched his lips around his fingers with fascination.

"It is your turn, my lord." She dropped her skirts and turned to face him.

With a chuckle he shook his head. "There's something else I had in mind, since we first met." He retrieved his cane and held out his arm to her. She followed him as they walked through the house to the ballroom. Anne had glimpsed it when taking a short tour a few days before, but she'd never expected to come here with Cedric.

"Husband, what are you up to?" Excitement fluttered inside her as she watched the moonbeams cut through the tall windows and light up the room. The floor gleamed invitingly, as though calling her to dance upon it.

Cedric paused in the center of the room and spun her to face him. He set his cane down on the ground and sent it sliding several feet away. Then he straightened and held out his arms.

"I believe you owe me a waltz, my heart." The smile on his face brought tears to her eyes.

How had he guessed her secret wish for this very thing? It didn't matter that they weren't in a lively assembly room full of their peers. No, what mattered was that she was here, right now with the man she loved, and they were finally going to have their dance.

She could have danced all night with him if he asked her to. Walking into his embrace, she guided one of his hands to her waist and clasped his other hand in hers. Then he tugged her close enough that their bodies brushed.

"We have no music," she murmured, studying his look of concentration.

"We don't need it." He began to hum, the notes soft at first *a cappella*, then, as though more confidant, he began to sing the notes, his voice clear and bell-like. He sang like an angel. She would never have guessed that about him. Grinning in delight, she followed his lead as he began. They moved together with such ease it surprised even her. Without anyone else in the room, he could guide her effortlessly and she could follow him.

Because I trust him. Even after what Crispin had done to her that night at Almack's she hadn't given up the belief deep inside that Cedric was her destiny. As broken as Crispin's violation of her had made her feel, Cedric had erased that pain. Not unlike a piece of pottery she'd once seen from Japan, shattered and then fastened back together with gleaming powdered gold or silver seams. *Kintsugi*, her father had called it. The act of fixing something, letting the break symbolize something that was stronger for its being repaired. The gold illuminated the breaks that had been mended rather than hiding them.

What had happened with Crispin no longer defined her. Moving on with her life, with love, with Cedric, were her gold seams holding her pieces back together, making her whole again. She was not simply another wronged woman. She was Anne Chessley, a woman who loved horses, the outdoors, and her husband. He let her be herself, and yet they shared all their joys and now all their heartbreaks.

And we have survived through them, finding our joy together again. Because we lean upon each other. We are partners, equals. The thoughts turned in her head even as they turned around the ballroom. It was the sort of marriage her father had wished for her to have, and although he was gone, she knew he would have approved.

"Are you all right, my love? I felt you shiver just now." Cedric's hand on her waist, so warm through the fabric of her dress, tightened a little as they continued to dance.

"Yes, oh yes. I've wanted to do this with you for years," she admitted. The darkness and his blindness hid her blush, but she wasn't ashamed of the truth.

"Perhaps we ought to dance every night before bed?" He winked at her and she laughed.

"I wouldn't argue with you on that." She squeezed his hand and he spun her out from him, twirling her around before pulling her back, which made her laugh in delight.

"Let's have a ball next month. Invite all our friends. We can dance all night, darling."

"A wonderful idea! We could let Audrey plan it when she returns from France. Perhaps she and Jonathan could plan it together."

Her husband chuckled. "Are you matchmaking, my heart?"

She lifted her chin. "You said yourself Jonathan is considering courting her. I think it would be an excellent way for them to spend more time around each other."

"Then it's settled," he agreed, and pulled her flush against him.

"This isn't a waltz anymore," she whispered against his ear. "There's no longer any music."

"No, but it's something much better, wouldn't you agree?" He nuzzled her cheek and then kissed her temple.

She shivered again, but this time from renewed desire. "Cedric, why don't we go upstairs to bed. I have a sudden need for you to fulfill your duties to me again."

"Yes—" But something had changed. Cedric's wicked grin faded and his entire body went rigid. His hands on her hips dug into her hard.

"Anne, did you tell the servants to leave a window

open?" His words were so soft, she almost didn't hear him. But she felt a faint breeze kiss the back of her neck.

"No. I didn't." She started to rotate toward the window when a sound froze her in place.

Someone was clapping.

"What a charming show you put on, Sheridan." A cold voice cut through the gloom of the ballroom.

"Who's there?" Cedric demanded, dragging Anne behind him, putting his body between her and the direction the voice came from.

A soft hiss filled the air, echoing off the wooden floors. It sounded like a blade being drawn back from a sheath. Her father had a sword from his days as an officer in the service. When she had been a little girl, he'd let her remove it once from its scabbard.

"It has been a long time, Lord Sheridan." A rich, accented voice came from the shadows by the open window.

"No..." Cedric's utterance of that single word made Anne's blood turn to ice.

"Oh yes." The man stepped forward. In the dim glow of moonlight, she could see the gleam of his white teeth against his skin. Something about that seemed familiar, but she couldn't remember why.

Cedric's body began to tense. He started to maneuver them toward the door halfway between them and the man with the sword. "Anne, listen to me very carefully. Get

Hartley and escape the house. Do you understand? Go, now!"

Cedric shoved her toward the door. After that, everything happened too quickly. She stumbled toward the door just as the man with the sword came toward them. By the time she reached the door, Cedric had positioned himself between her and the intruder. His foot brushed against his lion head cane, which he picked up.

"Cedric!" she screamed as the man lunged. Cedric swung his cane as though it were a broadsword. The man ducked, but not fast enough, Cedric clipped him on the shoulder.

"Anne, go!" Cedric's bellow jarred her out of her frozen terror. She needed to find Sean. Find help. She burst into the hall, right into a tall, hard body.

Sean gripped her shoulder, holding her steady. "My lady? What—"

"Find Ashton. We need help! There's a man attacking Cedric!" She couldn't think beyond that.

Sean was about to rush into the ballroom, but several men now emerged from an adjacent room, men who couldn't be their servants. Their clothes were ragged and they all carried pistols or knives.

"My lady, get back inside, it isn't safe!" Sean pushed her into the ballroom, as he turned to face the advancing men. She watched in terror as he charged the men, fists swinging. One man fell back onto the ground with a single blow. Sean then grabbed another's arm and broke it, causing him to let go of his weapon. He threw the screaming thug into one of his comrades and picked up the dropped blade. The man knew how to fight, but he couldn't escape all of the men, not forever.

"Hartley, behind you!" she shouted from the ballroom doorway, warning him just before a pistol fired. Hartley had dropped down an instant before the gun discharged, and the bullet sank into the wall with a crack. He sprang forward and plunged the knife into the attacker before he could pull out a second pistol from his brace.

"Get inside, my lady!" Hartley shouted as two men tackled him and a third got past him to run toward her. She slammed the ballroom door, pushing against the heavy wood to keep it shut.

Before she could recover, she was grabbed from behind, a blade pressed against her side as a warning for her to stay still.

"Don't move, Lady Sheridan, or you will regret it."

"Anne?" Cedric's voice was distant, farther away.

The man had evaded Cedric and gone directly for her. He gripped her by the back of the neck and dragged her in front of him. Two more men slipped through an open window.

Anne tried to warn him of the others coming up behind him, but the man holding her squeezed her throat. She dug her fingertips into his hand, fighting for breath while the invaders wrestled Cedric to the ground. He couldn't defend himself, lashing out wildly against unseen foes.

"Don't fight, Lord Sheridan. I have a blade to your wife's heart. It would be so easy to slip it between her ribs."

Cedric ceased his struggles and lay stomach down on the floor, the men pinning his arms and legs.

"Bind him," the man holding Anne barked. Two men used a coil of rope they had brought with them.

Once bound, Cedric was pulled to his feet. His blank eyes drifted in her direction, but she still couldn't make a sound. The crushing grasp on her windpipe was too much.

"Take them to the coach, and be quick. Dispatch anyone who sees you. We must get back to port in time for the morning tide."

The man strangling her then let go, only to strike her across the back of her head, and she knew no more.

✵ 23 ✵

Darkness. *Damn the everlasting black.*

Cedric hung from a rafter in the belly of a ship. At least, that was his best guess. The ropes around his wrists chaffed him where they stretched straight above his head. Whoever had strung him up had given him enough slack to have a sure footing on the floor, which was a good thing because the ship kept pitching and rolling.

The briny smell of seawater and aged wood filled his nose. He tried to think clearly. The last thing he remembered was being attacked in his own ballroom by Samir Al Zahrani, whose voice he would recognize anywhere. Then he'd been ganged up on by a number of his men. Then he'd lost consciousness.

Where was Anne? He called out her name, his voice hoarse and his throat dry.

"Ah. Finally awake, Lord Sheridan?" Samir's cool voice taunted from somewhere in front of him.

Cedric jerked on the ropes binding him. "Where is my wife?"

Samir chuckled, the sound a little closer. "She is entertaining my men. Fair-skinned ladies fetch a high price, and she is in need of the practice in satisfying multiple men. I left her screaming like the English whore she is."

Cedric jerked on his wrists, the beam above him creaking slightly.

"You bloody bastard, I'll kill you!" The roar vibrated through his entire body.

"Do be quiet, or I'll have the men bring her down so you might hear her screams yourself. Pity you cannot see. The sight of her body breaking might have blinded you."

Cedric fumed as he clawed at the rope to no avail.

Suddenly something sharp dug into his ribs.

"You once said you had a long line of men ahead of me waiting to kill you, Lord Sheridan. But I've never been one to wait my turn. Besides, I owe you a fate worse than death. I can envision much, but I'm willing to settle with my original promise—my mares returned and your life as a eunuch. I'll give you a few hours to prepare, Lord Sheridan. You might die, if you are lucky." Samir laughed darkly as he dragged the blade's edge down Cedric's body to just above his groin. He didn't cut Cedric, but the intention was clear.

"Now, stay quiet and I might spare your wife a few hours of my men's attention."

Cedric's heart withered inside. *Oh, God, Anne, my darling...*

A despair like nothing he'd ever felt before overwhelmed him. Loving him had become a death sentence for her. For both of them. They had both found happiness only to have it ripped away. Losing his sight was nothing compared to the crushing bleak truth of what losing Anne would do to him. He slumped in his bonds, giving up. There was no hope. Nothing he could do to save her.

"You are fortunate that my mares were well cared for," Samir continued. "I might grant you death sooner, as a way to express my gratitude."

"This is all about the bloody horses? Did you steal them back as well?"

"Soon. They are being kept in Brighton, waiting to be put on a more reliable transport ship back to my country. This vessel is fine for human cargo, but as we both know, my mares deserve much better."

A scuffle of boots announced someone new had joined them.

"I will join my men upstairs, Lord Sheridan, to take a turn with your wife. If she pleases me, I might keep her for myself. While I'm occupied with her, I wouldn't want you to become lonely. As it turns out, this fellow here is also familiar with your treacherous ways, as you were once intimately familiar with his sister, a lady's maid for Lady

Poncenby. He has volunteered to give you a sound thrashing." Samir's laughter made Cedric tense. He was strung up like a side of beef, unable to defend himself.

He couldn't prepare himself for the blow to his stomach. His breath whooshed out and he grunted as pain radiated out from that point of contact. Another crushing punch to his chest and he wheezed.

"Enjoy your stay aboard my ship, Lord Sheridan. It will only take us three weeks to get home, I believe." Samir laughed one more time, and then his booted steps on the stairs eventually faded.

"I swear to you, I never touched a hair on Poncenby's maid." There was a decent chance this was true. If he could only remember whether Freddy Poncenby's mother actually had a comely looking lady's maid or not.

"Shut up, Cedric," a voice hissed. "Wait until I'm sure he's gone."

It took him a second to recognize it. "Jonathan?"

"Sorry about hitting you. I had to make it look convincing."

"How in the blazes did you end up on Al Zahrani's ship?"

Jonathan's hands brushed over his. There was a rasping sound as the bonds on his wrists were cut. He slumped to the ground, his legs weak after hanging for so long.

"I overheard a few sailors in London discussing a plan to kidnap someone in Brighton. I feared it might be you.

There wasn't time to warn you, so I found a way to hop on the ship."

"The devil you did!" Cedric was so relieved that he nearly laughed, but he didn't have time. He struggled to his feet. "We have to find Anne."

"Don't worry. We'll find her," Jonathan said. "You have to take it easy and be careful."

Cedric frowned. "How many are there on this ship?" he asked. The odds were going against them. They were in the ocean on a ship with Al Zahrani and his crew.

Jonathan must have understood the unspoken question.

"Too many to handle on our own. I sent word to Godric before I left port, but I do not know if the message reached him in time, or what he could do for us now that we're at sea."

"Damnation," Cedric growled. "Where the hell is Ashton and that fleet he's always talking about?"

A distant cry from above their heads silenced them.

"Ship off the port bow!"

"What?" Cedric and Jonathan said together. They'd heard the shout, but even still he was too afraid to hope.

"Jonathan, I need your help. We must find the powder room. Lead me to it, and then we find Anne."

He had a plan. It just had to work. He refused to accept any other outcome.

Ashton rode up to Rushton Steading, glancing around at the lack of life inside the house. No groom rushed out to meet him. The hairs prickled on the back of his neck as he slid from the saddle and hastily looped the reins of his horse's bridle over an iron post by the door.

"Cedric?" he called out and walked up the main steps.

The front door was ajar. Ashton tried to push it open, but it only shifted a few inches. He rammed his shoulder into the door and it finally gave. When he was able to slip inside, he froze at the sight of blood streaking across the floor leading to the body of a young man, the body that had been against the door he'd just forced open. Sean Hartley, the footman, lay half-dead on the floor by the door. Around him lay two corpses of men Ashton didn't recognize. Their rough clothing and the weapons they still held in their hands identified them as dangerous men.

"My lord." Sean's words escaped on a raspy breath.

Ashton removed his hat and clenched his fist in rage as he tried to soothe the younger man. He'd been stabbed and wasn't long for this world.

"Can you speak, lad? Tell me what happened? Where are the other servants?" In a house this large, they should have been everywhere, seeing to their duties.

"It's the...sheik." Sean's ashen face scrunched with pain. "The staff fled to the Pickering estate...going to find help...safe I think...but they don't know..." He shuddered, his eyes briefly closing.

"Don't know what? Where are Lord and Lady Sheridan?" Ashton asked the question, surprised his voice was steady. With the rage burning inside him, he could barely think straight.

"Taken...ship in port. The *Maiden Fair*, heard one of the men say it as they left," Sean said. Ashton pressed a hand to the young man's wounds, but he'd lost too much blood. Still, he had to try.

"I'm sorry." The lad's eyes began to dim.

"You did well, so well, lad." Ashton tried to think of what to tell the dying man.

"Aye," the young man sighed, and his head drooped. It wouldn't be long now.

Ashton struggled to his feet as a loud clattering outside caught his attention. He moved Sean back from the door, hands trembling as he did so.

"What in God's name?" Lucien's voice cut through the haze of rage clouding Ashton's mind.

Ashton saw Godric, Lucien and Charles in the doorway, staring at him and Sean in shock.

"It's Al Zahrani. He's taken Anne and Cedric to a ship called the *Maiden Fair*. They'll still be docked in Brighton if we're lucky. We have to go."

Emily and Horatia followed their husbands inside. Emily gasped and Horatia covered her mouth at the sight of the dying footman.

"Who is that?" Horatia asked.

"His name is Sean, and he fought bravely," Ashton said. His damned blood-covered hands wouldn't stop shaking.

"The servants have fled. We have to go after Cedric and Anne."

Charles came over to Ashton and offered a handkerchief to clean the blood off of his hands. Ashton accepted the silent offering, unable to look at Sean again. The lad didn't deserve to die. His loyalty to Lady Sheridan had gotten him killed.

"Emily," Godric said. "You and Horatia tend to Sean. Make him comfortable if you can." Ashton didn't miss the significant look that passed between Godric and his wife.

"Of course." Emily took Horatia's hand and ran to get the necessary supplies.

Once they were gone, it was only the three men in the grand hall.

Another innocent death. Another casualty because of enemies they'd made over the years. Would it ever stop?

Godric headed for the door. "I'll get fresh horses from the stables."

Charles knelt by Sean, who looked at him helplessly, and sighed.

"I'm so sorry," he said, taking the man's hand. Sean seemed to be having trouble staying conscious. "Listen to me, Sean. *Listen.* We will find them. We will save them. And when we do it will be because of your actions here today. You have done a great thing."

Emily and Horatia returned with what they needed to tend to Sean's final moments. Charles stepped back and looked at Ashton, his gray eyes were like dark storm clouds. It was rare to see this side of Charles, the side of the man who'd nearly drowned, instead of the carefree joker they'd come to expect. Fear and anger sparked in his eyes, the only part of him that betrayed his fraying control. As long as they'd been friends, it was these small details that Ashton didn't miss.

"I have the fastest ships, and one of them is currently in Brighton, ready to sail. If Al Zahrani's ship is not in dock, we will track it to the ends of the earth if need be."

Charles rose and clenched his jaw. "And when we find him?"

Ashton's body was coiled like a tiger ready to strike. "Then we kill him."

❦

"I'M SURPRISED YOU DO NOT REMEMBER ME, LADY Sheridan." Samir Al Zahrani took a seat in the spacious cabin's only chair.

Anne was seated in the corner by the narrow bed, watching him the way she would a venomous snake. She clutched the tattered pieces of her dress to cover her undergarments. She'd been roughly handled, her gown ripped, but so far no one had touched her other than dragging her to this cabin.

"Remember you? Of course I do. You nearly ran me over in Brighton a few days ago." It had shocked her when she'd woken in the cabin and seen him.

Samir shook his head, leaning back in his chair. Dark eyes like polished onyx, without any warmth, stared back at her. "No. We met before that."

Anne searched her memory frantically, trying to recall what he meant.

"I tried to steal you away on your estate, but it didn't work. I struck you hard enough that you must have forgotten me. If I had had the chance, I would have taken you then, and enjoyed knowing Sheridan was robbed of his bride. But waiting has turned out so much better. I have you both, and the punishment will be much more satisfying than I could have envisioned."

Anne closed her eyes, trying remember that awful night when she'd fallen down that hill onto the rocky bank of Cedric's lake, wounded by a blow to the head. She'd believed she'd stumbled and struck her head. But it had been him. Opening her eyes, she raised her gaze to meet his. She knew what sort of man he was from Cedric's story, a slave trader. Anne had lived her life bottling up emotions, and now she was ready to unleash them upon this soulless creature that did not deserve the life he'd been given.

Samir didn't miss her changing attitude.

"I always believed fine English ladies were gently bred. Too sweet and weak. Yet there is fire in your eyes." He laughed softly and clapped his hands together. "It will be a great joy to break you. And even more rewarding to do so in front of your husband."

It took every ounce of her self-control not to lash out at him. She wouldn't win in a direct struggle. Surprise was her only ally. The question was how to accomplish a distraction so surprise would be available to her.

"You are the man he bested at cards. The *slave* trader. A beast among men." That story she'd been told at Emily's house seemed so long ago. So much had happened since then. So much had changed.

Samir stood and struck her across the face. Pain exploded where his palm connected. She flinched back, expecting him to come at her again. She wiped a hand over her mouth and tasted the tangy acidic taste of blood. Samir paced away from her, then turned back, his eyes twin burning coals.

"You are testing me, trying to provoke me to kill you. It will not work. I mean to enjoy this." His smile cut to the bone. "I mean to enjoy you."

The taste of blood lingered in her mouth, a hint of the torture she knew that was to come if she couldn't buy herself time.

"You do not know much about my husband, do you?" she asked. "If you did, you would not be so confident right now. You'd be looking out that window, worrying."

That caught Samir's attention, but he said nothing.

"My husband is a member of the League of Rogues."

Samir seemed a little confused. "Rogues? Does that not mean criminal?"

"It means they do not play by the rules. I doubt you've

ever heard of them. If you had, you would know what sort of man you are dealing with."

Her captor's lips twitched, amused. "And what sort is that?"

"A man who no doubt has already freed himself from your prison and is taking out the ship's crew one by one." She struggled to stand, still holding her dress together as she faced him boldly.

"Your blind husband? Stumbling around the ship, pawing at the doors because he can't find the handle? That does not frighten me." Samir started toward her, one hand raised. She struck a defiant pose only an English lady could muster.

"It should frighten you to the bone, because my husband is never alone. At this moment there are five others coming. And they have ships and men of their own. They will do anything to save us. Track us across the world if they must. You can run home and hide in the deepest hole you can find, but you will *not* escape the League." She was surprised at the bravado she'd managed to show, even knowing it wasn't true. They had stood a chance while still in England, but at sea there was no hope of rescue.

Samir threw his head back and laughed. "Oh, you do amuse me, Lady Sheridan. You jest, of course. They won't find you, and by the time I'm through with you and that filth you call a husband, you will be begging me for a death that I shall not grant." He raised his hand for another blow.

So this is to be my end. Defending Cedric's honor and the League. There were worse things in life than dying to protect those she loved, she supposed.

Samir was stopped short by a shout from outside.

"Ship off the port bow!" The cry was echoed a few more times, each shout coming closer to the cabin where Anne and Samir stood. A scruffy crewman burst in through the cabin door, sliding to a halt.

"What is happening outside?"

The sailor squinted and apologized. "A ship, sir. Captain says it's bearing down on us and you are to stay in the cabin in case we come under fire."

A ship? Anne was too afraid to hope. It wasn't possible that Ashton had been able to catch up with them, let alone find them. Samir grabbed her and thrust her into the sailor's hands.

"Tie her to the bed," Samir ordered before he stormed from the room.

The man turned Anne around, meaning to force her down onto the bed as ordered, but Anne dropped her ripped gown to the floor and lifted her petticoats high enough to knee the man in the bollocks.

The man crumpled to the floor with a piteous moan.

Anne gave him a second blow while he was down, then leapt over his prone form and into the narrow passageway of the ship. Sailors were scrambling to man positions, others shouted out orders about prepping the cannons. No one paid her any attention as she dodged the chaos on the deck. In the distance a ship was quickly gaining and would soon be upon them.

Was it someone who would help them? How could she find Cedric and escape?

Cedric, where are you? Fear sliced through her as she dashed back toward the lower decks. She had to find him.

24

Cedric leaned against a large wooden barrel bound by copper hoops. His nose picked up the fine acrid aroma of black powder—sulfur, saltpeter and finely ground charcoal. A deadly combination when stuffed into a ship's cannon.

"Jonathan, I have an idea."

"What?"

"This barrel is full of black powder." Cedric rapped his knuckles on the wood.

"Is this plan of yours going to get us killed?"

Cedric hesitated before answering. "There's always a chance."

Jonathan snorted. "Let us try to find the route off this ship that leaves us all breathing. Now, what's your plan?"

"There should be a light room close by. We prepare a charge, set it alight at the right moment and escape."

Cedric knew the plan was risky, but escape was not enough. They had to destroy this ship. But first they needed to find Anne.

"Let us be clear, you want to set fire to the powder room?" Jonathan moved closer, his booted steps echoing on the floor. Above them the sailors were scrambling to their battle stations.

"Yes. We wouldn't have much time after we set fire to the room. We need to find Anne and a way off this ship, but it's all for naught if this ship is still afloat."

Jonathan laughed, but it bore a nervous, edgy sound. "Are all your plans this insane?"

Cedric rolled his eyes. "Do you have a better one?"

"Very well." Jonathan sighed. "Stay here whilst I find the light room."

Cedric stumbled about, searching for a tool to open the barrel of powder. His hands came across a tool, something that felt a bit like a poker. He returned to the powder barrel and pried open the lid. The wood creaked in protest, but finally gave in.

Footsteps were Cedric's only warning that he'd been found out. He dodged to the right as something slashed his chest. It stung like the devil, but didn't feel deep.

"Cheating again?" Samir hissed. "You simply cannot accept when you are beaten." Cedric dodged again, Samir's words proving to be an invaluable warning to his actions. But he couldn't dodge the man forever. He needed to get hold of Samir's hands. Then he would stand a fighting chance.

"You need a sword to take me down? What, you don't have enough faith in your fighting skills to take on a blind man?" It was a small chance the man would be manipulated to do that, but it was worth it.

Samir snarled. "You don't think I can kill you with my bare hands?"

"You're the one in a hurry to run me through with a blade, Al Zahrani. Don't you want the satisfaction of strangling the life out of me? What sense of justice will you get with a sword?" Cedric held up his hands, fists loosely clenched in case he needed to grab his opponent rather than throw a punch.

Samir snorted. "You're right. I want to choke you slowly, make you feel every agonizing minute of your death. A slow death for a man who cheats," Samir replied smugly. The sound of a blade clattering to the ground echoed a few feet away.

The moment the blade was abandoned, Samir tackled him. They hit the open barrel behind him. Cedric hissed out in pain as Samir punched his lower stomach repeatedly.

Roaring, Cedric pulled his head back and thrust it forward. The crack of his skull against Samir's momentarily stunned them both, but Samir recovered quickly enough to stagger to his feet. Cedric got up and slammed into Samir, knocking them both to the ground. Pain shot through his head and for a second he thought he saw the hazy shadow of the man lying close to him.

Cedric didn't hesitate and hit Samir square in the jaw. A lucky blow if there ever was one. It was the advantage he needed. Scrambling off, he searched for the sword. When the blade nicked his hand, he cursed before he was able to grab the grip.

He heard scraping noises behind him as Samir struggled to get up.

"You English pig!" Samir shouted.

Cedric fell flat on his back, sword raised just as Samir landed on top of him. The blade met some resistance as it plunged into Samir's ribs. The man grunted and sagged on top of Cedric.

"You...cheated..." Samir panted angrily.

"That I did." He shoved Samir's body off him. "Just like that night playing whist. I don't play fair with slavers."

Cedric leaned against one of the barrels. His chest burned and his head ached. The gray fog about his eyes seemed to waver with black and white tendrils of color, like fleeting shadows, like the ghost of what he used to see.

Samir coughed, the sound a sickly gurgle now. "You... cheating...bastard."

"I prefer *rogue*," Cedric said. The rattling breath of his enemy finally ceased.

Just then, like a phantom's voice amongst the noise of the crew, Anne's voice echoed up the hall.

"Cedric?"

He moved in the direction of the sound. "Anne? Where are you?"

"Cedric! Thank God."

The sound of her slippered feet was music to his ears. He opened his arms and she wrapped herself around him.

Anne gasped. "You're bleeding!"

"Reminds me of the day you proposed," he said with a happy chuckle.

"Oh! Cedric!" She tensed in his arms. "Is Al Zahrani...?"

"Dead. Yes. I'll explain later, but we must go. Now." He held her in his arms, but let her guide him into the narrow corridor.

"Jonathan!" he shouted.

"I'm here! Stand back," Jonathan warned.

Heat blossomed close to Cedric's chest and he instinctively curled himself around Anne as they moved back. He thought for a moment he could see a filmy curtain of light, like glimpsing a fire through heavy woods. Flickers, shadows, but nothing more. Was he seeing the glow from a lantern? He was too afraid to hope.

"Jonathan, what are you doing?" Anne asked, her body tense in Cedric's arms.

"Well, my heart, we are going to blow up the ship."

"*What?*"

"There's no other way for us to escape alive," Cedric said. "These men will fire on that ship, and they will be forced to fire back. We don't want to be on board when the cannonballs start flying through the walls around us. You have to trust me on this."

"Yes, I trust you." Despite the touch of panic in Anne's voice, it was nevertheless resolute.

"Jonathan will set the fire, then we will run for the deck. If we can reach a longboat, we'll take that, but there may not be time. If I say jump, jump over the side. Do you understand?"

She grasped one of Cedric's hands in hers. "Promise to stay with me."

"I will," he vowed, holding her hand tight.

Jonathan interjected. "Right. I'm ready to light this. You two go ahead, I'll catch up with you on deck."

Cedric steeled himself. "Be careful, Jonathan. Audrey will never forgive me if she learns I let you blow yourself up." He meant to tease the younger man, but also knew Jonathan would understand all the things he didn't have the time, or words, to say.

"I'll find you when it's done," Jonathan replied.

Cedric turned back to Anne. "Lead me to the deck, lady wife. It's time to make our escape."

ANNE AND CEDRIC HURRIED UP THE FLIGHT OF STAIRS and burst out onto the main deck. He whipped his head about as though listening to the crew around him.

"What's happening, Anne? Be my eyes."

Men raced to positions and men shouted orders and reports.

"She's a large sloop, sir. We'll never outrun her!"

"No flag signals ordering us to stand down," yelled another. "Gun ports are open!"

Anne heard who she presumed was the captain bark, "Bring her to port! Load cannons! Load chain shot! Target her masts!"

It was chaos.

"How close is the other ship?" Cedric tugged her to the railing and they carefully, but quickly, worked their way across the maze of ropes and ship equipment on deck.

"Half a mile away. There might be another chasing behind it." She squinted in the bright light, trying to assess the distance between them and the ship. Thankfully none of the crew did more than glance at them with irritation as they rushed past.

"We don't have enough chain shot, sir!"

"Load the remaining cannons with grape shot!" the captain ordered.

"Aim for the decks!" a midshipman added.

"Belay that! Aim for the sails! We have to slow her down!"

She was terrified she and Cedric would be hauled back down into the hull of the ship by someone, but they were far more worried about the approaching sloop. When she focused on the ships in the distance she saw two flags. The

Union Jack flapped against the wind of both vessels. The larger and closer vessel also carried the flag of the Royal Navy at the rear. The ship just behind it was closing the gap, and she saw more clearly that ship's flag.

Cedric curled an arm around Anne's waist, keeping her close as they moved. "Do you recognize any of the flags?"

"There's a British flag and a navy flag on the first. The second has a dark blue flag with a white flower on it." It was hard to make out the shape in the distance with all the wind.

Cedric laughed. "Good God, he found us!" And then he whooped loudly and kissed Anne on the lips.

"Who found us?" She had no idea what he was talking about.

"Ash! That's his company flag. Must be one of his ships! He's brought the bloody navy with him, the sly dog!"

Before Anne could say anything she saw Jonathan run up on deck, shouting, "Jump! We don't have time!"

Jonathan sprinted across the deck, leaping over a pair of sailors bent over a cannon they were preparing to load.

"Fire in the powder room!" he bellowed.

That single cry and the ominous coiling of black smoke from below the deck sent sailors scattering like rats.

"What about a longboat?" Anne asked.

"No time!" Cedric glanced around, cursed under his breath. He thought he could make out some shadows, but even if it was more than just wishful thinking it wasn't enough to navigate by. "Is there a part of the deck without a railing?"

Anne glanced around. "Yes."

"Do we have a clear shot to run to it?"

"Yes. It's about fifteen feet." She swallowed hard. "We're really going to jump?" It looked like another twenty feet to the ocean.

Cedric cupped her face with his free hand. "Yes. Jump away from the ship as far as you can. Kick for the surface once you're in the water and get as far away as you can. Don't let go of my hand...if we become separated, I may not be able to find the surface." The desperate look on his face tore at her already battered heart.

"I won't let go," she vowed.

"Then run!" He propelled her forward and she guided him as they dashed across the deck. Jonathan met them halfway and shouted as he leapt over the railing and into the air.

Anne screamed, unable to contain the panic as her stomach jumped into her throat as she and Cedric fell. The dark water rose up to meet them, and in a hard smack she struck the surface, then sank below. Icy water swallowed her up. The shock of the cold water nearly made her scream. Her grip on Cedric's hand was tenuous, but she kicked away her petticoats weighing her down.

A heavy vibration rocked the world around her. Looking up through the water, blurred streaks of red and orange consumed the skies above. She kicked herself upward until she at last surfaced. White smoke cloaked the area just above the water, and fiery hunks of the ship's hull splashed around her. Cedric broke through the surface with a painful gasp a moment later. She reached out for him and grabbed his hand.

"Cedric!"

"Anne! What—" Cedric's cry was silenced by a mighty crash.

Burning wood singed her as part of the ship's wreckage fell on her husband. She cried out, and then her hand, the one tightly locked with Cedric's, started to drop as Cedric's head slipped beneath the waves. The weight of his body sinking was too much for her to hold on to.

"Cedric! No!"

She dove under the water, her eyes stinging as she searched for him. The water was thick with debris. She swam until her lungs burned and forced her back to the surface.

A piece of wood large enough to hold on to floated within her reach. Kicking and paddling over to it, she grabbed it and rested a few moments before diving back down to look for Cedric again.

I won't let go...I can't let go...

But he wasn't there. She couldn't see him. When she broke the surface a third time, her body had become stiff with cold and she didn't have enough strength to go back. The body of a sailor floated past, and when it touched

Anne, she flinched. She could barely see anything through the white cloud from the powder explosion.

Every part of her body hurt. She clung to that bit of wood, her cheek pressed to the roughened surface, blinking back tears. It was no use. She wept in silent grief.

The only two men she'd ever loved, she'd lost. Her father and now her husband. Too stunned to move, she allowed the sea to swallow her heart within its depths. Wherever Cedric was now, so went her heart and soul.

A longboat cut through the smoke, and the distant shouts hailed her. The navy sloop loomed out of the smoke, and only a short distance away, Ashton's vessel drifted closer. Men shouted at each other from the decks, pointing in her direction and preparing a longboat.

Anne couldn't breathe, let alone answer them. Her mind had shut down, unable to process what she was seeing. Faces, marked with blackened streaks of soot, peered down at her when the longboat drifted up.

"She's alive!" someone shouted.

Hands reached down, pried her viselike grip off the driftwood, and she was hauled into the boat.

"Anne, look at me," a gentle but stern voice commanded. She opened her eyes and saw a golden-haired man sighing with visible relief. Charles. The name came slowly through the pain. Another face, one just as wet as hers, Jonathan, leaned in by Charles.

"Where's Cedric?"

Lips trembling, she looked back to the wreckage. Her

throat felt as if she was swallowing glass shards. Every protective barrier she'd ever built had been obliterated in the wake of that explosion. She could no longer contain her pain, the rage at her loss. The only man who'd loved her for the woman she was, was gone.

Everything was gone now. She'd been rendered blind, not in her eyes, but her heart. She'd lost Cedric forever. Charles slipped his coat off and wrapped it around her shoulders, but she barely noticed.

"He's gone," she whispered.

The boat went silent. As one their gazes drifted toward the sea, which had claimed the life of the man they'd come to save. The memory of an old poem her father used to recite came unbidden to her.

"And the ocean claimed her lover,
The waves folding him in an endless blue embrace,
Mourn not this king of seas, this prince of tides..."

🍂 25 🍂

Pain...*excruciating darkness... stars...blue...*
Cedric's head throbbed as he fought to get away from whatever was dragging him deeper and deeper into the sea's vast depths. His strength was rapidly fading and his lungs would explode unless he could get to the surface. His shirt tore and the binding that had trapped him to the wreckage was gone. He fought as though nothing in his life had mattered until now.

All he could see was Anne's face, and his desire to live. His desire to see her looking up at him with love and endless wonder. New strength flooded his limbs. The water stung his eyes, burned them like hot pokers, but he kept swimming toward that brightening point of light that he knew had to be the surface.

When his head burst above the water, he sucked in a

loud, agonizing breath. A shocking white glared into his eyes, and he blinked, raised one hand as he treaded water, and looked about...*looked*...as gray shapes appeared in the fog.

"What in God's name?" Pieces of wood bumped into his shoulders as he breathed in the thick smoke. That was what made things gray. Not his blindness, but gunpowder smoke and burning wreckage.

He could see! Not well, but by God he could see! He started to laugh, but choked as he breathed in the smoke.

He saw several longboats drifting through the ship's wreckage. The one closest to him had several people in it, all of them facing away, their backs to him. A woman was in the middle, and her soaked dark hair hung to her waist.

Anne! She was alive. Not yet strong enough to call out, he started to swim toward the boat before it left him behind. As he drew closer he recognized Godric, Ashton, Charles, Lucien, even Jonathan on board. Just beyond them two ships, the HMS *Ranger* and Ashton's merchant vessel *Black Lily*, were drifting around the wreckage of the *Maiden Fair*. The entire League and Anne were on that boat, all staring silently at something he could not see.

Dread filled him. What had happened? It had to be something horrible, something he couldn't bear, if it had struck his friends and wife speechless. When he reached the longboat, he swam around to the side. He clung to the edge of the boat and searched the floating wreckage, trying to spot whatever had devastated his friends.

Anne's face was strewn with tears, and Charles had a comforting arm around her shoulders. Cedric forced his gaze back to the sinking ship.

They must think I'm dead...

It was Jonathan, the one nearest to him, who slowly turned his head and saw Cedric clinging to the side of the boat.

"Cedric!" His startled shout made everyone jump.

Jonathan rushed over to where Cedric gripped the side of the longboat. Exhausted, Cedric latched onto the younger man's arms and allowed himself to be hauled aboard.

No sooner had he righted himself did Anne launch herself at him, sobbing incoherently. They fell together in a wet mess.

Ashton wiped at his eyes and cleared his throat. "We thought we'd lost you." There was a rough catch in his voice. Everyone looked too strained, too devastated.

The admission of how much he was loved, not just by Anne, but by his friends as well, struck his heart.

"Takes more than a burning cottage, horse thieves, piratical slavers and an exploding ship to kill me, eh?" he teased, trying to ease everyone's pain.

Charles chuckled. "Right. Should have known better than to think that could take you down."

Cedric looked down at Anne, who stared at him with that look he'd hoped to someday see. An endless wonder in her eyes, and love, so much love, that simply seeing it now gave him wings enough to fly.

"My heart," he whispered, feeling suddenly shy, so damned shy of his own wife. It was as though he was looking at a familiar stranger. He'd grown so used to her touch, her taste, her scent. To see her, finally *see* her again after so long in the dark...

She raised a hand and stroked the backs of her fingers across his cheeks.

"Don't cry," she begged him. "Please don't. If you do, I won't be able to stop."

"To hell with it." He buried his face in her neck, curling his body around hers, clinging to her. His heart, his love, his other half. They were alive and safe.

"I can see you," he kept saying as he wept. Never in all his life would anything be as beautiful as his beloved Anne and his dearest friends. The last five months had been an awful nightmare.

But I've finally woken up. He brushed his lips over Anne's, tasting the sea and her tears.

He vowed from that moment on, she would never cry again except from joy.

❦

Ashton stood on the deck of the *Black Lily*, his captain, Ellis Bristow, beside him.

"Close call, Lord Lennox. We almost didn't reach the *Ranger* in time." The captain, his hat tucked under one arm, watched the rolling waves, his sharp eyes missing nothing.

"I know." Ashton held his breath a moment, trying to

erase the thoughts of what might have been if they hadn't gotten to the *Maiden Fair* when they did.

They'd learned at the port which direction the slaver's ship had gone, and in the race to catch her, soon learned a navy ship was also in pursuit. The joy at having an ally, however, became terror when their man from the crows nest called down that the *Ranger* wasn't ordering the *Maiden* to stand down, and instead was opening gun ports.

Captain Bristow desperately arranged for his own message to be raised, warning the navy ship that English hostages were on board their target.

The captain of the *Ranger* had heard them and ordered his crew to prepare for boarding instead, but moments later the *Maiden* went up in flames without a shot being fired.

Seeing the ship burn and the bodies floating among the flotsam had almost killed Ashton. He'd feared Cedric, Anne and Jonathan to be among the dead.

He glanced down from the top deck of the *Lily* to see Anne and Cedric heading to the cabins below. Cedric's arm was curled around Anne's shoulder, and she clung to him as though afraid to let him out of her sight. Cedric paused just beneath Ashton and glanced up, nodding at him in silent gratitude for the *Lily*'s arrival.

Miracles do happen. After everything that had been lost over the years, sometimes the world gave things back. Like Cedric's sight.

Ashton wasn't the sort to put his trust in faith, but he

couldn't deny their good fortune today. Still, he feared what tomorrow would bring.

When he'd spoken to the captain of the *Ranger*, he'd learned that he'd been given orders to sail to Brighton to find and sink the *Maiden Fair* without giving quarter to prisoners. He'd been told it was a slaver ship, but it was supposed to be devoid of human cargo.

The orders had been given through the proper chain of command, yet Ashton had the distinct impression he was playing a vast game of chess. One with a board that spanned the country, and that somehow, even with this, Hugo Waverly was his opponent.

"Ash." Lucien climbed the stairs to the deck and nodded at Captain Bristow. Bristow offered them some privacy and left to speak to one of his lieutenants.

"How's Cedric?" Ashton asked.

"Good. Better than good. He's seeing again and can't seem to stop smiling at his wife. Silly fool."

Ashton heard the note of love in those last two words. Last Christmas had been a dark hour for both Cedric and Lucien. But they'd weathered the storm and come out stronger.

"Horatia would have killed me if our baby had lost its uncle."

It would have devastated them all to lose Cedric.

"And Jonathan? How is the lad?"

They glanced at the lower deck where Jonathan was braced with his back against one of the masts, his sandy-colored hair blowing in the wind. He'd risked much to get to Cedric and save him, far more than Ashton had asked of him. And that had truly made him one of the League of Rogues now.

"He's a bit distant. I sense he's feeling lost, even after so many months of adjusting to his new position. He needs someone to ground him, keep him in high spirits. Give him a wife to chase and tame, and he'll settle down and be happy. I think it's time Cedric brought Audrey home."

Ashton laughed, easing the tension he felt. "I never thought you'd be the one to suggest a wife was good for a man."

Lucien turned his knowing gaze toward Ashton. "A good wife is good for *every* man. You ought to remember that the next time you let a Scottish lass get the better of you in a theater alcove."

Ashton blanched, causing Lucien to chuckle.

"You're not the only one with eyes and ears, Ash. The staff at the opera house see more than anyone realizes. Might I suggest you find some *other* way to deal with Lady Melbourne, before she brings your business endeavors down around your ears." With nothing more than a smug grin, Lucien left Ashton at the railing, pale as a white flag of surrender.

He was right, though. Ashton had to deal with Lady Melbourne before she did exactly that. Ruin his business interests.

CEDRIC LOUNGED BACK ON THE SETTEE IN HIS DRAWING room, arms folded behind his head as a white and brown puppy dragged one of his boots across the carpet. Little Forrest growled and snarled, his dagger-like puppy teeth making little scrapes in the leather. Cedric didn't care. Life was perfect, puppy teeth marks and all.

It had been two weeks since he'd been rescued from the waters off Brighton, and his sight had fully returned. Headaches had pained him the first few days, but once the swelling from the blow to his head had subsided, so did the pain.

The door to the study opened as Anne and Audrey flew in like a pair of doves. Anne looked ravishing in her rose-red gown trimmed with embroidered wildflowers on the van-dyked sleeves and hem. Her full hips accented her tiny waist, especially when she placed her hands on them now to glower.

"Cedric, you mustn't let him chew on your boots. You're spoiling him." She lunged for Forrest. The King Charles spaniel froze, as he always did when Anne got frustrated with his mischievous antics. After she snapped up the boot, the spell was broken and the dog ran in a wild scamper for her ankles, nipping playfully. Before he could damage her skirt, he tripped over his own paws and rolled onto his back, his pink tongue sticking out.

Audrey giggled. "Bit of a rogue himself, isn't he?"

Cedric couldn't help but beam at her. She'd come home from Europe early, only two weeks after their escape from Al Zahrani's ship. It was as though she'd known he needed her, because she and Lady Rochester had arrived before anyone from the League had contacted them.

"Forrest is a scamp, kitten, not a rogue," Cedric clarified as he rose from the couch.

Despite Audrey's presence in the room, his wife walked up to him and curled her arms about his neck, kissing him fully on the mouth.

"How are you?" Anne asked.

He returned the kiss for a long moment before he replied.

"Like a better version of myself," he said, then smiled. "A *much* better version."

Anne pursed her lips. "As long as you remain wicked in one or two areas, I shan't complain." Her laugh made his body hum with desire. It was so good to see her smile. She had no idea how much he'd missed it.

"Are you ready to come see Sean? He needs another reprimand for trying to leave his bed," Anne said.

"Of course. I'm half-tempted to tie the man down to keep him there. Bloody fool."

Ashton and the others had thought Sean Hartley to be dead when they'd left Rushton Steading. Yet as Emily and Horatia had tended to what they thought were his final moments, the man had stubbornly clung to life. Stanching his wounds and making him comfortable, they had fetched the village doctor, who had once again worked a miracle.

Following Anne up the stairs, Cedric entered a guest bedroom. Sean was pale, but his eyes were clear and alert. One of the downstairs maids was spooning hot broth into his mouth. The maid jumped to her feet and curtsied as Cedric entered, her eyes downcast, cheeks flushed.

Cedric held up a hand. "Please, don't let me disturb you. Stay."

The maid sat down in the chair by the bed and resumed her task. Cedric leaned against one of the bedposts at the foot of the bed and scowled down at the willful young man.

"Now, listen here, Hartley. My wife says you're doing your damndest to get out of bed before you should."

Sean began to protest.

"Don't argue with me, lad. You won't win. I never officially terminated your employ here before, and I'll be damned if you make me do so now. It is my *order* as master of this house that you stay right there and let lovely ladies tend to your every need for as long as the doctor believes you need to stay in bed. Understood?" The maid blushed at that.

With a nod, Sean eased back onto the pillows of his bed. Cedric glanced at the women.

"I'd like a few minutes alone with him."

Anne and the maid quietly exited the bedchamber. Cedric took the empty chair by the bed.

"I owe you a debt, Hartley. You defended us more bravely and truer than any soldier. And you saved both our lives by telling Ashton what had happened. Those are debts I can never repay."

Cedric stood and made sure Sean was listening. "There are dark times ahead for me, for Anne and the League. We'll need a good man like you on our side. I'm depending on you to get better."

Sean swallowed and nodded. "Of course."

"Good. Now, if I were you, I'd let that pretty little maid serve you as long as you can manage it. She has an eye for you, I think." He winked at Sean and then left the room, chuckling at Sean's flustered expression. Anne and the maid were outside.

"Go on and tend to him," he said. The maid ducked back inside. Once he and Anne were alone, he pulled his wife into his arms, dipping her down low, as if in a dance, and kissed her senseless.

She touched her kiss-swollen lips, her dark lashes fluttering. "What was that for?"

He lifted her chin so she could see his expression.

"It took me far too long to realize what joy I had within reach." His mother's favorite hymn came to mind, and he knew she would approve. "I was blind, but now I see."

Anne's eyes shimmered. "And what do you see?" she asked.

"A long and wonderful life with you, my heart."

He bent his head down and kissed her, letting go of every dark memory tainted by pain. All that remained was an all-consuming feeling of love for Anne and the possibility of having everything he'd ever wanted in life.

And it all started with one passionate kiss to build their lives upon.

EPILOGUE

Daniel Sheffield rapped his knuckles on the door to Hugo Waverly's study.

"Enter."

Daniel nudged the door open and sauntered in. This was not going to be good news he delivered, and he hoped playing calm would help to lessen his master's rage.

They'd had a perfect plan. It shouldn't have gone awry. Once their man in Brighton had sent word Al Zahrani's ship had docked and he was making his move, Waverly had informed the Royal Navy and dispatched the HMS *Ranger* with orders to sink the ship to send a message to slave traders operating in English waters. No prisoners were to be taken under any circumstances.

What Daniel hadn't expected, and neither had Waverly, was Lord Lennox's timely interference.

"Well? Is it done?" Waverly looked up from his desk

covered in papers, most of them bearing royal seals.

"No. The HMS *Ranger* was intercepted by Lord Lennox's ship, which informed them of British subjects being held captive on the ship."

"Lennox?" Hugo crumpled the sheet of paper under his hand.

"Yes, sir. A fire was set by someone on board Al Zahrani's ship and it sank. Now it's at the bottom of the sea, as you'd hoped, but Sheridan and his wife survived." Daniel kept one hand still resting on the latch of the door in case he needed to make a hasty exit.

Waverly sat back in his chair and frowned.

"That man is like a bloody cat with nine lives."

Daniel waited for the fury to spark in Waverly's eyes, or for the man to shout or throw something. Such displays of temper had happened in the past.

"The *Ranger* did recover this floating among the wreckage, however." He revealed the item he'd been hiding behind his back. A cane with a silver lion's head.

When he held it out to Waverly, the man's grim expression turned to a hard smile.

"Well now," he chuckled. "My property has finally been returned to me."

Daniel retreated back to the door of Waverly's study.

"I've been to the White House in Soho and handled the matter regarding the individuals that Al Zahrani sold."

Waverly steepled his fingers together. "And you made it clear that we don't hold for that manner of trade here?"

"Yes. They tried to claim the women were simply *employed* by the house. I made sure they understood how mistaken they were. They won't be purchasing anything of that sort anytime soon. But I learned one female was auctioned off before I arrived."

"Just one? I commend you on your speed."

"I believe you will be even more interested to learn who purchased her." This was the one bit of good news Daniel had. "Lawrence Russell."

For the first time in a long while Waverly smiled. "Well, that's certainly interesting. A Russell buying a slave? Look into it, but do not act. I do believe that's a card we shall hold until it's time to play it."

Waverly gazed out the window to the back of the garden of his townhouse. Lady Waverly was sitting in the garden with another woman, chatting idly while a nurse held a tiny boy's hand. The lad walked on chubby legs, clutching his nurse's fingers as they navigated the garden's gravel path. Waverly's son, Heath, barely a year old.

He had his father's dark hair, but his mother's delicate features, which would likely make him grow into a handsome buck someday. Daniel flinched when he realized Waverly was now watching Daniel rather than the boy.

"Forget Sheridan for now. Lennox's shipping affairs have become increasingly inconvenient. What is he currently up to? What does our man inside have to report?"

Daniel stood to attention and focused back on

Waverly.

"He says Lennox is quarreling with a Lady Melbourne. It seems she is intruding upon his business in the shipping lines. She's buying contracts out from under him and generally running amok over Lennox's carefully structured empire."

Waverly smiled again. "Excellent. Lady Melbourne? I haven't had the pleasure of meeting her. I want you to find out everything you can about this woman. If she can be manipulated into crippling Lennox, I want to know how. Enemies of the League are my welcomed allies."

"Yes, sir." Daniel paused just outside the door when Waverly spoke again.

"Bring me the chess pieces, Sheffield, and I'll put Lennox in a checkmate he cannot escape."

Thanks for reading *Her Wicked Proposal*. I hope you enjoyed it! Be sure to follow me for new releases at one of these places:
NEWSLETTER
BOOKBUB

DYING TO KNOW WHAT HAPPENS WITH ASHTON AND the Scottish business woman who thwarts him at every turn? This sensual enemies to lovers romance

will have you swooning! Turn the page to read the first three chapters or **GRAB IT NOW HERE!**

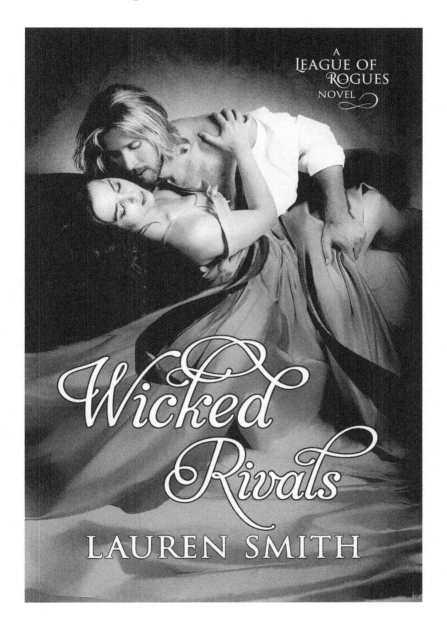

CHAPTER 1

L eague Rule Number 8:
    As a man's independence is inextricably tied
    to his wealth, it is vital that no woman should
be allowed to meddle with it, no matter how fine her eyes
might be.

EXCERPT FROM THE *QUIZZING GLASS GAZETTE*, MAY 29, 1821, the Lady Society column:

LADY SOCIETY IS ISSUING A CHALLENGE TO LORD LENNOX. She can't help but think he is afraid of a certain lady who is in direct competition with him.

Come now, Lord Lennox, what holds you in such fear and trepidation that you cannot be seen with her in public? At Lady

439

Jacintha's ball you turned tail and fled when the cunning lady stepped out onto the dance floor.

You cannot hide forever behind your fleet of ships, nor can you call upon your friends for support. The League of Rogues are fast succumbing to the charms of Eros and taking wives. Perhaps they know something you choose to remain ignorant of? For a man of such intellect and acumen, surely you cannot let that stand.

I challenge you, my cool, collected baron, to spend one night with the lady and be on your best behavior. Wedding bells, dare I say, shall ring shortly thereafter.

"YOU WANT ME TO DO WHAT, MY LORD?"

Ashton Lennox stared at the gray-haired banker sitting across from him in the offices of Drummond's Bank. He knew what he was asking of the other man was daring—and quite possibly illegal. Nonetheless, retaliation was required against certain players in his field of business. That didn't mean his demands wouldn't frighten any banker with good sense.

"It's as simple as I said, Mr. Reed. I want you to deny Lady Melbourne gold credit if she should come to you seeking a loan." As he spoke, he let his words come out in that cold, smooth voice that brooked no argument, and he finished by brushing his fingertips over his trousers, smoothing them out. By the age of thirty-three, Ashton had learned how to make men do his bidding with a cool stare and an imperious tone. Those who crossed him or dared to go against his wishes often ended up suffering a blow to their financial positions.

"But, my lord," Mr. Reed said, his eyes as wide as teacup saucers, "she's always been a valued client here—"

"I've no doubt of it, but you and I have an understanding, do we not?" Despite his tone, it was not a question. Ashton met Reed's now frightened gaze. "It was I, as you'll recall, who assisted you in selecting the consols to invest in last year. You were able to buy a country house in Sussex with the profits you made, were you not? I would think you'd like to keep my counsel on future matters."

The old banker's throat worked, and he managed a shaky nod.

"I am grateful, of course, but with regard to the lady in question, she is..." He struggled for words.

"Troublesome?" Ashton supplied, the word escaping on a growl as his cool demeanor threatened to unravel whenever he thought of *her*.

Lady Rosalind Melbourne was more than just troublesome. As owner of Melbourne, Shelly & Company, she'd spent the last several months stealing bids on shipping lines and purchasing other companies by underbidding him.

The woman was a menace. He'd done everything a reasonable man could do by offering to buy out her shares and attempting to go about his own business, but she'd undermined his every effort—or more to the point, every *legal* effort. Had she been a man, he would have admired her tactics, the way she outflanked him, outmaneuvered him at every turn.

But she wasn't a man, she was a woman—an intoxicating, beautiful, *infuriating* menace of a woman, with a fiery Scottish temper that pushed him out of his own control.

The situation was not acceptable. Control was his foremost weapon and his first line of defense. Where other men lost their bodies to passions, their minds to obsessions and their hearts to love, he always stayed in control of himself.

Except when it came to Rosalind. If she hadn't been a woman, he would have called her out long ago and settled their differences on a field at dawn. It took a moment for him to regain his focus on the matter at hand.

"Are we in agreement, Mr. Reed? You will do as I've asked?"

Ashton rose from his chair and towered over the banker.

Swallowing hard, the older man nodded. "We will, Lord Lennox. Lady Melbourne will find her requests for credit denied until you direct me to do otherwise."

Ashton inclined his head in approval and left Reed's office. He straightened his cravat and retrieved his hat from the rack in the corner outside the office. Once at the front entrance of Drummond's, he hailed a hackney.

"Where to, my lord?" the driver asked.

"Berkley's Club." Ashton climbed inside the coach and leaned back with a sigh.

"Very good, my lord."

After this morning, an afternoon at Berkley's was exactly what was needed. He didn't enjoy using such drastic measures, but there was more at stake here than professional pride. Lady Melbourne's companies were being used by the only man in England who worried Ashton enough to make him lose sleep at night.

Sir Hugo Waverly had been seen visiting with the captains of Lady Melbourne's ships, and his men, or men whom Ashton suspected worked for Waverly, had been on her passenger lists more and more frequently. He suspected Waverly was using Rosalind's companies somehow. It was unclear what Waverly was up to, but Ashton believed it wasn't good.

There was a secret war going on, one fought not with guns or swords but with eyes and words, and not on open plains but in the shadows. Hugo had declared this war some time ago, and Ashton had been mustering a defense in his own silent way. It was in the best interest of the League to take control of the situation, which at the moment meant taking control of Lady Melbourne's companies so that he could analyze her business activities and see how Waverly might be linked to them.

Ashton had visited five banks in the city this morning and had secured promises from each that Lady Melbourne would not be able to obtain credit. That way, when his friends called in their notes at each bank, she would not have the means to pay for their notes in gold.

It would crush her. At least temporarily. The woman would not be down for long; Ashton wasn't foolish enough to believe he could ruin her. But a temporary blow to her income and self-sufficiency would be enough .to bring her to heel.

Lady Melbourne brought to heel. A delicious thought indeed. *I will own you, Rosalind.*

Unable to stop himself, he thought back to the night when he'd caught her alone in an alcove of a theater. The intention had been to talk with her, convince her to leave his companies alone, but then he'd touched her and that plan had vanished, and something more primal had emerged.

He'd tried to use her body's response to his against her by bringing her to the brink of passion, only to let her suffer without relief as a reprimand for her unorthodox business tactics. It had been a foolish indulgence, yet in that moment he had been unable to help himself.

It also hadn't worked.

Instead, she'd turned the tables on him, and he'd come undone with the tight stroke of her hands. The memory of seeing her drop one dainty white glove at his feet, in a manner befitting a challenge to a duel, still made him hard. A duel of wits fought with seductive means... It was just how he liked to play his games. And now he'd met a woman who played as wickedly as he did.

Moves and countermoves, like a game of chess.

Grudging admiration for her was impossible to deny, but he was determined not to let her win.

The coach rattled to a stop in front of the elegant townhouse that had been the home of Berkley's Club for more than fifty years. Berkley's had not been the only gentlemen's club Ashton had gained an invitation to, though it had been the only one he'd accepted. It had appealed to him, for those moments when he wanted to escape business discussions, political issues, and other things most clubs were famous for. Berkley's was strictly a club for men who wished to escape the whirlwind of life in London.

The club was also the only place where he and his closest friends—the League of Rogues, as the papers had dubbed them—could settle in comfortably, away from the scandal rags and the gossip of that damned Lady Society. Her articles in the *Quizzing Glass Gazette* seemed determined to out their secrets for the amusement of London's elite. She'd been the one to make their nickname so famous over the last few years.

Ashton would readily admit that the League's title had always been an apt description of the original five members: Godric, Lucien, Cedric, Charles and himself. With the addition of Godric's recently discovered younger brother, Jonathan, they were now six.

Over the years, some of their activities had been ruthless, callous and even dangerous. But things were changing. The dark memories of the past were being buried by new ones, better ones. At least in some ways. They were settling down—a thing Ashton had never thought possible.

It had all started when Godric had abducted a young woman for revenge only to fall in love with her. Now, like ivory domino tiles, they were all falling one by one for women they could not live without. Lucien, one of the more scandalous rogues, had fallen for Cedric's sister, Horatia. And just last month Cedric had surprised everyone by proposing to Anne Chessley, the heiress.

Ashton had realized with some alarm that the League now stood equally divided between free men and those leg-shackled in matrimony. Their afternoon club discussions had changed from topics of seductions and conquests to the upcoming births of babes.

If we aren't careful, the League will change from a force to be reckoned with to a laughingstock. The power we've collected could be squandered, and our enemies will close ranks and try again to destroy us.

The thought made his blood freeze in his veins. The past year had been spent dodging one deadly event or another. The more the League let itself become divided by wives and children, the easier it would be for Waverly to harm the people the League loved the most.

It wasn't that he didn't wish well for his friends. They were happily, madly in love with their wives. But the power they'd all worked hard to attain since leaving university could crumble. New giants would arise from the dust of their fall and new enemies as well. Ashton could not rest until he was certain they were all safe.

Until then he slept with one eye open, and such a duty weighed upon him more and more each day. As the oldest of the members, he felt obligated to be the League's protector.

The cab halted at the entrance to the club. "Berkley's Club," the driver announced.

"Thank you." Ashton stepped out of the cab and paid the driver before walking up the steps. A young lad finely dressed in a Berkley's uniform opened the door for him. Ashton handed the lad his coat and hat.

"Looking for anyone in particular, my lord?"

Ashton tugged on his waistcoat. "Essex, Rochester or Sheridan." He waited to see if any of the titles registered with the boy.

The footman's face lit up into an almost reverent expression. "Of course. They are having drinks in the Bombay Room. Do you know the way, my lord?"

"Yes, thank you." He wandered through the club, passing tables and chairs of men drinking, talking and quietly enjoying a respite from the demands of society. The warm armchairs were welcoming by the fires burning in the hearths, and the smell of food and brandy teased his nose. Berkley's was like a second home.

The Bombay Room had Indian-themed décor and was located on an upper floor. The door was already ajar, and the sound of familiar voices inside filled him with warmth.

He allowed few things to matter deeply to him, but the League, aside from his family, was the most important thing in his life.

The first thing Ashton heard as he pushed open the door was Cedric Sheridan's chortling.

"Ash will be furious. Lady Society is calling him out." The viscount was leaning back in his chair, holding a copy of the *Quizzing Glass*, grinning.

"Again?" the others asked.

"It's a good thing whoever writes that column remains anonymous. Ash would destroy her."

"Nothing ruffles Ash. He's far too clearheaded." Godric St. Laurent, the Duke of Essex, reached for the paper and scanned it. "Wait until Emily reads this. She is convinced that Ash and Lady Melbourne need to meet in a proper setting where they are forced to be civil."

Lucien Russell, the Marquess of Rochester, stood by the window and turned at Godric's words. "That's all Horatia has been talking about for the last month. She said Anne invited them to tea with Lady Melbourne this afternoon."

Ashton stood in the doorway, listening to the three married members of the League discuss their wives with lighthearted amusement. He burst out laughing, startling his friends, who hadn't been aware of his presence. "Good Lord, you let your wives meet for tea?"

Lucien was the first to respond. "You know how much trouble it is to try to stop them. If I ever said no, Horatia would throw an embroidered pillow at my head. Followed by a vase."

"They are as bonded to one another as we are, I'm afraid," said Godric. "Even gave themselves that blasted name. The Society of..." He trailed off, forgetting.

Lucien moved his hands in the air, as though displaying the name in the air. "*The Society of Rebellious Ladies.*"

"Quite." Cedric chuckled and put his booted feet up on the nearest table. "So long as Audrey isn't among them, they can't get into too much trouble."

Ashton wasn't entirely certain he agreed with that. Audrey Sheridan was Cedric's youngest sister, and while she was trouble enough, Ashton knew the other ladies were almost as talented at getting into mischief.

"Ash, have a look." Godric handed the *Gazette* to him as Ashton took a chair next to him.

He glanced down at the article they'd been discussing when he arrived. His temper soon flared.

"*Hiding* behind my fleet of ships, am I?" The growl that escaped him was completely unexpected. Struggling for calm, Ashton closed his eyes and counted to ten in Latin as he'd done all his life when quelling his temper. When he opened his eyes again, he was smiling. It mattered naught. His plan was set in motion, and soon Rosalind would be dealt with.

"Well, she does have it right about you three." He checked the article again to recite the exact words. "'Succumbing to the charms of Eros and taking wives.'"

Godric plucked the paper from Ashton's hands. "I wish I knew who wrote this drivel. Probably some old bat on Upper Wimpole Street who can't find a proper way into the *ton*, exercising her vengeance for not being among the elite few." His slightly sarcastic tone hinted at his dislike of his own class.

Lucien swirled his glass of brandy and left his position by the window to take an empty chair by Cedric. Inspiration seemed to strike him.

"Why don't we put our darling wives on it? It would certainly keep them busy and out of our affairs for a change if they were off solving a mystery."

Cedric laughed. "I dare say they might even learn who she is, but there is no way Emily, Anne or Horatia would betray one of their own. And as hard as we try, there's no stopping them when it comes to our affairs."

Ashton nodded his agreement. But the problem that lay heavy upon his heart was the danger that one part of the League's past presented to the women in their lives.

As if echoing Ashton's trepidation, Godric crossed his arms, a grim look in his green eyes. "That reminds me, where do we stand on the Waverly matter?"

Ashton was seized with tension, every muscle knotting. Waverly always drew out dark memories and old fears, along with a tide of guilt.

There was a time that Hugo was merely an annoying privileged sod they'd met at Cambridge. But due to an old family vendetta, Waverly had attempted to kill their friend Charles, but another student had died that night instead. One who had been blameless and only trying to make peace. It was a moment that had changed all their lives.

Ashton's palms twitched, as though he could feel the taint of that innocent man's blood still coating his hands.

"He's been seen at the docks where my fleet is, but I haven't been able to ascertain what his intentions are at present. I suggest we all watch one another until Waverly's next scheme reveals itself."

Godric tried to hold back a scowl but failed. Patience had never been one of his virtues when he felt action could be taken.

Ashton reached into his waistcoat and pulled out a small pocket watch on a slender silver chain. It had been one hour since he'd given his instructions to the last of the banks regarding Rosalind's credit. In less than half an hour, the men he'd met with would be sending in notices to Rosalind's bank to demand their notes be cashed in for gold. The little Scottish hellion would pay for embarrassing him at the theater last month.

If only I could see her face the moment she realizes she's ruined.

Of course, he wasn't so cruel as to send her to debtors' prison. The woman would get her fortune back in time, after he learned what secrets Hugo held within her business, after she learned he was not to be trifled with. Lady Melbourne deserved such a lesson for challenging him.

"Good God, Ash is grinning. That's never a good sign," Lucien muttered.

Ashton broke out of the almost gleeful thoughts he'd been having.

"Ash." Godric's tone was full of warning. "Care to share with us what is going on in that head of yours?"

Cedric, Lucien and Godric all leaned forward, as though afraid to be overheard despite the privacy of the club's Bombay Room. The grandfather clock in the corner chimed the hour, but it did not distract his friends' rapt attention.

Ashton slipped his watch back into his coat pocket and met their stares.

"As of one hour ago, I set a plan in motion that will financially break Lady Melbourne. It will allow me to put a stop to her activities and therefore hurt Waverly."

"She's in league with him?" asked Cedric.

"All I know for certain is that he's been using her ships to his own ends, and I want to stop him. He's partnered with her in several companies, and I wish to gain access to her books as well as shipping manifests. But the only way I can review her companies is to have a claim on them myself. Therefore, I've bought up most of her debts—not that she had many. I will own her in all but name."

A low whistle escaped Cedric's lips. "Ash, our wives have invited her to tea this afternoon."

For the first time in a long while, Ashton felt gleeful. "If only I were there to see her face when she learns the truth." To see her beautiful gray eyes wide with shock, her lips parted as she sucked in a surprised breath... It would be almost as beautiful as having claimed her body in his bed. But since he could not have her body—one did not sleep with one's enemies, after all—this would have to suffice.

It was several moments later when his friends finally broke the silence.

"It's not because of the incident at the theater is it?" Lucien queried. "You're wanting revenge because she got the upper hand in that alcove?" Cedric snickered, and Godric cursed under his breath. It was not the response Ashton had been expecting. In the past, this would have been normal for the League. They would have been congratulating him for such a victory.

"What?" Ash demanded hotly when the others remained silent.

Godric rubbed a hand through his dark hair. "What if Lady Melbourne takes this too personally and brings those wild brothers of hers down from Scotland? I still have nightmares about the last time I tangled with them. One of them broke a bloody chair over my back. I was left to pay for the damages to the tavern we fought in."

"Three wild Scotsmen do not scare me." Ashton had never lost a boxing match, and he had never lost a tavern brawl either. While Charles was the group's true pugilist, Ashton's skill was on par with his, though he fought only when necessary.

"No, *one* should scare you," grumbled Godric. "Three should terrify you."

"Isn't anyone else worried that right now our wives are entertaining the victim of Ash's scheme?" Cedric asked. "If they discover we knew about this, I'm liable to be spending the next month sleeping in my study rather than in bed with my wife."

The murmurs of agreement from Godric and Lucien made Ashton scowl at the lot of them.

"I'm starting to believe Charles was right. You are all getting soft."

Charles had once said that love and marriage were tearing the League apart, destroying its strength. At the time Ashton hadn't been inclined to believe him, but of late...

A rap on the door made them all turn to the entrance of the Bombay Room. A young lad opened the door, his eyes wide and hands shaking a little with the letter he carried. Their reputation still held some in awe, at least.

"Excuse the intrusion, my lords. I have an urgent letter for Lord Lennox." The boy's face darted between them. He sensed he'd interrupted something and no doubt felt the invisible tension present in the room.

Ashton waved at the lad. "Bring it here."

The boy practically threw it at Ashton and fled.

"At least someone still has the good sense to be afraid of us," Godric sniggered.

The thin paper contained a short message from his youngest sister, Joanna.

ASHTON,

You must come home at once. Our two tenant farms caught fire last night and are completely destroyed. Thankfully no one was hurt. The families are safe but without shelter. Please come home. The farmhouses will need to be rebuilt at once.

Yours,

Joanna

ASHTON CALMLY FOLDED THE LETTER AND TUCKED IT into the inner pocket of his coat.

"Bad news?" Lucien inquired.

"It's from my sister. She says my two tenant farmers' houses burned down. I must go home at once." He rose from his chair.

"What about Lady Melbourne?" Cedric asked.

"What about her?"

Cedric raised a brow. "You set her up for financial ruin and now you're leaving London?"

A slow smile spread across his face. "If she decides to come grovel at my feet, please feel free to send her to my estate. I'll be happy to entertain her apologies there."

He swept his coat on and left the Bombay Room, leaving his friends behind.

If only it would come to that—Lady Melbourne on her knees, begging him for forgiveness, her gray eyes bright with pretty tears and her long dark hair swept back in a Grecian fashion. Those long curls caressing her neck…

Yes, Ashton had imagined the scene too often in the last week. How he'd tell Lady Melbourne that if she really wanted to appease him she could think of a few creative ways to make amends, behind closed doors. Not that he could trust her even in bed, and he'd certainly never coerce a woman to bed him, but such fantasies were worth exploring in his head.

Ashton departed Berkley's and hailed a hackney. He would have his valet pack light so they could reach his estate quickly. Joanna's note was troubling. While fires were common enough, the fact that both his tenants were miles apart was troubling.

I do not believe in such coincidences.

Once again he imagined a chessboard in his mind. A game was in play, the League versus Waverly, and the clock was ticking down to each move and countermove.

CHAPTER 2

Chapter Two
Hands sliding up her outer thighs, raising her gown, warm breaths soft against her cheek, bright blue eyes aflame with wicked desires and the fall of pale-blond hair...

"Lady Melbourne?"

Rosalind Melbourne came back to herself. She was sitting in a cozy armchair in a sunny parlor with blue walls. Three sets of feminine eyes were focused on her, all a little concerned. A moment ago, she'd been listening to her hostesses talk about the latest scandals and political intrigues when the conversation had turned to marriages and the men in their lives. It was only natural for her thoughts to turn to Ashton when his friends had been mentioned. And that had led to memories from the last time she'd seen him...at the opera...when they'd both lost control.

I should never have allowed that man to kiss me, nor should I have touched him. It was a mistake.

She reached for the cup of tea nearest her on the table. "I'm sorry. I was woolgathering."

"It's quite all right," Lady Sheridan said, smiling again. "We're so happy you've had a moment to meet with us."

Rosalind smiled back at her. Anne was one of the few women in the *ton* she tolerated. Most of the simpering fools did not particularly like her either. As a Scottish lady having come from a crumbling castle with three wild brothers, bless them all, she'd had no chance of ever fitting in with normal London society, even when she'd married Lord Melbourne, God rest his soul. The man had been in his sixties when he'd asked for her hand.

That day was never far from her mind. Whenever her brothers hadn't been around, she'd caught her father's attention, and he'd taken his anger out on her. On that last night she'd run from Castle Kincade, almost blind with pain. She'd walked nearly two miles barefoot to the nearest village. Her father's blows still burned her face and back.

She'd stumbled into a tavern in the village and fell into Lord Melbourne's lap when she'd tripped over a loose floorboard. He'd taken one look at her face and with a scowl had said, "No one should treat a lady thus."

He'd insisted on buying her dinner at the tavern. After

he'd seen that she was warm and fed and wearing a new pair of boots he'd bought from a barmaid, he'd taken her straight to a blacksmith and married her that night.

Poor Henry. Such a sweet man.

After her marriage to Henry, she'd moved into her new London home, and he had died in his sleep only a year later. It had been a long time coming, but now she was the mistress of her own destiny. The dear man had tutored her in the ways of business strategies and banking. She'd always had a natural knack for it, but he had helped foster in her a confidence and knowledge that left her strong and able to stand on her own after his death. His companies had become her empire and would remain hers unless she remarried. Under English law, it would then transfer to her new husband, and she would become property herself.

My life wouldn't be mine ever again.

She had no intention of letting that happen. Being a powerful widow was preferable to being a married slave.

"Lady Melbourne, I understand you have a number of shipping companies?" the Duchess of Essex queried before sipping her tea.

The duchess, who had insisted on being called Emily, was a lovely creature with violet eyes, auburn hair and a smile full of mischief and cunning.

"Yes, that is correct," Rosalind replied. "I took over my late husband's company and have been growing it by acquiring other shipping lines as they go on the market. Sea trade can be a risky endeavor, but it has proved fruitful so far." She smiled a little, happy to be talking about business. It was one of her joys in life, the pursuit of companies, the acquisitions, the shipping. The mental challenges of running the companies that formed her fortune had always been vastly rewarding.

The other two ladies, Anne, Viscountess Sheridan, and Lady Rochester, who insisted on being called Horatia, exchanged glances. Rosalind wasn't daft. The three women had been doing this from the moment she'd come inside the Sheridan household for tea. She suspected they'd invited her to Curzon Street for some purpose, and she wished they would simply come out and ask her whatever it was they were interested in.

"Do you do any business with Lord Lennox?" Horatia asked. Her cheeks had gone pink, betraying the direction Rosalind had feared the conversation was headed. Given their husbands' close friendships with Lennox, she had been expecting this.

Rosalind sighed. "Lord Lennox..." The infernal baron had an uncanny way of coming up. It was he who had been on her mind moments ago. The man who'd ruthlessly kissed her in a theater alcove. He'd been out to punish her for her interference with his business, but that chastisement had turned to an attempt at passion, no doubt with the intent of leaving her alone and longing for him.

She had to fight hard to contain the little smile at that particular memory. She'd seen through his ploy and turned it against him, and he'd been defenseless against her. She remembered dropping her glove at his feet, a parting challenge before she'd left him to handle the problem of his stained trousers.

Lennox would no doubt be planning something to obtain his revenge; his ego would not allow otherwise. But these ladies were married to friends of his, so she would need to answer carefully.

"Well, our business interests, while shared, tend to put us in direct competition." She hesitated to say more. It was possible that anything she told these three women would make its way back to him through their husbands. The secret behind her success came from the subtle balance of obtaining information from others and keeping it away from indiscreet ears.

On more than one occasion, she'd come across the jilted lovers left in Ashton's wake—widows, daughters or unhappy wives of those he was in competition with. They had provided him with information over the course of an evening, often in bed, and he had used it to his advantage.

But he had also left a fair number of women who were willing to talk about *him* and his tactics as well. Rosalind had used that information to her own advantage and had been able to track his movements and strategies, even anticipate his business goals and outsmart him on more than one occasion.

Emily nudged Horatia's elbow. Horatia spoke up.

"I'm sure you must think we are spies on behalf of our husbands, but I assure you that is not the case." Horatia set her teacup down. "The reason we are asking is to protect you, if we can."

"Protect me?" Rosalind set her own cup down, a flicker of unease darting through her like a startled rabbit in the underbrush. "Whatever from?"

Emily cleared her throat. "What we mean to say is that we know Lord Lennox. We know what he's capable of when he's in a mood, that is. All of us admire your courage and your ability to compete among the men. And we don't want Ashton, that is, Lord Lennox, to upset you simply because he has his trousers twisted. I adore the man, but like the rest, he can become harsh in his business matters where his pride is pricked. We only wish to protect you, Lady Melbourne. We ladies must stick together."

"Well..." What did one say to that? Rosalind plucked at her rose-colored day gown and glanced away, feeling a tad awkward.

"Have you any way to know if your finances are protected?" Anne asked quietly. "Cedric, that is to say, my husband, once said Ashton will challenge a man by dealing a blow to his banking abilities, such as his credit and his debts."

Rosalind felt her stomach drop out. These ladies were serious about Lennox. And she'd certainly pricked the man's pride. She'd bought three companies out from under him in the last month and had wooed old trading partners of his to her lines. But surely he wouldn't do something so drastic. But she had taken out credit lines to buy the last few companies, and her own bank was light in gold if any of her notes came due at this moment.

"But surely he wouldn't..." She went over the numbers and scenarios in her head. She saw it. A vulnerability. What if...?

Suddenly the room was too hot, too closed. She needed air.

"Quick, Anne, open a window!" Horatia gasped.

Rosalind rushed from her seat following Anne, who opened a window facing the back gardens. She leaned against the sill, her hands digging into the wood as she sucked in the fresh spring air.

"There, there," Anne soothed. "Breathe and you'll be fine."

Rosalind wished it were so simple. But if Lennox was setting that plan in motion, she would have little chance of stopping him, unless she could get to the banks and ask for more credit to cover the gold cash-outs. But that wouldn't solve her debt problem if he bought the debts. She would then still owe him everything.

"What can we do to help?" Horatia asked.

It took several long moments for Rosalind to recover. Her stays were too tight, and dizziness swamped her.

"I'm afraid I must go—" If she could get out in front of this, she might survive.

"Of course," Emily replied. "Would you like someone to go with you?"

"No!" Rosalind gasped, then recovered herself. "I

mean, no thank you, Your Grace. I'm afraid it would not do to have you walk into a bank with me. They act poorly enough when I go in—I should not like to see how they react to a duchess."

Emily grinned, her violet eyes twinkling. "Nonsense. I have no qualms about scandals. You forget who I am married to. Scandal is nothing new to me."

Rosalind debated her options. She wasn't all that fond of accepting help, but something about Emily was reassuring. Neither she nor Horatia nor Anne seemed to be the sort of women who allowed men to control them, not even their husbands.

"Well, if you wouldn't mind." She finally sighed and rubbed her temples.

"Not at all." Emily shared another of those secretive glances with Anne and Horatia.

"Might I ask, why are you helping me, Your Grace?" Rosalind closed the window facing the garden and focused on the three women. "I cannot help but notice you keep looking at each other."

Horatia blushed. "We've all had to put up with men in the past when they've caused trouble. We wish to help you, and we know Ashton can do great harm to your business."

"I'll ring for my coach." Emily rose from her chair and pulled a slender cord on the door.

HALF AN HOUR LATER THE COACH BEARING THE ESSEX coat of arms rattled to a stop outside Drummond's Bank. It was the bank where Rosalind kept the majority of her lines of credit.

Rosalind and Emily climbed out of the coach and proceeded toward the bank, ignoring the stares of men and women on the street. It had amazed Rosalind to learn on the ride over that Emily was a skilled businesswoman herself. She'd handled her uncle's accounts, then taken over her husband's once she married. Through the course of the conversation, Emily had told her a fantastical tale of abduction, intrigue and eventually love, which had resulted in her marriage to the Duke of Essex. The local papers had certainly not given any of *those* details.

As they reached the door to the bank, Rosalind drew them up short. "Are you positive you wish to go in with me? There will be talk—more than talk—if you do."

With a chuckle, Emily replied, "It's been quite some time since I've been considered scandalous, so it's time to dive back into the gossip, I think."

If Rosalind's nerves hadn't been so raw, she would have laughed with her.

The inside of the bank was filled with men of business and members of the peerage, talking, perusing papers and making business deals. A collective hush filled the room when she and the duchess entered. Women were not supposed to enter such a realm without a gentleman escorting them. It was something she'd gotten used to, the quelling gazes of men who wished to intimidate her into leaving. But she never gave in. There was nothing any of them could do to her. After living most of her life at the hands of an abusive father, she was done letting men dictate her life.

"Is it always like this?" Emily leaned in to whisper. "The way they stare at you?"

Rosalind answered with a faint nod.

Suddenly a tall, dark-haired man with honey-brown eyes stepped out of the crowd and approached them. Rosalind recognized the gentleman. She had half feared that Emily's husband or one of the other so-called Rogues would be here to intercept her, but this man was not one of their number, though he was an acquaintance of theirs.

"Your Grace." His smile dispelled some of the tension around them. There were still a few grumblings, but the majority of the men returned to their previous conversations.

"Lord Pembroke! How lovely to see you," Emily greeted the man and turned to Rosalind. "Lord Pembroke, this is Lady Melbourne."

Pembroke bowed over her hand and pressed his lips to her knuckles. "A pleasure. What brings you ladies to Drummond's?" Pembroke's eyes darted around them, but he did not seem entirely surprised at their being in such a bastion of masculine activity.

"We're resolving an issue," Emily said. "Rosalind, who is it we need to see?"

"Mr. Reed."

"Very well." Pembroke offered an arm to Emily and she took it, winking at Rosalind while he escorted them to Mr. Reed's office.

The banker was settled at his writing table, poring over several letters. He glanced up and froze when he saw Rosalind, Emily and the Earl of Pembroke in his doorway.

"Lady Melbourne?" Her name escaped the banker in a stutter.

"Mr. Reed." She took a seat in front of him and studied the older man closely. His skin had taken on a white pallor, and he began to shuffle all manner of papers and items on his table. This did not bode well.

"What may I do for you?" Mr. Reed asked as he slid a finger beneath his neckcloth and tugged on it.

"I wanted to see about extending my line of credit."

"Your credit..." Mr. Reed swallowed and smiled a little, but the expression was forced.

"Yes, I have several notes out, and I am afraid they may be called in." She hesitated when Mr. Reed's glance darted away and then back.

"Lady Melbourne, I do regret to tell you this, but I cannot extend any further lines of credit."

Knots formed in Rosalind's stomach. She leaned forward in her seat. "Why not? Do you need more collateral?"

Mr. Reed shook his head. "I cannot extend your credit under any circumstances."

"Why is that?" Lord Pembroke demanded.

Rosalind saw he had remained with her and Emily. He was now scowling as he leaned against the door frame to Mr. Reed's office.

"Well, it's bank policy to make decisions that protect our stability and—"

"Mr. Reed," Emily cut in gently, though Rosalind caught a hard glint in the young woman's eyes. "You have a daughter coming out this year, do you not?"

"Why, yes. Amelia. My youngest." Mr. Reed sighed and dropped his head a few inches.

"She's a lovely girl, I recall," Emily continued. "And she could make a good match if she had help, say if a *duchess* sponsored her?"

Rosalind blinked. Was Emily actually offering herself as a sponsor to the banker's daughter?

Mr. Reed's face lit up. "Why, that would be wonderful."

Emily raised a gloved hand. "It would be an honor to sponsor her, but I'm afraid that I simply could not do it unless I trusted you, Mr. Reed, in *all* things."

The banker stared at Emily for a long moment. "You would help Amelia find a good man, with say ten thousand pounds a year?"

Emily's smile grew. "I have quite a few suitable candidates in mind already."

When Mr. Reed spoke again, his voice was low and he leaned close. "You must not tell him that I betrayed his confidence."

"We shall not. Now, *who* has told you not to allow any credit extensions? I assume someone ordered that, correct?"

"Lord Lennox."

It was the name Rosalind had dreaded to hear. Hearing her worries confirmed sent spirals of panic through her. So Lennox was finally making his play, after a month of letting her believe she was safe following that night in the theater.

"Thank you, Mr. Reed." Emily glanced toward Rosalind.

Pembroke looked horrified. "Wait a minute. Lennox is trying to stop you from obtaining credit? Whatever for? I know him. He's a ruthless man of business, but not to ladies."

With a mirthless laugh, Rosalind fisted her hands in her skirts. "It seems I am to be the exception." *How fortunate am I?* Her inner voice was a tad impolite, but who could blame her? Lennox had her back against a wall, and she wasn't handling it very well.

"Lady Melbourne, I was advised *not* to give you details. However," Reed said, glancing at Emily again, "I've been informed he also bought the debts you have and will be sending demand payments through proxies this afternoon."

Rosalind sank in her seat. That was far worse than the gold demands she'd been expecting, but it was oh so clever as well. A personal touch, to let her know exactly who had bested her.

"Why that pompous, bloody bastard!" The curse did not come from Rosalind, but Emily. "Just *wait* until I get my hands on him. He's supposed to be the most gentlemanly of the League. *Ooh!*" Emily's hands were curled into fists, and anger sparked in her eyes.

Pembroke growled and looked at the two ladies. "That is indeed a very low thing to do. If you give me the nod, I'll have half the *ton* give him the cut direct by this evening, and he'll be tossed out of his club."

"Thank you, James, but that won't be necessary. I've a better plan in mind to deal with our misbehaving friend."

Rosalind laid a hand on the duchess. "Please, Emily, you need not get involved—"

"Nonsense. That is *precisely* what I must do. But first, we have to get you home, Rosalind."

"But I need to handle the notes—"

Emily smoothed out her skirts. "Let me see to that. You must handle Ashton."

"How on earth do you suggest I do that?" She had her own ideas, of course. Strangulation being at the top of her list. But she was also curious as to what Emily might say.

"You are rivals, correct?" Emily asked.

"Yes." Lord help her if they were rivals in anything besides business.

"And how would you handle a business rival?"

Finally Rosalind felt like smiling. "By finding his weakness. Breaking him down from the inside."

"And do you know any weakness you might exploit?"

Her thoughts went back to the theater. One heated encounter in that alcove and he'd lost his control, but she'd kept hers. She'd won.

And I can win again.

Emily clapped her hands at the sight of Rosalind's cunning smile. "See, you have the right of it. I'm certain you can use that to your advantage. Now let's get you home so you can change into something more suitable for seduction."

The banker sputtered in shock, and Pembroke covered a laugh with a polite cough. "Allow me to escort you ladies to your coach." Pembroke nodded his goodbye to Reed.

"Thank you, Lord Pembroke," Rosalind said, but her mind was still reeling.

Seduction? She hadn't necessarily thought of that sort of plan, but there was logic to it. If it could get her back what was hers, her life, her independence, then she would play him like a fiddle if she must. But she'd only ever been with one man before, her late husband. Sweet and gentle in bed he had been, but his touch had never *burned* the way Ashton's had, nor had her entire body felt as though it was on the edge of something dark and wild when they had kissed.

But she detested Lennox. He knew just how to prod her until her barely leashed temper snapped. How was a woman to enjoy herself in bed when she wanted to strangle the man with his own bedsheets? Was he even *capable* of being seduced? She doubted he ever let himself be free enough to fall completely for a seduction, but what else could she try?

By the time she finally parted ways with Emily and Lord Pembroke, she had become thoroughly agitated. No, that was not nearly a strong enough word, but the words that came to mind were most unladylike.

As she reached the front door of her townhouse, her butler was there, anxiously holding out a letter.

"What is it, Pevensly?" She took the letter from his shaking hands.

"A man under the employ of Lord Lennox delivered this. He told me you must read it immediately and that he would be back within the hour to see that the letter's instructions are followed."

With trepidation, Rosalind peeled off her gloves and broke the seal on the letter as she entered the hall. Pevensly close the door behind her.

The letter was written elegantly, and yet as she began to read, it felt more mocking with each stroke of the quill.

My dearest Lady Melbourne,

As I'm sure you are now aware, Drummond's Bank as well as every other bank within your immediate traveling distance has been given strict orders not to extend or offer you any additional credit. All of your notes will be cashed in by my proxies if I hear of you trying to buy them back.

Additionally, I have purchased all of your debts. At this moment, my accountants and solicitors are taking a full account of your affairs at your offices in London and Brighton. Your entire fate lies in my hands. The house you stand in at this very moment? Mine. The clothes upon your back? Also mine. I own you, Lady Melbourne, in all but name.

What does this mean? I am putting you on the street. Your servants may remain at the house and I will see to their continued employment, but you, my cunning rival, must seek home and hearth elsewhere until I decide what to do with you.

I own you.

CHAPTER 3

C hapter Three

I own you.

The words from Ashton's letter blurred as Rosalind struggled to breathe. No, he couldn't do this to her. Shock paralyzed her body, her muscles tensing painfully.

The past came rushing up from the depths where she had buried it, swallowing her in its icy waters, unable to stop the memories as they enveloped her.

The cold castle corridors, wind whistling through the faded, tattered tapestries. The booming shout of an angry father.

"You think you can tell me what to do? You little wretch! I own you, and you aren't worth the breath in your lungs!"

A cup of mead exploded against the wall where Rosalind, only sixteen, hid behind a half-opened door. The aching sorrow of her mother's recent death hung in the halls like an invisible cloud. It had sent her father over the edge.

"Rosalind," a deep voice chided from behind the hall. Rosalind jumped, but her older brother Brock steadied her. "Leave Father alone—he's been drinking."

The door crashed open as their father, Lord Kincade, launched himself at Rosalind.

He swung a balled fist at her, but Brock knocked the hand away.

"Oh! Think you're a man to take me on? No son of mine would dare!" He moved fast, too fast. The punch knocked Brock onto the floor. Rosalind too was hit, spiraling wildly as she bounced off the wall and fell beside Brock.

"Pieces of shite, the both of you! Not worth the clothes on your backs! I should sell you both for the uselessness you are to me." Their father snarled like a wild boar and stalked down the hallway, leaving them alone.

Tears leaked from her eyes as she reached for her aching jaw. It felt like it was broken. She knew it wasn't, but it hurt like the very devil.

A hand settled on her shoulder, causing her to flinch. "'Tis only me," Brock said gruffly, but there was a gentleness to his tone. It wasn't proper for a young lass to cry, but she couldn't stop. Living in fear of her father every day was chipping away at her soul.

"I can't do this anymore," she whispered. "He's going to kill me."

Her older brother was still no match for their father, but she knew he would keep taking blows for her. All of her brothers would.

"Rosalind, what are you talking about?" Brock cupped her chin, but she whimpered at the flash of pain and pulled away.

"I'm not staying. I have to get out of this house. Ever since Mother died, this hasn't been my home."

Her brother brushed the tears away from her cheeks, and his gray eyes, so like her own, were as silver as a waning moon up on the moors.

"Rosalind, this is your home. It will always be your home. And we shall protect you."

Rosalind believed him, but she was no fool. As the exact likeness of her mother, she could not stay here and continue to risk her father's wrath. She would have to leave one day. But she would need a way out, a place to land.

If only there was a man who could find in his heart to marry her, she might be able to escape. But who would want the broken daughter of the cruel Lord Kincade?

The past faded, leaving a bitter taste upon her lips and tiny thorns embedded in her heart.

This home was the one she'd made for herself, the one her late husband had let her run. It was her world, and that damned fool Lennox thought he had the right to take it all away from her? To cast her out?

She stared at the note and realized she hadn't finished reading it.

. . .

I AM NOT A CRUEL MAN. IF YOU WISH TO DISCUSS THE situation, you may join me at my estate. However, you may not take your coach as that too falls under my control now. I'm sure if you were to come to me, we could come to some arrangement that would benefit us both.

Lennox

"AN *ARRANGEMENT* THAT WOULD BENEFIT US BOTH?" SHE muttered. Anger and panic rippled through her, dueling for dominance. That damned bloody Englishman. She wanted to strangle him, but the truth of her situation was dire. He had full control over her and was toying with her the way a cat would a mouse. Something had to be done. Perhaps Emily's suggestion to seduce the man was indeed a good idea. Rosalind sensed an opportunity here. If Lennox desired her and believed she'd come to heel, she would prove just who was the one in control when she brought *him* under her command.

But she was taking her own coach, Lennox be damned!

I have to face him. Perhaps the duchess's advice about seduction wasn't so unreasonable after all.

"What is it, Your Ladyship?" Pevensly asked. His dark brows knit together in concern.

Rosalind stared at the address on the parchment, frowning, then handed it to him.

"You may read it, but please do not inform the rest of the staff—I don't wish them to worry. Would you please have my coach pulled around in an hour? I am going to sort this out. Rest assured I will come back. Please do not let the servants grow overly concerned." She left Pevensly gaping after her in the hall as she rushed up the stairs, calling for her lady's maid.

"Yes, Your Ladyship?" A woman not much older than her appeared through an open doorway at the top of the stairs.

"Pack my valise at once. The best clothes you can find. Don't bother with hats. I won't have space for the boxes."

Claire met her as they walked toward her room. "Is this about that man who came by earlier? Pevensly was near frantic when the man left. Seems he suggested you would not be happy when you returned from your errands this morning."

There was no point in hiding the truth from her. The woman's observations missed nothing; it was why she made an excellent maid.

"Lord Lennox has just tried to buy my life away through my debts. He's ordered me out of this house."

Claire raise a hand to her lips, but just as quickly that hand curled into a fist. "Surely you won't let that stand."

"I will not. I plan to travel to his estate at once to remedy this error."

Claire nodded. "Ah. Then I shall be accompanying you, of course."

"No, that won't be—"

"It will be," Claire insisted. "You're a *lady*. You must

have a maid accompany you, and none of the other girls know you as well as I do. I'll not lose my head in a time of panic."

That much was true. Claire was a mother hen who watched over the household, but the woman had a backbone of iron too.

"Very well, you alone may come. But be warned, the means I intend to use to regain my life are best kept private." She trusted her staff, but secrets were always easier when one did not have too many keepers. "Thank you, Claire. Pack as much as you can. We leave in an hour."

She left her maid to pack while she went to her study to write a few hasty letters. She had a number of business partners who would need to be apprised of the situation immediately. Rosalind could only pray that they would be forgiving given the dire situation. She knew Sir Hugo Waverly would be most understanding. He, more than anyone, was aware of her competitive history with Lennox. Indeed, he had fostered many ideas that had led her to triumph over Lennox in battles of bidding and company purchases.

She sorted through the letters on her desk and paused when she found a palm-sized package addressed to her. The ink on the return address was blurred from rainwater, but it seemed to be from Scotland. Her heart began to pound as she unfastened the twine and opened the parcel.

An object wrapped in a handkerchief fell into her

hands. She unbound the handkerchief and studied the object.

It was a pocket watch. Turning her attention to the handkerchief, she noticed an all-too-familiar letter K stitched into the corner. Kincade. Her father carried these. A lump grew in her throat at the thought. Had he finally discovered where she was? Had he known all along? Would he come for her and demand she return to Scotland with him?

She blinked back tears as she unfolded the cloth further, finding a single sheet of parchment tucked inside. A letter. She read it with shaking hands.

ROSALIND,

Keep this safe, keep it close. Take it home to Scotland. I've entrusted your brothers with a secret that even they do not understand. You may yet have the chance to undo the evils I have created in my life.

Montgomery

THE POCKET WATCH WAS A HEAVY GOLD PIECE WITH NO remarkable engravings upon it. She opened it to see a simple clock face, and it appeared to be broken. What sort of game was her father playing? Whatever it was, she had no desire to go along with it. She folded the watch up in the handkerchief and set it back in the parcel next to the letters. There wasn't time to worry about it now.

She hastily finished the letters to her business partners, and with a final curious glance at the package she left her study. She found Claire busy packing in her chambers.

"Would you see that the stack of letters in my study is also packed? I shall need to read them and respond as necessary while we are at Lord Lennox's estate."

"I'll see to it at once." Claire departed, and Rosalind sat down on her bed, her mind still racing as she decided what she was to do about Lennox. She would have to worry about her father and his enigmatic gift later.

⚜

JONATHAN ST. LAURENT STOOD AT THE ENTRYWAY OF A fashionable townhouse on Half Moon Street. The keys to the door felt heavy in his palm, and his heart gave a quick thump. The residence had once belonged to a baron, Lord Chessley, who had passed away in early April. His daughter, Anne, had married Jonathan's friend Cedric three weeks later.

"Scandal be damned," as Cedric had said. Since Cedric and Anne both resided in his London townhouse on Curzon Street, they'd had no use for a second house and had chosen to sell it.

Now Chessley House was his. He'd met with the butler and housekeeper, and it seemed the entire staff except for

Anne's lady's maid, who had agreed to stay on with him. Yet he felt strangely off balance being the one in charge of a household.

He'd spent his whole life as a servant of the Duke of Essex, only to discover that Godric was his half brother. After the late duchess had passed, Godric's father had secretly remarried his wife's lady's maid, and Jonathan had been the result of that union. The secret, but legitimate, son of a duke.

After that revelation his life had been turned upon its head. He was thrust into Godric's world and was even considered one of the League of Rogues. But now he was contemplating marriage and settling down.

He snorted. Perhaps not the settling down. The woman he was interested in was not at all tame, and she'd likely never settle down. But he'd wanted to at least have a home to offer her when he proposed.

"Sir." The butler emerged from the servants' quarters. "I did not know you'd be here today. Please come in and let me take your hat."

"Thank you." Jonathan handed his hat to the man. It was still strange to be a gentleman. He'd been a footman, a gardener, and a valet for the last ten years, and it was difficult to curb old habits, such as wanting to see to his own hat or shutting the door behind himself.

"How is the house? Do you and the rest of the staff have everything you need?" Jonathan asked.

"We're quite fine, sir. You received this note an hour

ago. I was just about to have it delivered to Lord Essex's townhouse."

A sealed letter was handed over, and Jonathan unfolded it. A familiar hand had scrawled a few lines.

JON,

Meet me at the Fives Court at two this afternoon. I'm of a mind to bloody a few noses in the ring. Should be good fun.

Charles

JONATHAN SNORTED. CHARLES. THE EARL OF LONSDALE was always up to something. Not that Jonathan was surprised. He'd grown up living on the fringes of the League's world and was well aware of the antics they got into. Now he was one of them.

He grinned. *Duty calls, I suppose.* It would be no hardship to join Charles to watch him box.

"Is there anything you need from me, sir?" the butler asked.

"Er...no, I'm going out again. I'm not sure if I'll be back for dinner, so don't let the cook worry about preparing anything. Cold cuts and a bit of wine will be fine when I return."

"Very good, sir."

Jonathan glanced at the clock by the base of the stairs.

Half past one. He needed to leave immediately. He waved off his hat when the butler held it out.

"No need for that where I'm going." He turned right back around and headed outside, relieved to see the hackney hadn't yet left.

"Are you still available?" he asked the driver.

"I am." The driver jerked the reins up, and the black mare stomped and chomped her bit in irritation.

Jonathan climbed up into the cab beside the driver, and the vehicle rocked precariously.

"Where to?"

"Fives Court on St. Martin's Lane in Leister Fields. You know it?"

The driver flashed him a grin and smacked the ribbons on his mare's flanks. "I do."

Jonathan then slipped into the hackney and it jolted forward.

By the time they'd reached Fives Court, the sounds of a wild crowd could be heard outside the old brick building that housed the boxing events. Nearly a thousand men could press into the building and surround the square sparring ring.

Jonathan hopped out of the cab and paid the driver before turning to face Fives Court.

"Three shillings!" a lad cried out at the entrance. "Just three shillings to watch the pets of fancy fight in the ring!"

Pets of fancy. Jonathan chuckled. Charles was no one's

pet and likely hated the nickname for the pugilists who fought there.

The little lad held out a grubby hand to him as Jonathan approached.

"There you are." He tossed the boy his three shillings.

"Thank you, sir. The fight just started."

"Oh? Who's up now?"

"Some blond-haired bloke. Lonsdale, I think, and another man who I don't know. He's a bit of the home-brewed if you ask me." The cheeky lad grinned.

"Lonsdale's fighting someone with little training?" That was unexpected. Fives Court matches were supposed to be between men trained and approved by Gentleman Jackson, London's finest boxer.

"He's a milling cove all right, Jackson approved, but he cheats if you ask me," the lad whispered conspiratorially.

"Well this should prove interesting indeed." Jonathan slipped through the doorway and glanced around the interior of the high-ceilinged building. Dozens of men near him were hollering wildly as two men on a raised platform circled each other, gloved fists raised.

Charles stood bare-chested facing a man equal his height. Charles was well-toned, strong, and muscled, but his opponent was a massive beast, a real bruiser. There was a fair bit of blood on the other man's chin, and Charles was dancing lightly on his feet and grinning like the devil himself. That wasn't a good sign, at least for the other fellow.

"Knock his block off!" a high-pitched voice cried out ahead of him. It stuck out over the low-voiced shouts of the men around him. Jonathan began weaving through the crowds, shouldering his way to the front of the platform. At the edge of the ring two lads were waving and cheering Charles on.

"Draw his cork, my lord!" the second lad cried as Jonathan drew even with them at the edge of the ring.

The profile of the first young man was one he recognized instantly. Tom Linley, Charles's servant and man-about-town, though barely old enough to be called a man. Jonathan had always felt something was off about him. He couldn't quite put a finger on what it was. The lad was... shifty, or perhaps simply secretive.

Secrets. The flashes of fear and defiance he had seen in the lad's eyes in the past had been a warning Jonathan couldn't ignore. There was something going on with Linley that puzzled Jonathan. But his loyalty to his master was equally evident now in the prideful expression he wore as he whooped and hollered.

"Give it to him, Charles!" The second lad's voice was... higher. Too high. Jonathan leaned forward to peer around Linley's face, and his heart pounded against his ribs. That darker-haired lad was no lad at all. The breeches he wore fit snugly around his...no...*her* full, feminine buttocks.

"Audrey?"

The dark-haired boy froze and slowly turned his way.

It was Audrey. Audrey Sheridan, Cedric's little sister and a notorious hellion. She was also the woman he was considering courting. There was certainly no taming that wild creature.

His possible future wife was wearing trousers, standing in a crowd of men who smelled like alcohol and was watching a boxing match at Fives Court.

Audrey's mouth parted as she wet her lips. She hastily reached up to check her costume and tuck a few stray wisps of her hair back under her cap.

"*Audrey*," he growled, stalking over to her. Linley finally noticed him.

"Hello, Mr. St. Laurent. Have you come to see the match?"

Jonathan barely spared Linley a glance. "Audrey, what in blazes are you doing here?" His fingers curled around her upper arm.

Audrey struggled in his hold. "Let go of me!"

"Not until you tell me what you're doing!"

Her eyes narrowed. "I'm practicing disguises." Her little pink, all-too-kissable lips formed a delicate pout.

"Disguise?" Did she have no sense of the danger she was in? If one of the men around her realized she was a woman, she could be hurt, she could be... He shuddered and shook his head. No. That would not happen because he was taking her out of this place at once.

"If you don't unhand me this instant—"

"You'll what?" he challenged. "I've half a mind to redden that little bottom of yours so that you cannot sit down for the next week!" His threatening tone attracted more than one glance from the men around him.

Audrey's warm brown eyes were filling with flames from her temper.

"Everyone is staring. You had better let go of me."

"She's right, Mr. St. Laurent," Linley leaned in to whisper.

Jonathan hated to admit they were correct. Several men were losing interest in Charles, and the other man in the ring. They had instead turned to watch him and Audrey.

"Hellfire and damnation!" he cursed and dropped his hold on her arm.

With a far too dainty huff, Audrey plucked at her little blue waistcoat and checked to make sure the cap on her head was still concealing what he knew was a coiling of silken dark-brown hair. He'd gotten addicted to the way her skin tasted and the honeysuckle sweetness that clung to her tresses. From the moment he'd met her, Audrey had tied him into knots.

Sighing, he forced his attention back to Charles. In the short time he'd been distracted by Audrey's ruse, it seemed Charles had suffered. One of his eyes was a dark red, and blood trickled down the side of his chin from a split lip.

"What's the matter with Charles?" Jonathan asked Linley.

The lad shrugged, but his blue eyes were narrowed as he focused on the two men in the ring.

"My lord is fighting fair, but the other fellow is set on fibbing him."

"Fib?" Jonathan hadn't had much experience with boxing.

"Fibbing is a beating," Linley explained.

"Poor Charles," Audrey murmured. The initial excitement in her eyes from the first part of the fight had faded. The bigger boxer swung a gloved fist and Charles ducked, but he was panting hard. That wouldn't do at all. Charles was not allowed to lose a match, not if Jonathan could lend some support.

Jonathan rested his palms on the edge of the platform. "Finish him, Charles!"

Charles's gaze drifted across the crowd as he danced away from his opponent. When he caught sight of Jonathan, he started grinning again. "Wondered when you'd show up!"

Jonathan almost chuckled. "Here we go."

Charles dodged back, then forward, then to the side, his blows coming swift and hard. The other boxer didn't see it coming. Charles was finally displaying himself to advantage. The crowd cheered, and the men were shouting wagers on the quickly changing odds.

A masterful uppercut caught Charles's opponent off guard, and then he stumbled back and fell like a stone. His body hit the platform with a loud smack, and every man with odds on the bruiser winced. Chest heaving, Charles whooped in triumph and peeled off his gloves, tossing them to a man just off the edge of the ring. Then he slipped under the ropes and hopped off the platform.

"Jon," Charles greeted, his gray eyes sparkling with delight. "Just stalling for time until you showed up." He reached for a cloth a man passing by held out, and he wiped sweat and blood off his face.

Audrey beamed at him, sidling closer. "Well done, Charles."

Jonathan tracked the movement, a strange prickling sensation under his skin. He did not like the way Charles was standing there bare-chested and not at all aware that he was flaunting that chest in front of a virginal woman who was barely past her debut season.

"What did you think, lad?" Charles asked Linley.

The boy pressed his lips together in thought before replying.

"You missed an opportunity to gouge his eyes when he had you on the ropes."

Charles burst out laughing. "That's not how pugilism works, lad. This isn't a street match, but of two men with honor."

"Humph." Linley grunted in clear dissent. "If he wasn't fighting fair, why should you?"

But Charles was focused on Jonathan again. "Glad you got my note. We need to talk."

Shooting a glance at Audrey, Jonathan nodded grimly.

"That we do." He planned to give Charles another black eye if he didn't have a good reason for bringing Audrey to a match like this.

"Don't you think we ought to send the lady home?" He jerked his head at Audrey.

Her eyes narrowed again, and she crossed her arms. "Oh no. I am staying here."

"Absolutely not." Jonathan eyed Audrey reproachfully and then looked to Charles. "Perhaps we ought to meet later?"

"I had a letter this afternoon that Ashton is in need of help at his estate. We ought to meet there this evening," Charles suggested.

"Very good, I'll see you tonight." He turned to Audrey. "Now, you're to come with me. I am going to escort you straight home, and you'd better pray your brother isn't there so I don't have to explain where you've been." He grabbed her arm again.

"Charles! You can't let him drag me out of here," Audrey protested.

Jonathan shared an intense gaze with Charles, who smiled. "Well, you remember my advice."

"I do."

"Advice? What advice?" Audrey snapped.

"That I carry you out of here and put my hand to your backside if you raise another word of protest."

Audrey bit her lip and tugged her arm, but Jonathan was adamant. She was not going to stay here where it was dangerous. Without letting her speak another word, he scooped her up and threw her over his shoulder. Ignoring the pounding of her fists against his back, he carried her out of Fives Court. She screeched like a little hellcat, spitting and clawing and drawing all manner of bad attention to the both of them.

"I'll get you for this!" she vowed.

"I'm sure you'll try, darling." He smacked her bottom in playful punishment as he headed for a waiting coach.

"Curzon Street, please," Jonathan told the driver and then opened the coach door and tossed Audrey inside. It was going to be a long ride, and he'd have to guard his loins from her little booted feet.

Grab Ashton's book now HERE to see what happens!

Turn the page to see a list of other steamy, romantic reads from me!

OTHER TITLES BY LAUREN SMITH

Historical
The League of Rogues Series
Wicked Designs
His Wicked Seduction
Her Wicked Proposal
Wicked Rivals
Her Wicked Longing
His Wicked Embrace (coming soon)
The Earl of Pembroke (coming soon)
His Wicked Secret (coming soon)
The Seduction Series
The Duelist's Seduction
The Rakehell's Seduction
The Rogue's Seduction (coming soon)
Standalone Stories

Tempted by A Rogue
Sins and Scandals
An Earl By Any Other Name
A Gentleman Never Surrenders
A Scottish Lord for Christmas

Contemporary
The Surrender Series
The Gilded Cuff
The Gilded Cage
The Gilded Chain
Her British Stepbrother
Forbidden: Her British Stepbrother
Seduction: Her British Stepbrother
Climax: Her British Stepbrother

Paranormal
Dark Seductions Series
The Shadows of Stormclyffe Hall
The Love Bites Series
The Bite of Winter
Brotherhood of the Blood Moon Series
Blood Moon on the Rise (coming soon)
Brothers of Ash and Fire
Grigori: A Royal Dragon Romance
Mikhail: A Royal Dragon Romance
Rurik: A Royal Dragon Romance

Sci-Fi Romance

Cyborg Genesis Series

Across the Stars (coming soon)

Lauren
SMITH
TIMELESS ROMANCE

ABOUT THE AUTHOR

Lauren Smith is an Oklahoma attorney by day, author by night who pens adventurous and edgy romance stories by the light of her smart phone flashlight app. She knew she was destined to be a romance writer when she attempted to re-write the entire *Titanic* movie just to save Jack from drowning. Connecting with readers by writing emotionally moving, realistic and sexy romances no matter what time period is her passion. She's won multiple awards in several romance subgenres including: New England Reader's Choice Awards, Greater Detroit BookSeller's Best Awards, and a Semi-Finalist award for the Mary Wollstonecraft Shelley Award.

To connect with Lauren, visit her at:
www.laurensmithbooks.com
lauren@Laurensmithbooks.com

Made in the USA
Monee, IL
07 September 2023

42304442R00280